CW00747054

# MASQUERADE

## BY

## KITTY COOPER

*To Loraine, love.*

*Kitty Cooper*

Published in 2017 by FeedARead.com Publishing
Copyright © The author as named on the book cover.

First Edition

The author has asserted their moral right under the
Copyright, Designs and Patents Act, 1988, to be identified
as the author of this work.

All Rights reserved. No part of this publication may be
reproduced, copied, stored in a retrieval system, or
transmitted, in any form or by any means, without the prior
written consent of the copyright holder, nor be otherwise
circulated in any form of binding or cover other than that in
which it is published and without a similar condition being
imposed on the subsequent purchaser.

A CIP catalogue record for this title is available from the
British Library.

# Chapter 1

The background babble of happy chatter from the audience faded to silence as Luapp and Oola entered the arena. The crowd's hushed surprise changed to excited anticipation as they walked to the platform. Expectation hung in the air like a plains mist, and despite the sun's warmth, he felt cold.

Goth stood on a raised platform looking exhausted. His eyes were glazed and sweat streaked his face. Noticing Luapp's approach Goth's stoop straightened and his expression changed from defeat to hopeful. Facing the crowd, he took a moment to gather his strength.

'Good people o'Pedanta,' he shouted. 'Dis ma last slafe, ma best. He like gold dust in de desert of Secuffra; a slafe so rare you'll no believe your eyes.'

He paused while Luapp mounted the steps and joined him on the platform. The silence in the arena was almost palpable.

With a voice fading from the day's exertion, he continued, 'gentle folk o'Pedanta - I knew you be amaze. Your eyes truly see dis vision; he Gaeizaan third generation slafe. Some older folk remember his kind, younger folk just legends.'

Goth half-turned towards Luapp and raised his arm full length; it was the only way he could reach the top of his head.

'See how statuesque he is and physique natural. Bodyguard definitely; no thief or assassin in right mind tackle him. He young, just thirty. Fit, strong…'

Luapp stopped listening to the rhetoric. Slave Master Goth's prattle faded to a background triviality as he stared out at the crowd. The steep sided seats were filled with the fawn faces of Pedantans, intermixed with occasional other skin tones.

From the platform, he couldn't discern one face from another, but scrutinising the crowd helped distract from the turmoil now assaulting his insides.

'All biddin' end? Sold!'

Goth's gleeful broke Luapp's concentration and he glanced in his direction. The rotund slaver's grin was so wide it seemed to cut his face in half.

'Go with Oola,' he croaked.

Luapp left the platform and joined the scruffy young woman waiting at the bottom. She led him past the small enclosure where he'd spent the day to a large tent beyond. Stopping outside she attached the chain from the anchor spike to his wrist cuffs and went in.

Sold.

He was someone else's property. A range of emotions coursed through him, making his stomachs volatility more violent.

As the other slaves had left the carrier on the journey to Trhaan he'd watched them go with some dispassion, and he'd expected to get through his own auction the same way. But composure deserted him the moment he entered the arena.

4

A group of interested passers-by gathered while Oola was away. Like the rest of the visitors to the slave fair their thin open weave clothing was damped with sweat. The heat of the day was the culmination of a week of cloudless pale green skies and no breeze.

The women giggled making comments about his stature and physique. As the group edged closer they dared each other to touch. The stench of the mingled sweat from the men and women was repugnant.

Oola's sudden reappearance saved him from being manhandled. Shooing them away with heated words she unchained the cuffs and led him inside.

At the back of the tent stood a table covered in papers. A middle-aged man was sitting behind it reading something on the desk. Beads of sweat covered his forehead and streak marks showed their path down his face.

'Yes,' he said, as they arrived at the desk, 'he seems healthy enough.'

He wiped his forehead with a small cloth and returned it to its place on the table. Staring at Luapp he frowned. 'Where did he come from?'

'Ouside Black Systems ; Goth bout from Zeetan ambassador.' Oola smirked. 'You wan do touch test?'

'No!' His eyes widened with horror. 'Uh...no. It's obvious he's physically....' his voice trailed off. 'I'll sign the licence and you can take him to the lady.'

Looking down at the papers he scribbled a signature, fitted them into a wallet and handed it to Oola. Taking the wallet, she tucked it into the large pocket of her jacket.

'Your owner waiting outside. You be respectful an obedient. Then you haf good life. Come.'

They left by the back exit of the tent. It led to a small paved courtyard where a young woman was waiting, a native of the planet, but slimmer and more attractive than usual.

Her curvaceous figure was encircled in what seemed to be one piece of multi-coloured material. It wound around her from her right shoulder to half way down her left thigh.

From the tip of the bottom point hung a string of semi-precious stones that reached to her ankle. The top part of the material hung over her shoulder and down her back, and had a similar string of stones dangling from it. Her shoes were little more than straps attached to a sole.

The black hair common to all Pedantans was divided into two. The lower part was plaited and hung over her shoulder, interwoven with a bright red cord.

The top part was curled and pinned and had small artificial flowers secured in it. A parted fringe fell over her forehead and the edges of her gold-brown eyes crinkled as her orange painted lips curved into a smile.

The minute he saw her a host of thoughts zipped through his brain. The first and foremost being, *I'm in trouble.*

Chapter 2


Luapp's eyes flicked open and he stared up at the ceiling. Irritation flooded through him; he'd had no intention of sleeping. But weeks on the road with very little food, and the tension of the sale overcame his efforts to remain awake. He'd been here for… he checked his inner clock …two hours.

He'd been taken to a large country house by his new owner, Lady Rhalin, the land craft pilot had called her. While a little sparse, the room he now occupied was luxury compared to the slaver vehicle.

After being put into what seemed to be a metal box on landing runners, his stomachs had finally stopped their gyrations. The occupants appeared to be waiting for something, and while in the vehicle, he'd managed to enforce calm on his rebellious insides.

Being in the back with a solid metal plate between him and the other passengers he didn't see the person they waited for. By the light tread approaching the vehicle, he assumed they were female. As soon as she got in they left the fair.

Now fully alert, his mind worked on his predicament.

*I'll have to formulate a meticulous escape plan or it will be a life shortening experience. I'll wait until I know more about the workings of the household and the people within it. When I'm into a routine, I'll look for opportunities to abscond.*

Leaving the bed, he stretched leg and arm muscles slowly. In the confines of the slaver vehicle on the journey from Farro to Trhaan, there had been little chance to exercise. To ease constricted muscles, he paced the room.

The sound of hurrying footsteps above stopped his pacing. A woman was running down the stairs. She came towards his door and went past. Another door further along opened and closed and there was silence. The door opened and closed again, and the footsteps ran back upstairs. That wouldn't be the mistress of the house running about, more like another slave or a servant.

He continued his pacing until faint voices above made him stop again. *Two females… one walking away. The other is coming this way… she's opened a door... coming down...*

A quick knock was followed by the door opening. A young Pedantan woman stood in the doorway. The fawn coloured skin seemed darker beside the pale blue dress she wore. Her shoulder length hair was held back from her face by a small stiff hat of the same shade. She paused in the doorway then smiled and stood to one side.

'The Lady wanth to thee you, follow me.'

She led the way up the stairs and through the door at the top. A short way along the corridor she turned right into a spacious lounge.

A set of six near ceiling to near floor windows ranged across the far wall, edged by long curtains of purple and silver. The carpet had a pattern made of different shades of purple, from almost white to almost black.

In front of a large sofa covered in the same material as the curtains, stood a low wooden table upon which two half-filled glasses stood. On the wall opposite the door hung a brightly coloured tapestry depicting a hunting scene. Against the door wall stood a highly polished side unit with a vase of flowers.

All this was taken in as he entered, and now his attention was firmly on the women sitting on the sofa. One was the woman who bought him. The other, a sollenite like himself, sent his blood pressure soaring. She stood up and walked over with an expression of disdain and stopped a short distance from him.

'I am Kaylee Branon,' she said, in Pedantan. 'Lady of the house and your owner. The quarters you are in are temporary. You will be allotted fresh quarters when you are clean and presentable.'

The second slow look over conveyed sheer disgust.

'You will bathe and then be given a meal which you will eat in the conservatory. There is a clensrom just along the corridor from your present room. Hopefully you won't contaminate anything too much.

After the meal Sylata, the key keeper will take you around the dwelling. Do you have any questions?'

Fighting the urge to grab her by the throat, he said in Gaeizaan, 'I suppose you thought this amusing?'

'Yes, I did,' she said in the same language. 'A small payback for past encounters.'

Lady Rhalin left the sofa and walked up behind her. 'What did he say?'

'Nothing much,' his owner assured her, switching to Pedantan. Returning her attention to Luapp she continued, 'many things are happening tomorrow. I want you fresh and in the relaxrom the tenth before. Don't be late.'

With a brief frown, she added, 'you will speak Pedantan when there are others with us, that is your native tongue I've been told. Where did you learn Gaeizaan?'

'When travelling with my previous owner I met others of

our genus. They taught me.'

'You speak it well. What is your name?'

'Mikim Var, lady.'

'I will see you tomorrow, Mikim.'

She tapped a small metal globe standing on the table and a few minutes later the same female servant arrived.

'Cleona, take Mikim back to his quarters. He is to bathe. I want those... rags washed and placed outside the bathroom for him to put back on.

Tell Sylata he will eat in the conservatory in an hour. When finished he will return the dishes to the kitchen. She will then show him around the house. After that he will return to his room.'

Her attention turned from the servant to Luapp. 'He looks like he could do with feeding. Then leave him to sleep. He knows what I want him to do tomorrow, so no-one needs to disturb him.'

'Yeth Madam.'

'Mikim, Cleona is a general house servant. You will go with her.'

'Lady Kaylee?'

Enegene raised a brow as an encouragement to continue.

'What happenth if hith clothth fall apart? I mean...they don't look...'

'I know what you mean Cleona; it's probably the grime holding them together. Let's hope they survive a wash. Tomorrow the problem will be rectified.'

'Yeth Madam.' Cleona glanced at Luapp as she led the way from the room.

Finding his way back to his quarters wasn't hard, but slaves obeyed orders or there were consequences. He'd learned that particular rule quickly.

Back below stairs she showed him the bathroom and left.

Inside there was what could only be called an antique, but at least the ceramic container would allow him to immerse himself entirely. The film of orange dust covering his clothes and skin would only be removed by being up to his neck in water.

The stiff faucets squeaked in protest as he turned them on, and as the bath filled he searched for soap. A solid bar of something that smelled vaguely of flowers was lying in a small wire basket attached to the wall.

His clothes were dropped outside the door then he stepped into the bath and lowered himself carefully into the water. With the warmth relaxing mind and body, he picked up the bar, dipped it into the water and started to wash.

A while later he found his clothes outside the door having survived their own wash. He dressed and left the bathroom, arriving at the foot of the stairs as Cleona appeared at the top. She signalled for him to come up and took him to the large kitchen at the rear of the house.

The light-hearted banter among the gathered staff stopped in surprise. Eventually the head cook nudged the girl beside her with an elbow and said, 'don't stand there gawping girl, give the slave the tray.'

Pulling the covered tray from the work table the junior cook handed it over from a position as far from Luapp as she could reach. As he took it she hastily retreated to her place beside her superior.

'Heth not going to attack you, Sthtell,' Cleona said haughtily, as she headed for the door. 'Thupid girl,' she muttered, as they walked along the corridor.

Arriving at the transparent add on Kaylee Brannon called a conservatory, Cleona watched him put the tray on the table and sit down. 'I'll be back in half an hour. I don't exthpect it'll take you long to eat that; you look tharved.'

He waited for her to leave before removing the cover. Picking up the utensil he looked down at the meal unenthusiastically. After weeks on curling leaves and dried out fruit and vegetables, the food before him now was too much. Even so, he had to eat something.

When she returned, and saw how little he'd eaten, Cleona made a clicking noise with her tongue.

'Cook won't like that; she thpent thome time making that meal. Thill, no need to tell her. I'll thneak it in the kitchen when we go back. We're going to thee Thylata now.'

Pushing down the rising irritation at the servant's troublesome speech impediment, Luapp made a mental note to adjust his inner interpretation as they left the conservatory.

They walked along the corridor, turned right and went down a few steps into a compact room. At one end were a small table and two easy chairs. 'Thlave's ready for the tour,' Cleona said, cheerfully.

A mature woman with short, curly, greying hair rose from one of the chairs with a frown. Giving Luapp a brief smile, she said, 'what is your name?'

'Mikim, Lady.'

'This way Mikim, we'll start at the top and work down.'

Half an hour later they arrived back at the basement steps.

'You know your way to your room?' Sylata said.

'Yes Lady.'

'No need to call me lady, I'm just the housekeeper. I'll send down a snack about nine. Don't return the tray tonight, bring it up tomorrow when you come for breakfast. We eat in the staff room.'

She watched him walk down the stairs and when he reached the bottom she said; 'don't be late tomorrow; Lady Kaylee doesn't like to be kept waiting.' She paused and finally added, 'sleep well Mikim.'

12

Luapp entered the room, walked over to the bed and undressed. He laid his clothes on a chair then slid beneath the covers and lay back. Closing his eyes he concentrated on the language interpretation area of his brain.

Inserting an instruction that changed Cleona's heavy lisp into clear language, he let out a sigh of relief. His body felt exhausted, but his mind was buzzing. It was occupied with Kaylee Branon. Just thinking about her made both his stomachs knot.

*She deliberately allowed me to think the plan had misfired… Choosing the venomous Swamplander might have been a mistake; perhaps she's not as reliable as I'd hoped, but she has the criteria.*

*She can think fast in tight situations and defend herself in a crisis. The knife she carries ensures no one in their right mind would trouble her.*

He smiled wryly.

*Her perceived wealth and status removed any possibility of rejection by the elite here. Being just another useless socialite, albeit an outworlder meant Pedantan high society would welcome her.*

*The duplicity of the Black Systems Governments is breath taking. They're happy for Enegene to stay on Pedanta despite being Gaeizaan. They're equally happy allowing the buying and selling of a third-generation slave.*

He let out a quiet humph of disgruntled resignation. *I shouldn't condemn a system that allows our mission to take place.*

A muscle twitched by his jaw as he remembered their last meeting on Gaeiza. *As she left GSC I warned her of the dangers of her assignment. Her reply was typical of her mind frame.*

*'Lighten your load Nostowe,'* she'd replied. *'The numerous possibilities of this mission haven't escaped me.'*

Guilt pricked his conscious as he remembered his thoughts watching her leave.

*A moment's deviation but it was unprofessional… She has a*

*shrewd mind and a determination as strong as micro spun cables. From the moment I arrested her she's managed to blight my life.*

Pushing the strange mix of emotions from his mind he took a few moments to meditate and release the built-up tension. It was only early evening but with immediate problems solved he fell into a deep and dreamless sleep.

## Chapter 3

The quiet chink of china knocking against china brought
Enegene to consciousness. She'd woken a couple of hours
earlier, but managed to get back to a light doze. Sitting up, she
pulled the tangled nightgown loose and accepted the bed
jacket Cleona offered.

She found it strange wearing clothing in bed, on Gaeiza
with its twin suns it wasn't needed. Wriggling to one side and
then another she pulled the restricting clothing looser. By the
time she was comfortable Cleona had positioned the pillows
to support her back.

A low mood descended as she watched the maid place the
tray over her legs and leave. Removing the heat covers
Enegene glanced at the food and picked up a fork. She ate
without enjoyment as her mind was occupied with confusing
feelings coursing through her.

*What's wrong with me? Everything's fine now the guardian's
arrived, so why do I feel this way? There's been little to concern me
since arriving in Denjal except Nix Pellan. With the guardian as a
protector Pellan will be taken care of. Not that I couldn't take care of
him myself, but it would sink the mission if I was arrested for
slaughter.*

She scooped some vegetable mash onto the fork and

chewed slowly.

*Nix Pellan hasn't caused this mood; he's more of an irritant than a problem; it's the guardian. I was expecting him to look the same; well-fed and neatly dressed. Possibly not as smart as usual but still wearing clothes that actually cover his frame.*

*He was gaunt; there was no life in his eyes… how could he let them treat him that way?*

Slicing the potato cake, she stabbed a small piece and put it in her mouth and stared across the room.

*What am I thinking? I'm a Swamplander, not his smothering mother, but he can't complete the mission underfed and lacking strength. I need Nostowe up to pinnacle or I'll be the next statistic. The slaves in Aylisha's dwelling are not so neglected.*

*What tuft sodden notion possessed me to agree to talk to his superior? I'd no intention of agreeing to help.*

A mischievous grin came and went.

*Not until I was told he was going to be my slave. Having Nostowe obeying my every word was too good an opportunity to miss. I had a list a light orb long before I left Gaeiza and going to the fair yesterday I couldn't wait to start.*

*Irritation's a good ploy; persistent niggling is easy. Despite his tight-fisted control I'm able to trip his breakers. But when he stood in front of me last evening I was shocked.*

The mixed flavours of the large open capped fungi the locals called fush, and another slice of potato cake were lost as the image of Luapp came up in her mind.

*Being a slave has left its mark… I know he's playing a part; too qessing well for my liking, but a little of the old stamina surfaced when he saw me.*

She smiled wickedly. *He didn't appreciate my little deception; unlucky for him he can't do anything about it. Even so, these feelings are bizarre; why should I concern myself with a Shadowman?*

Pushing down her growing concern with determination,

she plunged the fork into the remaining food.

Some minutes later she lifted the tray from her legs and placed it on the bed. She swivelled, slid from the bed and marched into the bathroom. Dropping the nightgown on the floor, she stepped into the shower and stood with the water pouring over her body.

*He'll soon recover once he's had a few good meals inside him. He can exercise and build strength in the pool. When he's back to normal I won't feel guilty about my plans. But for now, I'll be patient and concentrate on the mission. There's much to tell him; where can we talk without being interrupted?*

Her mind worked on that problem as she finished her shower, dried herself off and pulled on a bathrobe. Back in the bedroom she sat at the dressing table and brushed her hair. As she worked memories of their first encounter surfaced.

*Being raised in the swamps guaranteed I'd see guardians as a threat. Everyone there's on the slide one way or another; it's just a matter of degree. But Nostowe was different than expected.*

A hot flush crept up her neck to her cheeks but made no show against her skin colour. *The murkslider was rigid the day we met.* She stopped brushing momentarily then started more vigorously.

*Not the most intelligent thing I'd ever done; threaten a guardian with a knife. He carried me back and shoved me inside, even the other swampys laughed. I'm sure he intended the blood rush. I was so furious I couldn't speak...*

She frowned at her reflection in the mirror.

*I was scared that night in the cell, the rumours about what happened to swampy's in guardian detention kept going round my head...*

A cynical smile touched her lips and faded. *Nostowe's impressive. He's the only man to take my knife without getting stabbed or sliced.*

She stopped brushing again as the old anger returned.

*Ever since being released from the centre I've been waiting for a chance to get even. Now it's here I feel uneasy.*

'Gethsana Nostowe!'

She banged her fist on the table making things jump and clatter, 'why'd you have to look so... pathetic!'

A quiet tap was followed by the appearance of Cleona looking a little nervous. 'Are you finished Lady Kaylee?' she said, tentatively.

Glancing at the maid's image in the mirror, she said, 'thank you Cleona, I am finished.'

'You asked me to tell you when it was almost time...'

Enegene turned to face the maid. 'I won't be long. When is the smith coming?'

'Quarter past ten Madam.'

'Tell Farin to take him to the visitor room when he arrives. It will give me time to talk to the slave.'

'What clothes do you want today Madam?'

'I'll have the blue suit with matching leg huggers and shoes.'

'Do you need assistance with your hair today Lady Kaylee?' Cleona asked, from inside the wardrobe.

'No, I'll do it myself. You won't need to do it again; the slave will do it in future.'

'The slave?' Cleona appeared from the wardrobe with an armful of clothing, 'but he's a man Madam.'

'I had noticed. On my planet, it's customary for men to do women's hair.'

Cleona paused in placing the clothes carefully over the back of the bedside chair. 'But he's not from your planet, Madam, he's a generation slave from the Black Systems.'

'Even so, he had a Gaeizaan mother until he was sold, and I expect she would have taught him a few styles.'

18

'I heard the surviving children were very young Madam, perhaps his mother didn't have time to teach him.'

Changing subject, she added, 'I've placed your skirt, blouse and jacket on the back of the chair, and your tights are on the seat.

Enegene finished her hair adding a couple of diamond studded clips then applied her make up. She dressed and added an emerald pendant and broach. Satisfied with her appearance, she left the room and headed downstairs. She found Luapp waiting in the lounge.

*A good night's sleep has improved his looks. Some of the gauntness has left his face and his eyes are more alert.*

Mindful of being overheard she kept up the appearance of lady of the house.

'Good, you're on time. I like punctuality.' Raising a brow, she added, 'is that all you have to wear?'

'Slavers don't provide their stock with possessions, Lady.'

A cold shiver slithered around her insides. Referring to himself as stock caused Enegene unexpected revulsion.

*He fakes the part to perfection, at least, I hope he's faking it. What's happened to him over the past monspa?*

Controlling the urge to ask, she said, 'there are several things I want you to understand. The first is that when I speak to you, you will look at me, understood?'

His gaze dropped from a point behind her head to her face. 'Yes Lady.'

'Secondly, you are to be my protector. This means you will be with me every time I leave the dwelling unless I tell you otherwise. Also, you will soon be moving up to a room near mine. I want you close enough to reach me quickly should I need you.'

He frowned fleetingly. 'I could reach you quickly from the room I'm in Lady.'

'Unfortunately, the top and rear access doors to your room can be bolted, rendering you useless.'

She stopped as a young man dressed in the same colours as Cleona entered. He gave Luapp a curious stare then turned his attention on Enegene.

'The smith is here, Madam.'

With a brief frown, she said, 'he's early. Is he in the visitor room?'

'Yes Madam.'

'Tell him we'll be with him shortly, Farin.' She waited until the servant left before continuing. 'Although there will be times when I ask your opinion on something, and will expect you to respond to that request, where you are going to sleep is not one of them.

We'll be busy today. First, we must change the amulets you're wearing to ones bearing my crest. Then I must register you as living property with my syscred manager. Finally, I will take you to a clothes store and get you suitably dressed. What you are wearing is almost indecent. The smith is waiting. Follow me.'

Enegene led the way to a smaller room opposite the lounge. This was not as lavishly furnished, having just a few chairs and a low table. A man with skin like parched earth was standing by the table holding a case. Seeing Enegene he bowed his head as a sign of respect.

'Put your case there.'

She indicated the table as she walked over. Placing the case on the table he fumbled opening it. Enegene noticed Luapp watching the smith's trembling fingers and wondered about his interest.

When he finally opened it, she looked inside. There was a range of small plaques of various metals. Some were a single metal, others were combinations. There was also a small

20

book, which he pulled out and opened.

'This t'patterns; they surround t'amulet except for plain front piece. Your stamp placed there.' He flicked some pages over. 'Different lengths of t'amulets. These,' he flicked a few more, 'inside coverings. I've sample materials if want t'see them. At back -,'

He shut the book, turned it upside down and dropped it. Luapp picked it up and held it out. The smith took it and opened it again. 'Are stamps available. You look Lady Branon; I'll remove slave's bands and measure him up.'

Enegene sat on the nearest chair and looked through the book as the smith took out some vicious looking tools and a small bottle of liquid. Dripping a few drops around the bolt head, he picked up some pincers and tried several times to grab the head. Eventually Luapp took the tool, grabbed the bolt and held the pincers for the man to take.

Noticing the incident, she twitched a brow. 'There's no need to be nervous of my slave smith, he only acts if I am threatened.'

The man dropped the holding bolt into a battered tin he'd taken from his case. ''Tis not the slave Madam.' He concentrated on removing the amulet. 'I've met one before. Third generation slaves predictable.'

She looked up at the man concentrating on opening the band. 'Then what troubles you?'

Dropping the amulet into the same tin he looked up. 'T'day I was tested.' His eyes took on a haunted look. 'Had brush with t'destroyer.'

'The destroyer?' Enegene said incredulous. 'In your home? How do you know it was the evil servant?'

He concentrated on the other bolt as if not wishing to make eye contact. 'T'day I find it difficult to wake. But when I wake I see him. Jus in time I remember t'incantations and threw a glow coal at him an he vanish.'

'I can understand your nervous state smith.' She watched him drop the bolt and remove the band. 'Leave them off.' She added, and returned her attention to the book.

The man took out a metal ring with markings on it. 'He's not allowed in public without bands Lady.'

Enegene looked up again. 'How long will it take you to make the bands once I have chosen?'

'A day. They're pre-made. Only need t'be adjusted t'fit slave and have your stamp etched on. Could also have him branded with mark if you wish.'

He slipped the ring onto Luapp's wrist and squeezed it until it wouldn't close any further. Noting the mark it came to he did the same on the other wrist.

'Do you do the branding?' she said, as if considering his offer.

'Not here. Would have t'come t'my workshop. Best be put on other arm though. Two on one arm not good. Could damage muscles.' He removed the ring again and made some notes on a piece of paper.

'Two?' she said, surprised. 'I thought you said one.'

'I do one. Has already t'mark of Liani.'

Her primary stomach threatened to eject what remained of her breakfast. When she felt it safe to open her mouth she said, 'no, the amulets are enough.'

Enegene returned her attention to the book and concentrated on choosing a symbol for the bands. With the sizing done the smith moved closer to discuss the type of amulets needed. A short while later, he packed his case and left.

Telling Luapp to follow her she went to the study under the stairs. She put the sheet of information the smith had given her on a desk holding several machines.

'Where did you get the brand?' she said, in Gaeizaan.

'Liani, Lady. All slaves are marked with a birth brand.'

'It's safe to talk in here so drop the act,' she snapped.

'What is it? A laser dye?'

The blank stare became slightly more animated as he lowered his gaze to her face. 'It's a brand.'

She slapped her hand on the desk. 'I don't want you spouting your cover at me; tell me the truth.'

'The truth is it's a deep skin infusion.'

'You're expecting me to believe Guardian Strategic Control went to the trouble of branding you?'

'It was done in the medic centre and penetrates five layers. It's better than being slaughtered.'

A mixture of emotions surged through her as she assessed the truth of his statement. Disbelief. Respect. Confusion. But most of all an overriding anger at his agreeing to such a thing for total strangers.

*Outworlder strangers at that!*

'Where does duty end Guardian?'

Abruptly changing subject, she added, 'this internal room locks from the inside. When you're not protecting me, or helping Sylata in the garden, you'll be in here doing a historical search; that's what I told the servants. It's soundproof and safe to talk, especially in Gaeizaan.'

'Heard of translators?'

Enegene's lips twisted into a cynical smile. 'That's more like it Nostowe. The elite here have no time for such things. If someone doesn't speak the mother tongue, they're not worth listening to. Besides, very few outsiders have been in my dwelling, and none of them have been in here except Aylisha Rhalin and a couple of servants.'

'You trust the servants?'

'Yes. Especially the key keeper. Aylisha is a good friend

and totally trustworthy.'

'The language implant seems to be working well. Have you had any problems?'

'Not playing the brainless socialite. Commander Yetok is an excellent instructor. I can't understand why a man from such a gold syscred background would want to be a guardian.'

'Something about society parasites from what I remember. How do you know about his background?'

'One of the parasites announced it while we were waiting to board.' She smirked. 'He wasn't happy about that and told her so.'

Twitching a brow, he said, 'you've established yourself as a parasite?'

She gave him a cool look and touched a small machine on the desk. Before she could answer the viscom beeped. A man in late middle age with a plump, oblong face appeared on screen. As he recognised the caller he smiled broadly causing deep radiating lines around his eyes.

'Lady Branon, how can I help you?'

Fully facing the screen, she said, 'I have purchased a slave and wish to register him with you.'

'With pleasure. Is the slave there?'

She moved to one side allowing the manager to see Luapp.

'One of your own, how unusual. I heard they died in the plague…' He glanced down and then up again. 'Be still slave, while I get your picture.'

The manager murmured to a machine on his desk while working at a smaller machine in front of him. When he finished, he said, 'if you will kindly send me his details, and a copy of your stamp, all will be done. I'll send you one copy of the deeds and I will keep the other.'

'Thank you, Manager Klem, the details will be with you shortly.'

She removed the ownership documents from a drawer in the desk and fed them into the viscom machine. Next, she put in the amulet details and a picture of her chosen stamp and collected them as they slid out the other side.

Switching off the machine she sat on a chair and placed her feet on the desk. As Luapp remained standing, she let out a sigh of irritation and pointed to a second chair in the corner. He brought it over and sat down.

'So, everything has gone smoothly?'

'More or less. Soon after arriving I invited the neighbours to a gathering. That's how I met Aylisha. She gives the impression of a void but she's intelligent. She's become a close friend and her father Drew Rhalin advises me on purchasing certificates.'

'You're not supposed to use guardian credit to further your personal wealth.'

Her mouth tightened into a thin line as a surge of anger shot through her.

'Tempting the odds as they call it is common practice among Pedantan high society. Apart from giving me something to do, he's showing me how to distinguish good from bad. It's easy to get stripped, but if you're good it earns respect in the right quarters, especially as a single female.'

'Stop rattling your spines.' He managed a brief smile. 'As long as you keep your mind on the mission I've no objection to you earning a small amount. Apart from speculating on portions, how else do you spend your time?'

Enegene took a moment to calm her temper. 'Aylisha has been very useful. She took me to all the elite gatherings and gradually I've become known in the right spheres. Now I'm being personally invited instead of just coming with her.'

'Any suspicious characters?'

'Most of them are suspicious characters, it seems the nature of this society. While they have a veneer of respectability, very few are blemish free. Nothing is considered off limits unless they get caught, that's the one big transgression.'

She raised a brow and gave him a sideways look. 'Is it the same back home?'

'Why ask me?'

'You're friends with Commander Yetok, surely you've attended some functions with him.'

'Kym tends to avoid functions.'

'Much as I hate to commend guardians, I found their advice useful. Despite my scepticism, their instruction on mind control worked. I managed to alter Cleona's speech impediment so it could be clearly understood.'

Luapp raised a brow. 'I also found it a distraction.'

Allowing herself a self-satisfied smile, she continued, 'they have an odd practice here. If they have no life partner, whether they be male or female they have what they call an attachment. The attachment calls their wealthy host their mentor.

'The host takes their attachment to all the gatherings so they have a taste of top society. They live in their mentor's dwelling, and the mentor pays for their clothes, food and entry into entertainment.'

'Are these people slaves?'

'No, they're freeborn, but not of the same social strata as their mentor. What they do for the mentor in return for their benevolence can only be guessed at.

Slaves are a different matter. Most of the wealthy take slaves with them to the gatherings, but they're usually servant slaves, not protectors. Servant slaves can be ordered by anyone at the gathering, not just their owner.

Protector slaves are viewed in a different light. Only their owner can give them orders although they do tend to comply when asked to collect food or drink.'

'That's logical. If anyone could command a protector, they could be removed leaving their owner vulnerable.'

'That aside, slaves are generally considered to be public property.' The edges of her lips curled tightly. 'You'll have to accept physical contact Guardian.'

The cold look he gave her suggested otherwise.

'There are other customs about slaves I should tell you...'

'Tell me later. Have you come across anyone who might be a possible assassin?'

She paused. *Should I...?*

Swamplander rebelliousness seeped through the business façade. *If he wants to find out the hard way, that's up to him.*

'As you like. There's one, Nix Pellan. He's an attachment to a socialite called Antonia Benze. For some reason, he's trying to ingratiate himself with me. I came home one night to find him here. That was unsettling.'

'He forced entry?'

'Not the way you mean. He told the servants he'd an appointment.'

'Are your survivals alerted by him?'

'I'm uneasy when he's near...' She thought over the man's behaviour. 'He shadows me... I feel he wants something from me.' She slid Luapp a sideways glance. 'I have the urge to slit his throat.'

'That's not good.' Luapp rested back in the chair. 'Are you carrying your knife?'

A slow smile spread across her face. 'What's the matter Guardian? Afraid I'll lose control?'

Ignoring the remark, he said, 'genus?'

'I have no idea; he reminds me of a reptile.'

'Description?'

*He's becoming more guardian by the second...* 'Definitely

another outworlder. Almost tall as me, slightly taller than the locals. Skin pale green, hair brown, eyes gold and staring.

He's in his third decade at a guess. He's easy on the eye if that's your preferred type, but his habit of approaching from behind doesn't endear him to me. A ribglider comes to mind.'

'It'll be interesting meeting him, it will allow me to assess him from a guardian point of view.'

'You'll meet him tomorrow. I'm attending a gathering with Aylisha at the Pothery dwelling. Nix Pellan will be there.' She gave him a slow look over. 'But you can't turn up like that. We're retailing this afternoon.'

'Retailing? Why not use the mesh?'

'Not done your background Guardian?' she said, condescendingly. 'Not very professional. Pedanta's not on the same tech scale as us; intelmec are a relatively new concept.'

'But they have levitating vehicles; that normally comes after intelmec.'

'Obviously, they've done things differently in the Black systems. To continue; only the military, law enforcers and the government have unmonitored use of the mesh. Even large businesses still communicate by what they call the audiograph. If they're in the top two per cent they may have a viscom.'

'The elite don't have access to it even for communication?'

The question raised her suspicions. 'Problems?' She watched his expression carefully but couldn't gather anything from it.

Receiving no answer, she continued, 'the elite are the only other group who can use it; for communication only. It's expensive but I've subscribed. My reputation went up six points when they realised I had both mesh and viscom.'

A smug smile appeared briefly as she remembered the expressions of the women in the elite circle she mixed with.

'The elite have a points system for being an elite?' Luapp said surprised. Before she could reply he added, 'so what stops them from using the mesh for other things?'

'The government have a whole roomful of employees monitoring personal mesh holders. There's so few it's easy to do. Apparently, there's delicate negotiations going on and the government doesn't want dissidents using the mesh.'

Luapp gave her a thoughtful look. 'Are the elite likely to be dissidents?'

'From what I've learned about them - no. But there's always exceptions to the rule.'

'How do you know about current politics? Is there a contact in the elite group you're in?'

'This is where the socialite word net comes into being. Most of the females are joined to high powered males in all branches of elite occupations. At least two of the circle have husbands in the transnational government. We tend to know what's going on before the Coalition Master does.'

Watching Luapp stare across the room she frowned. *I can see the diodes sparking… what's going on in his mind?*

'I can't go out without bands,' he said, returning to current problems.

'No vex Guardian, Aylisha gave me temporary ones. They're in the top drawer of the wall store.'

He stood and scanned the various cupboards looking for a set of drawers. 'Does Aylisha Rhalin have an attachment?'

Finding the drawers tucked into the corner he opened the top one and retrieved a couple of plain steel bands.

'No. She's not independently wealthy. Her father controls her syscred.'

He returned to the chair and sat down. 'Have you met the metal worker before?'

'No, but he was recommended by one of the group.' His

examination of the bands prompted her to add, 'they merely clip together. Why are you interested in a craftsman?'

'Such people are not easily scared.' He clipped the bands around his wrists. 'Who or what is the destroyer?'

'It is some kind of evil entity that can steal their essence. It takes their shape and creates trouble for the entire family through criminal actions. It's one of their worst fears. Even the servants here carry small protective objects to ward it off.'

'It takes their physical shape?'

His sudden attentiveness caught her attention. 'Why are you interested?'

'We're hunting a multislayer that appeals to a wide spectrum of females across the galaxy. It's mystifying how this is possible. Something that can change shape, or appear to do so would be worth investigating.'

'The destroyer has been a legend here for millennia and tends to cover a wide range of misdemeanours. He's a good way of getting out of trouble.'

Enegene removed her feet from the desk and stood up. 'Come with me there's something I want to show you before we go; it'll be useful at times.'

She smiled at his confusion as they left the study and went up to her bedroom. Inside, she walked over to the wall behind the headboard. It was covered by wood panelling with inlaid square patterns of different coloured woods. Looking around, she said, 'close the door.'

When he joined her by the wall, she pressed the centre of one of the squares. With a soft click a door opened inwards.

Moving around her he looked inside. 'Where does it go?'

'All over the dwelling and only Sylata knows about it. It's one reason why I want you to sleep up here. One squeak and you'll be with me.'

Going a few steps into the dark passage, he said, 'and the

other reason?'

'I'm bait for a flesh carving multislayer and I don't want you the other side of the building locked in the pukka burrow below stairs.'

She watched him explore the passage with a raised brow and sideways smile. 'A further reason for wanting you up here will become clear later. This way,' she added, before he had time to question her last statement.

Returning to the room he looked at her expectantly. When she looked back puzzled, he said, 'close the door?'

'Press the release again.'

She crossed to the third door of the room opposite the entry door. Turning the handle, she gave it a slight push. It swung back to reveal another bedroom. This had a single bed, a bedside cabinet and a straight-backed chair. It also had a small wardrobe and a set of drawers. There was a further door in the opposite wall.

Pointing to the door she said, 'that's a basic clensrom. I assume Sylata didn't show you this on the tour?'

'No.' He glanced inside and then at her. 'What's it for?'

'Apparently for a primalin. When it's newly arrived, the carer sleeps in here with the qiver in its cradle. When it no longer needs a carer the qiver sleeps here alone.'

She leaned against the door frame, folded her arms and smirked. 'For those without qivers, or whose qivers no longer need to be close to their parents, it has quite a different purpose.'

'For a slave?'

'Quite possibly, I never thought of that. It's used for the attachments. It keeps them within easy reach.' The smirk widened as she noticed the brow twitch.

*He got the implications of that without further explanations.*

'Keep with me.'

Out in the corridor he followed her to a room painted a pale brown. Inside were a double bed and the usual bedroom furniture. It also had the wood patterned back wall. 'This connects directly to my room.'

She touched the relevant square and disappeared inside. A short distance further on, she pushed a button and a door opened to reveal her room. Stepping out she waited for him to shut it.

'That was your room. Any trouble and you can be here in seconds. Best of all you can't be locked in. Something can be pushed against the door in the corridor, but you can get through the passages to anywhere in the dwelling.'

'You've put your time to good use while you've been here.'

The fact he sounded impressed made her furious. 'Did you think I wouldn't be professional? It's my life we're offering and I'm making qessing sure I can escape when necessary.'

'I wasn't suggesting you were unprofessional.'

'No,' she screwed her hands into tight fists, 'you were just surprised when I was. How do you think I run a business?'

'I requested your help precisely because I thought you capable of assisting with this task.'

'Really? I thought it a good way to solve a problem. If the slayer got past you, no one important like a guardian would be lost.'

*Qess! I wasn't going to tell him that, but I couldn't stop myself...* She made a conscious effort to relax her hands as her nails were making painful impressions into her palms.

'You think you're unimportant?'

*He actually sounded surprised!*

'You think I'm unimportant.'

A vexed silence followed, then he said, 'I think you're an ache in the internals, but every life is important.'

*He's got to be fabricating; I can't believe he thought I'd be essential*

32

*to this mission.*

'Then tell me why a female guardian couldn't play the part of bait?'

He smiled briefly.

'They could, and very successfully. But this is a dangerous situation and they have two flaws you don't. As their superior, they address me accordingly. A slip like that would be fatal, especially if done at one of those gatherings. An owner calling their slave "Sir" would be noticed. And they would be more reticent in using a weapon first and asking questions later. As a swampy civilian, it's not a problem I consider you having.'

She couldn't stop the grin as her imagination played the scene. 'So nice to have my talents appreciated.'

Enegene left the bedroom and waited for him to join her at the top of the stairs.

'It's mealtime now Mikim,' she said, back in mistress mode. 'We'll go to town straight after lunch and get you something decent to wear. Tell cook I want you to eat now.'

'Yes Lady.'

Going downstairs, she frowned. *Why do I get this odd feeling when he calls me Lady? It doesn't make sense. I wanted his obedience so why do my insides squirm?*

As they went their separate ways Enegene resisted the urge to turn and watch him. She knew where he was going it wasn't as if he was going to get lost on the way. Entering the small dining room, she sat down and sipped the chilled juice waiting for her.

The rattle of plate covers on the hover trolley as it left the kitchen told her lunch was on the way. Farin opened the door a good five minutes later as Lydian guided it in. While Lydian put the trolley against the wall and removed the cover from the first course, Farin walked over with a bottle of wine and poured a small amount into the glass.

Taking a sip, she nodded her approval and he filled the glass. He and Lydian passed each other as he returned the bottle to the trolley and the girl brought over the first course.

Enegene had seen this dance many times before. The rigidity of the Pedantan serving of food had taught her a great deal about patience. The meal was served and eaten in silence.

*But I have a plan to break the monotony. With the guardian as protector I have an excuse to have him eat in the room with me. Even his barbed comments will be better than the isolation I now endure.*

With a sigh, she started eating. An hour later she escaped the dining room and went up to her bedroom. Collecting her card belt, she returned downstairs and met Luapp in the corridor. He paused for her to pass then followed her outside.

A much sleeker vehicle waited on the driveway than the one he arrived in. It had a rounder, more elegant top in burnished silver and highly polished black sides. At the moment, it was resting on its narrow engraved landing rails and the driver stood beside an open door.

'Mikim will be riding in the back with me Morvac,' she said, stepping inside. Sliding along the seat, she smiled broadly. *Let the fun begin!*

The chauffer left Luapp to close the door behind him. There were two sets of seats facing each other, and a glass divider between them and the front seats. He went to sit on the seat opposite Enegene, but she patted the seat beside her.

'Over here.'

She could tell by his expression he was going to argue but was prevented from doing so by a small panel in the divider behind him sliding back.

'Where to Madam?' Morvac said.

'Dermont's.'

Enegene gave Luapp a long look and raised a brow.

'Mikim, whatever you have been taught by previous owners has been useful, but look on this as a new beginning. I am your owner now, and I expect my orders to be followed without argument.'

Also, when riding in the Drifter...' she glanced around the interior of the vehicle, 'you will sit beside me. Move.'

Apparently aware of the small gap left when the driver closed the panel, he obeyed. The vehicle lifted off and both passengers fell silent as it glided swiftly out of the property's boundary and onto the open road.

# Chapter 4

Luapp's mood darkened with the progression of the journey. Retailing for him was buying food and clothes as necessary over the Skymesh. It was quick, convenient and aggravation free. While he conceded he needed clothes, his instincts told him Enegene was using this as an excuse to annoy. Pushing his irritation to the back of his mind he gazed at the passing scenery.

Apart from ignoring Enegene, he had an ulterior motive for noticing the countryside. At certain times during his stay he would need to leave the house and find a secluded spot to contact a space guardian patrolling the area. They were close enough to talk but not close enough to be detected by planetary defence systems.

This area of Pedanta was open and given mainly to farms. It was nothing like his home continent of Ailtaria. Apart from the capital city of Mohaib, the country surrounding the city was gently rolling grasslands going on to soaring mountains. Nothing was naturally flat; even at the coasts there were plunging cliffs, or slopes down to the shore.

*I've been in the Black Systems for monspa and I miss Gaeiza. If this is what being a space guardian consists of I'll remain a grey…*

Luapp pulled his mind back to the mission as the Pedantan farmland gave way to villages, small towns, outer suburbs, and then the city of Denjal. Once inside its boundaries, the driver slowed to the pace of the traffic.

A short while later Morvac turned off down a side street and then down a slope to an underground parking area. Stopping by a barrier he pressed a button mounted on a pole.

'Lady Branon entering,' he announced to the speaker and wound up the window.

Moments later the toothed barrier slid into the walls and a set of green lights lit up. Following the lights to a parking bay he stopped in front of some posts. They sank into the ground to let them pass then rose behind the vehicle.

'We will be approximately two hours Morvac.' Enegene swivelled and stepped out. 'You have some free time.'

Holding the door, the chauffeur smiled. 'Thank you Madam.'

As soon as Luapp was out Morvac locked the vehicle and left. He disappeared into the cavernous park as the Gaeizaans walked to the lifts.

It was a swift ascension to the floor they wanted in the executive lift. A ping preceded the doors opening and they were met by a female assistant wearing a pale green uniform.

'Welcome Lady Branon.' She smiled brightly. 'How may I assist you?'

~~~

The atmosphere in the vehicle on the return journey was frosty. Luapp stared out of the window all the way back, ignoring Enegene. If it hadn't been for Morvac being able to hear through the slightly open partition, she would have goaded a response from him.

Not that Morvac could understand Gaeizaan, but she doubted she could keep her voice calm when speaking to him at the moment. An elite arguing with her slave would not give the right impression, so she stored up the explosion for when they were alone.

Entering the house, she gave Luapp a curt order to fetch the housekeeper and went into the lounge. When Luapp and Sylata arrived, she smiled briefly at the woman.

'Sylata, Mikim will be moving from the basement room to one along the corridor from me; the one with the pale brown colouration. Also, from now on, he will eat with me.'

'I shall inform the staff. Will there be purchases coming?'

'Tomorrow. They had nothing to fit his height or size. He's wearing the only thing they could find but he won't be wearing it for long.'

'Understood Madam, is there anything else?'

'No, that will be all.'

The fleeting frown was noticed and she guessed something would be said as soon as he got the chance. Turning her attention to Luapp, Enegene added, 'after the frustration of this morning I feel in need of relaxation. I understand all slaves are taught such techniques. You will come with me to the therapy suite and help me relax.'

She left the room and passed Sylata in the corridor as she crossed to a door near the kitchen. It led down to a spa containing a sauna, massage room and swimming pool.

Enegene vanished into the changing room before he could air any grievances. When she returned wearing a robe she was surprised to see he had everything ready.

He watched her walk over to the table and sit on it. She had a moment of indecision before slipping her arms out of the robe and lying face down.

Tense seconds ticked by as she waited for him to refuse. *If he dares…* she seethed inwardly.

When he replaced the robe with a towel she was convinced

she physically left the table. Warm oil trickled across her back then she felt the touch of his hand.

'What are we doing down here?'

A frown creased her brow. *He sounds worryingly calm...*

'Apart from the study – aplirom,' she corrected, 'this is the only other place we can talk without being overheard. There's only one way in and they must come through three doors. We'll talk in Gaeizaan, I find it easier.'

'And the conversation with the key keeper?' he said, switching to their native language.

'General orders. As the key keeper it's her privilege to know.'

He added a little pressure as he rubbed the oil in. 'Such things could be done anytime.'

'Why are you being compliant?'

'If someone came in this is what they'd expect to see.'

She closed her eyes. The sensations created were causing a wonderful relief from the afternoon's tension. After a short pause to gather her thoughts she said, 'what was your interest in the metal worker?'

'We've discussed this.'

Long sweeps down and up her back was making clear thought increasingly difficult to maintain. Resting her forehead on her arms, she worked on controlling her voice

'I didn't receive a satisfactory answer. Shadowmen are masters of misdirection.' Biting her lip, she took a moment before adding, 'I thought you had something on your mind in the Drifter. Was I wrong?'

'I have many things on my mind to do with the task.'

Glancing back at him she saw no flickers of control on his face, it was just his normal non-expression. With a sigh of contentment, she rested her chin on her arms.

'This is good... so nothing about today concerns you?'

'Today?'

Her heart beat faster as she sensed a small victory. He poured more oil onto her shoulders and rubbed it in. Then his hands stopped next to her neck.

Leaning close to her ear, he said, 'where shall I start?'

*Yess! I thought he'd risen above it…*

The gentle manipulation of her shoulders change to a tighter grip, and the lighter tones of his voice became harsher.

'What was the point of today's excursion, apart from your acid observations?'

'I told you...' she winced as the grip tightened again.

'While I'm not fully conversant with this society, I'm sure someone of your perceived wealth could request a tailor come to the dwelling. If you're playing games Namrae...' the warning was unfinished but clear. He relaxed the grip and continued with the massage.

She supressed the grin with difficulty. 'It had a very real purpose, and that was information.'

He was now using a different method to the sweeps, but it produced equal waves of pleasure. She closed her eyes allowing herself to enjoy it.

'Continue.'

'I wanted it known I had a slave. Word will get around and Pellan will have some warning before you meet him tomorrow. Hopefully he'll keep away, but I doubt it.'

'Why do you concern yourself with him? I'll convince him of the futility of his actions.'

'I'm looking forward to that. It's been my experience he's so sure of his personal charm he doesn't understand the word no. But there's another reason. If Pellan isn't our slayer, then someone else at the gatherings is. I'm convinced of it.'

'Why?'

*Qess; he's stopped…*Enegene pushed up onto her elbows

and looked behind. 'Keep going, you're surprisingly good at this.'

He gave her a sour look. 'I asked...'

'I know,' she said, lowering herself again. 'Get on with it .'

She felt the oil trickle down her leg. His hand swept gently up from her knee and began to caress... *massage* it, she hastily corrected.

'There's a... presence... something... I feel it watching me. I'm not sure if it's Pellan or not. Whenever I look at him he's watching me, but he seems more void than slayer.'

He stopped again and then continued the massage. 'It could be a sham. Do you feel it when he's not there?'

'He's always there. Benze is like me and Aylisha, highly prized at society gatherings.'

'And the trip to the retailers, how does Pellan find out about me from that?'

'Did you see the two women in the store as we passed through?'

'Naturally.'

'They're informants. They tell the elite anything they think they might find interesting. If it's interesting enough, they'll get an invitation.'

Luapp stopped again.

'They're so desperate to be invited to the gatherings they wait around clothing retails?' he said, incredulous. 'This is a shallow society.'

'Not any clothing retail. That particular clothing retail. That's where the elite get their clothes. You've stopped again.'

He poured the oil onto her other leg and continued. 'What's the objective?'

'The aim is to let the group know. I wanted them to know about you, so I took you to the store. The informants waited until we left and then questioned the assistants. After that they call Benze and a few others and tell them I have a slave.'

'If they want to know, or you want them to know, why not just call them on the comunit?'

'Audiograph,' Enegene corrected. 'Because that would be crass. It's a word they use for not done in this circle of socialites. They wouldn't ask as that would be too intrusive, so they have to get their information other ways. But they must get it otherwise they are thought to be inadequate and are soon dropped from the invitation list.'

'It seems absurd, but they're salations and they tend to take the long route to a destination.'

'You'd be amazed at the information that flows around the gatherings. Between them the females are connected to every important male there is, from local law officers to the highest government officials. The Shadowmen have nothing on the Pedantan elite.'

'Why is it important for them to know about me before they meet me?'

'Because it would mean that the "network" as they call it had failed. There would be embarrassment all round.'

Silence followed as he did her arms. Enegene opened her eyes and frowned.

*What's he chewing on now?*

And then he stopped.

'Do the elite discuss crime?'

'You're not going to leave me half done?'

'Turn over,' he said, stoically.

Moving carefully, she was temporarily blinded by the towel he dropped over her face and chest. 'What are you doing?' she demanded, pushing it off her face.

'Adjust it.'

She pulled it across her breasts as warm oil dribbled down her torso to her navel.

42

'You didn't answer my question.'

You threw the dry cloth in my face.'

She stared fiercely into his eyes. *So dark and…*

'I wasn't as distracted as you supposed; continue.'

'Is that an order?' she snapped, pulling up onto her elbows.

'We are here to apprehend a multislayer, not to indulge your immature ego. I assume there's a point to this yarn and would appreciate you getting there quickly.'

They stared at each other in mutual annoyance before she slowly lowered herself again. 'Get on with the massage. Where did you learn such a skill?'

'GSC,' he said tersely. 'Answer the question.'

'They teach massage at Guardian Control?' she said, amazed.

'It's considered a useful method of relaxing tension. If you're not going to answer, I'll leave.' He stared down at her, mouth tight with annoyance.

*Nostowe is way beyond good looking. The unusual combination of red hair and brown eyes only enhance the natural allure already there. His hair is longer than I remember, and has lost its copper gold shine…*

The chill in his voice broke through her musings. 'Are you going to answer anytime soon?'

'They enjoy scandals, murder and political downfalls, so yes they do, especially if it is an unusual crime like a vicious murder. One of the husbands is a commanding officer in the law enforcers.'

'And nothing's been mentioned about such a slaying?'

'No… but there was something interesting. Two monspa ago a relative of Meica Larn, one of the group, went to her vacational residence and didn't return.'

'What's unusual about that?'

'She never stayed at the place longer than a towk;

apparently it's too cold. They've had several non-direct contacts by mesh and script, but nothing in visual or audio.'

'So nothing that would identify her as her. What about the scripted messages?'

'Meica claims they were genuine.'

'On this continent?'

'No, Yarim. It's near the northern pole.'

'Description?'

'It's white and cold.'

The edges of her mouth curled tightly. Noticing the unimpressed expression, Enegene's smile slipped.

*Lost his sense of humour along the way, if he ever had one.*

'Obviously female. In her third decade and obviously excessively wealthy. According to Meica she was "outstandingly beautiful".'

'Has she greater wealth than the last victim?'

'Hard to say. My monetary conversion between systems isn't perfect. If not greater, than equal to I would say.'

'She fits the profile.' Luapp made long sweeping strokes down both legs as he thought it over. 'Except for the wealth. There would be no reason to choose her if the financial situation is not improved.'

Closing her eyes, she bit her lip again. 'We don't know she's deceased. At the moment, she's still missing.'

He remained quiet as he poured oil onto her shoulders and gently rubbed it in. Enegene let out the sigh she couldn't hold in any longer.

*He doesn't think of me the way I think of him, if he thinks of me at all. What is it about Nostowe that stirs me?*

*Totally expressionless as he works; seemingly absorbed in the massage, I know the intelmec he calls a brain is working on six possibilities at once.*

'I don't understand the emotional attachment to a break in

44

the network,' he said, at last. 'It's not as if their lives depended on it.'

'No, it's worse; their reputation depends on it. Reputation is most important to a group like this. An example of this is my lack of attachments or slaves.'

'Certain members have been urging me to purchase slaves. To them I'm wealthy enough to buy slaves, so I should have them. I have been suitably resistant and have got around it because of my "difference". My justifications of being stronger than the males of this genus, and not understanding salations have been reluctantly accepted so far. But I was running out of excuses.

They see my lack of slaves as their lack of influence on me. As I'm one of the top three of the group, anyone who can influence my decision-making gains respect from the rest. Aylisha's position in the group rose rapidly as she got me to agree to a protector slave. And there are two others who can bathe in reflected glory for putting the idea into my head.

The embarrassment comes for the ones who considered me a lost cause on the subject and gave up trying. But if they know before the gathering tomorrow, they can have their excuses ready.'

Stepping back Luapp removed the oil bowl from the heat and replaced it with one of water. 'And it's important you listen to them because?'

'If I listen they're willing to talk about things not generally discussed in the group. They know I won't pass things on by salacious banter; gossip they call it. It's no good telling me anything they want to go public, but I will keep a secret and give advice if asked for it.'

He dipped his hands in the warm water to rinse off the oil and wiped them on one of the towels lying across her body.

'And you managed to infiltrate this tightly protected elite

network in a few monspa?'

'That's the time the guardians gave me.'

'The gem reserve they also gave you had no influence,' he added, dryly.

'It helped.' She grabbed the towel across her chest and sat up, 'and having Aylisha as a close friend helped also.'

'Can you trust Aylisha Rhalin?'

'One hundred per cent.'

'How do you know?'

'As I mentioned before, I invited the neighbours to a small gathering. According to Commander Yetok, that's a good way to meet and assess people.'

'And the reverse,' Luapp added.

'I felt... comfortable with the Rhalins. Aylisha and I have a lot in common although she's a couple of orbits younger than me. Her father, Drew, offers help and advice with no gain for himself.'

'Did you research them?'

'Do you think I'd be blinded by fake friendship?' she said, sharply.

'Discussion among guardians is so much easier.' Taking the bowls, he disappeared into the compact store room. Returning, he said, 'for a Swamplander you have an unusual inferiority complex.'

'I'm not inferior!' she snapped, her Swamplander accent becoming more pronounced.

'And your answer to my question?' he prompted.

'They've been in this city for generations. I looked them up in the status records.'

He folded his arms. 'Such things can be manufactured.'

'I know, but a whole family? Man, liana and three offspring? They're well known in high circles and there's visual documentation of their ancestors. Besides, they're too

46

natural to be dramatists.'

'And the other neighbours?'

'There are two other estates in this area. Both sets can be traced in the natal records. The Borvans, just a man and his liana, while extremely wealthy are not well thought of by the elite. They're not invited to their gatherings.'

'Why?'

'They're called opportunists. He was from the lower social strata, saw an opportunity to make a lot of gemstones and took it. The generation elites don't like that.'

'Then there are the Zumas. They're in their first maturity. Their family has grown and left, and he has retired from business. He is acceptable to the elite as he started as a mid level and worked his way up through the layers of seniority eventually buying the business.'

'I see no difference between the two.'

'It's down to what they call etiquette. On his way to the top, Farom Zuma had time to learn the correct way to behave. Yekob Borvan rose so fast he remains uneducated in their ways.'

'Neither the Borvans nor the Zumas fit the profile or have anything to gain by feigning. I've only met them twice and they are hardly boring their way into my confidences.'

A memory flitted through her mind making her smile fleetingly.

'Care to elucidate?'

'As I said, the Borvans are shunned by the elite, but I made them mingle with them. My first open house, as they call it, was most interesting.'

'The elite came because of my wealth and they were curious. Also, the Rhalins were attending and they are highly thought of. But as the Borvans were neighbours, I had an excuse to invite them.

47

It was most amusing. The socialites couldn't ignore them as it would be bad manners, but whenever one of them spoke to Tekor or Vikier they looked like they were sucking fire seed.'

'I can see that would amuse you.'

As Luapp turned off the oil heater a faint noise from outside made him look towards the door. 'Someone's coming.'

'Pass me the robe.'

Collecting the robe from the floor he handed it to her then took the burner to the store room. He arrived back at the same time as the hazel eyed maid called Lydina, entered. Giving him a quick smile she walked over to Enegene.

'Cook says she has to change the menu for the rest of the week. She asks if this will be acceptable.'

He gathered the towels from the table and took them to the box in the cupboard and returned a second time. Enegene handed the menu back to the maid.

'It seems fine Lydina, why did she feel the need to tell me of the changes?'

'She's trying out some different recipes and wanted to know if there was anything you disliked.'

'As I'm unfamiliar with the vegetables and fruit on Pedanta, I'll trust cook's abilities, she hasn't poisoned me yet.'

As the maid left she turned to Luapp. 'Mikim, collect my clothes and take them to my slember. Then go to the aplirom and wait for me.'

Giving her a long look he went to the changing room to gather her clothes. As he returned, he said, 'when do the servants retire?'

'When I tell them they can, but approximately the twenty second hour.'

'There are twenty-five hours in the Pedantan day...' he murmured, working on the timing.

Enegene slid from the table and tied the robe's belt. 'Why do you need to know?'

'I must contact a space guardian to let him know everything is going well so far. As no-one is hunting you yet, today is a good time.'

'Shall I wait up to let you in?'

'I'll have no trouble getting in, the locks are almost antique. Something I'll have to improve later. I assume my equipment arrived?'

'It's in the roof space. I'll show you where the entrance is.'

'It would look strange the lady of the house showing a slave where to find a place in the dwelling. One of the servants can do it.'

'Only Sylata and her husband know how to find it and even they wouldn't be comfortable going near it.'

Luapp stopped on his way to the door. 'Why?'

'I'll explain later. I must tell you about the procedures of an informal gathering for tomorrow.'

He held out the clothing. 'If you're going to your slember you can take your clothes with you.'

Enegene smiled smugly. 'It would look even stranger if the lady of the house carried her own clothes when her slave was with her.'

She headed out of the spa room with a feeling of elation. In the hall Luapp strode past her and was about to go up the stairs when there was a loud bang.

Both stopped.

Dropping her clothes on the stairs he said, 'go to your room and wait.'

As she continued up the stairs he headed for the front door.

~~~

Outside Farin and an elderly male were looking across the

front lawn. He was holding a three-barrelled missile projecting weapon. Going by the smell Luapp concluded he'd already fired it once and was holding it ready to fire again. Farin was leaning close to him, talking quietly and pointing.

'What's happening?' Luapp said, joining them.

The man looked at him frowning. 'Nothing to concern you lad, just a pokari skulking round.'

He looked in the direction Farin was pointing. 'Explain?'

'It's a large lizard,' Farin said. 'They come close when they smell food. Generally, they're not a problem; they run off at gunfire.'

'Why do you shoot at them?'

'Strange a third-generation slave from the Black Systems not knowing about pokaris.' The man glanced at Luapp then turned his attention back across the garden. 'They have a nasty bite; it can cause all sorts of problems.'

He lowered the weapon and looked around. 'It's a bit early for them yet, but we've been having unusually warm weather.' He looked around again. 'Looks like it's gone.'

Pointing the barrels at the ground he said, 'I'm Mevil Sylata, gardener, general handyman and husband of the housekeeper. Where did you spend your formative years?'

'Mostly outside the Black Systems with a Zeetan ambassador.'

'Never known a pokari try and get in the conservatory before,' Farin said, as they turned back towards the house. 'Normally they try to find a way round the back to get into the kitchen.'

'Anything unusual about the animal?' Luapp said, as they went inside.

'No,' Sylata answered, 'except he was one big bruiser. Usually they're small; the bigger ones generally stay away from houses.' Almost as an afterthought, he added, grinning, 'that's how they get to be big.'

The gardener watched Luapp collect the abandoned clothes. 'When you come to work with me I'll show you how to get rid of them without the gun.'

'That would be appreciated; your weapon makes a loud noise.'

'I suppose with your ears it does tend to make the brain ring.' Sylata chuckled quietly as he and Farin headed for the back of the house.

Luapp continued up to Enegene's bedroom. She was dressed and brushing her hair when he arrived.

'What was it?'

'Apparently a large sunseeker.' He laid the clothes on the bed. 'Have you had them here before?'

'No, but I've heard the servants talking about them, and so has Aylisha. She said her father puts cage traps out for them.'

'Indeed? I'll research them.'

She was humming quietly to herself as he left and except for a wide smile, she ignored him.

In the study, he sat down and looked at the computer. His first thought was to try and contact the enforcer assigned to him, but the short time until she joined him would be rushing a difficult process. Instead he shut out the outside world for some inner cogitation. The most pressing thing on his mind was Enegene.

*It appears from our recent discussion she's caught the interest of someone... but until we attend the gathering I can't do any assessments and therefore no preparation.*

*Could it be coincidental that shortly after I arrive there's been two suspicious incidents? First the smith is visited by a shape changing demon, and now the sunseeker appears. Taken separately they mean nothing; but together?*

His final briefing before leaving Gaeiza came to mind.

*I'll have to discuss the conclusions with the Spyrian as soon as viable, but it will have to wait until I've contacted the Tholman. After that, I hope I'll be able to confirm or refute their suspicions.*

Staring at the wall he switched subjects.

*Enegene Namrae is an enigma. On her release from detention she'd been a sullen, angry secdec with a sharp tongue. Despite her transition into a sophisticated business woman, when I requested her help on this mission her insular attitude appeared to show no change. Now she has a fixed grin, a light mood and is even pleasant on occasions, it's making me edgy.*

*I could almost believe she's been substituted, but the bio check I did confirmed it was her. So if she is Enegene Namrae, something else is going on… she's working on some scheme that involves me and I doubt if I'll like it…*

Footsteps approaching the study interrupted his thoughts. As she entered she gave him a bright smile and sat down next to him.

'This will take us until endeal,' she said, as an opening. 'If you interrupt with too many questions it will take until you leave tonight.'

She paused for effect and then continued. 'The metal worker will arrive at the tenth before to fit the amulets. Aylisha will arrive at half ten and she's always punctual. When we arrive at the Pothery's….'

## Chapter 5

It was one in the morning when he woke. Dressing quickly, he went down to the front door. An alarm of sorts was working but it took only minutes to bypass and unlock the door.

Outside, he placed his hand over the heavy metal lock and concentrated. A faint click indicated the lock was in place. Next, he put his hand over the top bolt. The visualisation of the metal bar sliding forward into the loop was accompanied by a soft dull thud. Then he walked up the path to the road.

Now he picked up speed to a jog. Even for a fit guardian it would take half an hour to get to the grassy hillside he had in mind. For him, still recovering from being with the slavers it took longer.

When he finally arrived, he walked up the medium sized incline towards a small copse. Sitting close to the trunk of a large tree he closed his eyes and relaxed. As yet unable to get any communication equipment from the loft, he was hoping the guardian patrolling was open to a biolink.

It took several minutes of deep concentration before he felt an acknowledgment of his presence. Once the guardian was tuned in it took less effort.

*'Name and rank, Guardian?'*

'Tholman Kerran Gyre, Sector East, Commander.'

'This will be brief Kerran. I'm now with Enegene Namrae and our cover is established. So far there's been no conspicuous candidate for the slayer. However, she's suspicious they may be part of the socialite circle she moves in. Has there been a firm decision on the Fluctoid theory?'

'Unfortunately not, Commander. As this is unresolved, High Commanders Bran and HaJaan suggest you continue under the assumption that is the case. It's better to be prepared for a Fluctoid and not have one, than the reverse.'

'Understood. Communication by bio at this distance is draining; if there's nothing more you can give me I'll close contact.'

'Other than no more corpses have been found fitting the method elsewhere in this sector; nothing. It's the consensus of GSC and Paduan Criminology Department this is the right place.'

'I'll contact you again when I've some hardware Tholman. Keep scanning the waves for anything that fits the methodology.'

'Noted Commander. Communication ended.'

He took a few minutes to give his aching brain a rest then considered what to do next. Somehow, he had to contact the local enforcer, but he'd have little time to do it in the next couple of days.

Getting to his feet he walked down the animal-worn path leading to the road. He was almost there when he stopped. Ahead of him in the darkness he could hear breathing. The person was waiting but relaxed. As he hadn't noticed them when he came up, they must have arrived while he was in contact with the space guardian.

'Nostowe?'

A tall man for a Pedantan stepped onto the path in front of him. He had the upright bearing of someone in the armed forces, and was holding a slim torch.

'Of course you are,' he said, coolly, 'you're Sollenite. I'm

Major Lyndon.'

Lyndon reached into his pocket and pulled out an oblong object. He flipped it open revealing a polished badge. Shining the light onto it he gave Luapp only seconds to read it and flipped it shut again.

'Come with me Guardian.'

Luapp kept his response non-committal. 'Who are you?'

The man started off down the path. 'Same as you; Intelligence.'

'You don't sound pleased to have me here,' Luapp said, walking beside him.

'In my opinion we don't need your kind interfering here,' Lyndon said, sharply.

'My kind?'

'Outside law. We can handle our own problems.'

The sneer preceding his next utterance was clearly heard. 'I've nothing against Gaeizaans, best damn slaves we ever had.'

Ignoring the derogatory remark, Luapp said, 'where are we going?'

'My employer wants to meet you, we're going to his governmental living quarters.'

'And your employer is?'

'Coalition Master Darl. We don't have much time for chat, so keep it until we get there.'

'He lives in this area?'

'No, but we have transport.'

Lyndon speeded up, attempting to stop the questioning, but Luapp easily matched his pace. The path got shallower and through the darkness a fence could just be seen.

'How did you know where to find me?'

Lyndon let out an irritated sigh. 'We've been watching the house where the woman lives. As we couldn't contact you without the servants knowing, we hoped you'd contact the local police inspector and we could intercept.'

'I haven't had time to do that yet.'

'We noticed the shopping trip.' The man laughed lightening the mood slightly. 'I suppose she told you the purpose of it?'

'The socialite's network.'

'Yes. It's very useful. When we want something known we tell one of our operatives to inform his wife. It goes through the network like a rat down a greased pipe.'

'She's aware of your manipulation?'

'Yes, she's an active operative herself. This way.'

Throughout their conversation neither man looked at each other. As far as Luapp was concerned it was pointless to look at someone he couldn't see clearly.

Lyndon headed off to one side bringing them to the fence. They walked beside it until they arrived at a gap and went through to another meadow.

Here a vehicle stood. It looked vaguely aquatic to Luapp. It had a slim, fish-like body with a bulbous top. As they got closer the high whine of engines started up, a door opened and a flight of steps came out.

They walked up to the doorway and Lyndon went inside. He pulled the front seat up and Luapp got in behind. As the engine noise rose steadily higher, wings slid out of the body, and engines came out of the wings. Finally, the machine lifted off and flew across country.

Raising his voice to be heard, Luapp said, 'how long will this take?'

'As long as the Coalition Master wants it to.' Lyndon turned and gave Luapp a dark look. 'I'll get you back before the servants wake up. Inspector Corder is there as well so you can meet him.'

There was a pause and then Lyndon said, 'I was told to inform you we have a bug in the house computer. If you want to speak to us at any time, input the code I'll give you and we'll make contact.'

'Computer?'

'The machine used for information gathering and communication,' Lyndon explained.

'Understood.'

Going by word connotation, Luapp guessed a "bug" must be a surveillance device. He also assumed Lyndon wouldn't have divulged this information unless ordered to.

The missing woman came to mind, but conducting a conversation at top volume didn't appeal to him. He decided to ask when it was a lot quieter.

The street lamps of the villages and towns below passed in a series of pink dots until finally they faded altogether. They flew on until a mountain loomed up in the craft's lights, and they appeared to be heading straight at its upper half.

Just as they reached its face, a sliver of light appeared. It widened and became large enough for the machine to enter. The door to the outside world closed as they touched down.

Lyndon jumped out and waited for Luapp to emerge from behind. They walked to an elevator at the back of the cavern and stepped inside.

*Obviously, the technology of this place is ahead of its civilian counterpart,* Luapp thought, as they travelled.

They stepped out into what could be considered the hall in an ordinary house. The deep piled carpet hushed their footsteps and the rocky wall had been covered in wood panelling and paintings. They passed a small table with a vase of flowers and entered a huge room with windows that filled the whole of the opposite wall.

In front of the windows was a large sofa on which a man in

his later years sat. He was grey haired and had a pleasant smile that broadened as they walked over. On another sofa adjoining the first sat a younger man with black wavy hair.

'Commander Nostowe,' the older man said. 'Let me express my gratitude for you taking such a risk to help us. Please sit down. My companion is police inspector Corder.'

He glanced up at Lyndon. 'Anyone notice?'

'No sir, the… guardian picked a useful area.'

'Go and have some coffee Kavyn, you'll be called when the commander has to go back.'

Major Lyndon left the room and Darl turned his attention to Luapp. 'Sorry about the subterfuge, but it's most important no one knows we're collaborating with outside law enforcers.

As you know the political atmosphere here is very delicate at the moment. That aside, I thought it important you meet the man who endorsed this mission. If it goes well, it will help my cause.'

'Your cause being?' Luapp said, as he joined Inspector Corder on the sofa.

'To drive out the external criminal element and bring the Black Systems into the Galactic Council.'

'An excellent aspiration,' Luapp said. 'I'm sure you're aware the governmental leader can't secretly enrol their electorate and tell them about it afterwards. Part of the council's treaty entails the population of a planet or system agreeing to, and voting themselves into its membership.'

Darl smiled, the whiteness of his teeth contrasting with the fawn of his skin. 'Chairperson L'Orieol made that perfectly clear Commander. I wouldn't attempt to drag my people into something they have no say about.'

'Last month we sent out carefully worded questionnaires to the entire population. The analysis suggests they would vote for it given a chance. I'll make sure you get to read it before you leave.'

'Major Lyndon appears less enthusiastic about my arrival.'

'Major Lyndon is of the old ways. He thinks we can handle everything ourselves. Fortunately, he also believes I'm a strong leader and is loyal to me. He won't do anything to wreck the mission.'

'If your people back your governance why all the secrecy?'

'Because on some of the planets not all the government officials are as honest as they should be. They are happily taking bribes from criminals to ignore their existence and would not vote for anything that would oust themselves or their backers.

Galactic Council rules state a majority of the population of the system must agree to joining, so it's vital the criminal element know nothing about your presence.'

'And how do you intend to get around their objection?'

'There are some crucial elections coming up shortly. Myself and selected heads of planetary governments are sending monitors to make sure the elections aren't rigged. Given a chance, there are some honest politicians standing for the offices coming available. I intend to give them a chance.

I've spent nearly two decades dragging my people out of the anarchy they've lived in; I don't want them descending into it again.'

'I understood you were a newly elected leader.'

'As Coalition Master of the combined planets of the Black Systems I am new, but I've been a politician for twenty years. And all that time I've been carefully putting laws in place one at a time. It's been a long drawn out affair. I could only act when the criminals in the governments were distracted with other things.

Now I have an equal number of honest politicians to dishonest ones. If the ones I want are elected, we'll be in the majority for the first time.'

'Why would my presence interfere with the elections?'

Darl frowned. 'If those in question find out about the investigation before it's concluded, they'll use it against me, my trusted politicians and the council. It would be suggested the council could force me to accept the galactic police on our planets in return for your help.'

He sighed. 'It's all very delicate and dangerous for you and your companion. If you're discovered, I'd be powerless to help you. You'd probably never leave again, at the very least your cover as a slave would become a reality.'

'Unfortunately, there would be no shortage of buyers for a Gaeizaan slave,' Corder said. 'They're still highly prized here, as you'll find out.'

'Is it not good I'm here to stop an external slayer from slaying the people of this planet?'

'Our history of combatting invasion from the wider galaxy has made us insular. The one thing the people of the Black Systems fear most is external control.'

'But they have no problem controlling unfortunate off worlders who unwittingly break the law or fall into debt,' Luapp commented dryly.

Darl's frown deepened. 'You're obviously familiar with the terms of the membership contract Commander; slavery is illegal. Making the wealthy give up their slaves is not an easy task. We'll have a few years to do it, but there will still be strong opposition.

We've been gradually strengthening the laws about slave ownership, and are now in the process of sending out a referendum on slaves. If it's a majority view to get rid of them, they'll accept it. If they think it's a clause in the membership treaty, they'll reject it.'

'What happens when they read the contract and find it's

part of it?'

'If they have already decided to relinquish the slaves, there'll be no problem. They'll just collectively shrug their shoulders and say so what.'

'And if they agree to losing the slaves, and the candidates you back are elected, what then?'

'Then, with the backing of our people, our systems police will seek advice from the galactic force on methods of removing alien undesirables. On occasions, inviting the guardians into the system to help remove them.'

He smiled and let it fade.

'We'll move towards the Council one step at a time, it will be a long and winding road filled with pitfalls. Dissidents are watching my every move and I have to be extremely careful.

But if you solve the case, arrest the killer and leave, I can use it as a positive motivation for joining. I can emphasise the fact you did not interfere with our lifestyle, merely apprehended a serial killer. The population would then see the benefit of your support. No one would condemn you for saving our citizens.'

'Politics is not my strength; I'm an enforcer, so I accept your judgement. My becoming a slave still seems extreme. Why couldn't I arrive as an elite with my assistant?'

'Women do not do law enforcement on this planet. That said, it's necessary to have women in the intelligence service for obvious reasons.

Your associate, as an extremely wealthy female, would not be considered a member of the police force. She can get away with careful questioning by being an eccentric alien. You, as a man would be instantly suspicious.

There are some highly dangerous galactic criminals living under the protection of a few dishonest officials, but they have contacts everywhere. We also have some extremely manipulative political backers. If you are caught here without the knowledge of the people, it could cause us to lose the elections we desperately need to win.'

'News about me being here will spread, if only by word of mouth. How do you intend to counter that?'

'Rumours of third-generation slaves surviving the plague have circulated for years. It allows your appearance without causing a problem.'

'And as I understand it, part of the secrecy was to prevent the murderer from fleeing before being caught,' Inspector Corder added.

'True, but I would not have needed to become a slave and have a burn on....'

'Branded?' Corder grimaced, 'you mean it's real?'

'The mark needed to seem old and real enough to convince a slave master. It's a deep tissue infusion, and was done by a medic on Gaeiza.

'Unfortunately, it was necessary,' Darl said, 'and I thank you for your dedication. As you are now established in your cover, there's less chance of your being thought a guardian.'

Darl's stern expression brightened momentarily. 'Your owner is a beautiful lady, I'm surprised someone from such a background could help you.'

'She's playing a part as I'm playing a part.'

'Really? Even so, when this is over I would like to meet her.'

Luapp twitched a brow. 'Does your female intelligence agent know I'm a guardian?'

'No, and I intend to keep it that way. The fewer people who know about you the better, less chance of being discovered. She's already suggested we investigate your assistant, and we've agreed. I hope her cover is good.'

'Both our covers are good; GSC set them up. I want to

know who she is.'

'Is there a problem with us having an agent in the group?'

'Not as far as I know, but I need to know why people are acting out of character. If it's because she's an agent I can dismiss her as a suspect.'

Darl nodded slowly. 'That's logical. I'll get Kavyn Lyndon to give you her name. Is there anything else you require?'

'What is known about Drew Rhalin and his family?'

'He's honest, hardworking and straight forward,' Inspector Corder said, before the Coalition Master could respond.

The speed of his answer made Luapp make a mental note to investigate his connection to the Rhalins.

'I'd agree with that,' Darl said. 'The Rhalins have been in Denjal for generations. They've had gem inheritance for at least ten of them. As an inheritor of a certain size of fortune Drew Rhalin has an automatic right to attend parliamentary debates and vote on various issues. He's one of the few who bothers to turn up. They are definitely trustworthy.'

'Nothing has happened recently to change your opinion of them?'

'I've had them thoroughly checked since the daughter became a friend of your assistant,' Corder said. 'They are who they should be.'

'And the other neighbours?'

'The Zuma's are from established country families. Although not native Denjallans they are from Pedanta. The Borvan's are newcomers from Farro, but they check out. He started by selling from stalls, noticed a place in the market and utilised it. He made his wealth over a period of five years. He's honest and trustworthy, but they're both still street sellers by nature and behaviour.'

'And what about Nix Pellan?'

'Him?' Darl's brows rose and fell. 'He arrived on planet

just over six months ago. He's a social climber of the worst kind. Certain women seem to like him, and he knows it.'

He leaned forward and touched a corner of the table in front of him. A small oblong in the centre lit up and he looked down, frowning at the image that appeared.

'But not dangerous?'

'He's a shifty character,' Corder said, 'but not violent.'

'Shifty?'

'He's always looking over his shoulder,' Corder explained. 'If he wasn't a social climber I'd have him down as a thief.'

Darl moved the display on the table several times, and then looked up at Luapp. 'Why are you so sure this… sadist is coming or is already here?'

Glancing at the table Luapp noticed a name from the files. Darl was reviewing the evidence.

'Because the first slaying took place on the planet Fythur, and has continued along a direct line between there and here. The last known slaying took place on Landrac, a planet on the edge of the Black Systems. The next logical place would be here on Pedanta.'

'Why not on Farro or one of the other planets of the systems?' Corder asked.

'The victims were each wealthier than the last, so it has been assumed by council profilers the slayer is attracted to wealth. Whether they gain by it, or merely hate the wealthy it's not known.

Pedanta is the prime planet of the Black Systems. It's here the highest wealth owners are gathered, so it is here they predict the slayer will strike.'

'And that's why you think they are likely to strike here in Denjal?' Darl said, scrolling the page again.

'They analysed the wealth of the citizens across the planet. The primary city has the most elites.'

'Hm.' Darl scrolled it up again. 'But you've no idea what he looks like or what type he's likely to attack?'

'As mentioned in the file, apart from all the victims being female and elite, there's no real pattern. They are all ages from the youngest at seventeen to the eldest at seventy-two.

They are different species and genus and the only other tenuous connection is their physical appearance. All were bipedal humanoids, and considered beautiful within their planetary standards.

That is the strangest point of all. If, as we assume, there is only one slayer, why are so many different females attracted to that person?'

Corder glanced at the picture on the desk and winced. 'He must be some sort of charmer.'

'It's not confirmed the slayer is male.'

Darl and Corder stared blankly at him.

'It has to be a male,' Darl said, incredulous. 'No female could perpetrate such… violations on another female!'

'The only reason we stated they could be male is the strength with which some injuries were caused. A few of the wounds show a knife tip forced right through the body breaking the skin on the other side, few females can do that.'

Darl's eyes widened. 'But to deliberately torture their victim for as long as possible? To keep them alive for their own pleasure until the body gave up? No, I cannot conceive of a woman doing that to another woman. It has to be a man.'

He pressed gently on the table edge shutting down the inbuilt computer. Sitting back, he added, 'naturally you have our full co-operation. Please apprehend this maniac before he kills again, Commander.'

The swish of the door drew their attention to a man wearing a dark suit. He walked over to Darl and whispered in his ear. As the man left the Coalition Master stood up.

'A problem has arisen and I must go. We will not meet again unless absolutely necessary until your mission is complete. Jym Corder is your first point of contact in Denjal. If you need anything beyond what he can do, call Major Lyndon. Goodbye and good luck.'

They watched the Coalition Master leave and then Inspector Corder smiled. 'Good, now we can talk shop; about the case,' he corrected, seeing the brief frown.

Glancing at the now clear table top, he then looked at Luapp. 'How could anyone kill so many women? In all my years in the force, the highest number of dead perpetuated by one killer is six. But sixteen?'

'Those are only the ones we know about,' Luapp said. 'There are gaps in the chain; planets they appeared to miss. It's possible there are yet corpses to be found.'

'I'm sure we would know if any of the elite went missing.' Inspector Corder frowned again. 'Anything you want to know?'

'Have any mutilated corpses been found?'

'Not so far. Have you heard anything to suggest they might?'

'Enegene mentioned a relative of one of the socialites going missing.'

'Betilda Cren by any chance?'

'I don't know the name, just a few details. She is related to Meica Larn.'

'We have her on ice... in the morgue. Definitely dead. She died in a fall; killed when her head hit a rock on the way down. Before you ask, I did go down and find the rock. It appears to be a simple slip into a crevice. All injuries correspond to that type of accident.'

'If it's so easily explained, why keep it a secret?'

Jym Corder smiled. 'Because you're looking for odd deaths,

and this one does have oddities. The woman was an experienced skier who knew the area well, and was aware of the location of the crevice.

It was a bright sunny day, so she didn't blunder into it, and if she accidently headed towards it she knew how to stop herself.

Also, she had a high concentration of Depithien, the fear hormone. We kept her for you to look at. After that, we'll release her body to her family.'

'I'll come to view the corpse as soon as possible.'

'It'll have to be late night; Pedantans don't like slaves wandering around without owners. Let me know when and I'll arrange everything.'

'Are you monitoring the intel - computer as well?'

'No.' Jym grinned broadly. 'I've been told you're a computer expert. I expect you to get into the system somehow.'

Kavyn Lyndon's arrival curtailed further discussion. 'Time to go,' he said, stopping by the doorway. 'It's the fourth. We must get the guardian back before anyone notices he's missing. We'll take you both to the police station and I'll drive the guardian to the house boundaries. Follow me.'

They walked to the elevator in contemplative silence. A few minutes later they arrived in the hanger and got into the machine. Jym Corder and Kavyn Lyndon chatted amicably during the flight, swapping stories of past events.

Luapp was content to mull over what he'd been told and was making mental notes about what to look for at the party the next day.

When the machine landed in the police yard, Luapp and the Major transferred to a land gliding vehicle for the rest of the journey. It stopped at the end of the drive and Lyndon pulled a card from his pocket.

'My contact number and the names of our agents,' he said, handing it to Luapp. 'If any mutilated bodies turn up we'll let you know.'

Leaving the vehicle, he walked quickly to the house and let himself in. He locked the door and went swiftly downstairs.

As he undressed he checked his internal clock. *Fortunately, I don't have to be up until the ninth before.*

Laying back on the bed he used a mind relaxing technique and was asleep within minutes.

# Chapter 6

The drone of a cleaning machine on the floor above woke
him the next morning. Taking a few moments to be fully alert
he rose and walked along to the bathroom.

The staffroom was empty when he arrived for breakfast,
but a tray with a covered plate was standing on the table.
With time to spare he ate slowly enjoying the meal and the
solitude.

When he finished he returned the tray to the kitchen and
then went to find the gardener. He was working in a large
transparent construction similar to the one he ate in on the first
night, but this was obviously used for propagating plants.
Luapp was right behind him before the man realised he had
company.

'Mikim?' A puzzled frown creased his brow. 'I thought the
smith was coming today.'

'At the tenth hour. I can work until he arrives.'

'Aren't you going out with the ladies when the smith has
finished?'

'Correct. Is there a problem?'

Sylata looked him up and down. 'You can't wear those
clothes to the type of function Lady Kaylee attends.'

'I can't wear anything else until the clothes are delivered.'

'They're already here; in the room you should've been sleeping in.'

Luapp's mind worked rapidly. 'The mistress said nothing about yesterday, I assumed she wished me to move today.'

'Deana, my wife was under the impression you were moving immediately. As Lady Kaylee wouldn't have checked on your whereabouts, you'd better move before she realises.'

'I have nothing to move except a wash kit. If I leave a short time before the metal worker arrives, I can be ready.'

Sylata scratched his beard stubble thoughtfully. 'I have some things for you to do, but not today. For now, I'll show you what I want done when you have the time. I'll also show you where things are kept.'

They walked to the end of the long garden to a patch of overgrown land. 'This needs to be dug over. It's hard work for me.' He looked Luapp over a second time. 'But you look capable of making short work of it. Ever done any gardening?'

'No, but I'll learn.'

'Yes,' Sylata said, quietly. 'I had you down as a fast learner.'

Luapp frowned. 'You distrust me?'

'Not at all lad. But I find it strange you appear several decades after your people died in the plague.'

'I've been off planet most of my life.'

'That would probably explain it. This way.'

Luapp's mind worked on what was said as he followed the man. *His word usage is careful, it suggests he doesn't believe me. I must be vigilant when working with him.*

They walked to a small stone building set against one of the walls. Its door was ajar and Sylata took Luapp inside. After a brief explanation of what was kept in there they moved on.

Walking back to the house he was taken into a side room

70

covered in floor to ceiling cupboards. Another explanation of the items kept there followed and finally Mevil Sylata pointed to a narrow wall mounted cupboard.

'This holds all the keys. Both to the sheds and the machines.'

'That also locks, who holds the key to that?'

'Deana. She has all the keys to the house.'

Sylata paused and gazed at Luapp thoughtfully. 'I don't think anything of mine will fit you. I'll ask Lady Kaylee to order you some overalls, gloves and shoes.'

'Why gloves?'

'Stops the tools from rubbing and protects your hands from the thorned plants. It also protects them from the poisons. Some of them are absorbed through the skin, although I don't know if you'd be affected like us.'

'Why do you use poison?'

'To kill the weeds and vermin.'

'Vermin?'

'Unwanted animals.'

'You kill animals?'

The tone in Luapp's voice made the older man frown. 'I suppose as a bodyguard you've never had to deal with rats before.'

A picture of a small mammal with a long thin tail flashed onto Luapp's inner vision. He'd refreshed his memory about Pedanta on the journey to meet the Zeetan.

'I've fed them.'

'You can feed them here lad; with poison, but not with anything else.'

The man rubbed his stubbly chin again. 'You sure you're cut out for protecting Lady Kaylee?'

'I'll have no problem protecting her. Sentient beings from higher species can make clear choices. If they make the wrong

71

one they suffer the consequences. The rat hasn't got the facts. It thinks you're being helpful, not murderous.'

Sylata stared at him incredulous. 'You'd like me to tell the rat that if it doesn't stop stealing food I'm going to poison it?'

'You could try. But it would take time waiting for each member of the rat's family to appear for an explanation. Alternatively, you could script a notice and place it where the rat could see it, but I doubt it can read.'

Mevil Sylata broke into a hearty laugh and slapped Luapp on the shoulder. 'You had me going for a while there lad. I was told sollenites didn't have a sense of humour.'

'Familiarity causes contamination,' Luapp said wryly. 'I could work the land for a while.'

'No, not today. You'd better go and get changed.'

Luapp walked through a connecting door to rear store rooms and down to the lower bathroom. Collecting the newly purchased wash kit he took it up to the room Enegene had shown him.

As Sylata had said, a large pile of parcels was laying on the floor by the inbuilt wardrobe. Opening the boxes he put away the clothes. By the time he finished he had just enough time to clear the packaging and change.

He'd made his choice as he unpacked and hoped it was right for the occasion. Enegene hadn't given him any hint on what to wear, but as it was a day gathering, he assumed smart was good enough.

On the way to the sitting room his mind went over his conversation with Sylata. *He possibly thinks I'm an illegal slave, but I doubt he'll do anything unless the enforcers arrive.*

*He takes Enegene to be genuine; there's no hint of suspicion when he talks of her. Another reason to be silent, not wanting to get his employer into trouble. The Coalition Master's perceptions are accurate…*

The two-toned ring of the doorbell interrupted his thoughts. He turned to leave but quick footsteps meant a servant was on the way.

A brief exchange between caller and servant told him it was the metal smith. The door closed and the smith was shown into the room. Giving Luapp a glance as he walked to the table, he placed a leather roll on it.

Enegene came in minutes later. She walked over to the chair beside Luapp and sat down. The smith pulled two amulets out and gave them to her to inspect. As she did he removed the clip-together bands from Luapp's wrists.

'Excellent work.' She handed them back to the smith. 'I shall recommend you to my associates.'

'Thank you, Lady.'

He clipped the gold edged silver amulet around Luapp's wrist with the holding loops above a square of leather. Working deftly, he pushed the long locking pin through the loops and sealed it in place with a hot iron. There was no sign of the nervousness of before.

Luapp watched the smith carefully, comparing the man's actions to his previous visit. They matched and he was satisfied the man was who he should be.

The smith looked up at Enegene. 'You test it Lady?'

'If you can get your finger between skin and metal I am sure I can. Carry on.'

As the smith took the second amulet she looked up at Luapp. Her expression was an odd mixture of distaste and concern. When the sealing process began, she looked away. Only when it was finished and the smith had packed his tools did she look back.

Fixing a smile in place she thanked him and said Farin would pay him on the way out. When he had gone, she stood up and grabbed Luapp's wrists, scrutinising each in turn.

'Are you unharmed?'

'The man's a professional,' he said, bemused. 'Concerned about me Spyrian?'

Her mouth tightened into a thin line. 'I don't want to be accused of collaborating in injuring one of the Brotherhood.'

The doorbell going a second time stopped him from replying. Cleona entered and came over to Enegene. 'Lady Rhalin has arrived Madam.'

'Tell Morvac to get the Drifter ready, and tell Aylisha we are coming.'

'Yes Madam.'

Enegene gave Luapp an icy look as she left. He followed her to the hall where Aylisha was waiting. She gave him a long approving look.

'He looks so much better in those clothes. I don't know where he came from but he arrived right on time.'

'On time?' Enegene said, surprised.

'Just when you needed him,' Aylisha explained.

Enegene smiled briefly. 'Shall we go? We don't want to be late.'

'What are you doing about Pellan?' Aylisha said, as they went outside.

'Nothing,' Enegene answered. 'Mikim's going to do it for me. If he comes over I'll inform him of my instructions to my slave. The rest is down to him.'

'And Benze,' Aylisha said, as they watched the Drifter glide up.

'Mikim is riding in the back with us,' Enegene said to Aylisha, as the driver opened the door. 'Morvac, Lady Aylisha will get in the other side.'

Morvac hurried around the car and opened the door as Enegene slid along the seat. Luapp stopped by the door but got in when her stare suggested trouble.

'This is cosy,' Aylisha said, smiling at Enegene.

Enegene's smile changed to a frown. 'And safe, no one would attempt to stop the Drifter with Mikim in it.'

'I think that was a one off,' Aylisha said. 'I've not heard of anyone else being stopped.'

With the women chatting Luapp turned his attention to the passing scenery.

A while later they travelled up the driveway of a large country residence. Three other vehicles came to the house behind them. A total of ten people emerged and started up the wide, semi-circular steps.

Following the women inside, Luapp was aware of whispering from the socialites behind. Despite the presence of many slaves his arrival in the room made conversation stop. It then continued in hushed tones.

Being head and shoulders above everyone else, he could see anyone heading in their direction. At the moment, that was the hostess, Lally Pothery. She was a short, slightly overweight woman with perfectly applied make-up.

'Kaylee, Aylisha, the party is always so much more interesting when you grace us with your presence.'

She smiled warmly as her fingers slid up and down the long pearl necklace. 'Slaves can go to the reception room and relax for a while.'

'He's a protector Lally; I want him to remain with me.'

'And we know who you need protecting from.' Lally's perfectly arched brows rose and fell quickly. 'Although I don't understand your reticence, I find him quite... amenable. It must be a species thing. So glad you took our advice.'

The smile remained as she gazed at Luapp. 'As he's not to roam free, he may have food from the main table. I must go and greet some others, but I'll be back to hear all about him.'

Lally Pothery drifted off to speak to other arrivals, the

pastel rainbow material strips that passed for sleeves floating behind her. Aylisha and Enegene wandered across the room to the long table covered in food.

'We're the centre of attention,' Aylisha said, grabbing a glass of wine from a passing tray.

'Yes, it must be difficult trying to look round corners,' Enegene commented dryly.

'You know the rules Kaylee, no staring.'

Aylisha sipped her drink while looking around. 'We're being approached.'

Luapp looked up from holding the plate Enegene was filling to see a middle-aged female heading in their direction. She was closely followed by a man whose skin was such a pale green it looked almost white. As she arrived, she looked Luapp up and down with an odd smile.

'Kaylee, what a turn up. Who is your superb companion?'

Enegene lowered the pastry to the plate. 'Aylisha Rhalin, I felt sure you've met before.'

'No games now, you know who I mean, this gorgeous man beside you.'

She looked him over again, several expressions blending into one another so rapidly he didn't have time to analyse them. Luapp gave her a quick glance then turned his attention on the man.

*Pellan, I assume. He's not from a race I recognise. The green tinge makes him look ill, and the impression isn't helped by the wide gold eyes.*

'He's my slave,' Enegene answered.

'Really? One of your own? What's his purpose?' The woman nibbled a sandwich, her brown eyes twinkling. 'I'm sure he doesn't work around the house; well, not all of it at least.'

Her sideways smirk gave Luapp the impression his clothes

76

had suddenly become transparent.

Enegene glanced at him then back to the woman. As Pellan was within earshot she said, 'he's a protector. I've been plagued with unwanted attention from certain males, so I decided to do something about it. From what I've been told he's a rare commodity.'

'Indeed, he is,' Antonia Benze couldn't keep the admiration out of her voice, 'he must have cost a fortune. But I'm sure he's worth it. Tell me, would you rent him out?'

Enegene coughed and swallowed hard. 'If I did that Antonia, he couldn't protect me.'

'No I suppose not,' she murmured. Then, as if she was aware of the situation between her attachment and Enegene she added, 'you'd better watch out Nix, or he will be doing something about you.'

The man combed a stray lock of his brown fringe back with his hand. Edging slightly behind his benefactor he said, 'he's a slave my lady. He's not allowed to touch a free born.'

'He can touch anyone I tell him to,' Enegene corrected. 'His orders are to protect my person with whatever force he deems necessary, right up to slaying someone if they have a weapon.'

Pellan frowned and sidled to the other side of Benze.

'I do agree,' Benze said, her eyes locked on Luapp. 'Ladies of our station do need protectors. We are incessantly targeted by all manner of freeloaders. I must get one of my own.' Her gaze came back to Enegene. 'It was very wise of you Kaylee.'

With a final appreciative look at Luapp Benze headed across to another group, closely followed by Pellan.

'Antonia's playing the "I'm too important to care about missed news card,"' Aylisha quipped Now we can enjoy the party.'

~~~

It was late evening when they returned to the house. Going

into the study Enegene leaned against the desk. Speaking Gaeizaan, she said, 'what do you think of Pellan?'

'Too early to make an assessment, but I felt no emanation from him. Everything I picked up came from expression. I'll hold judgement until I've met him several times.'

Enegene slid her hand up her sleeve and fingered the knife trigger. 'I don't like him.'

'You're probably right about him targeting you, possibly he wants to become your attachment.'

'I'll ask you again in a couple of weeks. I'm retiring now. Don't forget you've moved location.'

'I must leave the dwelling there's a corpse I must view.'

She grimaced. 'Whatever lights your star Guardian. Has the slayer struck?'

'Not unless they've changed their method. My local contact wants me to inspect it before they release the corpse for firing.'

'The relative of Mecia Larn?'

'Yes.'

'Don't be out all night, we have another event to attend tomorrow.' Pushing herself upright she left the room.

Luapp switched on the computer and spent half an hour getting around the detectors on the police computers. Jym Corder must have been on night duty as he got a reply straight away.

The return message told Luapp to meet him at the end of the drive in twenty minutes. He waited fifteen in the study then quietly left the house.

# Chapter 7

As the numbers of events increased Luapp gradually became more exasperated. The socialite's fascination with him was hampering his search.

Slaves were generally ignored as they catered to their owner's needs, and were only spoken to when orders were given. He'd expected this to allow him to observe the party attendees without problems. But the women drifted over like metal to a magnet.

To the Denjallan elite his presence was proof of other Gaeizaan slaves surviving the plague, and their anticipation of owning such a slave was troublesome. The continuous questioning about his origins tested his cover story and interrupted his search for possible serial-killer candidates.

The Major's female agent was proving to be more of a nuisance than most. He'd noticed her watching him and she'd spoken to him twice, expertly probing his cover.

The fact Enegene was also Gaeizaan was ignored by all, especially the agent. Her "good breeding" as they put it, along with her wealth endeared her to them greatly. He felt Ekym's instruction to Enegene on their journey to the Black Systems must have been remarkable.

Much to his annoyance, Nix Pellan often interrupted his concentration. The man didn't know when to give up, and he sympathised with Enegene's irritation with his persistence.

As he attended all the events he noticed the gravitation towards Luapp and opted to use it to his advantage.

The moment Enegene and Aylisha arrived at a party Pellan watched him. He waited until Luapp was distracted by one of the socialites, then he headed for Enegene.

At this event, he'd tried his ploy several times but only managed to get past Luapp once. Although he noticed Pellan's small victory, Luapp could do nothing about it as this particular socialite kept him busy.

While appearing to listen to the woman by giving her an occasional answer, he was actually listening to Pellan. Being close to Enegene, he could hear what Pellan was saying. As his hearing was more acute than humans, the background babble of the party attendees was only a minor distraction.

Keeping a wary eye on Luapp Pellan edged up beside Enegene. Her Swamplander instincts were obviously on high alert as she stiffened before he reached her. When he got the chance Pellan asked why she needed a protector.

'I don't like being sneaked up on,' she retorted, looking around for Luapp.

'Who would do such a thing to an eminent lady like yourself?' Pellan's mouth tightened into his version of an endearing smile.

'You seemed to have mastered the art,' Enegene answered, dryly.

The smile faded and he drew himself up to his full height. 'Madam, I don't sneak; I approach you quite openly.'

The lady with Luapp gripped his hand as a parting gesture and wandered off. Enegene noticed her departure with a smile.

'Really? Well Mikim's approaching you openly right now.'

He spun and looked around wildly. As Luapp was no longer where he'd last seen him, Pellan paled and hurriedly left. Arriving by Enegene's side Luapp spoke quietly in Gaeizaan.

'In my opinion he hasn't the approach of the slayer I'm looking for. I'm also sceptical he'd be universally appealing to females of many different species. Neither you nor Aylisha Rhalin like him. Unless he's an extremely good dramatist I doubt he's the person we want.'

Enegene frowned and surveyed the room. 'Do you sense anything?'

'Do you?'

He scanned the partygoers briefly. No one was looking in their direction.

'There's something...' She stepped closer to him.

Luapp opened his mind and caught a fleeting impression of anger before it faded. He faced the crowd again, everyone appeared to be busy talking to someone else.

'Yes,' he said, at last. 'But I couldn't locate it. Move around the room; I'll try to pick it up again.'

For the next hour they drifted between the different groups of party goers. Even joining Benze and Pellan briefly, but there was no sign of the intense emotional outpouring of before. Completing the round of socialites Enegene went into the garden and found a quiet place to talk.

'Well?'

'Nothing. I assume the person normally has strong control over their thoughts but were distracted causing a leak.'

'Any indications of gender or identity?'

'No, too brief, but you're correct; someone harbours negative emotion towards you.'

'I'm pleased you agree with me,' she said, sarcastically. 'I feel so much better knowing a psychotic slayer's targeting me.'

'It's the part you agreed to play. As your protector, I'll be with you most times. We must...' he looked towards the doors.

Seconds later Aylisha came into the garden. 'Here you are, why are you hiding out here?'

'Not hiding Aylisha, recuperating. It's so draining trying to discuss things when the person you are talking to have their eyes fixed on Mikim.'

'I find it amusing.' Aylisha's brown eyes twinkled. 'You can call them anything to their face and they don't hear you. Mikim is a great distraction.'

After a thoughtful pause, she added, 'Come on, back into the fray, they're about to announce how much has been raised for the charity, then we can escape.'

Following Aylisha back into the room they joined the rest of the guests gathered around the hostess. A short while later they were leaving in the Drifter.

~~~

For the next two events Pellan kept his distance. Several of his attempts to get past Luapp failed. He finally seemed to realise Enegene genuinely disliked him and he contented himself with giving her black looks across the room.

When she noticed him watching her she would try to listen into his emotions or thoughts, but being a novice at telepathic communication, got nothing from him or anybody else.

This didn't mean the person wasn't there, Luapp told her, merely that they were in control. She didn't find this reassuring.

The next meeting was the tenth, which marked the half way point of the season. At this party, a woman Enegene had never seen before brought an enhanced level of contact which caused Luapp to react.

After scanning the room for Pellan and being unable to find him, Luapp went to the buffet table to collect food and a drink for Enegene. While he was gone, one of the regulars, Jezine Ostler joined her, bringing the newcomer with her.

Smiling sweetly, Jezine said, 'Kaylee, this is Divanna, my cousin. This is her first season so I'm introducing her to all the influential people. She asked to meet your slave, I hope you don't mind?'

'In these awful circumstances, we all need guard slaves.' Divanna fiddled with her fingers while staring across the room at Luapp. 'But I never thought I'd meet a Gaeizaan one.'

'Indeed?' Enegene felt a stab of annoyance at being ignored. 'What awful circumstances?'

Jezine took a bite out of a pastry, chewed it and then smiled. 'Haven't you heard? There's been a murder.'

'No; anyone we know?'

'Of course,' Jezine said. 'It wouldn't be worth bothering about otherwise. Reena Kilmen...' Noticing Enegene's frown she added, 'short, fat, wears ridiculous eye watering outfits and drips with diamonds.'

'Oh, she doesn't attend often.'

Jezine's eyebrows flashed up and down. 'That's because she's not invited too often. Husband's a food chain owner.'

'She sometimes supplied the food for the charity events,' Enegene said, as her memory filled the gaps. 'Was it a robbery?'

'Possibly,' Jezine said. 'She wasn't wearing jewellery when they found her.'

'I hope it was quick.'

'Probably; her throat was cut.'

'He's coming back,' Divanna interrupted. 'He's so... well built.'

The woman watched Luapp's approach with a strange

sideways smile. He handed the plate and glass to Enegene and stood behind her, a tactic he taken up to stop Pellan reaching her unnoticed.

Divanna looked up at Luapp. 'He's so tall,' she gushed. 'Some of his facial features are different to ours, but the points on his ears and rising brows fit so well; he's sooo good looking.' She let out a sigh. 'I wish I could have a slave like him.'

She bit into her pastry while looking him over as seductively as she could. 'You're not considering selling him, are you?'

Enegene's smile froze.

*This woman's wittering is beginning to irritate. The Shadowman ignores being spoken about as if he's deaf. Despite our differences I despise him being treated like an object.*

'We must circulate.' Jezine brought her attention back to the now. 'Thank you for allowing Divanna to meet your slave.'

As Jazine went to walk away, Divanna stepped closer to Luapp and put her hand on his chest. 'You're sure I can't tempt you?'

She threw a glance back at Enegene then returned her attention to Luapp. 'My father can be *very* generous...'

Every muscle in Enegene's body tightened. The soft crack of the glass stem in her hand made her relax her grip slightly but not enough to drop either piece.

'He is *not* for sale,' she said, through gritted teeth.

'It's all genuine muscle,' Divanna enthused, as if she hadn't heard, 'perhaps I could borrow him for the week end just to see how he fits in our household?'

Enegene narrowed her eyes and allowed the smile to fade. 'Unfortunately, no. He's my protector, and he can't protect me if he is somewhere else.'

'Are the men from your planet as fascinating?' Divanna said, wistfully.

'He is a man from my planet.' Her mood darkened. *I'm not sure how much longer I can control the rise…*

'Is he?' She removed her hand and turned towards Enegene. 'You have slavery on your planet as well?'

'No. He's a generation slave from the Black Systems, but he's also an ancestral Gaeizaan.'

'Then he knows how things are done here,' Divanna purred. Her hand dropped to his thigh as she looked across the room. 'Someone is trying to attract our attention Jaz, we'd better go.' Smiling up at Luapp, her hand slid around his thigh as she left.

His only show of displeasure was a twitch of a jaw muscle as he watched her depart.

'Don't you do anything,' Enegene said quietly in Gaeizaan. 'I told you they touch. That was mild to what happens sometimes.'

His non-verbal response was to stare across the room. Enegene knew that expression well. The serene calm was just a thin lid on a bubbling interior, and she considered her escape options.

Looking around for somewhere to put the broken glass and finding nowhere she held it out to Luapp. 'Find somewhere to dispose of this,' she said, curtly.

Taking the glass, he walked across the room to where a small bin had been placed under the table. Enegene kept her attention on Divanna while he was gone.

She had wandered over to the other side of the room to join another group. From the occasional glances in Luapp's direction and the eruption of giggles, Enegene guessed Divanna was enthusing over her encounter with the guardian.

Bringing her attention back to Luapp as he re-joined her

she glanced around the room once more.

'No contact?'

'Not the same emotion,' he said puzzled. 'My concentration was broken momentarily, then I picked up... amusement. Unfortunately, it faded as soon as it escaped.'

'Time to leave I think. Aylisha has been giving me the let's go glare for the past quarter.'

As they headed towards Aylisha a sudden startled squeal cut through the chatter and everyone turned to look. Divanna was half lying across the buffet table.

Jazine rushed to pull her up revealing a face covered in the dripping pink sludge the hostess called tarnberry jello. Divanna flapped her hands and screeched at her cousin who frantically dabbed her face with a napkin.

Enegene fought hard to stop the grin. Forcing herself to give Luapp a black look, she said quietly, 'we'll discuss that later.'

Wickedly pleased, she allowed herself a final look at the food covered socialite as they continued towards Aylisha.

'Thank you, thank you,' Aylisha said, with relief, 'I thought I was going to die of boredom. Let's get out before someone waylays us.'

On the way to the door Aylisha added, 'did you see that woman fall over? What a fuss she caused. She must have slipped on something I suppose.'

'Possibly,' Enegene said, glancing up at Luapp.

All through the commotion his expression hadn't changed. If she hadn't known better, she would have thought him innocent.

As the Drifter drew up he moved forward and opened the door. Giving him a last black look Enegene got inside closely followed by Aylisha.

Travelling home, she looked out the window and smirked,

finally allowing herself to fully enjoy Divanna's embarrassment.

<p style="text-align:center">~~~</p>

The next couple of days passed in normal household routine. There were no events to attend meaning Luapp worked in the garden for Mevil Sylata.

When he wasn't doing that he was checking the local and international police files. After Enegene passed on the news of the murdered socialite he wanted to read the report. Accessing the files, he'd found three.

The murder in question had been put down as a robbery gone wrong, which he doubted. Thieves carried knives to stab, lasers to shoot or used their fists. Rarely did one cut the throat of a victim unless it was personal.

Putting in a discussion request to Corder he looked through the other reports. They appeared to be grudge attacks, nothing like the method of the serial killer he was looking for.

As he worked in the garden his mind went to the body in the morgue. *The female in the cool store was difficult. Her injuries were compatible with a fall down a deep ravine. Whether she had help falling is another matter.*

*There were no defence wounds suggesting a struggle, and no bruising that could clearly be identified with forcing her over…*

He bent to remove a stone, threw it onto the pile and continued. *While demise was not necessarily natural, it was not done by the multislayer I'm looking for. That being is a knife welding maniac with a taste for sadistic torture. A quick shove down a snow gully wouldn't satisfy their blood lust.*

*Most who fall don't have time to contemplate their fate unless it's a long fall; her's hadn't been that long… Investigations into her demise have been carried out on the continent she was found on, but without witnesses nothing can be proved conclusively. Corder was correct in releasing the corpse.*

He put effort into loosening and removing another stone.

*Distance investigating's frustrating. I'm used to the direct approach. Interview the various people involved, evaluate the information, come to a conclusion and make the arrest. Now I must inform the local enforces and wait for a response.*

*Lyndon's reluctant to assist and only does so because he's commanded. Jym Corder is more forthcoming; he has a good eye and I feel he's competent. Under this cover, all I can do is hope they notice the method and put anything suspicious online.*

Footsteps coming towards him broke his line of thought for a few minutes. Sylata stopped by the path, complimented him on his work and told him to stop. Collecting the tools, he carried them to the tool shed and locked them in.

With nothing more to do in the garden, Luapp went to the the office and searched the computer for contacts. A small red light was on so he sat at the desk and started it up. The screen lighting was so dim Jym Corder was barely visible.

'Sorry about the poor quality,' he said, quietly. 'But I'm in a cupboard. About your request; the woman was renowned for wearing large amounts of real diamond jewellery, so was a prime target for a thief.

While I agree it's unusual for someone's throat to be cut by accident, it can happen. But it wasn't a quick sneak up behind and slice; she was knocked about first. I got the feeling the attack came first and the theft came after, almost as an afterthought.'

'Personal?'

'That's one theory we're following. There are rumours of an affair so perhaps an angry husband...'

'None of the signs I'm looking for?'

'No,' Corder said eventually. 'But she did have a grimace.'

'Throat cutting doesn't usually give the victim time to think about it.'

'But going by her expression she did. And she had no chance of escaping. When we know more I'll call.'

'Understood.'

Luapp switched off the computer and sat back in the chair.

*I expected an attack shortly before or after arriving. Although there have been slayings, they don't appear to be by the multi-slayer I'm tracking.*

*The emotional leak is something I'd not expected in the Black Systems. Their society doesn't seem advanced enough for bio-speak to have evolved. While the leaked emotion suggests anger, I've not picked up the slightest hint of malice aimed at Enegene. Either they've regained full control of their emotions or the reason for the leak has gone...*

*Tholman Gyre wasn't able to clarify anything; should I inform the Spyrian about the Fluctoid theory or should I wait?*

Pushing back from the desk he stood up. *There's no logic in causing her stress without evidence, I'll keep it to myself for now.*

As he left the study, the gong in the hall was struck signifying lunch was ready. Walking to the dining room he waited for Enegene to arrive.

As she entered, she gave him a smile and he joined her at the table. 'What have you been doing all morning?'

Abandoning his problems, he concentrated on conversing with her. After the meal he returned to the study and spent the rest of the day re-checking backgrounds of the social group Enegene mixed with.

## Chapter 8


The events season was in the closing stages when Enegene
received a plea from the organiser asking her to host the
Grand Social. The original hostess had suddenly left the planet
due to the death of a relative.

This and one other event were the high points of the year.
Everyone of any social standing would be attending the
evening. Even people who rarely attended other events turned
out for this one.

Luapp asked for information on the death even though it
was listed as natural causes. The woman turned out to be a
frail octogenarian and had a history of heart problems. The
doctor had found nothing suspicious.

Having been on the planet for over five months,
frustration was beginning to set in. Lack of progress, in fact
lack of anything more than slightly suspicious, made him
wonder if the killer had skipped Pedanta and gone to the
next planet.

Enegene hosting this prestigious gathering meant a chance
to observe high society on home ground; some of which he'd
not seen before. Close friends, and a core of the top status elite
would expect to stay the night. This included Aylisha's

parents and, unfortunately, Lady Benze.

Sylata went into overdrive ordering all things necessary for such an occasion. The day before the event Luapp was required to help move furniture and erect a large marquee so people could spill into the garden.

The overnight guests would arrive early evening and were to be met at the door by Sylata, Lydina and Cleona holding trays of drinks. Luapp and Farin were to take their cases and direct any slaves to their owner's rooms. They would then be left to find their own way down to the gathering.

On the day, it became obvious few of those staying the night had brought their slaves, unlike those that were leaving.

With servants circulating with drinks or ferrying food to the dining room, and slaves carrying their owner's needs in food and drink, the house was fairly crowded.

Enegene was busy being the perfect hostess with Aylisha by her side so Luapp didn't need to stay close. This allowed him to go to the staff room and avoid unwanted attention from female socialites.

Occasionally appearing to check on Enegene, he would stand at the edge of a room and open his mind searching for malevolent thoughts, but found nothing.

It was because of these frequent disappearances he missed the arrival of Lady Benze and Nix Pellan. On his next appearance, he noticed them immediately. As far as he could tell Pellan was just as keen on watching for him, as he was watching for Pellan. Antonia Benze seemed to be searching for someone too.

Now Benze and her attachment had arrived, Luapp decided to remain among the guests. Circulating through the crowd allowed him to keep one move ahead of the usual over familiar socialites. Looking across the guests he could see when some female was heading towards him and took avoiding action.

He interspersed this with short stops to scan the crowd. If the murderer was on this planet and this continent, this would be the function they would not miss.

On one of the pauses he saw Pellan on his own. The man hadn't seen him and Luapp watched carefully as he once again headed for Enegene. He approached cautiously from behind so she didn't see him.

*That's the action of a man with purpose; is he truly as harmless as he seems? Yet someone who hides the fury of the slayer would leak their intention without realising. Pellan has no such mental leaks...*

Waiting until his quarry was distracted by a servant Luapp moved in. He approached from the side so Pellan would see him before he reached Enegene.

The move worked well. Just as he was about to touch her Pellan saw him and froze. Luapp picked up the "*Aaah*" thought from Pellan as he scuttled back to his benefactor. It was one of pure terror for a moment. As he watched him go Luapp's smile of satisfaction faded.

A cold emotion drifted to him like an icy draft in winter. He opened his mind further to pick it up and was surprised at the vicious intent of it.

It wasn't directed at him, and it was fragmented, as if the owner was trying hard to control their thoughts. He caught a hint of a female, but it was too faint to decide whether she was victim or slayer. Looking for a concentrated expression he found nothing out of the ordinary.

*My mind's so open I'm picking up thoughts from everyone; it's confusing. Salation brains are like sound boxes without off switches; always chattering about something...*

At this moment, they were echoing what was being said, so he was getting a double blast, one through the ears and one in the brain. He winced, at this volume it was painful, and he would have to tune most of it out. Unfortunately, that cut the leak as well.

Wending his way through the crowd, he tried to find the owner of the emotion. *The person was…* he waited, deciding on what he could feel, *they were unsettled, as if something had upset them. I'm closer to the source; if I keep going I'll…*

'Mikim, Sylata wants you in the garden.'

Farin's voice cut across his thoughts. Luapp tried to keep a grip on the emotion. 'For what reason?'

'Don't know, but she said now,' Farin said, and disappeared into the crowd.

Luapp cursed under his breath. The emotion was dissipating fast. Someone in the crowd close to him was the owner. As he looked around, just about every member of Enegene's inner circle of the elite were standing there talking.

Farin's interruption had somehow distracted them and their thoughts were now on something else. Closing out reception, he strode towards the back door and into the garden.

~~~

Enegene was talking to Drew Rhalin when she saw Luapp coming towards her. As he changed direction half way across she guessed what had happened. She assumed he'd achieved what he wanted when he turned away.

The noise of the party and the music from the two bands had covered Pellan's approach. While Luapp's presence had cut his attempts to reach her, his infrequent approaches were still an aggravation.

*It's time to implement another plan I've been brewing…*

Not only would it amuse her greatly, she hoped it would make Pellan think harder about approaching her again.

With Drew Rhalin moving onto someone else, she found herself free and looked around for Luapp. Seeing him by the stairs she headed towards him collecting glasses of wine on the way. As she reached him she held out a glass.

'Have a drink,' she said, in Pedantan and sipped her own.

Aware of the curiosity of the closest group, he said, 'Lady?'

'Have a drink. I doubt if you've had one all evening.' She thrust a glass towards him. Taking it he continued looking around.

'I assume Pellan had something to do with that action earlier on,' she said, changing to Gaeizaan.

'He thought he might try an unnoticed approach so I dissuaded him,' he answered, the same way.

'I want you to stick close, the crowd's thinning and he may try again.'

'As you wish.'

A wry smile touched Enegene's lips. She suspected Luapp's continuous scanning of the crowd had as much to do with predatory females as Pellan.

'You seem to have been moving around a lot tonight.'

'It's necessary if I want to avoid being mauled.'

She giggled. 'Unfortunately, that's seen as perks for the privileged.'

He frowned and glanced at her. 'Why don't they attack other slaves?'

'Because you're a novelty; the object of legends. They've got to touch to make sure you're real. Besides, the other slaves are all the usual type, so they know what they feel like. Drink up, I'll get you another.'

He gave her a puzzled look. 'I'm supposed to be a protector; I can't protect you if I'm inebriated.'

'And I'm your mistress.' She giggled again. 'In all senses of the word.'

Hearing a faint tune floating on the air, she took his hand, closed her eyes and swayed to the music. 'Shall we dance?'

He pulled his hand free making her open her eyes. 'I've enough distraction with the females and the servants without you clouding the issue. While I doubt someone here would use a weapon in public, it's not impossible.'

'You think I need protecting?' She sipped her drink, smiled at curious watchers, and sipped it again. 'You didn't mention Pellan.'

'You need protecting but not necessarily from Pellan. He has a purpose or he wouldn't risk meeting me. What the purpose is I can't tell.'

He scanned the room once more and added, 'I'm setting up the safe shelter soon and will need to get into the roof.'

Cleona wandered by with the tray and lowered it so Enegene could take a glass.

'Take the tray, Mikim,' she said, in Pedantan. To the astonished maid, she added, 'Cleona, go get another one.'

'Another tray, Lady?' She looked from Enegene to Luapp and back again. 'For you Lady Kaylee?'

'We have this tray so no-one else can have a drink. Go get another one and circulate.'

She sent Cleona away with hand flaps and turned back to Luapp. 'Well, if you don't want to dance, perhaps I can tempt you with something else.'

A series of giggles escaped her causing increasing interest from the surrounding groups.

Looking around the room a third time, he said quietly, 'what are you doing?'

'Getting alcoburned.'

Her eyes fixed on his face and she had a peculiar smirk that he was finding increasingly irritating. 'It'll take more than that with this brew.'

'There's plenty more where it came from. Besides, you're helping me drink them.'

95

'You think so?'

He spoke a little sharply but she giggled again. Turning to address the three groups surrounding them, she said, 'he's learned my native language and speaks it regularly just to make me feel at ease.'

Turning back to Luapp she returned to Gaeizaan. 'I know so. After which a good dose of fresh air will work wonders.'

She placed her empty glass on the tray he was holding and took a full one. He glanced down at her and then up at the crowd.

'What's the point of this drama?'

'I'm setting the stage and you're the main player.'

Her smile widened at his staid expression. Returning his attention to the crowd Luapp kept his opinion to himself.

After a few minutes of being ignored Enegene also turned her attention on the partying socialites. Apart from the occasional interruption from those leaving, they watched the crowd thin in silence. It would have made it easier to see Pellan, had he been there.

'The little mire sciddler isn't around.' She frowned. 'Perhaps he's retired, or better than that, left.'

'I doubt it,' Luapp said. 'Benze is staying the night. He'd have no better chance of getting to you than this.'

'Picked up anything?'

'A fleeting thought and it wasn't directed at you. It's been difficult with everyone here; they confuse the issue with their pointless mental gibbering. The previous incident involving you could possibly be a coincidence.'

'A natural biocom on this planet?'

'There's always a few within every civilization. It's how our people got started.'

Surely you would be able to pick them up? You're a trained talent and should be able to do so.'

'True; as bio-communication is rare here, they should be leaking information on a certain level. Only if they suspected another biotalent being present would they try to conceal their abilities.'

'Which suggests they're another alien.'

'Or they're used to travelling further than the Black Systems where biotalents are more prevalent.'

'That would rule Pellan in again. He's the only other alien at these gatherings.'

'It would seem that way. I must...'

'Stay here.' She exchanged glasses again. 'I'm going into the garden to see if Aylisha is there, I won't be long.'

~~~

Watching her go Luapp let out an exasperated sigh. Enegene wasn't the easiest person to protect. Placing the half empty tray on the nearest convenient table he walked through the various rooms looking for Pellan.

As he entered the large dining room he saw Antonia Benze helping herself to food and talking to another woman. The fact she was still up and alone made him uneasy. He doubted Pellan would retire without her.

Unfortunately, she saw him too. He was about to leave when she signalled for him to come over. He couldn't ignore the sign as it had been so clear.

'Ah, slave,' she said, looking up at him. 'I missed your name last time we met.'

'Mikim, Lady.'

'Mikim. It's a good name. I have met several unbonded people of your race, they always seem so... detached. Different to you....' She looked him up and down with a strange, sideways smile. 'But you are a third generation from this area, so I suppose you've adapted. How old are you?'

'Thirty.'

'Thirty is just right.'

Luapp felt the raising of a brow with the slow smile was meant to convey something but he didn't know what.

'For what Lady?'

'Anything Kaylee wants I should think.'

Her eyes swept over him slowly as she chewed the snack. It was an outward show of interest, but the total lack of emotion made him uneasy.

'Did you want anything in particular, Lady?'

'Yes, but I doubt if Kaylee will let you provide it. Did other Gaeizaan slaves survive the plague?'

Inner alarms went off and he opened his mind. He picked up a leaked knowledge of the Gaeizaan slave plague, and closed it again. Despite appearing more interested in choosing food than him, she was watching him carefully.

'I know nothing about them, Lady. I was a child when taken from the village and there were no other Gaeizaan children with me. I have been told there were others but I've never met another Gaeizaan slave. With your permission, I must go; the Lady Kaylee is without protection.'

She glanced up, took a bite of a titbit and put it onto her plate. 'When you see Nix on your rounds, send him back to me.'

'You can be sure of it, Lady.'

Out in the corridor he stopped, considering his reaction to the brief encounter. Benze had never bothered him before, but during that short exchange he'd felt strangely on edge.

Pushing the inexplicable response to one side he went out of the house. On the way, he added a tag to a previous decision on researching Benze' background; this time he'd do it through the guardians. She was too knowledgeable for a spoilt socialite for his liking.

~~~

Enegene left the house heading towards the marquee where the second band was playing light classical music. Not finding Aylisha she wandered around the grounds lit by the many candle lamps. Wherever there were groups of people she paused to look but was unsuccessful, and she decided to return to the house.

As she passed the large ornamental fountain in the centre of the lawn a hand grabbed her shoulder. She froze momentarily then gripped the hand hard digging her nails into the flesh. The whimper it caused gave her great satisfaction.

Staggering slightly, she released his hand, turned and lashed out. The slap caught Pellan full on the cheek knocking him to the ground. The sound of contact and his surprised yelp made all conversation abruptly stop.

'Don' grab meh,' she said. 'I don' like behing grabbed.'

Pellan covered the mark on his face with the napkin he had been holding as he hastily got to his feet.

'Lady Kaylee I....' seeing her hand move again he grabbed her wrist.

Two men from different groups made a move towards them but stopped. A hand on his shoulder made him jump, and then he stiffened. Taking a guess, he said, 'release me slave.'

'Release Lady Kaylee first.'

Pellan tried to prise Luapp's hand off but the grip tightened making him wince and squirm. Releasing Enegene's wrist, he turned to face Luapp as soon as he was free.

'This is a private matter between your mistress and myself.' He rubbed his shoulder gently. Pulling himself to his full height, he added, 'you will leave us.'

Luapp's only reaction was to twitch a brow. Being quite a bit shorter than the guardian Pellan's stance looked ridiculous and Enegene struggled not to laugh.

With Luapp refusing to move, Pellan's pupil slits rounded and his voice became shrill. 'You will learn respect for the unbonded. I demand punishment.'

He looked to Enegene for confirmation but her slight sway made him frown.

'Hehs my s..lave, in my house, following my orders.' She leaned against Luapp for support. 'No-one dis...ciplines him 'cept me.'

His sickly pallor paled to almost white. 'I will speak to Lady Benze about this... it is not ended.'

Enegene steadied herself on her feet and looked him up and down with a sneer. 'You dare speak to som-one of my s..tanding in that manner? Only Antonia invited; not you. Mikim, throw him out!'

Luapp took a step forward and Pellan several hasty steps back. 'I shall leave.' He pulled his clothing straight and glanced around the interested groups. 'It was not my intention to upset you Lady Branon.'

'Well you qessing did!' She sagged towards Luapp, and used his shoulder as a prop.

'Your lady requires your presence,' he said, pushing her upright.

Taking a step towards Luapp, Pellan hissed, 'this is not over.'

'Touch Lady Kaylee again and it will be over permanently.'

Pellan frowned and headed into the house. Enegene swayed slightly, looked up at Luapp and said, 'I think I need your assistance… take me in Mikim.' Slipping her arm around his, they went inside.

~~~

Luapp intended following Pellan but he was slowed by

Enegene. By the time they got in he was out of sight. She pointed to the lounge, which had been cleared for dancing and he diverted towards it.

He got the feeling she was looking for someone, possibly the same someone he was looking for. Passing from one room to the other they were intercepted by Aylisha Rhalin.

'Kaylee, where have you been? I've been looking for you.'

'An' I've been lookin' for you.' Enegene forced a smile and swayed.

Noticing her friend's behaviour Aylisha addressed her question to Luapp. 'Is everything alright?'

'Everything's fine now. Mus' go and bid farewell to leavers. Look after Mikim for me.'

'Gladly.'

They watched Enegene weave slowly across the room. 'Did Pellan have something to do with that?' Aylisha said.

'My lady's mood or the excess of alcohol?'

'Either.'

'Yes.'

Aylisha's smile was replaced by a frown as she watched her friend mingle. 'Do something for me next time you meet him Mikim, wring his neck.'

'I'm at your command Lady.'

Feeling Aylisha's sudden scrutiny he deliberately kept his eyes on Enegene.

'Have this, and come with me.'

Taking the glass offered by Aylisha, he followed her to the dining room. She filled a plate with food and handed it to him. Then she filled another and they returned to the lounge. He watched the crowd holding the plate and glass as Aylisha ate.

'Are you going to hold that for the rest of the evening?'

Glancing down at her he said, 'what am I supposed to do with it Lady? Is it not for you?'

'There are several things you could do with it.' The edges of Aylisha's lips curled tightly. 'You could throw it at someone you don't like. I would find that amusing, although I don't think Kaylee would. Or you could stuff it down Pellan's neck which all of us would find amusing but Kaylee would have to do something about. Or you could eat one and drink from the other.'

He studied her face for several moments trying to decide whether to speak or not. 'Do you find Pellan attractive?'

'Mikim!' Aylisha sounded genuinely shocked. 'That's not the kind of question a slave asks a lady of my standing.'

Aware of the hot blush rushing to her face she nibbled her sandwich and looked away. A few minutes later, she said, 'actually I feel the same about him as insects. A good dosing of insecticide would do wonders. Why do you want to know?'

'He's confident in his approach to females.'

'The little rat doesn't know when to take no for an answer. He was stalking me before Kaylee turned up.'

'Indeed? For what reason?'

'The usual reason I suppose, I never asked him. I was too busy running the other way. But he must appeal to a certain type of woman, otherwise Benze wouldn't tolerate him.'

'Is she particular in her tastes?'

Very.' Aylisha ate, and then added, 'before Pellan she 'hadn't had an attachment. Although the word is she wouldn't mind trading him in now.'

He continued his scrutiny of the revellers that remained until her expectant silence made him realise a response was required.

'Indeed? For who?'

'You. She's called Kaylee several times asking your price.'

He looked down at her. 'She needs a slave?'

She giggled. 'No Mikim. She can buy any number of slaves.

She wants you.'

Giving her a brief frown he returned his attention to the crowd. *More complications; I hope she doesn't get insistent.* He mentally shrugged. *I doubt she's a match for the Swamplander.*

Aylisha's continued scrutiny was beginning to annoy, but her next utterance disturbed him. 'You are an attentive protector Mikim, but there's something about you that's different to other slaves.'

'Possibly the fact I'm Gaeizaan?'

'There; you see? No slave would answer like that.'

*Keff... Langa's teachings appear to have deserted me...* 'Indeed Lady? What would they say differently?'

'They would become very nervous and try to placate me.'

'Did I say anything that offended you Lady Rhalin?'

'No, but that's not the point.'

'What is the point?'

She looked up, eyebrows raised in surprised. 'That's the point. You're too confident Mikim, not subservient enough. If I hadn't been there when Kaylee bought you I would doubt you were a slave.'

Luapp reverted to looking around the room, but his mind was working on the woman beside him.

*The Spyrian's correct, she **is** more intelligent than she acts.*

'I understand surviving the plague that eliminated your family would make you... stronger,' Aylisha said, looking up at him. 'But you were raised a slave in the Black Systems.'

He remained silent for some minutes thinking through a response. 'I apologise for any offence I might have caused you, Lady Rhalin. However, I point out most of my life has been spent outside the Black Systems.

When the Zeetan aristocrat bought me as a protector I rarely entered them. He instructed me to make my own decisions and act with confidence. I assume Lady Kaylee wishes me to continue this way as she hasn't complained.'

Aylisha sipped her drink and smiled. 'I don't want you to change Mikim; in fact, it's not my place, you're Kaylee's slave, not mine. Just be careful with it. The Denjallan elite sometimes realise things are different and then they react.'

Her smile broadened. 'Fortunately, they put it down to how she likes you to be.'

He placed the glass on a nearby table, took something from the plate and bit into it. Giving her a final concerned look he returned to crowd watching.

Seizing the moment Aylisha grabbed his hand and gave it a squeeze. He looked down as she looked up. She smiled and released him.

'Well, I've finally found something that makes you notice me.'

'I'm always aware of your presence, Lady. What was the reason for the physical contact?'

She sighed. 'Even when I get your attention you don't understand me. Kaylee isn't like this at all. Perhaps it's because she's never had to control herself as much as you. And possibly no-one  has ever treated you with compassion before. But you can't fool me Mikim, I know the real reason you ignore me.'

*This evening's turning into one qessing long miscalculation…*
Out loud he said, 'Lady Rhalin, I'm merely fulfilling my duty to protect Lady Kaylee.'

Aylisha wagged her finger to and fro and giggled. 'Now, now Mikim, don't fabricate. Kaylee is perfectly safe here in her own house with all these people around her. That's not the reason you watch her all the time.'

'Perhaps you would enlighten me Lady Rhalin.'
*If she's reasoned it out I'll have to do something…*
'You have real feelings for her, don't you?'

'Lady, I'm a guard slave; it's my duty…'

'Don't even try to deny it Mikim. Your eyes hardly ever leave her when she's around, and she feels the same.'

Aylisha shrugged. 'Inevitable I guess, you're both the same species…'

Luapp relaxed and shut out Aylisha's ramblings. She'd interpreted what she saw the wrong way, even so, she concerned him. Although Aylisha Rhalin was more controlled than the rest of the socialites, even she had the urge to touch.

His next scan of the room was interrupted by another hand squeeze, and it was slightly longer than before. 'I still don't like to be ignored, even though I know the situation,' she said, as he looked down again.

'May I ask you a question?'

Releasing him, Aylisha considered carefully before replying. 'As long as it isn't too personal.'

'Why do your kind feel the need to touch me?'

'I suppose because Gaeizaan slaves have passed into legend. We know they were real as there are many documents saying so, along with visual footage. And of course, people who leave the Black Systems have met free Gaeizaans.

But having a living breathing Gaeizaan slave amongst us again suggests the rumours are true, and there are a few more out there somewhere.'

'The Lady Kaylee is Gaeizaan; they don't feel the need to touch her.'

'Probably they do,' Aylisha said. 'I've seen many men gazing at her. But she's a freeborn; it would be terribly bad manners for us to walk up and touch her.'

Aylisha grinned. 'And there's the fact she could flatten Anybody, as demonstrated tonight.'

'You're saying they touch because they can.'

'Yes, but there's more to it than that. You are so much taller, stronger… You exude power, but it's contained. You're gentle and calm… it suggests… I suppose like a father figure…'

'What most of these females demonstrate around me is nothing like a child-parent relationship,' Luapp said, dryly.

Aylisha sipped her drink and grinned. 'You're right about that, but it's still linked to the power thing.

A strong and gentle lover is the next best thing to a father. Besides, when we do touch you, you feel different to our men. Your skin is soft as a baby's and you're nice and warm.'

'My body temperature is higher than yours.'

'Fascinating,' she said, sarcastically.

He scrutinised her face for a full five seconds longer. Giving her another puzzled look his attention went to the wider room. Aylisha followed his gaze and said, 'Kaylee's mood seems to have lifted now.'

They watched Enegene collect two drinks and head in their direction. She staggered over, taking sips from each glass. Smiling broadly, she said, 'wha's happenin?'

'I squeezed your slave's hand but he didn't appreciate it.'

'I hope he's not dishress…distres…rude.'

'No, just non-responsive.'

'Could order him to be.' She sipped one of the glasses again.

'You could order him to swing from the lampshades, but it wouldn't do much for my self-esteem.'

Enegene giggled and swayed slightly. 'Migh' be good t'see him swing from lampshades… highly amusing.' She giggled again.

Aylisha frowned then smiled at her friend. 'How many of those have you had?'

'Enough to enjoy myself. Only got to get upstairs.'

'Looking at you, you will be lucky if you get up one stair, let alone the lot.'

'Mikim can carry me, can't you?' She leaned against him grinning foolishly.

'If you wish, Lady.'

'Oh I do wish. I wish a lot, but I must shee the rest of the freeloaders off the premises.' She swept her arm around splashing wine from the glass.

Aylisha's smile widened to a grin. 'Does that include me?'

'You,' Enegene forced herself back onto her feet and swayed, 'are not a freeloader. You're my friend. My good friend. My best friend. My only friend.'

'That's not true; you get on well with several other people. We have quite a nice group.'

'But not like you. Your family's my family. I like your father.'

'Do you?' Aylisha laughed lightly, 'why?'

'Because he makes up his own mind. He's not predid… prejidid… he likes everyone.'

'He doesn't like Lady Benze.'

'A man of discerning tastes then,' Luapp commented.

Aylisha gave him a startled stare. 'Mikim, slaves are not supposed to air their opinion,' she said disapprovingly. Then added in a lighter tone, 'but in this case I forgive you.'

'So do I,' Enegene cut in. 'Fact…I tol' him to opin…pin..'

Watching Enegene swaying, Aylisha said, 'I think you really will have to carry her upstairs, Mikim.'

They were interrupted as the last couple leaving came to say their farewells. A short while later Sylata came into the room. Approaching Enegene, she said, 'that's it Madam.'

'Clear 'way food an' do quick brush shup. Rest done tomorrow.'

'I'll take Lady Kaylee to her room and return to help you,' Luapp told Sylata.

'The qess you will,' Enegene said, grabbing his arm.

107

Sylata and Aylisha exchanged glances, then her friend said, 'I'll be going to bed now Kaylee. I suggest you do the same.'

'Intend to.' She giggled as she watched Sylata disappear. 'I'm going to my s-leeper, and sho is Mikim.'

'It would be easier for your housekeeper if Mikim helped her,' Aylisha said, tactfully.

'I've many servants. Won't take long to clear 'way. Mikim's going to be occ..u - busy tonight.'

Aylisha looked her friend over. 'I doubt if he will,' she murmured. Then louder, she added, 'goodnight Kaylee, I'll see you in the morning.'

'Not early. Firseal's half ten.'

With a final smile, Aylisha lifted her gown and headed for the stairs. Luapp took the empty glasses from Enegene as she turned towards him. Placing both hands on his chest to steady herself, she looked up.

'Is there anyone around?' she said, in Gaeizaan.

'Not that I can see.'

'How did I do? Convinced everyone I was alcoburned?'

'Everyone but me.'

'Good. You'll still have to carry me upstairs; I'm in no fit condition to walk after all.'

Luapp narrowed his eyes. 'As you wish, Lady.'

He put the glasses on a nearby stool and turned back towards Enegene. In one swift movement, he grabbed her waist and lifted her over his shoulder. A grunt was forced from her as she hit his back. Pressing her hands against him she pushed herself up a little.

'Put me down you drypad city liver; put me down!'

With a shrug like movement he flicked her forward and lowered her to the ground.

'You required me to carry you upstairs.'

'Properly! You will do it properly.'

Reaching up she placed her arm around his neck. This time he lifted her into his arms and walked towards the stairs.

'Mikim.'

He stopped and turned towards the housekeeper. 'Don't do anything she doesn't want you to.'

Enegene laughed. 'Thas' not problem Sylata. Problem is getting him do what I want.' Resting her head on his shoulder she giggled merrily to herself.

As Luapp started up the stairs, he could feel Sylata's gaze on his back. He had the feeling she hadn't been surprised by the night's turn of events.

Outside her door he stood Enegene on her feet and turned the handle. She rested against the wall then slowly slid down it, giggling quietly. He caught her half way down and raised her to her feet again.

'Take me to sleeper Mikim,' she said, louder than he liked.

'It would be better for your guests if you kept the noise down,' he stressed quietly.

'Didn't hear you,' she said, sliding again.

Catching her a second time, he picked her up and carried her into the room. Placing her on the bed he turned to get a robe and notice a shadow under the slightly open door.

As he moved towards the door, the shadow rapidly disappeared. Then he changed direction and continued into the bathroom.

'Help me into sleeper.'

She pushed herself up onto her elbows. Sliding her legs off the bed she tried to get up and fell loudly into a heap on the floor. Hearing the noise he appeared at the bathroom door.

With unspoken descriptive words whizzing through his mind, Luapp went over to Enegene, and put his hands around her waist to lift her.

'You're heart warmer Mikim; glad you're mine.'

She wrapped her arms tightly about his neck and kissed him. Pulling free he stood up and pulled back the covers. Then he returned to her, picked her up and put her on the bed once more.

Extracting himself from her grasp again, he removed her shoes, undid her dress and slipped it off her shoulders. As he pulled it down her body and over her feet, it occurred to him it was fortunate she'd dressed in the style of the planet.

Next he collected the robe from the bottom of the bed and slipped it on her arms. It took time and effort as she was waving them around. He tied it's belt loosely around her waist and then removed the all in one under garment she was wearing. Finally he pulled up the covers.

Struggling into a sitting position she gestured to him. 'Come here Mikim.'

With his emotional control threatening to break loose he turned towards the door. 'Sylata needs my help.'

'Come or I'll scream an wake the whole qessing household.'

He hesitated, and then went to her side. 'You're taking this fiasco too far,' he warned in Gaeizaan.

'You are not helping Sylata tonight,' she replied in Pedantan.

'In that case, I'll retire.' He took a step backwards.

'Retire here.'

Caught unawares, his surprise showed. 'Lady Kaylee, you've had too much alcohol and your behaviour is unrestrained. It would be discourteous to follow your order.'

'Mikim, I've have jus enough... an know exactly what Iahm saying. I'll clarify...'

'Please don't,' he interrupted.

'Then I'll say it this way; you're ma slave, I'm your owner. You obey me an I'm giving an order. Get into sleeper now.'

He remained where he was for several seconds, then turned towards the door.

'You'd better not disobey me,' she warned, darkly.

'The door is open,' he said, walking over to it.

Shutting the door he returned, but before he could speak she raised her hand. 'Have they gone?' she said, in Gaeizaan.

Luapp listened. 'He's gone. What did you learn?'

'Learn?' she said, innocently.

'I'm assuming the inebriation act was so people would be less concerned about your presence.'

She smiled and propped her head on her hand. 'And I thought you were busy looking for predatory females.'

'Did you gain any useful information or not?'

'There's rumours circulating about Mercia's cousin. Apart from that nothing.'

'I'm concerned we have the wrong planet; or the wrong target,' he murmured, thinking of the leaked emotion.

'There are only two of us with such wealth,' Enegene said. 'Me and Benze. Perhaps wealth is not the reason for the slayings.'

She lay back on the bed and laughed quietly. Luapp gave her a puzzled look. 'You really believed my little performance just then.'

'Anything's possible with you,' he said, coolly.

'It's a necessary next step. As I'm solo and have a slave of my own genus, it would cause unwanted interest if my slave wasn't sharing my sleeper.'

Enegene watched the man in front of her with a mischievous smile. 'I'm not entirely dismayed at the necessary turn of events; I'm open to the idea of sleeper share.'

Studying her face for a few moments, he said, 'if you think this arrangement is going to be anything but a plains mist you're greatly mistaken. There's a possibility a slayer is in

111

this dwelling  and they could strike at any time.'

'And the slayer is the only one about to strike.' Raising a brow, she looked up at him. 'It's said when a guardian removes his uniform he reverts to being an ordinary male. So there's nothing stopping you taking advantage of the situation.'

His annoyance with her setting up the entanglement without telling him first caused a rapid mood deterioration.

'You're taking enough advantage of the situation for both of us.'

Pushing up into a sitting position she glared at him. 'You're supposed to be protecting me from a crazed slayer How can you do that from the other end of the dwelling?'

'I'm in the next room and I'm setting up the safe shelter as soon as possible. Then I will be with you permanently; actually above you.'

'You're going to be with me permanently now. Pellan's managed to creep up on me twice recently.'

'He's one of the weaker humanoids and doesn't carry a weapon. I don't understand your unease.'

'You said yourself you were reviewing your opinion of him.'

'He's not the insipid invertebrate I thought he was, but I doubt he could strike with the ferocity of the slayer.'

'He's determined to get to me. Why is that if not to slay me?'

'Each time it's been in a crowd. The person we're after doesn't slay in a crowd. Their aim is to take their time in the slaying and then escape.'

'So why is he so desperate to get to me?'

'Aylisha Rhalin said Benze was thinking of cutting him loose. Perhaps he's trying to find another benefactor before he's set adrift.'

'He can steer his reeder to some other shore. I don't want him.'

Luapp smiled. 'Perhaps he's attracted by your total lack of interest. Some males react that way.'

'You don't.'

'I'm on duty.'

A slow, seductive smile crept across her lips. 'Are you saying if you weren't on duty things would be different?'

'Why keep up this pretence? All you've done since we met is spit venom.'

Her relaxed posture stiffened. 'What did you expect? You arrested me and you've got my knife.'

'You were breaking. And if you think I'm going to return that flesh carver you tried to stick in me you're mistaken.'

'I didn't know I was breaking. And I didn't intend to harm you, it was just a warning.'

'You always carry that weapon for warnings I suppose.' He paused. 'As for not being a collaborator, you should have identified your employer. I gave you opportunities.'

'I'm not a carabac,' she snapped.

'Honour among the Swamplanders? It was a Swamplander who informed.'

'I know,' she said coldly, 'and I dealt with it.'

'Indeed? How?'

'None of your tehin business Guardian. Let's get back to the task in hand.'

Twitching a brow, he said, 'the women who were attacked were from different genus. It must be an unusual being to get close to such a variation without being rejected.

The slayer must be a person that's universally acceptable to many species and many age groups. From my observations Pellan doesn't have this universal appeal.'

'He could behave totally differently on a one to one.'

113

'Agreed. I haven't ruled him out, just pushed him off centre.'

'And if it isn't Pellan then who?'

'I'm not sure. The emotional leak clouds the issue. Until I can identify the owner I can't rule them out. But the problem is greater than you think. One of my superiors theorised the slayer is a shape shifter.'

'Shape shifter? What's that?'

'Exactly what the term implies. The most prominent genus is called Ominarian, known widely as Fluctoids. Generally, their shape is humanoid but they can change to look like something or someone else if they choose. If the slayer is a Fluctoid, they can make themselves appealing and trustworthy to the intended victim.'

As realisation sunk in Enegene's annoyance was replaced with fear. 'But that means I can't even trust you!'

'They can only take the physical form of a person. If they impersonated me, you would know. They wouldn't know my personality type or be able to speak Gaeizaan fluently.

They'd also make many mistakes thinking I was a slave. I can insert a mental tag to ease your concerns if you like.'

Enegene frowned and bit her lip. 'Yes, do that - now. At the moment, I'm convinced you're you... or I will be when you've answered two questions.'

'And those are?'

'Who is your closest friend, and what is their father's occupation?'

'Ekym Yetok. He's a Plac-cred Merchantman. Lie back and I'll place the tag in your mind.'

She closed her eyes and lay back. Luapp sat on the bed and put a finger of each hand against her temples.

'Relax; your tension will block the pathway.'

She made a conscious effort to do as required and

obviously failed; the biospeak comment that followed not only shocked her, but had her in fits of giggles.

As she calmed, the was a feeling of a gentle breeze coursing through the layers of her mind to the  very core of her personality. Here he placed a signature that represented himself, something that could not be replicated by anyone else.

No words would need to be spoken. But whenever he came into the same room as her, she would instantly know if it was him or not, and she would feel safe. As he removed his hands, she opened her eyes and looked at him.

'Your interest in the smith's behaviour – was that to do with the shape shifter?'

'He said it had taken his form. If the slayer is a Fluctoid, getting entry into the dwelling as the smith would allow it to assess me and the security of the building. If the man isn't in the habit of taking hallucinatory drugs, it's disturbing.'

'And the pokari? What was unusual about that?'

'It was the wrong time of year for the creature to be around, and it acted atypically by trying to get in the conservatory. Farin and Sylata commented on these things.'

'And the animal attack Aylisha mentioned?'

Luapp smiled. 'Your observation skills are well honed. Nothing except it confirms the animals are out earlier than usual. It helps to eliminate the one that arrived here.'

Enegene sat up. 'I'm not alcoburned and I'm not playing games, but I would really like you to stay the night.'

'I understand this information is unsettling. Knowing you're the target will put a strain on your nerves, but I'll be close enough to help you.'

'That has nothing to do with what I am feeling right now.'

A brief paused followed, and then he said, 'what happened to the attitude?'

'I reviewed my acrimony when I learned the truth about my sentence. You requested leniency; it was the consequentor who insisted on maximum.'

He considered his next words carefully. 'You and I are no longer the people we were when we left Gaeiza. The circumstances of the mission were bound to bring us closer. However, we've certainly not come far enough to allow me to accept your offer.'

'No would have done. But we're definitely carrying on the charade that you're now my monbliss as well as my slave.'

With a sigh, she lay back. 'Take the passage to the connecting room. Make sure you lock the outer door, so no one enters, and make sure you're back tomorrow morning for Cleona to find.'

'As you command, Lady.'

Leaving the bed, he pressed the relevant wooden square on the panelling. As the door opened he stepped through, but instead of going to his bedroom, he went along the walkway between the rooms.

At the end, he turned left and went on to Antonia Benze' room. Moving the sliding panel at face height, he looked in. She was in bed snoring. All he could see of her was the pink tipped black hair poking out from the cover. Pellan was sitting at the window table. It looked as if he was writing something, but most importantly, he was still humanoid in shape.

On the way back Luapp was about to enter his room when he changed his mind and carried on to the hidden staircase. He went down to the ground floor and emerged in the lounge. Going to the door he paused and listened.

Nobody should be around at this time in the morning but he was cautious. Hearing no movement, he quickly left the lounge, crossed to the study and switched on the computer.

He had done this so many times without any contacts from

116

the inspector or the major that it came as a surprise when a video was indicated. Clicking on it he was even more surprised as Jym Corder appeared looking tense.

'Commander, contact me as soon as you receive this; it's most urgent, I think we have a hit.'

Luapp consulted his inner clock. He doubted the inspector would appreciate his waking him at two thirty in the morning. If the slayer had struck the victim could wait. If Corder suspected a strike, he would remove the potential victim to a secret location. This could wait until later. Shutting down the computer he went up the conventional stairs.

Walking along the corridor he listened in on the other guests. All were sleeping peacefully so he continued to his own room. Inside, he allowed himself a brief smile. Judging by the fruit placed here, this was where she intended him to stay all along.

## Chapter 9

Luapp left the bed, felt around for his clothes and half dressed. Straightening the covers, he collected his shirt and boots and pressed the relevant square on the wall.

He later wondered whether he was tired, or whether he was subconsciously picking something up, but the panel he was about to open turned out to be wrong. He only realised his mistake because the release button was not where it was supposed to be.

Instead of entering like he intended, he pushed aside the small view panel and looked in. It was Benze' room again. She was still in the bed and this time Pellan was nowhere to be seen. He assumed he was sleeping in the side room.

He was about to return to Enegene's room when a shadow across Benze' window caught his eye. He was fully alert in seconds. Enegene's words about Benze being of equal wealth came to mind.

Looking around the room again he listened attentively. There was no discernible sound, not even breathing. Normally his hearing would pick that up. It would be disturbing if Benze had been slaughtered while he slept.

He lowered his clothes to the floor and carefully opened the door. Inside the room, he paused and listened again. There were no unusual sounds and nothing moved.

He approached Benze and stopped beside her. Despite covers being pulled up over her face, he could now hear soft breathing. The possibility something might have been in there besides them made him turn towards the adjoining room.

Quietly opening the door, he stepped inside. Pellan was sleeping face down snoring softly. Satisfied he was alright he walked back to Benze. He considered moving the cover to make sure she was fine, but he could hear her breathing clearly now and decided he was risking trouble. If she woke she would get the wrong impression, and he could do without more complications.

Back in the passage he went to Enegene's room and entered. Leaving his clothes on the floor he got in beside her. Still asleep she turned towards him and placed her arm around his waist. Emptying his mind, he allowed himself to drift half asleep for another hour until a faint sound brought him awake again.

Pushing her arm away he sat up and looked towards the shutters. He was trying to decide whether it was some night creature moving about, or even the wind. A few minutes of attentive listening told him there was no wind blowing, and now no sound.

Muscles tightened with anticipation of a forthcoming fight as a shadow crossed the shutters, but he relaxed as it moved away. The shadow had been humanoid in the fact it had a head and shoulders. There was nothing else to distinguish it.

Sliding out of the bed he approached the shutters with caution. It was getting lighter but not light enough to cast a shadow. He stood to one side and could see enough through the slats to know there was no moon.

*How had the shadow been cast? And where were they standing?*
*They couldn't stroll by a second-floor window with no balcony.*

He took several steps back and returned to the bed once more. This time he remained awake. An hour later Enegene woke with a sigh, and finding him beside her smiled happily.

'Now you're here, how about a little action?'

Luapp sat up and slid from the bed. 'The only action will be me leaving this room.' He collected his clothes and headed for the bathroom.

A short while later a knock on the bedroom door brought him out. He opened the door and received a quizzical look from Cleona as she passed. She went to the bed and placed the tray she was carrying over Enegene's legs.

'Good morning Lady,' she said cheerfully. Giving Luapp another long look, she left.

He waited a few minutes before following Cleona out. At the top of the stairs he watched her moving speedily down and into the dining room. As soon as she was out of sight he went into the lounge and through the hidden passageways. He stopped at the large dining room and slid back the view panel.

Some of the staff were laying the table and standing the heating containers on the sideboard. Sylata was supervising.

'Mikim's up early this morning,' Cleona said, pulling a trolley of food over to the sideboard.

'Oh? And how do you know?' Sylata said, watching Lydina lay the table for the guests.

'He was in Lady Kaylee's room when I took the tray in.'

Sylata focussed on Cleona just long enough for the maid to notice the derisory look. 'And from that you conclude he was up early?'

Cleona looked up from checking what was in each tureen. 'How else could he have got there before me?'

120

'If he was still there,' Sylata replied, 'I would say he was up late.'

Lydina chuckled quietly until silenced by a look from the housekeeper.

'Silly girl!' Sylata added, 'can't you read the signs?'

Cleona paused in transferring the tureens from the trolley to the warming plate. 'What signs?'

'Lady Kaylee was taken with Mikim the moment she brought him home. It was obvious.'

'I was quite taken with him too. Still am as a matter of fact, but I haven't found him in my bedroom.'

'Nor mine,' sighed Lydina.

'You and Lydina are human, Lady Kaylee is Gaeizaan. That's the difference.'

'More like I can't have him flogged for refusing,' Cleona muttered. A black look from Sylata sent her scurrying into the sitting room to tidy up there.

'No other owner would have waited so long, or have had to have been so drunk,' Sylata murmured.

'At least Mikim's good looking even if he is alien,' Lydina said. 'Lady Benze' freeloader is downright plain. I don't know what she sees in him.'

'He's a slippery one alright,' Sylata muttered. Then added quickly, 'get on with your work.'

Lydina brushed a wrinkle out of the cloth and left. Now Sylata was on her own Luapp could question her. Returning to the lounge he appeared in the dining room a few minutes later.

'Are you a light sleeper?'

'I beg your pardon?' Sylata said, surprised.

'Would you hear anyone moving around at night?'

'I would hear them outside, and on the ground floor, but not in the bedrooms.'

'Did you hear anyone moving around last night, or early

this morning?'

'No.'

'Do any of the staff walk in their sleep?'

'No. What the elite do during the night has nothing to do with us or you Mikim. Why are you asking?'

'As Lady Kaylee's protector, it is my duty to investigate unusual occurrences. I heard something last night; but it was very quiet.'

'I would have thought most of the guests were too drunk to be awake and wandering around.'

'So would I,' he murmured, more to himself than to her.

Their conversation was interrupted by the arrival of Drew Rhalin. He went to the sideboard, collected a bowl and helped himself to food.

Cleona followed him in and grabbed an ornate teapot. Moving to the table she asked what he would like to drink. As she departed again, he glanced up at Luapp.

'You are Mikim, yes?'

'Yes sir.'

'Kaylee bought you as a protector. Have you been trained to protect?'

'Yes sir.'

'You certainly look fit enough. Stick close to her Mikim, she seemed troubled last night; I have never seen her so jittery.'

'Jittery?'

'Nervous.'

'She's concerned about a certain individual.'

'Pellan. Yes, I know, but he is weak and ineffectual. He's a riser, nothing more. I don't discount her fears; I merely think she is looking in the wrong direction.'

Luapp was instantly interested. 'In which direction should she look, sir?'

'I'm not completely sure, but it's someone who moves in the same circles as Kaylee and my daughter. On the few occasions I accompanied Aylisha on the social circuit, I had the feeling there was someone harbouring ill intent. At first it seemed like it was directed at Aylisha, now it seems directed at Kaylee.'

'Did you feel this presence last night?'

'No...' he didn't sound certain. He sipped his tea and then said, 'did you hear anything during the night?'

Sylata's jaw dropped.

'Such as what sir?'

'It wasn't distinct. I thought it was leaves rustling against the windows, but there was no wind.'

'I heard the same thing,' Luapp confirmed. 'But I found nothing.'

Drew Rhalin gave Luapp a long look, but anything he might have said was curtailed by the arrival of his daughter.

'Good morning pap, good morning everyone,' she almost sang the words. Fixing Luapp with a bright smile, she added, 'good morning Mikim. Did you sleep well?'

She went to the sideboard and helped herself to breakfast then sat next to her father. 'Too tired to answer?' she said, mischievously.

Luapp considered his answer carefully. Whatever he said would be deliberately misconstrued by her. 'Not as quiet as I hoped,' he said, eventually.

She grinned wickedly. 'I'll bet it wasn't.'

Drew gave his daughter a disapproving look. 'Aylisha, if you have something to say, say it plainly, do not couch your meanings in riddles.'

'I'm sure Mikim understands me perfectly pap, he's used to interpreting hints.' Giving him a last grin she turned her attention to her meal.

123

Catailyn Rhalin entered next. As she joined her family more footsteps could be heard in the hall.

One by one the guests were arriving for breakfast so Luapp left the dining room to join Mevil Sylata in the garden. While he worked at removing the marquee and its contents, he took the opportunity to look around without being obvious. It also allowed him to think through the previous night's events.

His curiosity was roused by the fact someone else had heard something. A query crossed his mind about Drew Rhalin being awake at that time in the morning, but he discounted him as the shadow. Not only was he too old for such activity, he'd been investigated by inspector Corder and the major.

Being summer little rain had fallen and the ground was too hard to leave impressions. Much of the grass had been flattened by the many feet coming and going between the house and the tent, but not so many people had strayed away from that area. He found evidence of three only.

As he helped to clear up, he looked for anything that might have been dropped to give him insight. Again, he found nothing. Carrying the folded tent to the vehicle on the drive he continued his observations.

This time he found something interesting. Flattened grass in front of the conservatory and going around the outside edge. It looked as if someone was trying to find a way in. If that was the case, the intruder might not be one of the guests that stayed the night. That disturbed him even more. House security suddenly topped his list of things to do in the near future.

When he returned to the rear garden, Mevil Sylata told him he could go so he made his way up to Enegene's room.

She wasn't inside, but as there were several people milling around the house he doubted she would be in any danger for the moment.

Back on the ground floor, he tested all the external door locks. All seemed to be in good order, but replacing keys with a number system would be an improvement.

At the same time, he checked the alarms. They also seemed to be in good order, but he was going to recommend she had the number changed. This done he went around the bedrooms, and then down into the staff quarters.

The final check was on the windows. These had locks, but were seldom used, especially on the upper floor. At the front of the house he went out and looked up.

There were no plants growing up the wall for someone to climb up, no pipes and no trellises. The only things out there were the gutters just beneath the roof.

*I'd find it difficult climbing up there; even climbing out one slember window and into the next would be challenging. Anyone going past a window would have come down from the roof. I must go up and look.*

Passing quickly through the house to the rear garden he looked up. Here there were several methods of getting onto the roof. The high walls that separated the different parts of the garden were joined to the house, which then gave access to pipe work. It was not for the faint hearted, but he could do it easily.

There was also a large tree to one side of the lawn. Its branches reached out towards the roof, and it could easily be climbed. Careful moving along a branch would make it simple to get onto the roof. Also, a large creeping plant was attached to the back of the house. When tested he found it difficult to move. It would bear his weight with ease.

Just to satisfy his curiosity, he climbed the tree and went along the branch that almost touched the roof. He could nearly walk right onto it, except for a gap of about a stride.

The best way to get from one to the other was to bounce the branch and jump. This gave him a lift and he landed lightly. He realised when he did, this might have been the noise Drew Rhalin heard, as his room was in the back.

Climbing to the apex he looked for signs that someone had been there. After several minutes, he found some rope fibres around the chimney stack, and again, further down near the front guttering.

*This is how they managed to get outside the windows, and why they seemed to linger. If they wedged a beamstick at a certain angle on the roof it would also account for the shadow.*

Leaning back against the tiles he frowned. *Why didn't they enter? It's a lot of trouble to climb down just to climb back up and leave. Either someone was doing a trial run, or because of the gathering the intruder couldn't be certain who was occupying which room.*

He returned to the apex of the roof and was considering possibilities when a faint voice caught his attention. Farin was standing in the back garden waving his arms.

'Mikim! The Lady Kaylee wants you now!'

Putting both legs on the same side, he did a controlled slide to the place where the creeping plant grew and climbed down.

'What the hell were you doing up there?' Farin grinned broadly. 'When you first arrived, no-one knew you were here; now you're maized.'

'Where is the mistress?' Luapp said, diverting attention from the question.

'In the lounge with Lady Aylisha.'

They walked into the house and parted company. Luapp went through to the lounge where he found Enegene and Aylisha chatting happily together. Noticing his entrance, she said, 'Mikim, the guests have finished firseal and their

126

overnights are packed. Bring their bags to the vehicles.'

Aylisha and I are going retailing afterwards. I want you to inform Sylata we will not want lunch. I must say my goodbyes to the guests then we will be ready. Morvac will come out front when the last vehicle has gone so don't be late.'

The sentence concerning Sylata brought a brief cloud of depression. It meant they would be out for most of the day. As her protector, he would be required on the trip to town whether Aylisha was with her or not. His hopes of contacting Jym Corder and researching the guests faded.

Finding Sylata in the staff common room Luapp passed on the message. He noticed the strange look, but all she said was, 'we'll just arrange dinner then.'

Farin joined him in the hall and waited by the stairs as Luapp went up. He collected two bags and passed them to Farin who took them to the waiting vehicles. Returning upstairs he collected two more.

As it took longer for Enegene to say goodbye than for him to make six trips he retreated to the study to wait. He left the door slightly open so he could hear when the women were ready to leave.

Switching on the computer he found the recording again. The message was short and gave nothing away, but Corder was shaken.

The last of the guests were leaving and Luapp was about to shut down when another message popped up. This time from Major Lyndon, telling him to make contact. He took a moment to recall Lyndon's code and then keyed it in. As the picture cleared Lyndon looked solemnly out at him.

'I hope the cover of your assistant is good,' he said, dourly. 'Someone is looking it up.'

'Who?'

'I don't know, but it has to be one of the elite, they're the only ones with enough wealth and power to do so.'

'Any idea why?'

'You think they'd post it on the query?' Lyndon retorted. Sitting back in his chair he added, 'it's my guess they're looking for dirt.'

'Kindly explain dirt.'

'Mistakes, trouble, anything they can find for leverage against the lady.'

'For what purpose?'

Lyndon smirked. 'You're hot property. Several of the elite want to buy you.'

'I'm aware of this; Enegene has refused them all.'

'Hence the need for leverage. Whoever they are, they're looking for a way to force her to give you up. That could be a motive for murder.'

'I agree, but not the slayer I'm looking for. Are they researching me as well?'

'Apart from my operative, not so far.'

'Is there any way to trace the searcher?'

'We're working on it. They seem to know more about computers than the rest; like you.'

Luapp pondered that. *An intelmac expert?* To Lyndon he said, 'both our covers are good. My thanks for the information.'

'I didn't do it for you,' Lyndon said coolly. 'I did it for the Coalition Master.'

'Whatever your reasons, I still thank you.' Hearing the last guests leave he added, 'I must shut down.'

~~~

Enegene and Aylisha were just leaving the house as Luapp joined them. Morvac held the door as firstly Aylisha, then Enegene got in, then left Luapp to shut it.

'I expect you were pleased to see Benze and Pellan go this

128

morning,' Aylisha said, settling in the back.

'Yes,' Enegene replied. 'Strangely, it seemed as if she couldn't wait to leave. Perhaps I dented my reputation in her eyes last night.'

'You don't have to worry about last night Kaylee. I've seen hosts of that particular party do far worse things when zoned. At least you're single and only slept with your slave.'

Aylisha gave Luapp a brief smile as the Drifter started off. 'He's your own race and good looking with it. I don't know what Benze' excuse is.'

Enegene grimaced. 'I have heard members of our circle say how "irresistible" Pellan is.'

Aylisha smiled and looked at Luapp. 'Mikim was really concerned about you last night, weren't you Mikim?'

Giving Aylisha a brief glance, he said, 'yes Lady.'

'I can't think why.'

Enegene smiled and placed her hand on his knee. A cool emanation flowed towards her and her fingers began to tingle. Her smile faded as she hastily removed her hand.

*If looks could slay I'd have withered on the spot. The trouble with guardians is looks can slay, or at least, seriously embarrass as demonstrated with Jezine's cousin Divana ...*

'Now that barrier has been crossed,' Aylisha said, breaking into her thoughts, 'I hope normality will resume.'

'You don't sound surprised,' Enegene said, puzzled.

'Until you arrived the record of keeping celibate with a handsome young slave in the house had been three weeks, not several months.'

Enegene's smile re-established itself. 'Does that include you?'

Aylisha's expression became serious. 'Pap never has handsome young slaves in the house. But unless the attraction went both ways I wouldn't follow the trend. I don't condone forcing a slave into bed if they're not attracted to the owner. That's a crime, but it's ignored because they're a slave.' Her disapproval was almost tangible. 'But the way Mikim was fretting over you last night; it's obvious he has feelings for you.'

'Really? He hides it well.'

Enegene and Luapp held eye contact for several seconds until he looked away. She glanced at Aylisha then out of the window. Her friend frowned. 'Is there something else bothering you Kaylee?'

Enegene looked at her friend again. 'It's only minor; it's not worth bothering over.'

'Spill,' Aylisha said, forcefully. It's bothering you so half it.'

'I had an odd dream last night...' Enegene's voice faded, and she only continued because of Aylisha's frantic hand signals. 'No pictures, just words; like someone whispering my name. They were close and just kept saying Kaylee, Kaylee, over and over. Then they added beautiful Kaylee and it faded.'

'That was it?' Aylisha said, surprised.

'It wasn't a harsh voice; it was the kind of voice your mother uses to wake you up gently...' She rubbed her hand slowly. 'But it didn't make me smile; it made me feel... threatened.'

'Was it a man or woman's voice?'

'I don't know... somehow between.'

Aylisha looked at Luapp. 'Did you hear anything Mikim?'

'Nothing, but I can't hear what's in the mistress' dreams.'

He looked at Enegene who returned the look, frowning deeply. Their mutual stare was interrupted by Aylisha.

'A little creepy,' she said. 'But at least Mikim was with you all night .'

'Yes.' Enegene forced a smile. 'As I said, it's not important.'

'When we get to Dermont's I need to find a dress...' Aylisha said, changing the subject.

~~~

Aylisha's chatter faded to a background murmur as Luapp considered Enegene's revelation. He could tell by her tone she doubted it was a dream, and he was inclined to agree.

The minor annoyance of Enegene being right about the slave-owner situation paled in comparison to someone in the house being the slayer. This should have narrowed it to six groups, but it didn't.

*If High Commander Brann was correct, they could have been any of the guests, even those that left.*

*It wasn't the shadow maker that spoke, I'd been there both times and they were silent. Someone else was roaming the house and trying to frighten Enegene; one of the multislayer's traits is to confuse the mind and unsettle the victim...*

His mental meanderings were briefly interrupted as the Drifter stopped in the subterranean park of the shop. Following the women to the lift, he turned his attention to the safe station.

The fact that they moved through several different shops was lost on him. The tension she was hiding from Aylisha was being exuded empathically. His efforts to shut out her fears and continue his inner cogitations made the outside world fade into the background. He only really became aware of the world around him when the Drifter stopped outside a restaurant.

Aylisha looked up at the brightly painted sign from the vehicle's window. 'What made you choose this place Kaylee?'

'Talin Urber recommended it.' Enegene turned in the seat and stepped out. 'She said it had the best food in Denjal.'

Emerging from the vehicle, Aylisha said, 'I can't fault that statement. Did she also say they were pompous about slaves?'

Enegene gave her friend a thoughtful look. 'She neglected to say anything about slaves, was she being humorous?'

'Not exactly...' Aylisha let it drop. 'Shall we go elsewhere?'

'No, I wouldn't like her to think I'm easily intimidated.'

Enegene headed for the door, followed by Luapp, and after a slight hesitation, Aylisha.

Luapp shared Aylisha's doubts about the place, but not for the same reasons. As a Swamplander, nothing spurred Enegene Namrae into doing something faster than someone trying to embarrass her. He hoped she would just rise above the intended slur, but had the feeling this wasn't going to end well.

Inside it had the quiet, respectful atmosphere usually found in libraries. The room was painted pale yellow and had a bar at one end. The tables were widely spaced with just four chairs around each.

The under tablecloths and chair seats were matching gold, and the over tablecloths were a starched, pristine white. At the moment, there were only three tables occupied in a room that could hold twenty.

They were met at the door and escorted to a table. As the women perused the menu, Luapp opened his mind. The moment they entered he'd felt a change in atmosphere.

As the emanations gradually changed from displeasure to anger, he assumed it to be disapproval of his presence.

None of Enegene's social set occupied the other tables, so why would total strangers be antagonised by their arrival? He needed time to check each mind and discount it, but following events overtook his efforts.

The arrival of the gold uniformed waiter broke his concentration. The man's question about ordering set off a chain of verbal exchanges that brought Luapp's already frayed mood to a new low. All went well until Enegene asked Luapp what he wanted to eat. Taking the order, the waiter gave her a strange look and left.

Minutes later a senior waiter, denoted by his purple jacket, arrived. He bowed slightly, pulled his mouth into a tight smile, and looked down his nose at Enegene like someone examining slime under a microscope. In response, she gave him a bored glance .

Clearing his throat, he said, 'madam, I find myself in an awkward position.' He picked an invisible something from his sleeve and dropped it.

Enegene raised a brow. 'What makes you think I want to know about it?'

With the previous night's disconnected voice, and the apparently attempted affront by one of her circle, Enegene's building tension was ready to explode. The waiter's obvious disapproval just added fuel to the fire.

Judging by her expression, Luapp suspected she was about to show her feelings in her own unique manner.

The senior waiter tried his smile again. 'It's rather a delicate matter.'

'Is it a mental or physical matter?'

He stopped in surprise and tried again. 'It's your slave, Madam.'

'He's a "he", and I'm fully aware he's mine, I bought him.'

The senior man went for the direct route as the deferential one was not working. 'We do not serve slaves, Madam.'

Enegene's serene expression remained unchanged. 'I didn't order one.'

The man looked flustered by her refusal to understand. He grabbed his small crossover tie and tugged it slightly. Taking a breath, he tried again. 'We don't serve them in the restaurant.'

'I should think not,' she said, in mock horror. 'Apart from

being rather tough, it would be cannibalism!'

Aylisha covered her mouth with her napkin. Even so, a muffled giggle escaped from beneath it.

A quickly stifled sound from behind suggested others within hearing distance were also finding the situation amusing.

Luapp calmed his rising irritation and reached out with his mind again, but the anger had gone. The scene Enegene was so carefully manipulating was amusing everyone except the guardian and the waiter.

'We do not serve slaves with food, Lady,' he said, through gritted teeth.

'What do you serve them with? High explosives?'

His face reddened and his eyes bulged slightly. 'Slaves are not permitted to eat in the restricted areas.'

'Kindly do not shout; I am not deaf,' she said, haughtily.

By now all other talking had ceased as ears strained to catch every word of the dialogue without their owners turning to stare.

'Who is your superior?'

Surprised with her sudden return to normality his mind went blank. He stared across the room, his mouth opening and closing fish-like.

Pressing her advantage, she said, 'that's not very good; not knowing the name of your superior.'

'I-I do know it...' he stammered, desperately looking for help from some quarter.

'Yes?'

There was a pause before Enegene spoke again. 'No matter what his name is, I want to speak to him, bring him here.'

'Yes Madam.'

With an opening for escape the senior waiter made a hasty retreat. Aylisha now allowed herself to laugh openly.

'That's showing him Kaylee,' she gasped, between giggles.

Enegene looked at Luapp. He hoped his expression conveyed what he thought of her game.

The wine waiter came and went without incident. As he left he was passed by the manager coming to the table. Giving the waiter a long look, he focussed on the women.

'Ladies, I believe someone requested my presence.'

Enegene looked up at the thin man looking down his nose at her and took on a more sober expression.

'Yes, I did.'

He raised both brows and smiled coldly. 'How can I help?'

'You can tell me why you have such ludicrous rules.'

'Which ludicrous rules?'

'The ones stating slaves cannot eat with their owners. Where are they supposed to eat?'

'We have a section for slaves to eat down there.'

He indicated a screened off area at the other end of the restaurant with a quick flick of the wrist.

'And how is he supposed to pay for it? Slaves don't carry gems.'

'You pay for it,' he replied, as if explaining to a child.

Luapp took a long breath in. A muscle twitched by his jaw as he fought for control. Treating the Swamplander like a child had repercussions. It made him wish he were anywhere but here.

'Me? You expect me to pay for something I can't see? How do I know he ate what it says on the bill?'

The man was thinking of a plausible answer when she started again.

'He's my protector. How can he protect me if I'm up here and he's hidden behind that barrier down there?'

'Why...'

'Are you going to protect me if I am attacked? I don't

135

think so; you're even further away than him. What am I going to do then?'

'Madam, we do not object to him sitting there, merely eating there. This area is for high class individuals like yourselves; not slaves. Slaves eat in the cordoned off area...'

'He has to sit here starving merely because of a silly rule?'

'He can eat down there; it is only a short distance...'

'Do you know how long it would take for him to get here if someone attacked me?'

'No,' he answered truthfully.

'Too long. By the time he got to me I could be deceased. If I end up deceased because you forced him to eat down there, I'll sue you for every gem you have.'

He was speechless as he tried to unravel what had just been said, but she didn't give him the chance.

'Does anyone object to my slave sitting here protecting me from who knows what, and eating at the same time?'

She stood up and looked around. Also looking around the senior manager saw people shaking their heads in disbelief, or something.

'See? No one does.'

'Madam...'

'Branon,' she said. 'I am Lady Branon, and this is Lady Rhalin.'

'Ladies Branon and Rhalin?'

The frigid expression slipped as he realised two of the most influential women on the whole continent were in his restaurant. The consequences of upsetting both were too awful to contemplate.

'But of course your slave can eat with you Lady Branon, I did not realise he was a protector, I thought he was a house slave. Protectors are welcome to eat with their owners as long as said owner states so at the time.'

'I did state so,' she answered, sitting down again.

'Just an unfortunate misunderstanding. Your meals will be with you shortly, and because of the disturbance, they are on the house.'

'I would rather have them on the table.'

'What? Oh, very droll Lady Branon. I hope everything is to your satisfaction.'

'So do I, because if it is not, you will hear about it.'

The man bowed slightly and left.

Aylisha laughed. 'Kaylee, that was priceless. Just wait until Talin Urber hears how her trick misfired.'

Enegene's satisfied smirk changed to a scowl. 'I'll enlighten the manager as to how I found his restaurant on the way out,' she said with malice. 'I doubt he'll forget me or Talin Urber.'

Their meals arrived shortly afterwards, and it was obvious from the nervous glance of the waiter he was relieved normality had resumed.

Leaving the restaurant a while later, Luapp was looking forward to returning to the house, but was disappointed. The women returned to the malls and continued shopping. Enegene seemed determined to annoy him for the whole day.

Her insistence he needed more clothes resulted in his being measured and trying on what seemed like every suit that was around his size.

*It must be some form of punishment for a misdemeanour I can't remember,* he decided, changing clothes for the tenth time. *Sometime in my pretweens I got away with something and the galactic entity has caught up.*

Collecting the unwearable suit, he emerged from the changing room and handed it to the assistant. 'It's too small.'

The man murmured his regrets and looked at Enegene for further instructions.

'I'll just take the three evening suits I ordered,' she said, apparently as bored as Luapp. Standing up she signalled her intent to leave.

As they arrived at the vehicle Morvac appeared from inside and opened the door for them. Entering the Drifter, Luapp wondered whether Enegene was trying to wear him down so he wouldn't bring up the restaurant affair. If that was the case she'd failed. He was now so incensed he was fit to explode.

Aylisha was dropped at her door and they arrived at the house a short time later. Instructing Morvac to let Sylata know they were home, Enegene headed straight upstairs telling Luapp to follow. When they arrived in the room, she went over to the bed and flopped onto it.

'What do you want?' he said, icily.

'I'm giving you the chance to air your grievances,' she said in Gaeizaan.

'Such adolescent behaviour only confirms the opinion I had of you on Gaeiza.'

Sitting up she studied him carefully. 'So you approve of the way slaves are treated.'

He took a moment to control his temper. 'Do you think you made a difference? All you've done is show your contempt for the customs of the planet you are living on.'

Enegene pursed her lips and glared at him. 'Slavery is vile and shouldn't be allowed.'

'I agree, but it exists here and we are working with the permission of the Pedantan government. Only if we gain their trust will we be able to help them change. Making a mockery of their law only makes the population more determined to keep apart from the Council.'

'Aylisha didn't agree,' Enegene answered defiantly. 'She enjoyed it.'

'I doubt her father would have. Nor would he have been pleased with her approval. He is trying to change things from within, the correct method to use.

The Coalition Master is of the opinion slavery is losing its appeal for most of the population. The staff here confirm it. But it is not for you, an outworlder to interfere.'

'So, you advocate sitting back and doing nothing?'

'I act when it's possible and relevant. That's the reason I'm here trying to stop a sadistic slaying by another outworlder. I assumed you agreed for the same reason; if not you should return to Gaeiza.'

Her eyes flashed angrily. 'Are you going to send me back? You're my slave and subject to my commands.'

A cynical smile appeared briefly. 'It doesn't take long for your high morality to slip when it suits you.'

Enegene narrowed her eyes. 'This is your set up Nostowe. live with it.'

A frosty silence followed as she moved from the bed and walked over to the window. Leaning against the wall, she folded her arms and looked out.

'I understand why you reacted this way,' Luapp said, 'and it had nothing to do with the morality of slavery. Taking your emotional distress out on the restaurant staff was not logical.'

'Logical!' She turned and looked at him. 'That's typical guardian. I don't feel logical. Someone is tracking me, and I needed an outlet.'

'At the expense of someone else naturally.'

'Just think yourself lucky it wasn't you. It's your fault I'm here and a target for something we have no description for.'

Ignoring the outburst, he decided rational discussion would be the best course.

'You were never without support. For the three monspa you were here without me you were monitored by a space guardian, a local enforcer and an intelligence operative. Since arriving, I'm your constant protector.'

She flicked him a look but said nothing. He turned towards the door, and then stopped. 'I was beginning to doubt the slayer was here after so long without a show.'

She frowned, walked back to the bed and sat on it 'Beginning to doubt it? What changed your mind?'

'Drew Rhalin. He said he'd felt "evil intent" directed towards his daughter but he didn't know where it was coming from. While reading the reports at Padua I met a relative of one of the victims. He said she'd also mentioned a presence.'

She frowned at Luapp. 'It's a weakness to admit to fear in the Swamplands.'

'You're offering yourself as a victim; you're bound to be apprehensive. It's the reason you dislike Pellan. He has surprised you on a couple of occasions and you have no ability to strike back. But I pick up no hatred from him, merely confusion.'

With a sigh she said, 'I've thought about him many times and you're right. He's not menacing; just irritating. Swamplanders rely on their instincts and he messes with mine.'

'That's understood, but I'm with you. They'll have to slay me to get to you.'

Enegene let out another sigh then forced a brief smile. 'I'm not used to relying on guardians; more like hiding from them. What are you doing with the rest of the day?'

'I have to speak to Jym Corder, he left me a message last night. Then I'm starting the safe station when you show me how to get up there.'

'So soon?' Then she said, suspiciously, 'why?'

'It was always a part of the plan. But as we've picked up a few malignant thoughts, now is as good a time as any.'

'I'll come with you.'

The tone of her voice suggested his attempt at casual indifference had failed. Leaving the bed, she went to the door and looked out. 'All clear,' she said, heading for a cupboard across the corridor.

He followed confused; this was where the maids kept spare linen for the beds. Once Luapp was in she quickly shut the door enclosing them in total darkness. He put his hand on the wall and felt for the light switch. A few minutes later he concluded there wasn't one.

'Open the door so we can see,' he said, annoyed.

'Someone might come along and wonder what we're doing in here.'

*That makes a strange kind of sense…*

Ignoring her proximity, he reasoned there must be some sort of lighting if it led to the roof. Obviously, it hung from the ceiling. Reaching up and finding nothing he gave up.

'Switch on the light,' he said, tersely.

'How about giving me something first?'

'Like an indictment for wasting my time, you mean?'

She slipped her arms around his neck. He gripped her wrists and was about to pull her hands away when the door opened.

'Oh!'

A surprised and embarrassed Cleona was holding towels and blushing. Fortunately for Luapp, the equivalent blood rush didn't show on his skin.

'Don't just stand there Cleona,' Enegene said, smiling. 'Close the door he might escape.'

'Yes Madam,' Cleona replied, and promptly shut the door.

Enegene laughed softly. 'Fortunate you have a tight grip on your expression, guardian!'

'I've had enough of your adol behaviour this afternoon,'

he said, heatedly. 'Two minutes an adult then back to being a qiver again.'

'Do you want my co-operation or not?' she retorted, her amusement evaporating.

'This is for your protection; if you don't want it say so.'

'And I'm only on this mission at your request; I can leave any time I want; finished or not!'

'Switch on the light and let's get up there.'

'You know your trouble Nostowe? You've had a humourectomy.'

With a quick snatch in the air she pulled the chord, flooding the room with light. Next she reached between the shelves and pressed a concealed switch. The hatch opened and a strap fell out.

Luapp took note of what she did so next time he wouldn't need her help. Then he turned and looked up. Grasping the strap, he pulled it gently causing the ladder to unfold and slide down. He climbed the first three steps, felt inside for a switch and turned it on. Then he continued into the loft.

Enegene followed him and pressed a second switch on the roof beam to bring up the ladder. Luapp was already pacing out the distance to her room and she watched bemused. Finally, he lay on the floor and looked down.

'No visual points,' he said softly, his mind now on work.

She knelt and looked down. All she could see was the floor.

'I'll have to make an opening so I can see what's happening.'

He stood up and went to the other end of the loft to the luggage. Collecting the small case he opened it and released a concealed compartment. In there were two compressed sleeping bags and two floor mats. He carried them to a place he thought would be above her bed and laid them flat.

'We'd better go. I'll have to work in short intervals or someone will get suspicious.'

'Where will you be if I need you?'

'I must contact Jym Corder…'

He headed for the hatch and stopped. 'Why don't the servants know about the roof space?'

'They obviously know it's here but they don't know where the opening is. It's one of their odd superstitions. They believe a… demon, they call it, lives up here. When the dwellings are built, they fix an effigy to the wood to keep the demon in. If someone comes up here the demon can find its way out and cause havoc.'

'How did you get the cases up?'

'Morvac and Farin brought them upstairs and left them in my room so I could unpack. Then I took them up one at a time during the next week.'

She smiled. 'Cleona told me the demon was restless because there was a new owner. Apparently, she heard me moving about one night. I convinced her it was one of the small mammals that sometimes run around.'

'Rats,' Luapp replied. 'That was clear thinking.'

His mind ticked over the possibility of the shadow maker getting into the roof but dismissed it. There were no holes to show an external entry or internal leaving.

To get in the normal way they would have to come through the cupboard without being heard. On the other hand, to risk going into the loft suggested they were not native to the planet…

Enegene's unlatching the hatch broke his chain of thought. He waited for her to lower the steps and go down. Following behind he switched off the light and pushed up the steps. Once the hatch was closed Enegene opened the door and strolled nonchalantly to her room.

'You can go now Mikim,' she said, in louder than normal voice.

With a glowering look at her back he headed downstairs.

Chapter 10


It had taken quite a while to work his way around the police checks, but finally Luapp had managed to connect to Jym's computer. Sending a brief answer to the request he added a sound marker to attract attention. To his surprise it was answered immediately. Jym was looking just as strained as before.

'Commander, I'm relieved you got my message.'

'I received it last night, or early this morning, but I decided you wouldn't appreciate being disturbed at half two.'

'You're right about that; I'd had a hell of a day. Can you get down here at all today?'

'Not unless you can invent a good reason why Enegene needs to go to your headquarters.'

'That's a tricky one,' Jym replied. 'It would be easier for me to come to you. I'll be there in about twenty minutes.'

'Understood. Have you found a corpse fitting the method?'

'No, but it was close. I'll explain when I get there.'

Jym Corder closed the connection and Luapp turned his mind to the guest list. Drew Rhalin's mention of a presence along with the restaurant incident got his mind working.

*Why is the presence only felt at certain times? Is it connected to their emotional state, or because they were concentrating on their intended victim and had thought-leak?*

*People don't normally meet strangers alone unless it's for some forced reason like blackmail. Nix Pellan is a point in fact to this.*

*Enegene detests him, and there is no way in this universe she would meet him in a secluded place. So how was the slayer getting to their victims?*

*If it was the slayer last night, why were they observing Lady Benze' room? True she fits the description. She's gold syscred at least; she's mid-span for a Pedantan, and fairly attractive for her age… but the window observation doesn't fit the slayer's method.*

*How could they be in the restaurant today? How could they know Enegene would be there? Coincidence?*

*Was the female Talin Urber the slayer? Did she take a chance Enegene would arrive and went to the restaurant in a different guise? Or did Talin Urber send an associate to observe Enegene's embarrassment?*

A wry smile touched his lips. *If she did the jape didn't work as intended.*

Scanning the list he worked on the party attendees. The neighbours he ignored because they hadn't attended any of the events except for last night which left him with the social elite Enegene mixed with.

Over the months he'd been on the planet he'd researched every one of the core group thoroughly. While each of them was a possible target for blackmail simply because of their wealth, he'd found nothing murky enough to force them into a meeting. The only two he knew of were the agents working for Major Lyndon, and they knew how to take care of themselves.

Next, he considered the floaters, the ones who attended most parties but not all, and finally, the prestigers, the ones who only attended events like last night.

146

*Strangely, I discounted Talin Urber as she was on the periphery of the group. Not as familiar with Enegene's character as she thought.*

*Her hoax on the Swamplander spectacularly rebounded...*

Like most planetary social structures, the wealthy married the wealthy and most of them were easily traced. Only a minority had ever been outside their own system and those that had been were on the major's files. The only outsiders listed did not match the profile of the murderer.

He frowned as he considered Pellan.

*My instincts are usually accurate. Pellan doesn't fit as the slayer; he doesn't have the personality for it. I've seen him furious, and even then there was no evidence of the multislayer. Pellan's ineffectual; he needs someone like Benze to protect and pander him.*

His thoughts then turned to Drew Rhalin.

*How had Drew picked up negative emotions? Was he a natural biotalent and was it something Aylisha did that gained their attention? If so, why hasn't she repeated this behaviour since I arrived?*

*If the slayer is one of the socialites they must be a Fluctoid. This aristocratic band of platcreds don't socialise with strangers easily. They don't even socialise with their syscred equals if they consider them untrained. So the slayer had to be someone they were familiar with and had the social skills to blend in.*

*Enegene Namrae being accepted within three monspa was an anomaly... possibly because she was an off-worlder and wealthier than most of them. And she was introduced by Aylisha Rhalin who is one of the top socialites...*

*If the slayer is not one of her group how have they managed to get into the dwelling and unsettle the Swamplander? To be established, or even to be connected to a socialite they must have arrived on Padua before Enegene. If so, it's possible a slaying has already taken place and not discovered.*

*Was the deceased socialite a failed attempt? It would be ironic*

*if she ceased trying to escape the slayer. Was Aylisha saved because
she refused to meet a stranger?*

He interlaced his fingers behind his head and stretched.

*If GSC is correct, she would have been meeting a friend, or
at very least a well-known acquaintance. And now the being is
interested in Enegene…*

Returning to the list he also discounted several other
names as they attended only a few of the parties the two
women had been to. This left the same core of about ten that
always attended the same social activities.

*Now Enegene has apparently been chosen as a victim, the sooner
I get the safe station set up the better.*

Shutting down the computer he was about to leave the
study when the doorbell rang. He pushed back the chair but
stopped as he heard one of the female servants answer the
door.

A few words were spoken and she hurried off. She returned
and took the visitor to the sitting room, a male, by his voice.

Finally, she came back a third time and knocked on the
study door. Opening it Luapp saw Cleona. She flashed him a
grin and said, 'Lady Kaylee wants you in the sitting room
Mikim.'

Leaving the study, he walked across the hall. Cleona
watched him all the way smiling broadly, but saying nothing.
For that he was grateful. He could imagine what the topic of
conversation circulating among the servants was now.

Entering the sitting room he saw Enegene talking to a man
he didn't know. Looking up at his arrival she smiled.

'Mikim, the detective sergeant has requested your
assistance. As you are a trained protector and you know the
area around the dwelling I agreed. They're tracking a thief
and the sergeant thinks he entered the grounds.'

'Understood.' Luapp glanced at the man. 'Where do you

wish to start?'

'In the front and work our way around to the back. Lady Kaylee, could you instruct the servants to lock all the doors and close the windows please? If he's here and knows we're searching for him he might try to hide in the house.'

'Should I get a servant to search the building?'

The sergeant stood up. 'The probability is that he's not here and merely crossed your land, but it wouldn't hurt to check. Do you have some male staff?'

'Yes, two,' Enegene said, 'and of course Mikim.'

'Then get your young female staff members to team up with the two men. One team can search the upper floor, and one this floor. Then one of them can search the lower floor. I won't keep your slave long.' Turning his attention on Luapp, he added, 'come with me.'

Leaving the house, they went up to the entrance gate. 'Right,' he looked around. 'From here anyone would be seen. 'Where's the nearest hiding point?'

'This way.'

Luapp led him across the front grassy area to a place where shrubs and trees grew close together around the boarders of the property. They spent an hour searching the grounds ending up back at the front of the house.

He was beginning to wonder if this was a genuine hunt when the sergeant drew him to one side behind some bushes. 'Nothing hiding here,' he said, looking around.

Turning his attention on Luapp he slid his hand into his pocket and pulled out a small machine. 'I'll just dictate the search.'

After speaking into the machine, he returned it to his pocket and held out his hand. Confused, Luapp touched the sergeant's hand in the way he'd seen Pedantans respond. To his surprise, as the man's hand closed around his he felt a small package pressed into it.

Giving Luapp a long look he said, 'I don't know what this is and I don't want to know. It's delivered and done.'

Luapp pushed the package into his waistband. 'Why couldn't the inspector come himself?'

'He didn't want to be seen in case the place is being watched. He said the Lady Kaylee would understand. I must go.'

Back on the path they went their separate ways. The sergeant walked up the long drive to the road and Luapp returned to the house. Inside he went straight to the sitting room but Enegene wasn't there. Then he tried the lounge and found her standing by the windows looking out.

'Did you find anyone?'

Noticing the tension in her voice, he said, 'the grounds are clear; do you want me to stop the servants searching?'

'They finished before you, but you can tell them the result and stop their anxiety.'

'Understood. What's concerning you?' he said, switching to Gaeizaan.

'What makes you think anything's concerning me?'

'Your voice, your posture, your emanations. I'm picking up… unease.'

'Then I suggest you stop listening in.'

Taking a guess, he said, 'there was no intruder. My contact in the local enforcers organised the search as a way of getting something to me.'

As she turned to face him he pulled the package from his waistband. Without a flicker of emotion, she walked over to the sofa and leaned against it.

'I'm not sure that's the good news you intended it to be,' she said, quietly. 'When I thought there was a genuine intruder it explained…' She left the sentence unfinished and looked about the room.

'Explained what?'

Moving around the sofa she sat down and indicated for him to do likewise. 'Remember my dream? Well now I know it wasn't a dream. While you were out searching with the enforcer, I heard the voice again.'

Handing her the package, he said, 'where were you?'

'In the visitor room.'

'Have you heard it in here?'

'No.'

'What was said?'

'The same as before.'

'No threats?'

'No. That's what I can't understand. They make no threats but I feel threatened.'

'That's the intention. Did it sound natural or like a recording?'

'A recording wouldn't have bothered me. It sounded like they were right behind me, whispering in my ear.'

'I'll search the visitor room and then the hidden corridors. It's possible someone else knows about them.'

Pushing herself upright she said in Pedantan, 'when you've done that I want you to join me in the study Mikim, there are a few things I want you to do for me.'

Luapp continued speaking in Gaeizaan. 'Lock yourself in and wait for my contact; I shouldn't be longer than a half.'

Leaving the sitting room, Luapp stopped in the hall and watched Enegene enter the study. Then he went along to the staff room. Sylata, Lydina and Farin were chatting quietly about the policeman's arrival. They stopped and looked up as he walked in.

'The Lady Kaylee wishes you to know the search is ended and nothing was found.'

Farin looked relieved. 'Didn't he come here after all?'

'It's the enforcer's opinion he merely crossed the property and carried on. They're continuing their search.'

'That's good,' Sylata said. 'We can unlock the doors and windows then. Are you joining us for tea Mikim?'

'Lady Kaylee wants me to join her in the study.'

'Better not keep her waiting then,' Sylata said, and sipped her tea.

'It's bigger than the upstairs cupboard anyway,' Lydina said with a giggle.

Luapp twitched a brow and left the room. *How long are the salations going to find the situation amusing?*

Entering the sitting room, he looked around. While in here, Enegene would have sat down to wait; it was not her habit to stand around aimlessly for long periods of time.

A visual search of the sofa found nothing, so he ran his hands over it, turning it around and upside down as he went. As he turned the back to face him he noticed a corner of the material lifted. Pulling it back he found a small round disc. It had two thin wires that poked out of the top allowing them to be free but unseen.

He raised a brow as he examined the object carefully. It was the kind of thing he would expect Major Lyndon to place. Yanking out the wires, he left the room and went to the study.

In front of the door he projected her name. Seconds later it was opened and he walked in. Pulling up the spare chair he joined Enegene at the desk.

'That was quick,' she said, in Pedantan.

'It took less time than anticipated Lady.'

She turned and looked at him in surprise. Putting his hand on the desk, he opened it allowing her to see what he was holding. She frowned and looked up.

'We will talk Gaeizaan for a while Mikim, the practice will

152

do you good.' Changing to Gaeizaan, she said, 'what is it?'

'Some sort of transmitter. It had fibres lying on the top of the seat. They would have been just behind your head.'

Enegene held out her hand. He dropped it in and she studied it closely. Giving it back she said, 'it looks professional.'

'I thought the same.'

Putting the device on the desk he smashed it with his fist and brushed the remains into a bin. Then he looked at Enegene with an expression of expectancy for a few moments. She stared back and then mouthed, Oh!

She picked up the package and pulled off the cover. Removing the box inside, she took out a micro-thin square sliver and slid it into the computer drawer. 'Whose your contact in the enforcers?'

'Jym Corder, a high-ranking officer; we couldn't operate without local assistance.'

'Would they have set the device?'

'Not the local enforcers. I know there's a listener in the intelmac, but that was for me to contact them.'

'There's always the possibility the shape shifter has taken the place of an enforcer,' Enegene said, watching the title page come up.

'Yes. I'll make some enquiries when I make contact again. Let's see what Jym Corder has sent us.'

The recording opened showing a man sitting in a room that was empty apart from a desk and two other chairs. He was agitated and looked around at the slightest sound.

Enegene squinted at the screen. 'Is that blood on his clothes?'

'Looks like it, but it's difficult to tell on this limited clarity.'

'Commander,' Jym's voice was hushed. 'I thought this would be the best way as you can't be here in person. There was an incident last night.

 We were called to Jae Garber's residence at seven. He was distressed and his wife was hysterical in an upstairs room. She says he tortured her and was going to kill her.

He denies harming her and said he returned from work only a few minutes before finding her. On this recording is her statement from the hospital and our interview with him. His is the one I find incomprehensible.'

The scene with the man in the room was replaced by one showing a woman sitting on a bed being tended by a doctor. He was  swabbing several slashes to her arms, and one down her face. She winced as the damp swab was gently moved down the wounds.

'This better not take too long,' the doctor warned. 'I have to seal these quickly or she'll be scarred.'

'We need her statement while it's fresh in her mind,' said the curly haired policeman.

He stood by the bed pushing buttons on a small machine. Moving to and fro to avoid the doctor he glanced at the person holding the recorder to make sure they were ready. It was the same man that had come to the house.

'Tell us exactly what happened this evening,' he said, returning his attention to the sobbing woman. 'Try not to leave anything out.'

She sniffed, and then took a deep breath. 'I – I'd been to a political fundraiser in the morning. We were going to the event at Lady Branon's house that evening so I came in about four …'

She stopped, swallowed hard and took a few minutes to control her emotions. 'I was putting on my make up when I heard footsteps coming up the stairs - '

Tears streamed down her face and they paused for her to regain control. 'I called out "Is that you Jae". It was early for him but I hadn't heard the doorbell ring. As he walked into the room he was scowling.'

Her voice broke and she sobbed some more. 'Jae is the gentlest man I've ever met, but he – he called me such vile names… I tried to reason with him, but it just made things worse. He – he –'

She dissolved into shoulder trembling sobs again. The sergeant waited patiently until she was ready to continue.

'He what Madam Garber?'

'He hit me so hard he knocked me out!' She stared at him for several minutes. 'That's what caused this.' She touched the large black swelling on her cheek.

'And then?' prompted the sergeant.

'Whe - when I woke up I - I was tied to a chair. My - my wrists and ankles… I couldn't move. Jae was nowhere in sight. I thought he'd gone out to calm down, but he came back…'

There was a look of horror on her face.

'He had knives; said he was going to show me what living with me had been like; then – then he cut me! It hurt so much, I begged him to stop but he seemed to like it when I begged. He – he said he was going to enjoy inflicting as much pain on me as I had on him.'

'So what stopped him?' a female voice said.

The woman shook her head slowly. 'Don't know. I was feeling faint from the pain.' She frowned. 'I thought I heard the front door open again. He left the room and I heard a strange noise…'

'Do you know what the noise was?' said the sergeant.

'No... then I heard footsteps running up the stairs and Jae burst in. He just stared…'

She went to brush back a strand of hair but was stopped by the doctor.

'I pleaded with him not to hurt me; said I'd try to be a

better wife.

He kept saying something over and over again but I couldn't understand him. He picked up the knife and came towards me. I thought he was going to cut me again and I passed out.'

She swallowed hard. 'When I woke up I was on the bed and there were towels on my arms. A stranger came into the room and said they were the police. That's all I know.'

'You're sure it was your husband that did this to you?' the sergeant said.

'I'd know Jae anywhere. It was his voice, his mannerisms and his body twin. Unless the destroyer had taken his place, it was him.'

'But you also said it was not his nature to harm you,' the woman's voice said.

'No...' Tears ran down her cheeks. 'But he did. Why did he do it?' She searched their faces for an answer. 'Did he have a brainstorm?'

'We don't know Madam Garber, but we'll find out. At the moment he denies he did it. We'll be back tomorrow after you've had some rest. Perhaps you'll remember something else.'

The sergeant looked straight at the person doing the recording. 'Sergeant Oklad and social helper Pegath ending the interview. Let's go.'

'That was her version,' Jym said as the recording stopped. 'Here's his.'

It started again in the room they saw at the beginning. This time the camera was pointing straight at the man at the table. Two police officers were facing him, but the picture only showed their backs.

The man's hair was standing on end where he'd scraped his hands through it and his face was stained with blood and tears. 'Why are you holding me here?' he said, weakly. 'I want to see my wife.'

'She doesn't want to see you,' Jym said. 'She says you attacked her with a knife.'

'What?' The man looked astounded. 'I wouldn't attack Cyna; I love her. She knows I love her, why did she say that?'

'She said it because she believes it,' the other man said. 'Tell us your version of events.'

The weary expression changed to a scowl as he slapped his hand on the table. 'No! I won't co-operate until I've seen her and talked to her. This must be some mistake; I found her…'

'Mr Garber,' Jym said patiently, 'it's true you called us. You obviously cut your wife free and placed her on the bed and tried to do something about her injuries. But we also have her statement that you attacked her, and we have the knife with your fingerprints on it.'

'Of course my fingerprints are on it!' His furious glare lessened. As he wiped his tears on his sleeve his voice wavered. 'I use it to cook with and I used it to cut her free.'

'Tell us calmly what happened and we'll try to unravel this,' the second detective said.

'Then can I see my wife?'

'Not tonight. A councillor will be talking to her tomorrow. If she agrees you will be taken under guard to see her,' Jym said.

Garber considered this for a few minutes. 'Alright.'

He frowned, wiped his forehead on his sleeve and began. 'We were going out to Lady Branon's social event, so I intended to leave the office early. But being preoccupied with a contract I forgot the time.

When I finally looked up it was six o'clock. Despite being later than intended, I was slightly earlier than usual. Because of this the traffic was much lighter. I drove up to the house and turned around ready to leave that night.

I opened the front door and then remembered I'd left some important paperwork in the flycar. I went back to collect it, came back to the house and...' He stared across the room.

'Continue,' Jym said.

'I - I saw my reflection as I walked to the stairs.' He frowned as if not believing what he'd just said. 'As I went upstairs I heard an odd noise...'

'What kind of noise?' the second detective said.

'A kind of shuffling... scraping... so I came down again. A pokari bolted out of the dining room straight at me but it couldn't get out as I'd closed the door.'

'It attacked and I had to use my work case to fend it off. Then it ran into the lounge. I opened the front door hoping it would go out. When it found itself trapped in the lounge it came out, saw the open door and escaped.'

He scraped his hand through his hair again. 'I shut the door behind it and then went upstairs. I thought it was a good thing Cyna hadn't seen it as she hates those lizards...' He paused staring across the room again.

'Go on,' Jym prompted.

'When I got to the bedroom the door was open. I saw - ' His face crumpled. Tears flowed again and he wiped them with the heel of his hand. 'I saw Cyna... she - she was tied to a chair. I thought she was dead, but as I came in she lifted her head and started crying. She kept saying "don't hurt me, don't hurt me".

There was blood running down her arms, her beautiful face...' He sobbed. 'I - it was gaping open. I asked what happened but all she said was "don't hurt me I'll be a better wife."

I looked for something to cut the ropes and found the knife lying on the chair. I picked it up, she screamed and fainted.

I cut her loose and carried her to the bed. Then I got some towels to her arms and face. I locked her in the bedroom and called the police and medical services.'

'Why did you lock her in?' said the second policeman.

'She was hysterical,' Garber said. 'She had to be. I wouldn't do that to her, I love her. I was afraid that if she woke up she'd try to leave the house.'

'And you saw nothing but the pokari in the house?' Jym said.

'And my reflection.' Garber stared at the wall behind the police.

Enegene paused the recording. 'Sounds swamp gas fazed to me.'

'Going by his expression his equilibrium appears unbalanced,' Luapp replied.

She started it again.

'Why did you find your reflection so disturbing?' Jym said, picking up on the last statement.

Garber's stare was relieved only by the raising of one brow. 'We don't have a mirror in there,' he said, distractedly. 'But I saw… me.'

'How long after you saw your reflection did you see the lizard?' Jym said.

'Minutes. I passed the doorway on the way to the stairs. I saw my reflection, started up the stairs, heard the noise, came down and saw the pokari.'

'There's nothing you want to add to your statement?' the second policeman said.

'If I attacked my wife, why would I call the police and try to help her?'

'Perhaps you had a moment of insanity and realised what you'd done,' the second policeman said.

'No! I didn't leave the office until six; I can prove it. There are security cameras in the lobby of the building and on the external wall of the house. Check them.'

'We will,' Jym said. 'In the meantime, you're staying with us. Interview ended at 8.30.'

The second policeman got up and led Garber from the room and the recording stopped.

When Jym spoke again it was almost a whisper. 'Sorry there's no picture, I'm back in the cupboard, otherwise there'd be awkward questions.

Some final notes. Garber continues to deny attacking his wife, and although she says it's not his normal behaviour, she insists it was him.

Also, we've checked the security cameras. He did leave the office at six, and there's no way he could have tampered with the recording; they're kept in a secure room by a security guard.

The house recording shows him driving up and parking right at six thirty. He couldn't have got there any sooner, so he couldn't have left the vehicle somewhere, arrived on foot, attacked her and then arrived again. The camera also caught the pokari escaping along the drive minutes later.'

'Finally, after the initial entry by the fly patrol we arrived and looked around. There's no mirror in the dining room nor any sign of one being there. I'd like to hear your thoughts on this.'

Enegene ejected the sliver and shut down the computer. 'What are your thoughts?'

'Either it can travel at great speeds or there's two of them,' Luapp said, quietly.

Frowning, Enegene said, 'you need to explain that.'

'I'm sure the slayer was here last night. When Pellan tried to approach you I picked up leaked thoughts and emotions, they were what I'd expect from a multislayer. I was trying to

160

find the source but Farin distracted me.'

'Would they have time to run from the Garber's dwelling?'

'It would depend on how far away their dwelling was, and how fast the multislayer could travel. I'll have to check the details with Inspector Corder.'

'If they were here, do you think they stayed the night?'

'It's possible as we don't know who they are. Have you met this female? I have no memory of her attending the gatherings since I've been here.'

'I've heard her mentioned. They're not within the same wealth bands as myself, Aylisha or Benze, but they're close. From what I understand she's selective about the events she attends. Also, she goes with her husband when he travels for business.'

'He has to work? That would mean they're not in the same wealth sphere at all.'

'No, he chooses to work. It's his business and he makes sure it runs smoothly. You said something about a shape shifter; that would fit with his account.'

'Yes.' Luapp sat back in the chair. 'But how did they get here so quickly? None of the guests were late.'

'Perhaps they flew.'

He studied her expression and decided she wasn't being flippant. 'Too much body mass; they wouldn't get off the ground.' After some thought, he added, 'it's essential I set up the safe station.'

'You get started, I'll put this somewhere safe. Then I'm going to rest; my head is pounding.' As he walked to the door she added, 'don't be away too long.'

'You should be safe during the day with so many people around. Just don't go meeting anybody without me.'

Leaving the study, he headed for the back garden. At the outbuilding where Sylata kept his tools, he used telekinesis to open the lock. He couldn't ask Deana Sylata for the key as she would want to know why.

It didn't take long to break in as the locks were designed to keep humans out, not sollenites. Inside he found the tools he needed and headed back into the house.

Outside Enegene's bedroom he put his hand on the door and sent a message. Receiving no answer, he opened it quietly. She was asleep. He entered and looked up at the ceiling. After completing his calculations he went over to the bed, removed his boots and stepped on.

Standing astride her he cut a small circle. Even though the cutter made very little noise, it half woke her. He'd just finished when he felt her hand slide up his leg.

'So nice of you to return,' she murmured sleepily.

He looked down. Her eyes were closed but there was a smile on her face.

'Let go.'

In her semi-conscious state she was in a co-operative mood. She did as told and he got down. Collecting his boots, he left the bedroom, crossed the landing to the cupboard and went inside. From there he went into the loft.

Rummaging in the smallest bag he found the camouflage kit and opened it. Inside were several pieces of self-adhesive blending material. He selected a piece slightly bigger than the hole with a gripper. He poked it through, pulled it back sharply and held it tight against the ceiling until it stuck.

After a few minutes, it stiffened and changed to the same colour as the ceiling. He put his face against the floor and looked through the hole. The open weave material was impossible to see through from a distance, but up close it was easy.

Then he went to the large bag and opened the false bottom. From this he took several packages, most of which he stored further over by the hole. From one of the remaining ones, he pulled out a small box and a tube.

A digiviewer and its connecting cable were removed from the box, accompanied by a flexible neck with a lens at one end. Attaching the neck to the box, he poked the lens into the hole. When he switched on, the small screen at the back of the box showed a perfect picture of the room, but it was dark.

Removing the cap of the tube, he squeezed a small amount of clear gel onto his finger and waited. When it was semi solid he pressed it to the bottom of the lens neck. Next he adjusted the neck and pressed it on the floor. The gel stabilised it but gave it enough manoeuvrability to move around.

Then he took the long thin cable with a connector at one end and faceted glass at the other. Plugging the end into the back of the box, he played out the cable through the low eves of the roof.

Gently easing the faceted end through the fibre lining and tiles he pushed it out enough to catch the sunlight. It twisted in his hand as it turned to face the sun. Immediately several buttons lit up indicating its energy cells were charging.

From the medium case, he unpacked a fold down screen and cable and attached both to the charging box. The dim picture of Enegene sleeping got brighter as the cells gathered power.

From another compartment in the case, he removed a recorder and a box of panes. The recorder was plugged into the screen and a pane entered. It flashed to indicate it was recording. Then he stopped it.

Taking out the recorder pane, he inserted an instructor pane, which told the recorder what and when to record. When this flashed, he removed it and packed it away.

With everything set up he left the loft and went back into

her room to clear up. Finally, back at the out building he replaced the tools, shut the door and pushed the lock into place. As he returned to the house he met Mevil Sylata in the passageway.

'Is everything alright, Mikim?' he said, curiously.

'Yes sir.'

'You seem to be preoccupied with house security. Deana said you thought you heard movement last night.'

'Yes.'

'It was probably rats.'

'Not unless they've started using rope.'

'Rope?' Sylata sounded bemused.

'As Lady Kaylee's protector, it's my duty to maintain her safety which obviously includes the security of the dwelling. While checking this morning I found new rope fibres caught in the brickwork.'

A thoughtful pause followed before Sylata spoke again. 'Is there any reason to think Lady Kaylee is in any kind of danger?'

'She thought so or she would not have felt the need to purchase a protector.'

'And what do you think of the house security?'

Luapp chose his words carefully; he knew the elderly man was previously responsible for security.

'It's good. However, there are entry points that need to be eradicated, and changes that will make her feel more secure.'

'And this was prompted by last night?'

Considering how much to tell the man Luapp said, 'it was always my intention to survey the dwelling security, but last night brought the decision forward.'

'Merely because you heard a small noise?'

'I wasn't the only one to hear the noise, so did Lord Rhalin, and it disturbed him enough to mention it to me.'

'Yes, Deana did comment on it.'

'Also, there was someone moving about last night.'

'Moving about?'

'I saw a shadow cross the shutters of Lady Kaylee's room. It was not a bird in flight, or a small creature climbing the wall, it was humanoid.'

'How could a human be up there?' Sylata said, concerned.

'It's why I was on the roof; looking at possibilities.'

'And did you find anything?'

'Discounting rats, enough to convince me someone had been there.'

Sylata contemplated that statement. 'We'll instigate the improvements you have in mind. Don't discuss what you've said to the rest of the staff. The girls can be imaginative and will start seeing things.'

'Understood.'

'What are you doing now?'

'More research.'

'Fine. Go.'

Luapp returned to the study and switched on the computer again. Carefully circumnavigating the police tracing programmes, he logged onto Jym Corder's computer.

Accessing his files, he keyed in his thoughts on the video.

*I consider Freeman Garber innocent. People's personalities don't flip to homicidal and back to normal unless they have a history of mental imbalance. As to the seemingly inexplicable behaviour of a caring husband to his wife, I suggest we meet to discuss the matter properly.*

He added a couple of lines about the incidents at the restaurant and the party and shut down Jym's file. Keeping the connection going, he accessed the general report files of the duty sergeant. He was searching for reports about women being followed or approached by men they didn't know.

There were several of these, but in all but three cases it

turned out to be a private investigator or an acquaintance they didn't recognise. In these three cases the women were unnerved by an unseen stalker.

Reading the details, only one was a wealthy female. The other two were a shop worker and a student. There had been no second report, so he assumed it had been resolved.

*Probably a Pedantan breaker and not a galactic one,* he thought, shutting down the computer.

He left the study just as Sylata came out of the lounge carrying a tea tray. 'Where is Lady Kaylee?'

'She told me she was going to rest.'

She studied him with a frown. 'Mikim, are you alright?'

'Explain?'

'Physically well.'

'I'm in perfect health.'

He watched her place the tray on the small hall table.

'What about mentally?'

She straightened up and scrutinised his face.

He frowned, wondering where this was leading. 'As far as I'm aware I'm sane.'

'At the party the other night you kept disappearing.'

'That was self-preservation.'

'Lady Kaylee bought you because she needs protection. You can't protect her if you are hiding in the staff room.'

'Has she complained?' he said, abruptly.

'No, but...'

'She did not reprimand me. Within the walls of her own dwelling, surrounded by friends and servants she was not at risk. I put in enough appearances to make sure she was safe, and the only time she needed me I was there.'

'Excuse me,' Sylata started heatedly. 'I am a freeborn and you...'

'Are her slave,' he finished, 'not yours. I'll do what's

necessary to protect her.'

Sylata paused to calm her rising indignation. 'Has something upset you? You're not normally so... forthright.'

'I'm a slave subject to the orders of my owner. What could be troubling me?' His gaze was steady on her face. 'Did you need something?'

'Take this to Lady Kaylee.'

She picked up the tray and thrust it towards him. Taking the tray he started up the stairs. Half way up he mentally rebuked himself.

*Sylata is right, I say too much for a slave. Today's escapades must have annoyed me more than I'd thought. I must do some emotional control exercises.*

Tapping on her door lightly he entered Enegene's room.

# Chapter 11

With the grand social gone the season of events was coming to an end and Enegene had more time on her hands. Aylisha was her constant companion and rarely missed a day.

When she arrived on this day, she was in an unusually quiet mood. She watched Lydina place the tray of tea and cakes on the table with her hands tightly clenched in her lap.

Enegene noticed her unease and took the opportunity of a break in their conversation to question her. 'Since the gathering here you've been like my shadow. Now you're displaying anxiety.' She watched her friend fidget for the third time, 'what's wrong?'

Taking a cake, she said, 'now or since the party?'

'Both. We're good friends but you didn't used to turn up in the morning and follow me all day.'

'I've only just arrived...'

'Only because your father took you to Javith.'

'I thought you were... unsettled at the party.' Aylisha peeled the case off the cake. 'I know Mikim was there to protect you, but you were acting out of character. It's not normal for you to get drunk Kaylee. At first I thought it might be to do with taking Mikim upstairs...'

168

Enegene frowned. 'What do you mean by that?'

'You were obviously attracted to him from the moment you bought him.'

'I think you're misunderstanding what you saw; what else did you conclude?'

'Possibly that dream upset you. Despite being your bodyguard there's some places Mikim can't go with you, so I thought I'd go along.'

Enegene smiled. 'There are places you can't come with me either, or you could but I wouldn't let you.'

Aylisha blushed. 'I didn't mean there, I meant changing rooms and such.'

'So what's got you wriggling at the moment?'

Grabbing her bag Aylisha produced a crumpled envelope and held it out. As Enegene took it Aylisha warned, 'it's from Pellan.'

With a slight frown Enegene opened the letter, read it and then looked up. 'He wants to meet me on a matter of business.'

'You're not going to meet him, are you?'

'I'm interested as to what business he thinks he and I share.' Enegene picked up her cup and cradled it in her hands.

'You're not connected to him business wise, are you? I thought pap was advising you.'

'Not as far as I'm aware...' Enegene drifted in thought for a few seconds. 'I shall meet him, but it'll be here and Mikim will be with us.'

'Do you want me to take him a reply?'

Enegene looked at her friend, frowning. 'Why did he script it and give it to you anyway? Why didn't he just contact me over the viscom?'

Aylisha shrugged. 'He's scared of Mikim.'

A broad smile replaced the frown. 'Mikim can't reach through the wires and grab him by the throat.'

Aylisha giggled. 'Pity. However, you can be overheard on a visual.'

'Yes,' Enegene agreed. 'That's a consideration. I think I'll contact him in the normal way; I wouldn't want someone to think I'm meeting him secretly.'

'I certainly wouldn't want to meet him secretly,' Aylisha said, shuddering.

'That's enough about him,' Enegene said, 'let's plan our day out.'

~~~

Hearing the doorbell ring, Luapp had waited in the study in case he was required. As no one came to get him, he relaxed. That meant he had some free time. Neither Deana nor Mevil Sylata wanted his help so he'd retreated to the study to search the police files.

So far he'd been unable to meet or contact Jym Corder about the Garber incident, but felt his written reply was enough. For now, he had another problem to solve. He retrieved his comunit from a drawer in the study desk and contacted the Tholman.

'Are there any references to the victims of the slayer being verbally taunted before the attack?'

'There were the tactics of moving household objects, but there's nothing mentioned about verbal manipulation, Commander. I'd have to get a Paduan connector to ask the different enforcers.'

'Understood. In that case I have information you can add to the files. We've had an incident of a female being viciously attacked. She claims it was her husband, but at the same time is adamant it's not his nature to be violent.

He denies the attack, but claims he saw his own reflection in a mirror where there wasn't one. Minutes later, he found a large sunseeker in the dwelling.

Due to the conflicting evidence given by the partners, the odd sighting and the pokari, I suggest evidence of a Fluctoid of some description has been found. Pass it on to the Paduan profilers and Supreme Commander HaJaan, and get their opinion.'

'Noted. I'll contact you as soon as I have an answer to your question. Contact ended.'

Luapp sat back in the chair and considered the Garber case. Initially it appeared promising, but the fact the woman was less wealthy than Enegene was confusing.

*Why was she chosen instead of Enegene? If the Spyrian isn't the target, why is she being menaced? Previously the slayer attacked one female at a time.*

*Nix Pellan has finally understood I'm adept at being a guard and has kept his distance except when Benze joins us.*

Luapp stared at the blank computer screen. *As far as Enegene Namrae is concerned it's a good result. But Pellan holds no possibilities for me… Benze is the one whose depth I can't see. She acts the bored aristocrat, but she's artful; she questioned me skilfully at the gathering while portraying indifference.*

*She also made me… what? Uneasy? And yet she did nothing. As a Shadowman very few have made that impression on me; was I reacting to a subliminal? I didn't pick up a leak from her…*

He mentally shrugged.

*I've made a request for a more detailed background search and I can't do anything more for now. Therefore, I'll work on something I can do something about; dwelling security.*

Leaving the study, he went into the loft and collected a scanner from the luggage. Starting in the bedrooms, he went through the house surreptitiously scanning the furniture, walls and fixtures for any sign of monitoring devices.

Finding none, he changed the setting to biological and repeated the exercise, this time including a distance search of the servants. Everything registered as normal.

Putting the scanner in a cupboard in the study, he decided it would be prudent to watch the monitors in the safe station above Enegene's bedroom with increasing frequency.

~~~

As soon as Aylisha left Enegene pressed the call bell. When Lydina answered, she told her to find Luapp. He arrived a short while later. As he entered she held out the note.

'You were taking your time, where were you?'

He took the note, read it and handed it back. 'Reviewing security.'

'What do you think? This is the kind of thing we've been waiting for, isn't it?'

Switching to Gaeizaan he answered, 'possibly.'

'Possibly? The slayer lures their victim into a meeting. Should I meet him or not?'

'It would be useful to know what he wants, but don't agree to an isolated setting.'

'And why do you think he wrote to me instead of using the viscom?'

'He didn't want someone in the dwelling knowing he's contacting you.'

Giving him a dark look she said, 'I know, but why?'

'There could be several reasons. He may have no business interest and merely wishes to gain access with your permission. He has assets that he alone knows about and wants to keep it that way, or he could be wary of someone finding out he is seeking outside help for some purpose.'

Enegene frowned. 'Who would he be wary of?'

'I would say Benze. Even though he's an attachment, he still ranks higher than the servants. He shouldn't be bothered by them unless he thinks one might report what they see and hear to her. I suspect his benefactor is not the kind of person who'd take kindly to him seeking advice elsewhere.'

'But where did he get information on my business affairs?'

'Have you told anyone of your interests at the gatherings?'

'No, not even Benze. Wealth or the making of it is not discussed.'

'Why do you mention Benze?'

'Because I know she has investments.'

'How do you know if it's not discussed?'

'The depository manager....' her voice trailed off.

'If he's prone to being indiscrete then he probably told Benze about you. She in turn possibly mentioned the fact to someone else in Pellan's presence.'

'He's supposed to be dependent on Benze for his living, how has he managed to gather syscred for investment?'

'It's the question Benze would ask. On the occasions I've watched him he's demonstrated anxiety around her; almost fear. Either Benze has a strong personality or she has some unusual connections.'

'Do you mean breakers?'

'While the elite here are a law unto themselves, I doubt if it's legal for the average citizen on Pedanta to partake in violence, even if they threaten it.

I've been researching his background. All I can find is the usual immigration record of his travels around the galaxy, some of which coincide with the slayer's path.

Given his conviction about his ability with different genus females, I'm going to do a deeper search. Perhaps that will give me a better insight into him and Benze.'

Enegene placed her hand on the seat beside her and looked up at him. He deliberately sat in the chair opposite.

'Here,' she insisted.

'I'm remaining where I am.'

'In that case I'll come and sit on your lap.'

'And you will be on the floor seconds later.'

Enegene got up and walked over to him, smirking. 'Then I will come to you.' She sat on the arm of the seat and placed her arm around his neck.

Gripping her hand he pushed her away. 'Cease trying to take advantage of the situation.'

'So,' she sighed. 'If the slayer's not Pellan who is it?'

'If I knew that we could go home tomorrow.'

'Why are you so convinced it's not him?'

'In my opinion it's ninety per cent certain we're looking for a shape shifter. It's the only way I know for one person to appeal to such a varied female group.

While Fluctoids find it relatively easy to keep a shape while awake, when they sleep and lose consciousness, they generally revert back to natural shape.'

'And this helps us how?'

'On the night you hosted the gathering, I used the concealed passageways to observe Benze and Pellan. Benze appears to feel the cold as she was completely hidden beneath the covers, but Pellan was visible. Both times I saw him, he kept the humanoid form.'

'Also, a shadow appeared outside the window while I watched. I immediately visited Pellan in the inner room. There was no way he could be outside then get into the room without me seeing him. It couldn't have been him.'

'You didn't tell me about this shadow,' Enegene said, tersely.

'You were unsettled by the voice; this would only have made things worse. I've now reviewed dwelling security and there should be no way for anyone to enter without being detected.'

'Do shape shifters always lose control when they sleep?'

'Not all of them, but it takes an exceptionally strong will

and definite purpose to keep control. Usually they need mental training to do it, like a covert agent.'

Enegene stared across the room, then looked at Luapp. 'From now on you're sticking close. I can handle things I see and know about, but this is a different nest of spitters.'

Luapp twitched a brow. 'If the slayer is a Fluctoid, how do you think they get close to their victims?'

After some consideration, she said, 'by taking the form of someone they trust.'

'And apart from me, who do you trust?'

Her eyes widened. 'Aylisha and the servants.'

'So we must do something about them. I've been considering acting for some time, but until recently there was no real evidence the slayer was on the planet. Given current events I think the time has come to strengthen our defences.'

'What current events?' Enegene said, suspiciously.

'The Garber incident, and the fact I picked up a leak I would most definitely link to a slayer, plus the shadow outside the windows - '

'How do we mark them?' Enegene cut in.

'I can't mentally tag them all; that would interfere with my ability to act swiftly when needed. But in the equipment you brought I have some devices to cope with a Fluctoid's abilities.

One of them is in essence a vaccination kit. I can inject a biotracer which records the biological working of the people vaccinated. If this changes a warning is sounded.

There's also a wrist monitor you can wear and check whenever they enter the room. Normal is green, abnormal is yellow and absent is red.'

Her brows rose in surprise. 'Absent?'

'If Sylata is vaccinated, and is standing in front of you but the monitor flashes red, you know the Fluctoid is with you.'

'What am I supposed to do then?'

'Act normally and call me using biospeak.'

'I thought you had some form of machine that picks up Fluctoid biotraces.'

'I do, and I've been using it. However, it only works when the Fluctoid is in an original or living shape. If it copied an inanimate object or fluid it's extremely difficult to detect without the tracer.'

'Why? Isn't it easier to pretend to be a table than a person I know?'

'If as we suspect it's part of your circle of elites, it has been studying them and has a good idea how they move, react and think.

It would be almost impossible to "think" like a piece of furniture. It would have to stop all thoughts altogether. It's not much easier to think like any animal whose shape it takes.'

'How do we set up the vaccinations? We can't ask them to queue up.'

'I intended doing the staff first, they have easy access to you, and we have access to them. Once they retire I'll use a mild anaesthesia to keep them unconscious and then administer the tracer. They will wake in the morning no wiser. Aylisha Rhalin is the problem.'

'I can set up an outing. I know Aylisha likes them and we can put something in her drink.'

'You contact Aylisha. We'll do the staff tonight.'

'And Pellan?'

'If Pellan isn't the slayer, you still want to know what he thinks his business connection to you is, don't you?'

'Possibly,' Enegene said guardedly. Then she added, 'if all goes well, you could be a free man in a very short time.'

'I doubt things will move that quickly,' he said, despondently.

A hint of sarcasm came through as she said, 'not looking forward to your freedom Guardian?'

'You can't imagine how much,' he said, with feeling.

'This charade is such perfect cover.' Smiling broadly, she placed her hand on his knee. 'We can talk freely without suspicion being raised. Everyone knows how much I appreciate you.'

Brushing off her hand, he said, 'you're enjoying the cover too much for my liking.'

'As your owner, I consider myself to have shown great restraint. The situation could have been much worse for you.'

She leaned against him. He gave her a frosty look and pulled away.

'You can't go any further,' she whispered. 'You're trapped.'

She knew he was uncomfortable playing a slave. He also disliked the new turn of events. As there wasn't a better way of explaining their closeness, he was stuck with it, and Enegene intended to make the most of the situation.

Abruptly standing up he left the room. Now alone, her smile faded. Annoying the guardian helped ease her concern with being bait, but when on her own she felt vulnerable.

Enegene looked around the room and shivered. She stood up and went over to the window. As she gazed out across the front lawn, her mind went over his reaction to her teasing.

*I'm surprised at Nostowe's tolerance; I've seen him in action and he isn't someone to cross. Even more surprising is the insight he's shown with my anxiety, has he studied mind sifting or something?*

The view from the window was uninspiring and she paced the room, her mind occupied with her role in the masquerade.

*It's looking increasingly likely I'll be the next victim; my ease with the socialite life is ended. I'm always on edge now, watching out for… what? Something that can change its appearance at will? How would I recognise it? Or even worse, how will we capture it?*

*When I thought it was Pellan I knew who to watch, but if it isn't him we're back to the start. I realised Pellan was weak when I hit him, he went down like a poroth in a breeze.*

*He's annoying but Nostowe's right; I could easily injure or slay him, but he doesn't need to be strong to use a knife, I should know.*

*If he is the slayer, surely he would change into a form more pleasing to me, a certain Shadowman for instance…* She stopped pacing. *Don't go down that track.*

The pacing started again. *Instead he repeatedly approaches me in a form he knows I find irritating.*

Her hand slid up her arm and touched the reassuring frame of her knife holder. *If it's someone connected with Pellan, what part do they play? Are they partners? Did he pick the victim and they slay them? Or was he a victim also?*

*Perhaps it's revenge. If so Benze might be in danger. Even though they're together it's obvious he has no real feelings for her. If he began secretly meeting me I would become a target. What am I thinking, I **am** a target. My mind's going around in circles.*

*I know Nostowe's capable of defending me, if he's conscious or breathing. I can never tell what he's thinking with matters connected to work, that guardian facial mask blocks all estimations.*

She shivered again. *A shape shifter could be anyone. Nostowe is right. That's the only way someone could get close to so many different species of women and slay them.*

Suddenly the house which had been her sanctuary for a year seemed a lot less comforting.

*The guardian was right about that too. It could be Aylisha, the servants or any of the guests. Before this I'd felt safe with the servants around me, now I'm beginning to see them as a threat; I'm becoming paranoid…*

*The only person I know I can trust for sure is Nostowe. I know him better than any shape shifter could, especially since he became my slave. If they changed into him I'd notice the difference instantly. So I'll grab the befrin by the beard and contact Pellan.*

Walking to the study, Enegene decided to be open about the contact. She switched on the computer and input his name and the personal code he'd placed on the letter.

Her message was simple: *Have received your note. Tomorrow at the eleventh hour. Bring details.*

After a brief consideration, she added her name. No sooner had she sent it than an acceptance was flashed back. She paused her next task in surprise.

*He must have been waiting by the machine.*

Pushing Pellan to one side she contacted Aylisha and organised a day out. She felt a pang of guilt about that. Her friend was so trusting it would never cross her mind she was being lured into a trap.

The early evening was spent in the pool room trying to relax her mind and body. She found the pool to be a great relaxant. After swimming around for an hour she then called Cleona to fetch Luapp.

He arrived a short while later, and the deathly silence suggested he was still annoyed about her previous transgression.

'I've contacted Pellan, and until we have the servants tagged I want you to stay with me.'

She waited for a reply but there was none. Enegene gritted her teeth as he went into the back room to collect the equipment for the massage.

Being a Swamplander, she hated being ignored; a result of Drylanders indifference to their plight. She decided that if he was going to brood, she would do something to make him respond. Turning to face him she smiled.

'I never thought you would be one for negative silences.'

Giving her a dark look he said, 'if there's nothing to say, there's no logic in speaking.'

'If you won't talk to me, I'll have to find some other way to amuse myself.'

She curled her arm around his back and began to stroke her fingers down it. He frowned but remained silent. When her actions got no response, she dropped her hand lower. Before she could even touch him, he grabbed her chin and held it tightly.

'That's enough for today.'

'If I have a bruise you'll regret it.'

Enegene knew she'd over done it but defiance was her default response. Pulling the towel tightly around herself she was about to leave the table when he scooped her into his arms, strode into the poolroom and threw her in.

'Cool off in there,' he said, scowling.

After the warmth of the massage room the pool room felt cold. Hitting the water, she let out a shriek of surprise and sank. Surfacing spluttering and furious, she was going to give him the full force of her opinion, but he'd left.

Fortunately, the pool room was almost soundproof, so none of the servants came rushing in to find out what happened. 'I'll even the score,' she muttered, wading over to the steps.

Seething over the indignity caused by the guardian, Enegene dressed and went to the lounge. While apparently watching the visual, she occupied her mind trying to think up a suitable revenge. It was a great distraction from her stress.

Time flowed unnoticed as she worked through several plans. Schemes of retribution were interrupted by Lydina's arrival in the lounge.

'It's Mister Pellan Lady Kaylee; he asks to be admitted.'

Enegene's mood plummeted to a new low. The idea he'd

deliberately misread the message sprung to mind, but she contained her anger while answering the servant.

'Show him into the visitor room Lydina, then send Mikim to me.'

Switching off the visual, Enegene waited until she heard Pellan go into the other room before leaving the lounge. She stood in the hallway until Luapp arrived. His expression had set into the mask, but when she said, 'Pellan,' it softened.

When they entered, she was shocked at Pellan's appearance. The usual healthy green of his skin had faded to a sickly yellow and his eyes were dull and expressionless.

'Excuse me for calling on you in this unexpected way Lady Branon, but I have just had an unnerving experience.'

His lip trembled and he glanced anxiously up at Luapp.

She tried sounding sympathetic as she walked over to the sofa opposite him and sat down. 'Indeed? Remain seated and explain.'

'I borrowed Lady Benze' vehicle for a trip into town. I was on my way there when it became completely uncontrollable. It accelerated to top speed and the steering locked. I was very nearly killed.'

He brushed back a strand of hair with a shaking hand.

Enegene was interested despite her annoyance. 'How did you escape?'

He swallowed hard. 'The control unit burned itself out and it slowed enough for me not to be killed when it hit a tree. I managed to free myself from the wreckage, and as I was not far from you, I walked the relatively short distance here.'

Enegene watched his every move. 'You must be shaken. Mikim, call Medic Cyle.' She glanced back at Luapp. 'Then call a vehicle collection unit. Ask them to search for sabotage.'

Luapp went to the side unit and told the viscom to switch on. As he made the two calls she discussed the accident with

Pellan. When Luapp finished the call, she said; 'also call Lady Benze. Tell her about the accident.'

By now Pellan had started to wilt. Seeing Luapp finish the last call she beckoned him over. 'Take Freeman Pellan up to one of the spare rooms and return to me.'

~~~

Luapp waited until Pellan dragged himself to his feet. Taking a few minutes to steady himself, he took two steps and his knees buckled and he fell back onto the sofa.

Moving closer, Luapp offered his hand and hauled him up again. Pellan glanced pathetically up at him as he trudged to the foot of the stairs. After another near collapse on the first step, Luapp turned Pellan around and lifted him over his shoulder.

The man's only response was a muted grunt. He then lay limply down the guardian's back. Carrying him up the stairs he took him to the nearest empty room and placed him on the bed.

'Remain here.'

Pellan's tight expression suggested he knew it wasn't a recommendation. He attempted a weak smile then lay back and closed his eyes. Returning to Enegene, Luapp found her pacing. Seeing him arrive she sat down.

'This is one of two things,' she said agitated. 'Someone's now tried to kill Pellan, or Pellan has cleverly found a way of gaining entrance here.'

Raising a brow, he said, 'if this is a ploy, I think it went wrong. He looked genuinely terrified. Unless these vehicles are different from everywhere else in the civilized galaxy, acceleration is designed to cut out in failure, not increase. For it to increase uncontrollably it must have been tampered with.

There is of course another possibility; the vehicle is owned by Benze and she could have been the intended victim. She is of equal wealth to you-'

'Not quite.'

'And she would be an equal target for the slayer,' he continued, ignoring the interruption.

'Perhaps he's got reasons to be careful after all,' Enegene murmured. 'Even if they are after her, he's usually with her and becomes a target as well.'

They were interrupted by Lydina's arrival again. 'Doctor Cyle is here lady.'

'That was quick,' Enegene remarked. 'Show him in.'

The doctor bustled in and looked relieved to see her up and apparently well. 'Lady Branon, what can I do for you? Or is it your slave?' He looked at Luapp and frowned.

'Neither of us medic, we are in good health.'

She explained what had happened to Nix Pellan, and then Luapp took him up to the room Pellan was in. Sometime later he re-joined them in the lounge.

'Apart from some scratches and bruising, he has no physical injuries. He was extremely lucky to get out alive. However, he is very shaken. I have given him a mild sedative. I hope you don't mind him staying the night.'

Enegene forced a smile. 'Of course not. I'll inform Lady Benze of the situation. I hope you don't mind me asking, how did you get here so fast?'

'I was in the area making another call, and yours was sent through. Now I'll continue to my original destination. Goodbye Lady Branon.'

Lydina came in response to the bell being rung and showed the doctor out. When they were alone again, Enegene turned to Luapp. 'What happens now?'

'About what?'

'About vaccinating the servants.'

'That goes ahead. I'm not leaving anything to chance.'

'What about Pellan?'

'He's been given a sedative. With that and the shock he should sleep most of the night. We can lock him in if you're anxious.'

'I'm coming with you,' she said, firmly.

'It's not necessary, I can do this alone.'

'Maybe, but I'm coming with you.'

Going to the viscom on the side unit, Enegene called Benze' personal number. When Antonia appeared, she told her about the doctor's visit and that Pellan would be staying the night. Stating her driver would return him in the morning, the meal bell cut off any further conversation.

As soon as the meal finished Luapp disappeared to the loft. Enegene went to the lounge and tried to occupy her time watching the entertainment screen, but her mind kept wandering to Pellan.

*Has someone really tried to slay Pellan, or is he playing games? Whatever happened I'm not comfortable with him being in the dwelling. The guardian's warning on Gaeiza was prophetic; this isn't turning out to be as amusing as I thought.*

*Apart from the first arrest I'd always thought of myself of being in control when Nostowe and I met. I'd been the aggressive and assertive one; he'd always backed off. Only occasionally had he answered my outpourings. I'd seen that as weakness, now I know he couldn't be bothered. Since the incidents started happening here I've reconsidered my opinion of him.*

*Now the spectre of an unknown and unidentifiable assailant is a reality I hope he's going to demonstrate the tenacity guardians are known for...*

Having watched nothing, she finally switched off and went upstairs. She'd only been in her room a few minutes when Luapp arrived. He handed her a small case containing the vaccination kit, and he carried a gas cylinder and hose.

'We use bio-speak while we work.'

'I've never really done that before,' she said, anxiously.

'You have, but on a sub level. Just keep your mind open; I'll do the communicating.'

Opening the door, he stepped out and listened for several seconds. As all was quiet he went down the main staircase, along to the door of the basement stairs then down to the servant's quarters. At the bottom, he stopped and listened again.

With it still quiet he attached the flexible hose to the cylinder and went to the nearest door. Squeezing the hose under the door he turned the top allowing a small amount of gas to hiss out and closed it again. Then he moved onto the next door and repeated the action. In a few minutes the bedrooms were finished.

Listening at the bathroom door he made sure no-one had escaped. With all the rooms done he detached the hose from the cylinder and placed both by the stairs.

Enegene opened the case and handed him a gun-like device and a long vial of red liquid. Pushing the liquid into the handle, he used a small touch screen to input human biosigns.

*'Point this at the person in the sleeper,'* he sent, handing the screen to Enegene. *'If they're not salation it will flash red.'*

Enegene stared at him. His words had been so clear she'd had to check he wasn't speaking normally. Following him to the first room she watched as he tried the door. It was locked.

Her grudging respect for his abilities grew as he opened the door with telekinesis. *'Won't we be affected by the gas?'* She had only just formed the question when he replied.

*'It's weak and will have dissipated by now.'*

The person in the room was Lydina. Enegene held the scanner over her and nodded. Luapp pressed the gun against her neck and pulled the trigger. Removing the empty cannister he picked up the case and moved on.

Having worked their way along the servants, Luapp collected the gas cylinder and hose and they returned to the second floor. Taking the equipment to the cupboard he hid it just inside the loft door.

*'Not returning it?'*

*'Pellan was only given a mild sedative. While I expect him to sleep until morning, he might wake if he hears someone moving about above him.'* Shutting the door, he added, *'I'll check on security before retiring.'*

*'Do you suspect uninvited guests?'* she sent, anxiously.

*'It's possible. If it was a genuine attempt on Pellan's life, the assailant may have followed him here.'*

*'Don't be long; I don't feel safe.'*

He glanced at her arm that held the knife. *'It's anyone you meet that's not safe.'*

She smiled wickedly. *'Anyone breaking in here deserves what they get.'*

Luapp left to do his circuit of the house and Enegene went into her bedroom.

~~~

Finishing a quick search upstairs, Luapp went down to ground level. He was on the way back to the stairs when a voice stopped him.

'Mikim? What are you doing in Antonia's house?'

Luapp's suspicions rose. Someone who'd been given a sedative wouldn't be as alert as Pellan was now.

'You're mistaken; this is Lady Branon's dwelling.'

Pellan placed his hand on his head and frowned. 'Then what am I doing here?'

'Your vehicle crashed. You came here for assistance.'

'Oh, that explains why things seem odd.'

He attempted a smile. Noticing the slave's unimpressed

expression, he let it fade.

'You were sedated by a medic; you should not be wandering around.'

A flicker of annoyance crossed Pellan's face. 'I do feel... weak...' He put his hand on Luapp's arm as if to steady himself. 'But before I return, your mistress, the Lady Kaylee, is she free?'

The suspicions reasserted themselves. 'Explain.'

Releasing his arm, the man placed his hands together as if praying, brought them to his mouth, then away again. 'She has no husband? No permanent partner?'

'No male partner has called here. As to a husband, I have no knowledge.'

Pellan watched him keenly. 'What about me?'

'I don't understand.'

The golden gaze was steady on his face. 'Has she spoken of me?'

'Several times.'

Pellan frowned. 'What did she say?'

'Her words on you were only of general things. Anything else she does not confide to me.'

'But you spend a lot of time in her company.' Pellan smiled slyly. 'Day and... night.'

'I'm her protector. At this time she requires me to be close. I don't question her orders, I obey them.'

'Naturally. I did not mean to imply otherwise. The lady has not spoken about our business arrangements?'

'Only to state she did not have any.'

The man fidgeted from one foot to the other. 'Should she speak of me in your presence I would be grateful, very grateful, if you were to tell me the nature of her conversation.'

'I don't pass information about Lady Branon to others.'

'Of course,' Pellan said hastily. 'I merely wish to know if

the lady thinks kindly of me.'

'Then I suggest you ask her sir. It's late and you've had an unnerving experience, I'll escort you to your room.'

'My head has cleared a little,' Pellan said, backing away. 'I can find my own way.'

He turned and limped to the stairs. Luapp watched him go yet again considering the plausibility of Pellan being a serial killer.

When he was out of sight he followed him up. Noting the door to Pellan's room was closed, he continued on to Enegene's. As he entered she turned towards him.

'You were a long time,' she said, sleepily.

He walked past the bed to the chair. 'Nix Pellan was downstairs. He was asking about you.'

She was fully alert within seconds. 'What about me?'

'He wanted to know if you had a liana and what you thought of him.' He pulled off his boots and unfastened his shirt.

Propping her head on her hand she watched him. 'And what did you tell him?'

'The truth; I didn't know. I avoided what you thought of him.'

Having removed all the clothing he intended to, he went to the bed. When he got in she slid closer. 'Why is he asking questions about me?'

'Perhaps he's thinking of acquiring a liana, I didn't listen in to his thoughts.' Luapp slid down and made himself comfortable.

'If he is looking to me for that he's going to be sadly disappointed.'

She pushed his arm gently, a sign that she wanted to move even closer. He considered ignoring it but decided her continuing the signal would keep him awake, so he obliged

188

by raising his arm and lowering it around her back after she closed in.

'Whatever he's up to I'm still of the opinion he is not a multislayer. However, if you are unsettled by his presence, I'll stay the night.'

With his arm around her she sighed contentedly. 'I'm extremely unsettled by his presence,' she said, sleepily.

Luapp looked down at her. She didn't look unsettled but he knew she could hide her feelings well at times. Closing his eyes, he did a mind relaxing exercise.

Gradually the tension ebbed from his muscles and a feeling of calm drifted over him. Enegene let out one last sigh and settled into soft regular breathing.

Quiet footsteps approaching the door stopped his own drift into sleep. They stopped outside then went away several minutes later.

If Pellan had been the Fluctoid, Luapp felt certain he would have come in the moment he thought they were asleep. Pushing thoughts of Pellan to one side, he performed one last mental exercise allowing him to finally, fully relax.

## Chapter 12

Luapp had lain awake listening for the footsteps of a maid for the last half an hour. When they finally became noticeable he was relieved. Cleona knocked the door and entered, not waiting for a reply. Enegene woke and sat up in bed.

With a bright, 'good morning Lady Kaylee,' Cleona paused by the bed, then following Enegene's indication placed the tray on the table by the window.

As soon as Cleona left, Enegene moved from the bed, slipped on a robe and sat down to eat. When he moved, she smiled and told him to join her.

After breakfast he left to start the various jobs Mevil Sylata had lined up for him that day. While busy at the vegetable patch he had the feeling of being watched. Finally, he stopped and stood up.

'Is something troubling you?'

Mevil Sylata straightened up from leaning on the fork and scratched the beard he'd been growing.

'No.'

Luapp carefully assessed his body language. He seemed relaxed. 'Am I doing something wrong?'

'No.'

Dusting the soil from his hands he said, 'then why are you observing my every movement?'

'Strange you should ask. Every other slave I've met would have kept on working hoping for the best.' He paused. 'Are you aware you upset Deana a couple of weeks ago?'

'I regret causing her distress. But as long as I obey orders and carry out tasks assigned adequately, what's inside my mind is not for discussion.'

Sylata folded his arms. 'Who told you that?'

'My previous owner; Zeetan aristocrat Third Order Langa Char. How many slaves have you overseen?'

Sylata rubbed his stubble covered chin and scratched it again. ' a few over the years.'

'Salations, humans?' Luapp corrected at the slight frown.

'Mostly.'

'Gaeizaans?'

Sylata smiled briefly. 'I think you know the answer to that.' The elderly servant looked him over. 'I get the feeling you don't know how slaves behave here.'

'Although Lord Char was my fourth owner, he is the one who taught me from an adol until the time he sold me. His philosophy was that I should never allow another to subdue my character nor invade my thoughts. It's the way I always conducted myself with him.'

'All I can say is it's lucky your present owner is a Gaeizaan. A human wouldn't appreciate your... directness. The Zeetan aristocrat did you no favours.'

'It's my nature to require perfection. I would appreciate instruction if I'm doing something wrong.'

'You appear to be a decision maker.' Sylata's gaze was unwavering. 'Another unusual trait for a slave.'

'I'm a protector. That involves making decisions.'

'You speak like a slave, but you're not fully slave subdued,

191

especially for a man raised in these parts. There's something different about you. I'll figure it out sooner or later.'

Luapp twitched a brow and returned to work. *Sylata's suspicious... hopefully he'll ignore the oddities.*

'How do you feel about the night duties for the lady?'

Sylata's question made him stop digging. 'Resigned,' he replied, starting again.

'It was inevitable she be attracted to you. You're the same race, more or less the same age, and she understands how you think.'

'She has many qualities I respect. Therefore, it would be illogical to cause her grievance for a minor irritation.'

Sylata chuckled quietly. 'Given time, I'm sure that minor irritation will be replaced with something else.'

Luapp turned and gave him a long hard look. *Perhaps his suspicions follow other directions.* 'If I'm not displeasing you I'll finish this task.'

'Go ahead.'

Walking over to the vegetables Luapp had pulled up, Mevil Sylata laid them on a sheet of paper. Picking up a brush lying beside them, he gently brushed off the soil and placed them in the small boxes put out for them.

When packed for storage Luapp carried them through to the pantry, passing Farin as he went. The manservant's face crinkled into a broad grin as he approached, and he made a comment about night exercises. Luapp ignored the remark. Understanding the meaning he had no intention of replying to it.

As he stacked the boxes in the larder, he picked up emanations from Enegene. She was uneasy and anxious. He left the kitchen and headed for her room where she was dressing. Seeing him she smiled her relief.

'Is he still here?' She said, watching him in her mirror.

'I've no idea; I've been in the garden.'

'The sooner he leaves the better. He may not be a multislayer, but he brings my survivals alert.'

Tiding her hair, she pulled her clothing straight. 'Let's go and see. As soon as he's out the door we're picking up Aylisha.'

Luapp turned as she walked past him. 'For your trip out?'

'Yes. We're going to a small uninhabited island. It was her suggestion. Make sure you bring the kit.'

'Yes Lady.'

She flashed him a dark look as they left the bedroom and headed downstairs. Luapp looked in the lounge as he passed and returned to her.

'He's not in there,' he said, as they headed for the dining room.

Pellan was in there, sitting at the table apparently enjoying his meal. As she entered, he stood up and dabbed his mouth with a napkin.

'Lady Kaylee, I was told by the staff you would eat in your room, so I continued on my own.'

'I will have Morvac bring the Drifter to the door. ' She forced a tight smile. 'We'll leave as soon as you've finished.'

'I thought that as I was here we could discuss business.' He smiled again.

Enegene's disapproval was almost tangible. She watched him sit down and he ate another couple of mouthfuls apparently unaware of her condemnation.

'As long as it does not take too long,' she said, eventually. 'I have an engagement with Lady Rhalin this morning.'

Looking at Luapp she added, 'Mikim, contact Aylisha and tell her I will be delayed by a quarter, then get Morvac to bring the vehicle around the front.'

Enegene sat at the table opposite Pellan. She seemed calm

at the moment, so he carried out her orders and then returned the cylinder to the roof.

Back in the cupboard he collected the vaccination kit. Taking it down to the kitchen he covered it with two mats he'd brought down for them to sit on. As he entered the kitchen he noticed the collective smiles from the staff. Even Sylata who was normally controlled, smiled as he approached.

'Is the pack meal ready?'

She pulled it from under the table and handed it to him.

'Have a nice time,' the cook said, her eyes twinkling.

'And have a nap on the beach,' Cleona said. 'You could probably do with it.'

There was a ripple of giggling from the maids before Sylata stopped it. 'That will be enough from everyone.' Looking at Luapp she added, 'take no notice of them, they are behaving like children.'

'Is there something I should be aware of?' he said, looking around the smirking group.

'Nothing the passing of time will erase,' Sylata assured him.

Out in the hall, his keener than human hearing caught the light rebuke from Sylata to the servants.

Continuing out to the Drifter he placed the kit, mats and food in the boot. Looking up he saw Morvac watching him silently.

'You wish to say something?' he said, defensively.

Morvac shrugged. 'Only that it's about time. The suspense was making me jittery; not that it's any of my business.'

Luapp frowned. 'The entire staff is amused by something I know nothing about.' He shut the rear door and came around the side.

Morvac lifted his cap, scratched his head and replaced the cap. 'I hope you know what they know, or something mighty funny is going on around here.'

Luapp paused on his way up the steps and turned to face the driver. 'What do they know?'

'You and Lady Kaylee. Cleona saw you in her bed this morning and her tongue hasn't stopped wagging since.'

'This is a surprise to them? I thought they knew before.'

Morvac leaned against the Drifter. 'Before it was merely speculation. Now it's fact. We're all very pleased for her.'

'Indeed? Why?'

'She's lonely. She puts on a bright front for the guests, but in her quiet times it was obvious she missed the company of her own kind.

Lady Rhalin keeps her cheerful, but she isn't here all the time. You're the same as her and you don't go anywhere. She's been a lot happier since she bought you.'

Luapp turned to go when Morvac spoke again. 'Is that sleazy little weasel going home soon?'

He turned towards the driver once more. 'This is Pellan?'

'How many sleazy little weasels do you have in there? Yes Pellan. If ever someone was up to something it's him.'

'What do you think he's up to?' Luapp said, interested.

'Getting himself installed here I would think.' Morvac laughed quietly. 'But you've put paid to that. I bet he's steaming about it.'

'You dislike him.'

'Mikim, that's the biggest understatement I've heard this week.'

'A lot of the freeborn seem to dislike him.'

'Probably because he's always on the lookout for the next mentor.'

'Indeed? Is he not content with Lady Benze?'

Morvac laughed. 'That's a good question. Lady Benze keeps him on a short reign. Maybe he wants more freedom, or perhaps he's just after her money. Either way, interest soon wore off.'

'Has Lady Benze expressed a desire to be rid of him?'

'Not that I know of, but he's always on the sniff for a fuller gem store. The only socialites higher than Benze are the Lady Rhalin and Lady Branon.

Lady Rhalin has a father who knows what he's up to, and Lady Kaylee now has you. He's stymied!'

Morvac chuckled happily as Luapp headed towards the house. 'I heard she gave him a smack in the eye the other night,' he added, gleefully.

Luapp didn't bother to turn around. 'She was inebriated.'

'Don't believe it! She probably felt like smacking him.'

Morvac's amusement was cut short by the arrival of the people being discussed. He stood upright and opened the door to the vehicle. Meeting them halfway up the steps Luapp stopped.

'We are picking up Lady Aylisha and dropping Freeman Pellan off at Lady Benze residence Morvac. Mikim, get in the back with me.'

*Judging by the way she's giving orders, Enegene's not in a good mood*, Luapp decided. He followed her back down the steps and cut off Pellan's rush to beat him inside the vehicle.

As they waited for Morvac to start off, she planted her hand firmly on Luapp's knee. With a grip of iron, she showed how happy she was with Pellan's presence. Luapp's only reaction was to stare straight ahead.

Pellan lounged back and sighed. 'I would have thought that you of all people would be above such foolish fashion following.'

As the Drifter glided up the long drive to the road, Enegene glared at Pellan on the opposite seat. 'What are you talking about?' she asked, testily.

Pellan glanced at her hand. 'Having an affair with your slave is soo yesterday.'

Her position became rigid and the atmosphere cooled by several degrees.

'Keeping company with my slave has nothing to do with fashion and everything to do with enjoyment. As my personal life is not your concern, you will leave the subject alone.'

Pellan ignored her response and continued, 'but Lady that is just taking advantage of a man who is incapable of refusing you.'

The fact that Luapp was in silent agreement with the man didn't help the situation. The meteoric rise of her temper was felt as her nails threatened to pass through his trousers and into his leg.

'And you are the expert in taking advantage of others, are you not Freeman Pellan?' she snapped. 'Someone who relies on wealthy females for a living.'

The rest of the journey to the Rhalin's place was done in icy silence. Only when Aylisha entered the vehicle did the atmosphere lighten. Pellan's presence appeared to affect her mood as she was abnormally silent.

She returned to her normal effervescent self the moment he left. Enegene relaxed and released Luapp's leg, making the rest of the journey more genial.

At the pier, Morvac and Luapp collected the equipment from the boot and loaded it onto the boat. Then Luapp helped the women aboard.

'We will be back at five, Morvac,' Enegene announced. 'Go and enjoy yourself.'

'Thank you, Madam.'

He gave them a wave as the boat picked up speed then returned to the Drifter and drove off. Aylisha gave Luapp the location of the island and they headed out to sea. Some miles out, he increased the speed lifting the boat free of the water onto three hydrofoils.

It was the perfect day for a trip. Bright and sunny with the sea calm. The acceleration of the boat whipped the women's hair behind them, making it flick into curls and out again.

Sea birds circled and called overhead, and as they got further from the harbour a shoal of brightly coloured fish leapt from the water and glided on large fins before dropping back into the sea. The flash of sunlight on iridescent scales was almost blinding if looked at.

'It will take about half an hour to get there,' Aylisha said, raising her voice to get above the sound of the engine.

'You said it is uninhabited?' Enegene said.

'My father bought it and had a one storey house built there. We use it for escaping to when everything gets too much.' She glanced at Luapp standing in front of the control panel. 'Is there anything he can't do?'

'The Creator knows what he did for his previous owner, but he has a range of useful skills.' Enegene smiled and then said, 'Pellan doesn't know about this island, does he?'

'No why?' Aylisha turned towards Enegene causing her face to be covered in her long black hair.

Holding her own hair down, Enegene answered, 'I wouldn't put it past the man to turn up.'

Aylisha gathered her hair into her hands pulling it away from her face. 'Why was he in the Drifter and what has he done to upset you now?'

'He turned up at my place yesterday afternoon. He crashed Benze' glider and staggered to my home. To be fair, the medic did say he had been shook up.'

'Couldn't you ship him off home earlier?'

'The medic gave him a tranquiliser. But now Mikim is with me I'm not so anxious. The best thing I ever did was to listen to you about a protector slave.'

Enegene slid a sideways look at Luapp but his attention was on piloting the boat. 'He was in a particularly ingratiating mood this morning,' she added. 'But all it did was estrange me further.' Frowning briefly at the memory she let it fade.

Aylisha raised a brow. 'Trying to hook you as benefactor, was he?'

Enegene's lips tightened into a thin line.

'No, he wanted advice on share purchase. I don't know how he knew I invested but he was quite knowledgeable about the leading companies. I gave him a couple of names and he as much as told me they were about to fail!'

'You can relax on the island,' Aylisha said, smiling. 'Pap had security monitors put all around it. Only those who know the code can land without half the Pedantan police brigade turning up.'

The conversation stopped as the women turned their attention to watching the sea. A while later an island appeared on the horizon and the boat began to decelerate.

The island quickly grew larger until a small jetty could be seen jutting out into the water. As the boat pulled up beside it, Luapp stepped across the narrow gap between boat and pier carrying the equipment. Then he turned to help the women.

'Set it for four,' Aylisha told him as he went back into the boat to adjust the programming. 'And send it off to the cave around the coast.'

That done he stepped out again, unhitched the mooring rope and watched the boat back away from the jetty. When it was a fair distance out he turned towards the women and picked up the basket, vaccination kit and mats.

'It's only a short walk from here.'

Aylisha walked up the path towards some trees. Just in

front of a low hanging tree stood a metal pole with a top cover. Flipping up the lid she quickly keyed a code and closed the lid again.

'We can carry on now.'

The women walked along the path through the trees chatting happily while Luapp followed. A short walk later a large building could be seen in a clearing ahead. Going up the steps Aylisha unlocked the door and led them into the one reception room.

'Put the mats on the floor, Mikim, and bring the food through to the kitchen.' Glancing at the case in his hand she looked up at Enegene. 'What's in that?'

'A medical kit,' Enegene replied. 'Being an evolutionary vegetarian on a planet that eats meat, I have to carry a medical kit in case of contamination.'

'You've never carried one before,' Aylisha said puzzled. 'Does Mikim carry one?'

'That's because we've always been in a place where I can get medical help if needed. As for Mikim, he doesn't need to; the one kit covers both of us.'

'It never occurred to me being a vegetarian could be dangerous,' Aylisha murmured. 'I always thought it was healthy.'

'You are native to this planet, Mikim and I aren't -' Enegene stopped abruptly realising her mistake.

'I suppose even though he's a third-generation slave, he is still a biological Gaeizaan. What's poisonous to you is poisonous to him.'

While they talked Luapp dropped everything except the basket on the floor. Giving the kit a last puzzled look, Aylisha headed into the kitchen. Luapp followed and put the boxes of food into the frost unit. When he returned, he noticed the kit had gone.

'Where would you rather go?' Aylisha's voice said from the kitchen. 'To the beach or the waterfall?'

'How cold is the pool?' Enegene said.

'Freezing; it's fresh running water,' Aylisha answered, appearing from the kitchen.

'In that case, let's head for the beach.'

With no sign of the kit Luapp finally looked at Enegene and noticed her glance towards a sideboard by the wall.

'That's a bedroom,' Aylisha pointed to a door. 'Water suits and tanning  liquid are available if needed.' With a grin, she added, 'we have men's water suits too.'

Turning his attention from the sideboard to Aylisha, he said, 'I cannot protect Lady Kaylee up to my neck in water.'

'You don't have to get in the water, on the beach will do.'

'It's not necessary to change my clothing to remain on the beach.'

Enegene laughed. 'Stop teasing Aylisha.'

Aylisha pouted and headed for the bedroom. 'You bait him all the time.'

'He's my slave,' Enegene replied, as she disappeared into the second bedroom.

Luapp went straight to the sideboard and looked inside. Behind a pile of narrow boxes, he could just see the case. Going to the sofa, he worked on possibilities for vaccinating Aylisha while he waited for them to change. He came to the conclusion the best time was when they returned from the beach.

His mind then ran through the possibilities of the biotalent being the murderer and who they were. The fact he'd not seen anybody he recognised from Enegene's social set at the restaurant had kept his mind active on several nights.

When the women returned, he picked up the mats and they headed for the beach. This was a few minutes' walk down a well-worn path through the tall, wide branched trees. Their flowers were in full bloom now, and the sweet scent from their pure white, hand sized flowers lingered in the air.

They emerged from the lush blue-green forest onto a small white sanded beach. Laying the mats near the trees he sat on one. The women untied their colourful wraps and dropped them beside him. They walked to the sea happily discussing friends in their social circle.

Resting his arms on his knees Luapp watched them testing the temperature. Once in, they swam and talked. His eyes and mind remained on Enegene. Not because he suspected she might suddenly disappear, but because his thoughts were occupied with her.

*Since arriving on Pedanta I've seen a different part of her. On Gaeiza I've seen her furious, determined and ready to fight anyone.*

*The knife she carries would be used without a second thought; sometimes without a first thought,* he corrected, remembering a very close call in the early days.

*I'm used to the brash and defensive Swamplander, but here I've seen her vulnerable. Despite her irritating game playing, she's somehow penetrated my defences and stirred up carefully buried emotions.*

*If the slayer is a Fluctoid, protecting herself will be almost impossible. Being the first line of defence I'm determined no harm will come to her.*

Watching her swimming and playing in the water his mind drifted from the mission.

*The water and sun gives a healthy bloom to her skin and brings out the lighter shades of her hair…*

Suddenly aware of the direction his thoughts were taking, he brought them to an abrupt halt. Apart from the fact he was on duty and such thoughts were unprofessional, it was the second time he'd caught himself thinking that way. Shocked by his lack of discipline he took a slow look around the area to get his mind back on the mission.

Satisfied nobody was around he relaxed and lay down, his arms beneath his head. Although his eyes were shut he listened to their voices. The words were drowned by wind and waves, but their laughter was easily heard.

*Waves lapping the shore, breeze rustling leaves, sea birds calling and the women laughing. Nothing around to disturb them or me.*

The warmth of the sun and the constant gentle rush of water onto the beach lulled him into a semi-stupor. Not fully with it, but listening just the same.

A while later he noticed the women's voices had stopped. Sitting up he looked around and saw them walking along the beach. Occasionally one of them bent down and picked up something. Shells, he presumed.

Having checked on their whereabouts he laid down again. Although he continued listening their voices were now inaudible, being drowned by the sounds of nature. Very little could land on the beach without him being aware of it so he remained where he was.

It came as a surprise when he suddenly felt water dripping onto his face. Despite a cloudless green sky, long trickles were falling randomly.

Looking up, he could see nothing until a few large drips appeared from the branch overhanging his position. He got quickly to his feet and walked to where the trunk arched out over the sand. Among the branches and thick foliage, he could just see the outline of a female. Thinking it was Enegene he pushed it hard.

There was a squeal of surprise as the trunk shook. First to fall was a shell. Next came a body. Neatly sidestepping the shell, he caught the body before it hit the ground. It turned out to be Aylisha. She laughed and put her arms around his neck.

'You don't have to put me down Mikim,' she chided, as he lowered her feet to the ground.

Looking into the tree he saw no sign of Enegene, so he glanced up and down the beach. She was nowhere in sight. After several seconds of waiting for her to appear, he became concerned.

'Where's Lady Kaylee?'

His words came out sharper than intended. Busily wrapping her gauze material strip around her waist, Aylisha failed to notice.

'She said she was heading back to the house for a shower.'

Snatching up the mats and second wrap he strode towards the path. 'I must find her.'

'She'll be alright Mikim,' Aylisha called after him. When he didn't stop, she ran to catch up. 'Nothing can get onto the island without the code.'

Luapp barely heard her, his mind was swinging between berating himself for not watching Enegene, and telling her what he thought of her when he got the chance.

As they entered the building everything was quiet. Dropping the mats on the floor he went to the nearest bedroom. A quick glance showed nothing and he continued onto the bathroom. The door was open which told him she wasn't there.

Next, he tried the kitchen. Not finding her there either he went to the second bedroom and its attached bathroom. Aylisha followed slowly plaiting her hair.

Finding both bedroom and bathroom empty, he returned to the first bedroom. A quiet moan drew him towards the bed, and another moan located her position. Moving towards the window, he saw Enegene lying on the floor. Scooping her into his arms he lifted her onto the bed. He sat beside her and scanned her body for wounds.

'Are you alright?' Aylisha said, arriving beside the bed.

Enegene turned her head, winced and opened her eyes. 'Something hit me,' she said, weakly.

Luapp searched through her hair and found a bleeding wound on the side of her head. He fetched a wet cloth from the bathroom and pressed it on the wound.

'What hit you?'

She took a sharp breath in at the cold and pain. 'I don't know.' She raised her hand, only to have it brushed away. 'Something fell... I heard it falling and then it hit me.'

Luapp looked around the room. There was no sign of anything having fallen. There was nothing in the room but them and the usual furniture. Counting the chairs and bedside tables, all seemed correct, but he was only guessing. He hadn't entered either of the bedrooms.

Returning his attention to Enegene, he said, 'where were you when it hit you?'

Aylisha gave him a strange look and was about to speak when Enegene said, 'in the relaxrom.'

Closing her mouth Aylisha frowned. Glancing at her as he stood up Luapp said, 'kindly stay with Lady Kaylee.'

He went through to the lounge and looked around again. Everything looked normal. On a second scan he focussed fully on each piece of furniture. Here he had a chance; he'd sat in this room. Still nothing looked out of place.

He returned to Enegene now sitting up on the bed. Taking the cloth from Aylisha, he refreshed it with cold water, wrung it out and brought it back.

'What hit me?' she said, glancing at Aylisha.

'Why ask me?' Aylisha said, surprised.

'You were here,' Enegene replied, closing her eyes.

'I wasn't; I was on the beach with Mikim,' Aylisha said, indignant.

Enegene opened her eyes and looked at her friend. 'You walked up to the dwelling with me. In fact, it was your suggestion to come here.'

'You told me you were going to the house to change,' Aylisha countered. 'And to tell Mikim to come later.'

Enegene winced again as Luapp dabbed the wound. 'I think the sun's gone to your brain. We were walking along the beach and you said you were thirsty. You suggested we came back to the house to get a drink.'

Aylisha shook her head. 'As we walked along the sand you suggested playing a trick on Mikim. You said you would watch him while I went down to the shore to collect water in the shell I found.'

Luapp worked silently until Aylisha dragged him into it. 'Mikim can tell you I was with him, can't you?'

Enegene's expression was sombre as she looked at Luapp. 'The Lady Aylisha was with me on the beach. We came back when I asked where you were.'

'But she was with me...' Enegene protested. She stared at Luapp confused.

'Perhaps the blow has blurred you.' He dabbed the wound again. 'It's not unusual to hallucinate with concussion.'

'I'm not concussed,' Enegene said, frostily.

'Lady, despite you saying you heard something fall, nothing is out of place and you're in the slember. Possibly an animal got in and felt trapped. It could have bolted and tripped you.'

'That sounds plausible,' Aylisha said, 'even though we didn't see one when we came in.'

Enegene glared defiantly at Luapp. 'It wasn't an animal and I didn't trip. I was in the relaxrom and something hit me from behind. I have the wound to prove it.'

'But how would an attacker get on the island?' Aylisha

said. 'They would have triggered the alarms. And why would anyone attack you anyway? Why drag you in here?'

Luapp gave up hope of keeping the assault low key.

'Possibly they assumed she was you, Lady Rhalin, the daughter of a wealthy man.'

Aylisha looked amazed. 'Kaylee and I look nothing alike.'

'They don't have to know you to attack you,' Luapp said. 'Some thieves attack because they're disturbed. Whatever your security, a determined thief can get past it. They could have been here for days.'

'They couldn't possibly know I was coming,' Aylisha said. 'I didn't tell anyone except Kaylee.'

'They wouldn't need to know. In fact, they probably preferred you not being here; there would be no chance of being found,' he said, slightly exasperated. 'And they attempted to hide the evidence by moving Lady Kaylee in by the sleeper.

'Possible I suppose,' she murmured. 'We had better get Kaylee to a doctor, she could have a serious injury.'

'By the time you call the boat it would be coming anyway,' Enegene said quietly. 'We might as well have our meal and catch the boat as planned.'

'Will you be alright here while we get the meal?'

Enegene closed her eyes again. 'As long as you shut that window.'

Aylisha looked at the window. 'Did you open it?'

'The window was open when we arrived.'

'It shouldn't have been. That's the way the attacker entered and escaped.'

Luapp looked around again as Aylisha closed the window. The sign he was looking for was absent. With a glance at Enegene he followed Aylisha into the kitchen.

While she went around to the various cupboards getting

out plates, cutlery and glasses he watched her carefully. She seemed to know where everything was, which would indicate this was the genuine Aylisha Rhalin.

'Take those through to the lounge Mikim and lay the table.' She spoke as she worked without looking at him.

Collecting plates and glasses he went into the other room.

While laying the table he looked up every now and then. No matter how many times he looked, the room still appeared normal. His observations were disturbed by Aylisha coming in with the boxes she'd retrieved from the frost unit.

He helped remove the contents and put them onto the large plates then took the boxes back to the kitchen. When he returned with the bottle of wine he saw Aylisha standing by a window looking out. Walking up behind her he did the same, but saw nothing unusual.

'What troubles you Lady?'

She turned and looked at him with a worried expression.

'What's going on Mikim? I know I didn't come here with Kaylee, why did she think I did?'

'The blow has confused her thoughts. She was thinking of you and possibly thought she came up here with you.'

'Try again Mikim.' Aylisha's lips tightened into a thin line. 'I have the feeling you know more than you're saying. Your concern with Kaylee's protection borders on obsession.'

Stepping forward she placed her arms around his waist and held him tight. 'Whatever's going on I'm glad you are here.'

'So am I.'

Gently placing his hand on her shoulder, his fingers touched her neck. Before she could question his actions, a small electrical charge shot through his hand and up into her head. The sudden rush of bio-electricity temporarily short-circuited her brain, and she fell unconscious into his arms.

Laying Aylisha on the sofa, he took a minute to recover from the loss of energy. The collection of power from cells was only normally done in emergencies, but this small amount only caused a minor dip in muscle mobility.

Kneeling beside her, he put his fingers against her temple. With the briefest burst of concentration, his mind found the deepest recesses of her thoughts.

Luapp was confused. He'd expected to find the usual non importance of a wealthy child from a wealthy family, with a certain attitude to slaves. While the rest was true her attitude to slaves differed to her actions.

She detested slavery, but outwardly played the part of a feckless elite. Aylisha knew slaves well and had her suspicions about him. Luckily, her concerns were on Enegene's behalf. Whatever else she was, her friendship and affection for the Swamplander were real.

Coming back to normality he stood up and looked down at the unconscious woman. A nagging little thought whispered that had this been the Fluctoid, it might not truly have been unconscious. Attempting to read its mind in that way would have been incredibly dangerous. Irritated by his lack of precaution, he went into Enegene.

'How are you feeling?' he said, in Gaeizaan.

'Apart from the headache; embarrassed.'

She slid forward slowly and swung her legs over the edge of the bed. 'I know we discussed the possibility of Aylisha being... copied, but it didn't occur to me...'

'You were fortunate. Did you tell Aylisha Rhalin to play the stunt?'

Enegene smiled mischievously. 'Yes. That must have been when it happened. She said she would get the water, and I should wait on the path.' Her smile slipped under his disapproving gaze.

'She went to the shore and I went along the path and waited by the division to the dwelling. When she arrived she said you were sleeping, and she wasn't going to risk waking you suddenly.'

Enegene frowned. 'I thought that sounded unusual coming from someone used to dealing with slaves. Almost as if she thought you might do her an injury...'

She thought about it for a few seconds and shrugged. 'We walked to the dwelling, Aylisha went to the kitchen to get a drink, and I went to the slember. Next thing I know you're looking down at me.'

He held out his hand. She took it and stood up shakily. Following him back to the lounge she steadied herself against the sofa. Luapp went over to the windows and looked out for a few moments.

Glancing at Enegene he said in Pedantan, 'I'll shut out the light. Perhaps the darkness will relieve your headache.'

A puzzled pause followed until Enegene caught on. 'I'm sure it will help.'

She watched him close the shutters and the bedroom and kitchen doors. Then he retrieved the case and returned. Removing the immuniser he fitted the serum into the handle.

'Aren't you going to scan her?' Enegene said, surprised.

'This is Aylisha Rhalin,' he said, in Gaeizaan.

'How do you know?'

'I tapped her mind.'

He pushed the immuniser against Aylisha's neck and pulled the trigger. Then he removed the empty container, dismantled the devise and returned it to the case.

'Give me the armband and I'll add Aylisha's reading to the memory.'

When nothing happened, he glanced at Enegene .

'I didn't think we'd need it here,' she said, apologetically.

'I'll add it when we return.'

She looked down at Aylisha. 'How long will she be out?'

'Only a few minutes, it was a small surge.'

He collected the basket from the kitchen and placed the case in one of the empty boxes. Then he took it to the corner of the room behind the table. It was in plain sight but away from doors and windows.

'Don't let the basket out of your sight.'

Enegene moved to a chair and sat down. 'It seems your theory about a shape changer is correct. I definitely walked up with someone I thought was Aylisha.'

He opened the shutter slats then sat in the chair opposite. 'You know you're a target. Ignoring advice could be fatal.'

'Apart from the attack, it did me no harm. If I was the target, why was that?'

'Perhaps we interrupted it, or this time it was after something else.'

Enegene glanced at her friend on the sofa. 'Aylisha?'

'Perhaps, but her father said he thought the malicious intention had moved from her.'

'You then.'

'It had opportunity to attack me earlier. I wasn't asleep but I was drifting. I let my guard down thinking you were safe. It won't happen again.'

'Just as you were beginning to thaw out Guardian.'

Giving her a long look he said, 'how long before we got here were you attacked?'

'I can't be certain but I think it was only minutes.'

'Fortunately Aylisha was quicker than anticipated. You could have been another statistic.'

Enegene put her hand to the swelling on her head. 'Don't stress Nostowe; I won't let you out of my sight from now on.'

He looked around the room and then back to Enegene.

'Come into the slember.'

Puzzled, she went with him. Opening the door, he stepped to one side. When she passed him he remained in the doorway watching the lounge.

'Look around. Is there anything different? Something not here that was here before or something new?'

Scanning the room, she looked back at him. 'A chair is missing.'

'It's definitely missing?'

'There was a chair between the window and the robstor. I thought it was an odd place to put one; it was somehow misplaced.'

'That means the attacker left.'

Returning to the lounge they saw Aylisha was stirring. She opened her eyes and sat up. 'What happened?' she said, looking at Enegene, 'why's it so dark?'

'You fainted,' she lied. 'Mikim closed the shutters to allow me to recover. Do you feel well enough to eat?'

'I think I can push something down.' Aylisha slid her legs off the sofa, gripped Luapp's hand and stood up.

'I'd appreciate it if Mikim could open the shutters. I don't want to fall over the basket in the middle of the room.'

Luapp turned but saw nothing. 'Basket?'

Enegene also scanned the space between the chairs and sofa. 'There's no basket,' she said, puzzled.

Aylisha rubbed her neck. 'I must have been dreaming.'

As he opened the shutters Luapp looked out across the area in front of the house. Seeing nothing out of place he returned to the women by the table. The basket was still in the corner where he left it.

'This trip hasn't quite gone as planned,' Aylisha said, apologetically. Stretching her neck, she added, 'normally it's so quiet and peaceful here.'

'Don't blame yourself,' Enegene said. 'This isn't your fault.'

The meal was eaten in contemplative silence except for the occasional request for Luapp to pass a plate or the wine. With little to distract him his mind worked on how close Enegene had come to being the next victim.

*Being bait has worked too well. The final preparations must be put in place tonight,* he decided. *To leave it any later could cost the Swamplander her life…*

Enegene's voice telling him to sit down and eat cut through his thoughts. Pulling out the chair he helped himself to food.

When the meal finished, the women went into the bedrooms to collect their clothes and change. Luapp packed the remains of the meal into the empty boxes. Collecting the basket from the corner he stood it on the table and packed the containers inside.

As he picked up the beach mats he had the sensation of being watched. Dropping them on the sofa he glanced around the room. It was so carefully placed, he almost missed it. An extra chair had appeared around the table making an even number.

Scrutinising each chair in turn, he finally saw it. The end chair had a faint shimmer; although in its position, the glow could have been dismissed as sunshine.

Luapp was formulating a plan of action when the women reappeared. Both apparently having got over their surprise at recent events, they were discussing their morning swim.

'I'll carry the basket Mikim, you take this back to the boat for me. I'm swapping some clothes over.'

Walking to the middle of the room, Aylisha glanced at the table as she put the large, cloth covered case down.

'Strange,' she said, quietly. 'I'm sure pap put that spare chair in the cellar.' She shrugged. 'I suppose he forgot. Carry it down there Mikim.'

Aylisha went into the kitchen as Luapp walked to the end chair and gripped the top tightly. It was far too heavy for a piece of furniture. The top looked like wood but felt like skin. It was also warm. Lifting it away from the table, he felt movement beneath his hands.

Aylisha returned with a key strip and opened the door under the loft stairs. The clack of her shoes got fainter as she went down.

The chair back was moving more quickly now. Tightening his grip, he looked around for some method of containing it. With her footsteps getting louder he gave up hope of concealing its presence.

She appeared smiling, but her expression changed from cheerful to horror. Despite Luapp being between her and the chair, she could still see its legs moving. Her hands went to her face as her voice rose to a shriek.

'What's happening to the chair?'

Standing by the door Enegene hadn't noticed the chair but Aylisha's shout made her look back. With a second scream, Aylisha ran towards the kitchen as Enegene backed towards a bedroom.

Luapp was too concerned with trying to stop the Fluctoid escaping to care about its shape change. Feeling the weight slide downwards he saw the legs slither across the floor. The chair back thinned in his hands and parted.

Tightening his grasp on the writhing ends, he held on. It was now a brown blob with several manically waving tentacles. One lashed towards him making him duck and lose his grip. Hastily moving out of reach, he worked on a way to capture it.

His scrutiny of the room was interrupted by a hiss. The creature now was changing into a pokari. With its head formed it let out a low growl. The speed of change suggested it would

214

soon be developed and free.

Grabbing Aylisha's case, Luapp lashed out while he had the advantage. It connected with the head knocking the half formed lizard onto its side. It let out another rumbling growl as it scrabbled to right itself then fixed Luapp with a stare.

'*Get on the table,*' he sent to Enegene.

Its legs and tail now formed, it watched Enegene hurry to the table. Seizing the opportunity, Luapp swung the case again. The pokari ducked, turned and whipped at his legs with its tail.

He dropped the case, caught the end and held on. The creature snarled and twisted trying to free itself as he heaved it towards him.

Throwing itself into a roll, it yanked its tail from his grasp slicing his hands on the upright scales on its spine. It scuttled around to face him, its tongue sliding out to smell the blood.

A hiss and scrape of claws gave a brief warning as the animal leapt forward, mouth open wide. Grabbing the case Luapp shoved it into the gape. Its fangs pierced the cover and lodged in the top.

'Go to the table Lady Rhalin.'

Edging past the thrashing reptile Aylisha ran to Luapp. He gripped her waist and lifted her onto the table. Then he worked his way around the writhing creature looking for an opportunity to strike.

With a final twist, it shifted the case with its claws. Free again it rushed at him. Turning at the last moment, he helped it on its way with a backhanded swipe. The blow added momentum and sent it careering into the wall across the room.

It staggered drunkenly as it righted itself then turned to face him. Snatching up the case again, Luapp moved between the lizard and the women.

A rapid tongue wave preceded another charge. Connecting with the pokari's shoulder the case  knocked the animal onto its side.

Dropping the case he moved closer. Deftly avoiding its tail, he tried to grab its neck. A second unseen tail lash knocked his legs from beneath him. He landed face down. Momentarily face to face with the animal he rolled to avoid a pounce. It followed, slashing at him with its claws as he  scrambled to his feet. Reaching for the case, another tail lash sent it sliding out of his grasp.

Keeping eye contact with the pokari, Luapp backed towards the table. With a hiss, it attacked.  He twisted, grabbed a chair and swung it back hard. It connected with the creature's head and shoulder, lifting it from the ground. It landed hard on its back with a grunt.

Dropping the remains of the chair, he picked up a sharp-ended leg ready for the next rush. The pokari righted itself, sidled towards the door, and scuttled from the house. Striding to the doorway Luapp watched it run down the path into the trees.

'What the heak was that?' Aylisha exclaimed.

Luapp saw no point in trying to deny the evidence before them. 'A shape shifter.'

He glanced at Enegene. She was as shocked as Aylisha. Discussing such a being was one thing, seeing it in action was something else.

Aylisha looked around as if expecting another to appear.

'What's a shape shifter?'

'A being with the ability to look like other creatures and objects. It uses its skills for hunting,' Luapp said, watching the door. The truth was now the only course. 'I think that was the only one, Lady Rhalin, it's safe to come down.'

'Are you sure Mikim?'

She stared around the floor as if afraid it was going to change into something else. Seeing Enegene crawl to the table edge she added, 'it must have been that thing that attacked you Kaylee. That's why you thought you were with me.'

'You're right,' Enegene said, accepting a lift from Luapp.

Bringing Aylisha down the same way he watched for the Fluctoid returning. As soon as she was on the ground he picked up her case and headed for the door.

'I suggest we keep together going to the pier. Normally animals give up and keep away after being defeated, but it can't be guaranteed.'

'I'll lock the cellar,' Aylisha said. 'Kaylee, can you lock the shutters? Mikim, check around outside. It will speed up our leaving if we all help.'

Luapp went to the doorway and looked out. There was no sign of the Fluctoid anywhere, but it would be more difficult to see in bright sunshine among the trees of the forest.

With the light cut out by Enegene closing the shutters, it was also now difficult to see inside. But he was reasonably confident it couldn't get past him a second time.

Aylisha collected the basket and stopped at the doorway. She gave the room a final look around, stepped outside and locked up.

'Let's get to the pier,' she said, hurrying past the Gaeizaans.

They walked in tense silence until the pier was in sight, then Aylisha relaxed slightly. The boat wasn't there yet but it could be seen heading towards them. Looking up at Luapp she said, 'do you think it is native to the island?'

'No.'

He watched for anything moving in their direction as he spoke. 'You've never heard of shape shifters, so they're not native to this planet.'

With a quick look around Aylisha frowned and looked up at him a second time. 'How do you know so much about them Mikim? You're a third-generation slave.'

'My previous owner was a Zeetan ambassador. He travelled with his duties. As his protector, I travelled with him.'

Aylisha scanned the forest nervously and then looked at Enegene. 'I suppose Mikim has told you about his travels Kaylee.'

'The first thing I did when I had the chance was to find out about his previous owner.'

Aylisha's eyes were now fixed on the nearing boat. 'But how did it get on the island? Or even to the planet?'

'It can mimic whatever shape it sees so it can easily board a ship without being noticed, and just as easily disembark. People here are not familiar with shape shifters, it can move around without anyone suspecting. As for getting on the island, I doubt if the sensors are triggered by animals.'

'No.'

Watching the boat manoeuvre into position, Aylisha added, 'that thing gives me the same creeps as Nix Pellan. You don't think he's one, do you?'

She smiled briefly at Luapp as he took the mats from her and helped her in.

'I doubt it.' Enegene followed her friend into the boat. 'He would have changed into something better looking.'

As he stepped into the boat Luapp looked towards the trees one final time. There was no sign of the Fluctoid. In one way he was relieved, in another concerned.

*If they're not following us, what are they up to? I'd had them in my hands, but couldn't hold onto them. The equipment in the roof is the only way to capture this being.*

Casting off the line he took the boat out to sea. The women

218

watched the waves and sea creatures silently until Aylisha broke their trains of thought.

'That thing might have come over on the boat with us. It makes me shudder to think of it. Is it with us now, Mikim?'

'It's not with us,' he said, shifting his gaze to her.

'How can you be so sure?' she said, nervously.

'I watched for it as you boarded. Nothing came aboard with us.'

Aylisha sighed with relief. 'Well, at least it's marooned on the island.'

Keeping his eyes on the direction they were going, he said, 'not necessarily.'

She stared at him wide eyed. 'What makes you say that?'

'It can change to any shape it pleases. All it has to do is to change to a swimming animal and it can leave the island.'

'I wish you hadn't said that,' she said, staring at the water around the boat.

'We are quicker than it is,' Enegene said. 'We are on a fast boat, and we have Morvac in the Drifter. Unless it has an engine attached to its rear end it has no hope of catching us.'

She looked at Luapp mentally daring him to correct her statement. 'Now we've left it behind, it will probably hunt something else.'

'Do you think we should report it to the authorities?' Aylisha looked up at Luapp for an answer.

'Is it likely they would believe us?'

'Probably not.'

'Then we would be wasting our time.'

'This has turned out to be one of the worst day's outings I've ever been on,' Aylisha said, gloomily.

'Then things can only get better,' Enegene said, trying to sound positive.

'How can you be so cheerful after what happened?'

'Considering how things may have turned out, I'm fortunate to be still breathing.'

The boat slowed as it approached the quay and came to a halt as the ropes were caught by a harbour worker. Climbing up the steps they found the Drifter waiting for them.

From the quay to their homes was a rapid journey with a tense atmosphere. As they dropped Aylisha off Enegene said, 'if it reassures you, tell your father what happened. If he doesn't believe you tell him to call me.'

'I'll do that,' Aylisha said. With a quick smile, she went into the house.

Luapp's mind was occupied with the Fluctoid as the Drifter pulled away from the Rhalin estate. It disturbed him how easily it managed to find and attack Enegene on an island in the middle of an ocean.

*How did it follow us without me noticing? Did it come with Pellan to the dwelling? It will be even harder to lure out now, but I must do so before it attacks Enegene or some other socialite again.*

## Chapter 13

'Will it attack again?'

Enegene's question brought Luapp out of his reverie.

'It's a sentient member of the genus, and if you are the target, most certainly. We must get the final preparations done today.'

'At least we know it's after me,' she said, despondently.

'It may not have been after you. It had time to slay you but didn't.'

'You and Aylisha came back too soon.' Enegene sat on the massage table staring across the room. 'You interrupted it.'

'Yes.' Luapp pulled himself onto the massage table beside her. 'Perhaps that's the reason; we interrupted the ritual.'

'What ritual?'

'You saw the digistils. It doesn't just kill, it mutilates. From the wounds and blood flow we know it does most mutilation when the victim is alive.

Also from the high levels of adrenalin and comparative excretions in the different genus' we know the victim was conscious when mutilated. That seems to be confirmed by the Garber incident. It's sadistic and enjoys the fear and pain it causes. Just slaying you quickly wasn't what it wanted.'

'Why come back? It knew you were there and it wouldn't have time to slay me as it wished. Why risk getting caught?'

Luapp glanced at her. 'Perhaps it wanted to test me,' he said quietly. 'It knew you couldn't tell the difference, and it wanted to know if I could.'

'And now it knows you can?' she said nervously. 'Is it on to us?'

'Not in the way you mean. If it suspected you of assisting guardians it would have killed you then.'

'Or think up an extra special termination just for me.'

'As you said before, it doesn't like changing its plans. I'm going to the loft to complete the safe area.'

He got off the table and Enegene did the same. 'I'll join you when I've showered and dried my hair.'

They left the spar area together and parted company outside her bedroom. He continued into the loft as she went in. Dropping the towel outside the shower cubicle she stepped in and switched on the water.

Half an hour later, she sat at the dressing table brushing her hair. Inserting a couple of flowery hair clips, she headed for the door.

Just as she got onto the landing the doorbell rang. The door was answered by Lydina, and recognising Benze voice, Enegene turned away from the cupboard. Descending the stairs, she met Lydina at the bottom.

'Lady Benze has called to see you Madam.'

'Did she say why?'

'No Madam. I've put her in the sitting room.'

'Thank you Lydina.'

Enegene crossed to the sitting room with her mind furiously working on why Antonia Benze would call on her. Pausing outside the door, she pasted on a smile and went in.

'Kaylee,' Benze said, as Enegene crossed to a chair, 'I've just heard the news and I had to come to make sure you were alright. It must have been quite a fright.'

'What news, Antonia?'

'That you were attacked by a pokari on the Rhalin's island; it's gone around the group like wildfire.'

'Really? How did anyone find out?'

'Oh you know us Kaylee, nothing happens in Denjal without the network hearing about it.'

'To be honest Antonia, we weren't in any real danger. Mikim was with us and he persuaded it to leave.'

Antonia Benze smile seemed to freeze. Then she added, 'I must say he's been worth his price. I've got a few inquiries going to try and locate another Gaeizaan slave for myself.'

'From what I understand they are few and far between.'

'True, very true. Are you sure you won't part with him? I'll give you twice his price.'

'As you said, Antonia, he's proved his worth. I wouldn't part with him no matter what anyone offered.'

'Well, it was worth a try. My other reason for visiting is to ask you to a private little lunch party.'

'When?'

'Now.'

'Oh... I – '

'There's just three of us, myself, you, hopefully and Petulla.'

'Not Aylisha Rhalin?'

'No, I understand she's elsewhere today.'

'And Pellan?'

'Visiting his cousin. She arrived on the planet a month ago, and has remained on an extended visa.'

'Yes, I'd like that. I'll send a servant to fetch Mikim.'

'There's no need, it's very secure. The place has its own

223

security staff.'

'Still, after my experience on the island, I'll take him.'

Enegene pressed the servant call on the table and tapped it lightly. When Farin arrived, she sent him to find Luapp.

*Luckily he's in the roof space and he won't be able to find him,* she thought as she sat down.

It came as a  surprise when Luapp entered a few minutes later. Giving him a puzzled frown she said, 'tell cook we'll be out to lunch and come back.'

They were waiting by the front door when he returned. As it was Benze personal glider, Luapp sat in front by the driver.

A couple of hours later they returned to the house. Telling Luapp to follow her Enegene went straight to the lounge.

'What do you think that was about?' she said, as they sat down.

'I have no idea. The discussions were about everything except the incident on the island. Didn't she give you any explanation for the meet?'

'Only that they'd heard about what happened and wanted to cheer me up.'

'It's suspicious timing.' After some thought, he added, 'it's possible that wasn't Antonia Benze.'

'The shape shifter? But Petulla was waiting for us.'

'If it was the Fluctoid, it had to have a back-up plan in case things went wrong. It probably assumed we'd be unprepared for a second attack so soon after the first, and you would go leaving me behind.'

'Would it have killed Petulla as well?'

'I doubt it, it would probably have found an excuse to get you alone.'

'But if your ritual theory is correct, it would have wanted to get me somewhere private where it could take its time killing me.'

Luapp shrugged. 'It lured you away before without you being suspicious.'

'But my insistence on bringing you spoiled the plan.'

'Probably in two ways. I'm more likely to recognise it, and I can fight it off. Or, it could have been Antonia Benze wanting to get all the information for the next event so she is ahead of the group.'

'Did you see anything suspicious?'

'The glow is more difficult to see in open spaces in the daylight, it would be easier to see in dimmer light; perhaps -'

Before he could say more the doorbell rang. A few minutes later, Cleona arrived in the lounge.

'You have a visitor, Madam. Kyrita Chrona; she says you've met before. She's the cousin of Nix Pellan and she wants to talk to you.'

'They're coming in like blosips...' Enegene muttered. Then louder, she added, 'where is she?'

'The sitting room, Madam.'

'Thank you Cleona.' The maid disappeared and Enegene glanced at Luapp. 'What do you think she wants? I've only met her once.'

'More to the point, why is she here? He's not native to the planet, so she either followed him or came with him. It's an opportunity to find something out about Pellan.'

'Where will you be?'

'In the garden. Freeman Sylata wants me to do planting.'

Enegene smiled. 'You're getting good at plant tending.'

As he left for the garden, the look he gave her conveyed his thoughts on her remark.

Enegene entered the sitting room quietly and observed the short, slightly plump female with yellow hair. The young woman was standing by the window looking out. She only realised Enegene was there when she deliberately shut the door hard.

Kyrita Chrona looked around startled. 'Lady Branon, so apology for encroaching on valuable time. Unsure you remember me.'

Enegene sat on the sofa and the girl moved to a chair opposite. 'What is it you want?'

'We need help, and thought I could help you also.' She smiled and let it fade.

'We, who, and what help?' Enegene said, coolly.

'Nix tries free himself from Lady Benze. She ignoring request for reference. Unable to free himself if no other lady to go to.'

Enegene's relaxed posture stiffened; she could guess where this was leading. 'What has this to do with me?'

Kyrita Chrona clenched her hands in her lap nervously. 'Nix suggest you be next benefactor.

Most important event impending. Sure you'll be invited. Hostess man second chief to planetary head man. Nix want you tell Benze you need escort. She believe you, no strife.'

Enegene raised a brow. 'And after the gathering? As we know, I am not actually going to be his benefactor.'

'He tell me has someone marked for her place. When free of Benze he go to new lady.'

'Why are you on this planet? Nix I can understand, but you have no real reason to be here.'

'Nix and I very close. Like brother and sister. Raised in same sett. I go where he go.'

Enegene relaxed back against the chair. 'There are two complications in your plan. I usually go to such gatherings with my friend Lady Rhalin, and I always take my slave.'

'No strife,' the girl said happily. 'Lady Rhalin not object so sure. Slaves always go with owners, it overnighter, wealthy can't function without slaves.'

Enegene detected a note of cynicism that made her feel Kyrita Chrona disapproved of slavery. 'And what help do you think you can give me in return?'

Pellan's cousin held Enegene's gaze then slowly smiled. 'How can I not offend?' she asked coyly. 'Understand slave more than just slave... have feelings for him.

No misunderstand, not judge, it natural. You stranger here and men must seem... weak beside him. To find slave of own kind seem like god's offering. You destined to find interesting.'

Enegene watched the hand movements almost mesmerised. Although Pedantans used their hands as they spoke, this woman seemed to use them as a second language. Pulling her gaze up to the girl's face she was about to speak when she started again.

'Understand he not enthusiastic; obstructive even.'

'You are mistaken,' Enegene replied icily. 'He is co-operative.'

'Reluctantly obedient?' She put her head on one side and smiled. 'He does as necessary. I help banish that.'

Enegene's annoyance at the airing of her affairs was escalating to anger. 'My social group do not discuss such affairs, therefore I assume Pellan is the source of your information?'

'Not matter. Only importance is if true or no. If so I help you.'

'Indeed? How?'

The young woman opened the bag on the chair beside her and pulled out a small vial of blue liquid. 'This. It make him very obliging. Will remember nothing.'

She held it out. Enegene took it and looked through the transparent blue of the liquid. Then she lowered it again.

'Put on pillow just before he lay down. You not breathe in. Fifteen minutes, he yours. Next morning, no memories.

Give this sample you try. You want more call me.' Pulling out a card she handed it to Enegene. 'All we ask is you take Nix to shaylie.'

Enegene glanced down at the card. 'Shaylie?'

'Happy time; party.'

Returning her gaze to the girl's face Enegene observed her expression carefully. 'And why does your cousin think I would be willing to upset Lady Benze?'

'She no close friend of you.' Kyrita sounded almost indignant.

'Neither has she done anything to upset me.' Enegene placed the vial on a side table. 'I don't like Nix Pellan spreading unsupported rumours about me.'

The girl bit her lip nervously. 'My clumsiness offend,' she said miserably. 'Nix not tale teller. We discuss means of escaping Benze only.

I appeal to sense of justice. Nix is cousin and must help him. His life not easy; only trying to live. She treat him worse than slave. Expects complete obedience and taunts with other males. He desperate to leave.'

Enegene maintained the unsympathetic expression. 'As to how he is treated, from what I can see Benze is most generous with her wealth. He is dressed well, goes to the most prestigious meetings and has good food to eat. For all of this he must expect to give her some service.

The males he complains of may amuse her, but it is him she keeps in the dwelling. Unless of course, she is the one thinking of changing the arrangement and not him.'

The girl looked horrified. 'No, definitely him.'

'Then tell him to get his new benefactor to take him to the gathering. Why should I become involved?' She picked up the vial. 'For this? I have my own methods of getting my slave to co-operate. Your story is too thinly spread for the truth, and I

228

don't like being lied to.'

Her skin turned a deep green, and she hung her head. Tears welled up in her eyes and trickled down her cheeks.

'You correct,' she whispered, looking up again. 'I lie, not good at lying, but desperate. Don't know to trust you.'

'Probably the same as I trust you,' Enegene replied, coldly.

The gold eyes scanned Enegene's face, looking for some sign of softening, but finding none, she decided to speak anyway.

'Nix and I from poor family. Hard to make living. He realise ladies attracted to him. They gave him gifts for little return. Realised could earn with rich benefactors.

I warned many times he get trouble, but he see no other way. Benze to be last. He save prudently from exploits, and wants to invest.'

'The business advice I gave him he promptly discredited. If he is so knowledgeable why come to me? There must be wives of businessmen in Benze' circle, why not ask them?'

'He need trustworthy person who not tell Benze. Many friends with the lady and they tell her. Also, not many understand investments as you and Benze. If she know she stop his allowance. She not want him leave but not care for him either. She threaten accuse him of theft if he leave.'

'I can see that would curtail his efforts,' Enegene said dryly. 'She has a great deal of influence here and he is an outworlder. So who is his benefactor?'

Kyrita Chrona's skin darkened again. 'No benefactor. Only ploy to show he no bother you. We know we match pair. Nix concerned Benze have me imprisoned or worse.'

'Worse?' Enegene frowned. 'I could see Benze might be annoyed enough to make a false statement, but worse?'

The slight contortions of her face suggested Kyrita was trying to stop herself crying. 'Nix say jealous. If he getting

229

friendly with other females she organises an accident.'

'If he has evidence of such behaviour he should go to the enforcers,' Enegene said.

'And they believe him over Benze?' The girl's words came out sharply. 'He trying for a life for us.'

'So instead you would rather I be the next accident.'

Kyrita Chrona's eyes opened wide in innocent denial. 'Not at all. You more powerful than Benze. She not dare attack you, especially with such slave. Nix says excellent at protection.'

Enegene couldn't stop the smirk. 'And he should know. I will think over your request.' She held out the vial but the girl shook her head.

'Keep as trial.' She stood up and put the bag strap over her shoulder.

'I have received no invitation.' Enegene also stood up and walked to the door with her.

'They come this week.'

Enegene stopped just in front of the door. 'You are very well informed.'

'I work as assistant for lady host. Must go; my thanks for seeing me.'

'If the drug works as you say, why does he not use it on Benze to gain his release?'

'We unable use that drug on her - ' she stopped abruptly.

Suspicions rose in Enegene's mind once again. 'Why?'

'It meant for slave... highly expensive, couldn't afford more.'

'If this is so important to Pellan, why did he not speak to me himself?'

'Nix know you find him… less desirable.' She smiled. 'Cannot understand, he wonderful personality.'

'His approach needs work,' Enegene remarked. Pressing the servant bell she waited for one of the maids to arrive.

When Cleona appeared, she said, 'show the Freewoman out.'

Watching the young woman leave Enegene felt she had a genuine affection for her cousin. Looking at the vial again she placed it in a draw of the sideboard by the door.

Kyrita Chrona's revelation about Benze piqued Enegene's curiosity. Up until then, she had never heard any mention of the woman being anything other than the usual socialite.

She left the sitting room and headed for her study to do some research. Concentrating on work gave her mind something else to focus on other than being bait.

Some hours later the bell rung for evening meal. It was with some relief that she stopped her research. Despite following every mention of Benze activities, she found nothing to indicate a darker side.

Arriving in the small dining room she found Luapp waiting. As they sat down she kept the conversation to generalities, outwardly seeming the genuine article of owner talking with her slave.

After the meal Luapp disappeared again, and Enegene went back to the study to check on her investments. She wanted to know how the companies she recommended to Pellan were doing.

His dismissive comments had stung her confidence. By the time she stopped again it was almost midnight. Going up to her room, she saw Luapp arranging pillows in the bed.

'I don't think that'll be necessary tonight,' she said, pulling the pins from her hair.

He looked up at her in surprise. 'And your reasons for this assessment?'

'It knows you can see it, and after the island confrontation it will know you're expecting it. I would think it would wait for a week or so before trying again.'

He straightened up and stared at her. 'Where does your

sudden insight into its actions come from?'

'Nowhere. I've had time to think things through calmly that's all.'

'And you would rather trust your civilian reasoning than my guardian experience?'

'You'll be with me. It ran from you before.'

She brushed out her hair while watching his reaction in the mirror. 'Besides, such a low-tech ruse would hardly fool a multislayer.'

'From a distance in the dark it would be enough to draw them in.' Returning the bed to normal, he added, 'but as you will, it's your life we're risking.'

Undoing the many buttons down the front of her dress she said casually, 'Pellan wants me to pretend to be his benefactor.'

She watched Luapp take the extra pillows back to the side room. When he returned, she added, 'if it's him, he won't attempt anything until I've done that.'

He stopped by the end of the bed. 'And if it isn't Pellan?'

Enegene shrugged. 'Like I said before, they'll lie low for a while. That's what happens in the swamps.'

'I agree. But generally Swamplanders are smugglers, confidence fraudsters and thieves, not multislayers.'

Instead of her usual sharp retort, Enegene forced herself to be calm. 'I've forgotten to switch off the intelmac in the aplirom,' she said, 'you go in the clensrom first.'

His perceived belittling of Swamplanders gave fervour to her decision on the way down to the sitting room. Retrieving the vial from the drawer, she muttered, 'I'll show him what Swamplanders are capable of.'

Back in the bedroom she dripped three drops onto his pillow and placed the vial in the drawer of the bedside cabinet. Then she retreated to the window. As soon as Luapp reappeared she slipped into the bathroom and took her time preparing for bed.

She emerged half an hour later and he appeared to be asleep, and he didn't stir when she got into the bed. Turning towards him she quietly called his name. Receiving no answer, she gripped his shoulder and shook it.

'Mikim.'

With no response, she sat back against the headboard arms crossed and tight lipped. 'Fine drug that is,' she muttered angrily. 'All he does is sleep.'

Looking down at him she said, 'why can't you put your arms around me just once, Luapp?'

To her surprise, his eyes opened and he stared up at her. Sitting up, he pulled her gently into an embrace.

'I thought you'd never get around to showing your feelings...'

As she pulled back to kiss him she realised he was not relaxing his grip. She was trapped. 'Mikim... Luapp... let go!'

Fighting to pull loose, his sudden release caused her to end up flat on her back. Furiously struggling to a sitting position, she glared at him.

'If you thought that was funny - '

Luapp wasn't smiling or even looking at her, he was staring straight ahead at the windows.

'Look at me Mikim.'

His fixed stare didn't waver. She waved her hand in front of his face without the slightest reaction.

'He's only responding to his real name,' she murmured. 'Good thing he won't remember this in the morning. Lie down and sleep Luapp.'

Watching him do as he was told, she sighed and wriggled down beside him. Switching off the light she tried to sleep.

It was a restless night. Luapp slept as if dead and that disturbed her. For all she knew the drug may kill him. Guilt stung her conscience for trying it on him without telling him, and she doubted he would be amused if he ever woke up in the morning.

Half way through the night she woke, noticed he was still in the same position, and realised he'd been totally immobilised. If the shape shifter arrived it could kill them both, and that would have been her fault. With that thought floating around her head it took a long time to get to sleep again.

The next morning she woke feeling edgy and with a pounding head. Turning towards him she watched for any sign of stirring. By eight she was beginning to think the worse.

Just as she was about to panic he stirred. Taking a deep breath, he opened his eyes and sat up. Seconds later he leapt from the bed and headed for the bathroom at speed.

He remained there for at least quarter of an hour and when he reappeared it was obvious he wasn't well. Sitting on the chair he held his head in his hands with his eyes closed.

'Unwell?' she enquired tentatively.

'It must have been something I ate,' he replied weakly.

'Or breathed in,' she muttered.

Obviously it hadn't been quiet enough as he straightened up and focussed on her with narrowed eyes.

'Meaning?'

Enegene slid from the bed and tried to position herself between it and the bathroom as she considered her options. She could bluff, but the chances were he'd know and want to know why. Or she could tell the truth and risk his reaction.

He would have to know about the drug anyway in case it had side effects. This wasn't going to be pleasant, and could be a little dangerous, so she might as well get it over with.

'Pellan's cousin gave me something to use on you, by way of payment for me helping him. I thought it was a fake.'

He closed his eyes for a few minutes then opened them again. 'What was it meant to do?'

'Suppress your will.'

She watched his every movement. He was inexplicably calm. The guardian was either feeling too ill to care, or building up to an explosion.

'And did it?'

'Don't you remember?'

'I have a pounding headache and feel like a reactivated corpse, but I have no knowledge of why I'm like this.'

'I honestly didn't think it would work.'

A muscle twitched by his jaw and he took a long breath in. 'What part of the phrase "homicidal outworlder" did you not understand?'

'I – I know it was thoughtless...'

'Thoughtless?!' He stared fiercely at her. 'Try tehin void; we could both have been killed!'

Wincing with pain he gave her another glare and fell silent. To her surprise that seemed the extent of his lecture about the danger she'd put them in.

*He's enough ammunition to rant for hours; I got off lightly.*

Leaving him sitting on the chair trying to control the nausea she went to the bathroom. By the time she came out, he had obviously succeeded, as he was dressed.

'Where's the drug?' he said, sounding more alert.

Going to the bedside cabinet she pulled out the vial. He took it and looked at it for a few seconds.

'I'll keep this and get it analysed.' He closed his hand over it. 'For now I'll put it up with the rest of the equipment in the roof.'

'She told me to call her if I wanted more.'

Enegene went to the dressing table and picked up a brush. She held it out and he walked over. Putting the vial on the dressing table, he gathered her hair and brushed it.

'You should contact her and see what turns up,' he said.

'As soon as I get the invitation I'll call Pellan. Just make sure you don't leave me alone with him.'

'I'll do my best; as long as you don't incapacitate me with any more drugs.'

She forced a smile as she waited for him to finish the thorough brushing. 'I'm having my hair down today, just weave it loosely.'

A knock on the door made him put down the brush and walk over to it. Cleona smiled as she walked in and put the tray on the table. As she left, she pulled the door to but didn't quite close it.

Enegene moved over to the table, lifted the lid and looked at the meal. 'I hope you realise I exercised great control last night, I didn't take advantage of the drug's effect.'

The room temperature dropped by several degrees. Cursing her stupidity under her breath, she looked up. He glanced at the door and to her horror it swung shut and locked.

Being trapped in the room with a furious guardian wasn't a good prospect, she knew. In the Swamplands, there were tales about what guardians were capable of just using the power of their minds.

The slow flexing of the fingers on both hands was a bad sign, as was the keeping of a distance between them. It suggested he didn't trust himself to keep his hands off her.

'Ever since it's been my misfortune to know you I have suffered at your hands,' he said, in a quiet, controlled manner.

'From the knife wound in my leg to the poison you administered on Padua. And now this. Do you realise I could have been under anyone's control, even the slayer's?'

Dropping the meal cover she backed towards the bathroom. 'I didn't give you that drink; it was the android.'

236

The door shut behind her cutting off her sanctuary.

'Under your orders,' he said, moving towards her.

She changed direction and headed for the bed. 'It was made by the guardians,' she shot back. 'They had no right...'

'Programmed by you!'

Words of warning from other Swamplanders ricocheted around her mind. She had to escape him somehow. Climbing on the bed she sidled across it. He abruptly changed direction and went the other way making her slide back again.

'I should have known you were game playing when you insisted on remaining here last night.'

Progress to the edge of the bed suddenly halted. Panic rose as she felt an invisible force holding her. As Luapp was getting on the other side there was no escape.

A squeak of fear escaped her as he grabbed the lapels of her top and pulled her close. They were now kneeling on the bed face to face, her whole body tingling like she was touching a low power source.

'This is a life threatening situation for me as well as you,' he said, lowering his voice to a furious whisper, 'and you are playing tehin games. Don't kec around at this gathering or I might lose control.'

With a slight shove he released her. Striding towards the door he reached out and the vial shot from the dressing table into his hand. The door swished open and then shut after him. Only when he was gone did she feel it safe to leave the bed.

There was not a shred of doubt in Enegene's mind what she'd experienced, was only a small portion of what he was capable of. Luapp Nostowe installed more fear into her in those few seconds than the threat of a multislayer ever had.

Looking down at her trembling hands she decided she would wait until she could hold them out without shaking before leaving the room.

When finally in control, she straightened her hair and clothes and went downstairs. The study was the safest place to be for now, she decided.

Sitting at her desk she went through her business files. A short while later, Lydina interrupted her work with the mail. Quickly sorting through it she saw what she was looking for.

She input Benze' number on the viscom and was surprised at Antonia's opening question. Forcing a smile, she waited for Benze to stop speaking.

'It was unexpected but those creatures appear to be everywhere at the moment. Fortunately Mikim was with us. But onto other matters; I am calling to ask if I could borrow Nix Pellan for the Vian gathering.

Normally I am happy with my slave, but Aylisha is accompanying me and she has no escort, so she has requested using him. Naturally if you are attending I understand that you will need him yourself.'

The slow smile that crossed Benze face made Enegene wonder about the meaning behind it; she seemed almost relieved.

'Several off planet business trips have left me fatigued. Of course you can borrow him, and don't rush him back, I will enjoy the solitude.'

Benze' excuse didn't make sense, Antonia had been lively enough at their meal the day before. She would have to discuss it with the guardian, when it was safe to go near him.

Next, she called Aylisha and explained about taking Pellan to the event. She wasn't happy about Pellan, but said, 'I don't mind you using me as an excuse, but we'll have to palm him off as soon as we arrive.'

With arrangements made, Enegene went back to work. She hoped Luapp would have calmed down by the time they met again.

# Chapter 14

Luapp retreated to the garden. He deliberately missed breakfast; he doubted he'd be able to keep it down. He also wanted to avoid Enegene for as long as possible; he didn't trust himself to remain calm in her presence. As he worked his mind went over the incident.

*Until today I thought she'd matured enough to be reliable, now I doubt her. Why did I expect anything different?*

Unable to answer that question, his thoughts changed direction. *The drug controls the victim leaving no memory of its use. But if she's correct, the person is in a trance-like state. While this is passable inside, outside it would be noticeable to passers-by.*

*It needed to be tested, but what's so keffing annoying is she neglected to tell me. She put both our lives at risk at a time when she knew the slayer is targeting her...*

He stopped and stood upright. *I must alert the space guardian.*

With this task finished, he went to the roof and pulled out a narcotics tester. Once again, he mentally thanked the genius who thought of everything when they packed the kit.

Sticking the probe into the liquid he pressed the buttons and waited. Some minutes later the screen lit up with a message: *Combination of five known synthetic drugs. Previously unknown mix.*

He frowned. *A new drug? It's probably untraceable…*

It went on to list the drugs and side effects, most of which he was aware of. The next piece of information caught his interest.

*This combination only effective on sollenites.*

*Where would Pellan's cousin get such a specialised drug, especially a new one?*

Leaving the loft, he headed for the study, but just as he reached the door he heard a noise from inside. Enegene was in there. The only other place he knew to be secure was the exercise area, so he changed direction.

Making sure all three doors were closed he sat on one of the massage couches and closed his eyes. It took a few minutes before he felt the guardian answering his mental call.

'Biocontact?' he sent, confused.

*'Unable to use the machine Kerran. I've come across a new synthetic drug for use on sollenites only. It's made from five already known drugs. I need you to post a warning on the guardian comlink.*

*I don't know its name. No doubt some research will supply you with that. I need some information on it. I want to know how long it's been around, where it originated and for what purpose. I also want to know if it's restricted and what the restrictions are. I'll send the analytical break down of the drug.'*

'Understood Commander,' Kerran sent. *'Have you identified the slayer yet?'*

*'No, but we've encountered a shape shifter. It used its ability to follow and attack the Spyrian. This makes me fairly sure it's a sentient member of the species. The biotalent could be connected. The appearance of this drug suggests the slayer wants me out of the way.'*

*'Be watchful sir. I'll send answers as soon as I have them.'* Tholman Gyre then passed on further information on the killer from the Galactic Council.

*'There have still been no murders following the configuration*

240

*since your arrival on Pedanta. The past pattern suggests one is due anytime now. Also, there's been no comeback from any enforcer group about the victim being verbally taunted prior to being attacked. However, they are reviewing their files and are interviewing close family and friends.'*

*'Noted. Sending drug breakdown now.'*

Forming a mental picture of the information from his narcotics tester he sent it to Kerran. An acknowledgement returned seconds later.

*'Contact me when you receive the required information.'*

It took several minutes to recover after breaking contact. Then he returned to the garden. He'd only been working a short while when Sylata appeared and watched him digging the rough ground.

'When I said I wanted that turned over lad, I meant only once. You've done it three times now.'

'I assumed you wanted it ready for planting,' Luapp said, continuing.

'I do, and that's enough. Is anything bothering you Mikim?'

A loud clang immediately followed his question. Luapp stopped and lifted the fork. Neatly stabbed on the end of a prong was a hand sized rock. Grabbing the rock, he yanked it off and looked at Sylata.

'Why do you ask?'

Sylata eyed the rock and scratched his chin thoughtfully. 'Little things.'

'Nothing concerns me.' He threw the rock onto a growing pile. 'If this is completed to your satisfaction, perhaps there is something else you want me to do.'

'Judging by your temperament at the moment, there is one thing. Come with me.'

Standing the fork by the wall Luapp followed Sylata to a patch of lawn at the front. On it stood a tree stump.

241

'I've wanted to get this out for some time. As you seem to want to lose some energy, perhaps you can do it. I'll give you the tools; I've got some reinforced ones you can use. I'll bring them to you.'

'I'll collect them,' Luapp said. 'Show me where they're stored.'

Returning to the tool store in the back garden Sylata pointed out the axe-like tool, along with a specialised saw, fork and spade.

'Hopefully you won't break them Mikim, and it will help you work off what's bothering you.'

Sylata gave Luapp a pat on the shoulder and left him to work on the stump.

When the meal bell rung several hours later, Luapp decided the elderly man had been right. He'd managed to remove the stump and in doing so work off his fury.

On the way in he locked the tools away and then headed for the small dining room. Enegene was already drinking her soup as he entered.

'Where have you been all morning?' she said, in Gaeizaan.

'Working.'

She rested her spoon on her plate. 'On what?'

He walked over and sat opposite. 'Removing tree roots.'

Picking up a slice of bread she said, 'is that all you did?'

'I contacted the Tholman.'

Enegene dipped her spoon in the soup and paused. 'Checking the drug?'

'Yes.'

He'd switched to Pedantan making her glance towards the door.

'Before you disappear next time  you will clear it with me.' She paused as the handle moved, then continued, 'remember that while you are on loan to Sylata and her husband when not

242

protecting me, I do not expect to have to search for you when I wish to speak to you.'

'Understood,' he replied, following her lead.

Cleona entered and went to the table to pour Enegene a drink. With her duty done the servant left again.

'Is this place secure?' Enegene said, in Gaeizaan.

'It's safe against everything except a Fluctoid.'

'Why can't you secure it against the shape shifter?'

'It would take guardian equipment I'm not supposed to have. Besides, that would defeat the purpose of our being here, we need evidence of the Fluctoid slaying. Keeping them out won't allow us to gather that evidence.'

'I thought I was merely bait to draw it in,' she said, sarcastically. 'I didn't realise I had to be a victim as well.'

A tense silence ensued until she finished her soup. As she pushed the empty plate away, she said, 'get something to eat.'

Luapp remained where he was. Under her constant stare, he added, 'I'm not hungry.'

'You haven't eaten all day.'

'Monitoring my movements?'

'Sylata mentioned it, she's concerned about you.' After a pause, she added, 'what good are you if you're too weak to defend me?'

'Missing a couple of meals will not diminish my strength. Also, there's no point taking food in, if it is likely to be coming up some minutes later.'

She gave him a guilty look. 'You should try something, it might settle your stomachs.'

'That would be highly unlikely, both are feeling rebellious. What did you want to discuss?'

She stared at him puzzled. 'How do you know I want to discuss anything?'

'You were complaining about being unable to find me, I

assume it was because you wanted to discuss something.'

Giving him a long look she said, 'do you think Pellan had anything to do with that drug?'

'Exactly what are you asking?'

'Do you think he put her up to it?'

'If you mean did he obtain it for her, I don't know. If he did, then he is more sophisticated than I judged him to be. Are you going back to the original supposition Pellan is the target?'

'You still think he's not?'

'In GSC the supposition is the slayer is a Fluctoid. We know there's a shape shifter on the planet and it's targeted you. It would be a remarkable coincidence if it had nothing to do with the case.

If it was Pellan, he would have to be a Fluctoid, and I'm reasonably certain he's not. What did his cousin tell you when she arrived?'

'That he was trying to break away from Benze, and they wanted to be together.'

'They who?'

Enegene related her conversation with Pellan's cousin.

After a silent contemplation he said, 'Benze could be the presence that Drew Rhalin picked up. Salations can project negative feelings without being a biotalent if they are angry enough. But if she has no real feelings for Pellan why is she unwilling to release him?'

'He's definitely hiding things from Benze,' Enegene said. 'His cousin suggested she had connections to breakers. She said accidents had been arranged for those who got in Benze' way. Pellan's recent accident makes it almost believable.'

Luapp frowned. 'That's not the impression I got of her.'

'You haven't been here long enough to get any impression of her.'

'My enforcer contact told me Benze' family is as established as the Rhalin's. But I'll search again.' After a pause  he added, 'I analysed the drug. It's a synthetic mixture of five other drugs and is designed for sollenites.'

Enegene frowned. 'I thought there was something odd when she handed me the sample. I asked why Pellan didn't use the drug on Benze to get away.

She became agitated and said it was only for you. She covered her mistake by saying it was expensive and they could only afford one. It means you were the target.'

'Or you. If we assume you were the original target, when first studied you were solo without a slave. Then you bought me and I'm now an obstacle. The drug was ordered to incapacitate me allowing access to you, or possibly so I could be used as a weapon against you...'

He stopped, thinking that through. 'But if that's the motive, the slayer has changed their tactics. Normally they choose a female without complications and slay them themselves.'

'I was without complications before I bought you. Perhaps they don't like changing victims once they've chosen.'

'Possibly, but as Freewoman Garber has been moved to a protection site they've been forced to. I've kept a sample of the drug locked away. When you get the new one we'll compare them. If my suspicions are correct, the second dose will be much stronger, possibly fatal. Anything else you forgot to tell me?'

'I did forget,' she said defensively. 'Only when you mentioned it I remembered.'

'Have you contacted Pellan yet?'

She left the table and returned with dessert. 'No I contacted Benze.'

'And what was her reaction?'

'She was exhausted and couldn't attend the gathering.'

'When is it?'

'Just over a week.'

Poking the spoon into the dessert, she pulled it out and licked it.

'And she knows she would not be recovered in that time? This being second only to the gathering you hosted, not attending would be unthinkable. Benze must have more urgent matters to attend to; perhaps she's planning something for Pellan.'

'There was one other thing,' Enegene said, 'Benze asked me if I had recovered from the attack on the island.'

Luapp studied Enegene's face for any signs of amusement and saw none. She was obviously as troubled by that question as he was.

'I think you were most fortunate when you insisted on taking me with you,' he said at last.

Silence followed while Enegene ate and Luapp thought. He seemed absorbed in staring at the table. Eventually she could stand it no longer. Putting the spoon into the empty glass she said, 'what are you thinking?'

'That several new lines of enquiry have opened up. I'm beginning to think the slayer is connected to Benze even if not Pellan. It's been established that Benze and Pellan were at every gathering when a presence was felt. Now I need to find out how long they have been together and what each was doing before they met.

I must also trace the route the drug came to Pedanta. I need to find out if it was made to order, or whether it was purchased on the submarket and sent to Pellan or his cousin.

Further, I want to know if Benze is suffering with a serious complaint. Finally, if the slayer is here, why are they waiting?'

'I thought you decided it was because you are in the way.'

'I'm constantly reviewing the situation. Originally, I was to be your protector to stop an attack. I'm convinced you're still the primary target, but to get to you, they must remove me.'

High Commander HaJaan and I discussed the probability of me becoming a target but secondaries are not the usual method of the slayer. Somehow, they manage to get the victim alone and trusting which is why we came up with a Fluctoid.

However, if the slayer had a salation version of the drug they gave you, then it could be administered and the victim told to come to an isolated location. It may have been given several times without the victim remembering it.'

'But they still would have had to be close enough to administer the drug. You had to breathe it in.'

'Maybe the salation form could be placed in food or drink. Also, not all previous victims were salations. They were different genus. As this drug is a mix, it would be possible to tailor it by altering just one component. And then it wouldn't be necessary for the slayer to be a shape shifter.'

'I would think there are very few places they could get that here, which means they had to contact the breaker society off planet.'

He twitched a brow. 'Not hard given there's a community of galactic breakers dwelling within the Black Systems. I'm sure several of them have contacts useful to a multislayer.

The sample Pellan's cousin gave you was a controller. If three drops did what you say they did, there was enough in that vial for an orbit. Why would you need more? The only reason to mention it was to plant in your mind it would be unavailable in the future.'

Enegene pulled the napkin from her lap and dropped it on the table. 'I suggest we travel to town.'

Luapp looked at her in surprise. 'For what reason?'

'Information. Through my business and social contacts, I have many influential people as associates and friends. I can talk to them and get the answers we need. It will be faster than you contacting your law enforcer; and as you're a slave, they'll happily talk in front of you.'

'Good strategy. When do you want to go?'

'Straight away.'

Leaving the table, she headed for the door. Realising he wasn't with her she turned and looked back. 'Well?' she said, impatiently, 'do you want answers or not?'

Pushing back the chair he followed her from the room.

~~~

The trip to town took all afternoon and most of the evening. Through her contacts Enegene found Benze was not the local they thought her to be. She'd arrived on the planet only a year before the Swamplander herself.

According to certain individuals, Benze was the granddaughter of one of the wealthiest people on the continent. She only arrived in Denjal after the estate had been left to her.

Although her family origins were on Pedanta, Antonia Benze had been sent off planet for an education. After leaving her socialite training college she moved around the Black Systems doing various charitable works until she inherited the estate.

This was common practice among the wealthy; it was a way of keeping their progeny out of trouble and empathizing with the less well placed.

All the papers she'd given the solicitors had appeared correct within a degree, but not as perfect as they should be for a close relative. The solicitor at the time suspected Benze had died and her place had been taken by a daughter or niece.

This was not illegal, it often happened. The legal profession tended to allow it to pass rather than going through the tedious process of proving who they were before they inherited.

Therefore, although she inherited under the name of Benze,

248

it could be she was not actually the Benze named in the will.

The gossiping servants of various households provided the information that Pellan and his cousin were indeed blood relatives. She was from his mother's side, and quite a way back in her ancestry there was a mixed species marriage.

Whatever the mix had been, Pellan's family was ashamed of it even though it was so far back the mixture was unnoticeable. Pellan had told Benze this along with some other minor indiscretions when he was drunk. She'd used the information to blackmail him into staying when he tried to leave her.

Nobody knew whether Pellan and Benze had known each other before arriving on the planet. But certain people remarked that Benze displayed a raging fury when faced with the possible loss of him. This confirmed the jealousy statement Pellan's cousin made. It also suggested that her indifference to him was just an act.

*Nothing is done simply in this society*, Luapp thought, as they returned to the house. *We couldn't just turn up and ask questions as on Gaeiza. There's a lot of social banter to be gone through between questions. Even so, despite the meandering route it was worth it.*

Back in the safety of the study, Enegene sat at the desk and smiled. 'I told you the network was good.'

Luapp raised a brow. 'This was not the intel we got on the Black Systems. We were told they were still in the throes of an anarchic society. While it's only the wealthy that partake in this exercise, it shows the emergence of a more sedate civilization.'

'I assume it wasn't guardian observation that gave you this information,' Enegene said, with a wry smile.

'Guardians couldn't enter the Black Systems to get an accurate assessment, so we relied on multi-species personnel.'

'If true, Benze could be the terminator,' Enegene said.

'To be the multislayer she would have had to travel across the galaxy. There's been no suggestion she's done that. We know she's travelled between the planets of the Black Systems, which would give her an excellent opportunity to meet the resident breaker element. Unfortunately, the same could be said of most of the elite of her generation onwards.

However, it does explain her knowledge of the Gaeizaan slave plague.' Noticing Enegene's raised brow, he added, 'she questioned me about the survivors.'

He paused and then added, 'Pellan has been here for two orbits, she's been here one. He must have been with someone else before she arrived. I wonder if he remained on Pedanta for the whole two orbits or if he moved around?'

'His mentor couldn't have been anyone higher than a mid strata gem holder,' Enegene rested back in her chair and put her feet on the desk. 'Otherwise Petulla would have named her.

While there isn't a gem holder in the upper and elite strata's she doesn't know, she has no interest in the lower levels. He doesn't come to their attention until Benze takes him on. If he's been here all that time, he can't be the multislayer. The last victim ceased just under an orbit ago.'

Luapp glanced at the boots on the desk with a hint of irritation. 'The same applies to Benze,' he said, thoughtfully.

'Although the law speaker's wife confirmed she often went off planet on business trips, she apparently kept to the Black Systems.'

He considered the information gleaned from the trip. 'It could be his cousin. It would be useful to know what the joining mix was and why they were ashamed of it.'

'She wants to be with him but can't,' Enegene said, following his line of thought. 'They may be working together to choose wealthy victims and dispatch them.

When he started targeting me I researched Pellan. Despite

what he says, he's been to each of the planets a corpse was found.'

'When were you going to tell me?' Luapp said, irritated.

'When I thought it relevant; like now. And I'm not the only one keeping information to myself, am I?'

'I'm the professional enforcer. I appreciate your efforts but pass on what you know. Lack of co-ordination can cause fatal mistakes.'

His mind turned to new possibilities. 'If he's working with his cousin, he may want Benze to think you're the new benefactor so she doesn't see the link between them. They could also be implicating Benze to take attention off themselves. I'll get Kerran to trace their movements.'

'If Pellan and his cousin are working together, why don't they get rid of Benze?' Enegene said.

'Possibly because she's too well known, or for the moment, too useful.'

'I'm just as well known.'

'Yes, but not connected to Pellan. You've made it clear to all around you want nothing to do with him. If you were killed the spotlight doesn't instantly fall on him. And if they are working as a team, it would allow him to be seen while the victim is being dispatched.'

'It could be the cousin working alone. We only have their word she can't utilise the ancient talents hinted at. And that also allows Pellan to be here while the slayer continues her work.

It's possible he might not know about her activities. While he slips away from Benze, his cousin will be over here trying to cut my life line. That's gratitude for the financial advice I gave him,' she added petulantly.

With a brief smile, Luapp said, 'you *are* the bait.'

'Whoever it is has had one try at me already.'

'And I got in the way. I know what to look for, therefore I must go.'

'Pellan's cousin comes here and gives me the drug. I ask for more, use it and slay you myself. I like their style.'

Enegene sighed. 'The trouble is, High Commander Bran's briefing said the slayer was most likely to be male.'

'We assumed they were male because of the ferocity of the blows, but if it is a Fluctoid, it can become male for the attack even if it's female.

The only thorn in the fruit is the two females interested in Pellan think you're interested in me. Your charade at your gathering guaranteed that, so neither of them sees you as a threat.'

'Benze has seen me turn him down on numerous occasions. I remember her being particularly amused about me buying you. And his cousin said he'd told her I wasn't interested in him.'

'Perhaps the attack on the island was a test to see whether I was capable of defending you. Then they realised I could recognise a Fluctoid when I saw one. But that leaves the question of who is manipulating Pellan's cousin...'

Luapp drifted into silence as his mind worked on the problem. Enegene stood up and headed for the door. 'I'll call the cousin and tell her to bring some more of the drug to the gathering.'

As she closed the study door she was met by Farin. 'Sorry to disturb you Madam, Lady Rhalin is on the video communicator.'

'Which room?'

'The lounge Madam.'

'Thank you, Farin, I will come straight away.' She watched Farin leave then returned to the study and opened the door. 'Has Sylata anything else for you to do today?'

'Not at this time in the evening.'

Enegene smiled broadly. 'Then I will meet you down in the health rooms in a quarter. I feel like a massage.'

Giving Enegene a dark look, he left the study and went down to the exercise area. The frequent use of the massage room annoyed him as he was convinced Enegene was game playing. But it was safe to talk down there. He knew the moment anyone came through the first door and by the time they reached the third all was as it should be.

He'd just completed the preparations when Enegene entered. Going through to the changing rooms she undressed, slipped on a robe and returned to the table. Luapp unfolded a towel, put it in place and removed the gown.

'This is one of the better ways of discussing the mission,' she commented.

He collected a small jug of warmed oil, walked over to the table and poured some onto her back. She closed her eyes as the scent drifted around the room. The gentle movements of his hands relaxed tense muscles and made her feel drowsy.

'Where did you learn to do massage?' she said, dreamily.

'We've been through this; GSC.'

'Oh yes it would be,' Enegene answered sarcastically. 'Along with exotic dance and fehy music.' Unable to see him smile, she continued, 'I didn't believe you then and I don't believe you now.'

'Your belief in my answer doesn't change facts.'

'Why would guardians teach massage?' she said, suspiciously.

'I told you that also. What did you want to talk about?'

Enegene took a deep breath. 'The first thing I want to say is... I apologise. I realise it was an incredibly shallow and dangerous thing to do last night, especially as you knew nothing about it. But your comments about Swamplanders just sparked my embers.'

'It wasn't meant as an insult; I merely meant that guardians don't normally see Swamlanders as psychotic slayers.'

'It sounded like and insult; but I should have been more mature in my response.'

She was expecting another rebuke, but only silence followed. 'Nothing to say?' she prompted, after a while.

'I said what I wanted to say. Words will not change the past. What else is on your mind?'

'Well…'

'Mission-wise,' he clarified, before she could say anything else.

A throaty laugh was followed by her turning her head to look back at him. 'You're getting to know me too well Guardian.'

Facing forward again, she said, 'Aylisha is also invited to the gathering but she has no male escort. Although it's not necessary to have an unbonded, it is necessary to have a male of some description.'

Luapp raised a brow at the "some description" part. 'And?'

'You're to be her escort.'

'If a slave isn't good enough for you, why is it good enough for her?'

'You would have been perfectly adequate to go in with; solo females frequently use slaves as escorts. My excuse for using Pellan was that Aylisha was using you and I had no escort. It's the one part of the plan Aylisha likes. Once inside she's hoping to pick something up.'

He poured more oil onto her legs and rubbed it in. 'Like food poisoning?'

Enegene chuckled. 'Why Guardian, that's not like you.'

He picked up a second towel and handed it to her. 'I doubt if you know what is like me.'

254

She turned over to face him with a huge smile. 'You're right, but every time I try to find out you stop me.'

Catching the gleam in her eyes he paused for a split second, then continued pouring the oil onto her skin.

'There are two other things; Aylisha should be arriving any moment. She couldn't get over fast enough when I told her you we're doing massage. I'm sure we could make a business out of this.'

'And the other?' he prompted.

'We're going retailing tomorrow. We haven't got the right class of clothes for this kind of event.'

'This is less of an event than the one you hosted. If our clothes were sufficient for that, they are sufficient for this.'

Enegene smiled. 'Unfortunately, the two events are too close to each other to be seen in the same clothing. It would suggest I can only afford one collection. Equally, my slave must be adequately dressed.'

Luapp was about to comment, but stopped. Light footsteps hurrying along the hall warned him of Aylisha's approach. Seconds later she burst in and hurried past Enegene.

'Won't be long Mikim,' she called from the changing room.

By the time she reappeared he'd collected another set of towels and returned to the second table. Enegene left her table, put on the robe and sat back on it. Luapp offered three small jugs to Aylisha, and when she chose one he started on her.

'You know Kaylee, Mikim is better at this than any of the parlours in town. He's worth his weight in gems.'

Watching Luapp work Enegene said, 'what kind of man are you looking for Aylisha; just so Mikim knows what to seek out.'

Aylisha grinned. 'Well, let's see now, he has to be tall, good looking, reliable, rich, gentle and have a good sense of humour…'

Enegene swung her legs absentmindedly. 'That's effectively cut out most of the males that attend these events.'

Aylisha turned her head to look at her. 'Why?'

'Most of them are joined, and if not, they are not independently wealthy.'

'There must be some unmarried men around that have a reasonable bank balance.' Aylisha sighed. 'This is just heavenly; I bet you have a massage every day.'

'Mikim wouldn't get any work done if I did.'

'So, what's the plan for the occasion then?' Aylisha said dreamily.

'You and Pellan are coming here so we can all go in together. Once in I will lose Pellan and you will try your best to find a victim.'

'Do you mind?' Aylisha said, in mock indignation. 'I object to the word victim.'

'We'll go retailing tomorrow; Mikim's really looking forward to it, aren't you?' She grinned broadly at his glowering look.

'I take it by his silence he doesn't agree with you.' Aylisha turned and looked up at him. 'I thought as much.'

'Fortunately, Mikim does as he's told. Don't you?'

This time he didn't bother looking up. 'Yes Lady,' he murmured.

'I hope you don't mind Kaylee, but as we were going shopping tomorrow, and would probably be all day, I told pap I would be staying overnight.'

'I have no problem with that, we can try out that new holistic I bought.'

As Aylisha went to get dressed, Luapp cleared away the equipment and washed his hands.

Enegene slid off the table and walked towards the changing room. She met Luapp as he returned from the store room.

'You have some free time, Mikim, we'll see you at supper.' Then she continued into the changing room.

Luapp went up to the ground floor, collected Aylisha's bag and took it to a spare room. From there he headed for the roof. The free time was spent making sure all the surveillance and recording equipment was working perfectly.

Finally satisfied, he retrieved the specialised weapon for a Fluctoid. Turning it over in his hands he familiarised himself with the firing sequence.

*After my experience on the island I appreciate the Council's foresight in requesting this weapon. As Fluctoids can spread themselves thin and make openings in their bodies, normal weapons are useless against them.*

Replacing the weapon in the case, he left the loft and went down to the study. Here he attempted to contact Inspector Corder to verify the information gathered with Enegene.

He also wanted to know about Pellan's cousin, as little was gleaned about her. While he waited for the connection to be answered his mind went over the questions he wanted to ask.

*If Benze is the slayer, what happened to the real Antonia Benze? If it's not her, how long has she been missing? Pellan's route across the galaxy closely followed the slaughter trail. Was he following the slayer, or were they following him? Could Pellan possibly be the slayer after all?*

He dismissed that.

*Multislayers have a mental aberration, no matter how well hidden, there is always a tell. Pellan hasn't displayed anything that could be interpreted as unstable...*

With the contact going unanswered Luapp left a message and continued with other tasks.

Finally satisfied everything was as ready as it could be, he went down to the lounge. While waiting for the women to arrive, his mind worked on a plan to capture the Fluctoid alive.

The door opened and Cleona came in carrying a tray. Placing the cups and a plate of biscuits on the table, she picked up the small bell on the tray and rang it. Leaving the tray on the sideboard she passed Enegene and Aylisha on the way out.

Luapp waited for a break in conversation to ask to be excused. Before Enegene could answer Aylisha interrupted.

'I expect Mikim would be good at these games. From what I've seen he's quick on the uptake.'

Noticing Luapp's expression Enegene said, 'it's too late to test his gaming ability tonight. We could try tomorrow after retailing.'

His tension eased. By tomorrow he would have had time to think of a way to avoid it.

'Shall I clear away Lady?' he said, watching them finish their tea.

'Yes, it's been a long day and I'm ready to retire.' Enegene held out her cup and he put it on the tray.

'Mikim seems very deep in thought a lot of the time,' Aylisha said, as she handed him her cup. 'Are men on your planet usually so intense?'

'He certainly outshines the Gaeizaan males I've been in contact with.'

'I guess he's had to live on his wits before you bought him.' Aylisha stood up and yawned. 'If you will excuse me, I'm tired and I'm going to bed.'

'Probably,' Enegene murmured, as Aylisha headed for the door. As soon as her friend had gone Enegene stood up. 'You do that so naturally,' she said, in Gaeizaan.

He walked with her to the door. 'I've had my own dwelling since I graduated as a guardian.'

'No liana at home? No doting mother?'

'I've just answered that.'

He paused, waiting for her to precede him. She was

showing unwanted interest in his private life, but he saw no reason to be harsh.

Leaving the room he went to the kitchen. He hoped she would continue upstairs and abandon this line of curiosity. But when he returned he found Enegene waiting. Her expression suggested more questions were coming.

'What happened to your mother?' she said, as soon as he joined her.

'Why should anything have happened to her? I'm thirty; old enough to live on my own.'

'Your reaction told me.'

He considered telling her his private life was his business, but that would cause heated words and wounded feelings. Starting up the stairs he said, 'she ceased when I was a qiver.'

When he said nothing more, she said, 'how? Why?'

'She contracted a terminal illness before my arrival. It claimed her life soon after.'

Enegene stopped abruptly. Her expression displayed disbelief. 'I don't want your cover story,' she snapped, 'I want the truth.'

He continued up the stairs, irritation growing. *If I'd told her to mind her own business it would have caused friction. Now telling her the truth has done the same.*

'That is the truth.'

Running to catch up Enegene said in a softer tone, 'do you remember her?'

He turned up the corridor towards the bedroom. Vaguely.'

'What do you remember?'

They reached her room and went in. Sitting on the chair Luapp started unfastening his boots. He paused and thought about the question. A picture of his mother reaching out to him slipped into his mind.

'She laughed a lot. I also remember her singing as she put

259

on her face colours.'

Enegene lounged on the bed watching him undress. 'Your father never re-joined?'

'No.'

He pulled open his shirt and took it off. Then he stood to remove the trousers.

She sat upright. 'Why?'

'He said after my mother every other female would be a disappointment.' Putting his clothes on the chair back he added, 'while Aylisha is here I will sleep in my room.'

'I haven't finished yet,' Enegene protested, watching him press the relevant square on the panelling.

'Yes, you have.' He stepped through the now open doorway. 'I'll return in the morning.'

Seconds later he entered his room. He frowned as he pulled loose the covers. *Why did I tell her that? Such revelations are kept for my closest friends...*

Removing the final piece of clothing he got into bed and pulled the covers up. Giving the puzzle a few seconds more thought, he gave up. He was too tired to figure it out tonight, and had more important things to concern himself with anyway. Touching the lamp, he switched off the light and relaxed.

# Chapter 15

The next morning started bad and got worse. Luapp arrived in Enegene's room just before the maid. He left as soon as Cleona finished much to the Swamplander's annoyance. His mood was low and Enegene's snide comments degraded it further.

This made for a strained atmosphere in the Drifter. Aylisha chatted happily all the way to town apparently unaware of Luapp's discontent and Enegene's irritation.

The shopping session took several hours with the women deciding what clothes to wear, and then Enegene involved him, which annoyed him even more. By the time they finally headed for the Drifter again Luapp had been close to insubordination.

When they arrived back at the house he went to the kitchen to inform the cook. The meal was served immediately and afterwards the women decided to swim, which gave him free time. As Mevil Sylata hadn't got any tasks he went into the study and pulled up the police files. Some answers to his questions had been sent and it was so far, so good.

No other incidents using the murder's method had been recorded. Mr Garber had been released. He'd been told the attacker had disguised himself as him, and Mrs Garber told the attacker was a criminal hypnotist. This allowed them to be reconciled and taken to a police safe house.

In answer to his other questions Jym Corder insisted the Benze family were natives to Pedanta. They originated in the country and moved to Denjal over two centuries ago.

He also confirmed it was normal practice for the rich to send their children to different planets to broaden their education.

Their records showed that Benze had done a few more than most, and then settled on Lappina, the fourth planet of the second system.

Pellan's cousin was taking longer. Corder had looked up her arrival files and was now back tracking them. Leaving an acknowledgement Luapp closed down and shut off. He was just leaving the study when the viscom buzzed. Touching the on switch he was surprised to see Lord Rhalin. On seeing Luapp he smiled.

'Mikim, I understand my daughter is with your mistress.'

'Correct, sir.'

Luapp frowned briefly. Drew wasn't looking directly into the viscom, but somewhere slightly above it. 'Can you call her to the machine?'

'She is swimming with Lady Kaylee, do you want me to bring her to a viscom?'

'No, that's not necessary; just give her a message. Tell her we are taking a short break on the island for a few days.'

'Has Lady Aylisha told you of the event on the island?'

'Yes she did. I had a security team sent out to sweep the whole place.'

The screen went blank and he quietly contemplated the message before going to the pool. Both women looked up as he entered.

'Something wrong Mikim?' Enegene said, noticing his

pensive expression.

'There's something I need to discuss with you Lady.'

'I'll only be a moment, Aylisha.'

Making her way to the edge of the pool she climbed up the steps and walked with him into the changing room.

'What is it?'

'Drew Rhalin just called to tell Aylisha the family are going to the island.'

'Is that safe?'

'I asked if Aylisha mentioned the event there. He said he had sent a security team to the island.'

'So?'

'So, no Pedantan security team would know what a Fluctoid looked like nor how to capture one.'

'Perhaps Aylisha described it to her father.'

'A moving chair? The sunseeker? He probably thought she'd had too much sun and wine. In fact, I was relying on him thinking just that. Also, Drew Rhalin was not looking at the viscom when he spoke; he seemed to be looking at something beyond.'

'What's going on? Is he trying to send a sub-message?'

'It's the impression I got. I think I should check on the family. Ask Aylisha whether she told her father about our trip, and check your wristband while with her. I don't want to leave you here alive and come back to find you deceased.'

'If it's with the family it won't be here.'

Enegene went over to a cupboard and pulled out a towel. Wrapping it around her shoulders she moved to her pile of clothes and took out her wrist band. Slipping it on her wrist she looked up at him.

'And I'm capable of taking on anything that bleeds.'

Pulling her knife from the pile she strapped it to her arm and released the holding loop.

'And what if the Fluctoid is here and an accomplice is with the family?'

Enegene stopped on her way back to the pool and gave him a long look. 'Perhaps you should get the weapon.'

'Not until I know this is Aylisha Rhalin.'

He collected a second towel and walked with her back to the pool. Standing slightly behind her but close enough to see the wrist band, he watched the light as she pushed the button. It turned green and Luapp started to walk away.

'Perhaps you'd better hear her reply,' Enegene said, in Gaeizaan. Changing to Pedantan she called Aylisha over. 'Your father called.' She glanced at the band again. 'He said the family are going to the island for a few days.'

Aylisha waded over and stopped by the edge. Pushing back her fringe she looked up at Enegene. 'But they can't,' she said, starting up the steps.

'Can't what?' Enegene said, puzzled.

'Go to the island.'

Enegene looked at Luapp as he moved forward to give Aylisha the towel.

'The Lord Rhalin just contacted us on the visual Lady Rhalin. He asked me to give you a message stating he was taking the family to the island.'

Aylisha took the towel and wrapped it around herself. 'I told him we were attacked and he said he was going to have it cleared. It will not be safe to visit.'

'Are you sure he has not already done it?' Enegene said, as they headed back to the changing room.

'He sent the decontamination crew over three days ago. No one can land on the island for the next three weeks.'
Aylisha rubbed herself gently then dropped the towel. 'I'll dress and call him back.'

'His inference was that he was leaving immediately.'

'And he told me he wasn't going anywhere when I left yesterday,' Aylisha said. 'And if he's out mam will be home.'

'You're sure your family were home when you left? They hadn't gone anywhere?' Enegene said.

Aylisha looked up smiling. 'Do you think I saw an imaginary family before I left? They were definitely there.'

Glancing at Luapp, Enegene said, 'Mikim, continue with that errand while Aylisha and I get dressed. We'll call Drew and find out what's going on. Meet us in the study.'

As he arrived outside the cupboard door, he paused to look around for servants. Seeing nobody, he entered and went to the loft. From the medium sized case he pull out a weapons belt with several pockets and an area of rough material. Then he retrieved the three items for use against Fluctoids.

The weapon he pressed onto the rough material, and the detector and immobiliser were pushed into pockets. He returned to the cupboard, and then down to the study. He'd only just got inside when he heard hurrying footsteps. A sharp knock followed and the door opened and Farin peered around the door.

'Lady Kaylee said to go and see her in the lounge.'

Farin moved back to let Luapp pass with a wide-eyed stare at the belt.

As he entered the lounge, he saw Enegene and Aylisha standing beside the viscom. Glancing up the Swamplander watched him come over. On the screen was a young boy with dishevelled hair and staring hazel eyes.

'We've had another call,' Enegene explained in Pedantan. 'At first we thought it was a hoax as no one was there, now this pretweener male has appeared.'

'That's my brother Ovar,' Aylisha said, puzzled.

The boy looked over his shoulder and then back at the screen. His expression was one of pure terror. 'Please help us,'

265

he whispered. 'Someone has attacked pap. Mam and Skye have disappeared. I don't know where the servants or slaves are.'

A faint noise in the background made the boy look wildly around. 'He says he's going to kill us all if he doesn't get what he wants.'

The boy's face was stained with tears and his voice trembled. 'Please send your protector to help us Lady Kaylee.' Another tear was wiped away with the heel of his hand.

A second noise was heard; more clearly this time. He glanced over his shoulder then back to the screen. 'Must shut down or he'll know I've called.'

Before she could answer the screen went blank. Aylisha's face had paled and her voice trembled as she said, 'we have to go over there.'

'We are Aylisha. Mikim are you ready?'

'I have what I need,' he said. 'But it would be safer if Lady Aylisha remained here.'

'No chance,' Aylisha said firmly. 'They're my family.'

'Get Morvac to bring the Drifter around,' Enegene said quietly.

Luapp found Morvac in his usual relaxing place. He had a comfortable chair wedged into an alcove in the staff room and it was possible to overlook him with a quick glance.

Returning to the lounge he told the women the Drifter was being brought around and they headed for the door. As they got in the back Enegene gave Morvac his instructions.

'To the Rhalin estate Morvac and hurry.'

He took the vehicle swiftly up the long drive onto the highway and then engaged top speed. 'When we get there stay in the Drifter with the doors shut. Don't have anything open, not windows or vents.'

At the pace they were going it took only a few minutes to get to Aylisha's home. Travelling up the tree lined drive to the house, Enegene glanced at her friend. 'Aylisha, stay with Morvac. This could be dangerous.'

Aylisha jutted out her chin with determination. 'No, I'm coming in with you and Mikim.'

'In that case, stay with me at all times, don't go anywhere without me. The minute we enter your house we put your family in danger, so be silent.'

'You talk as if you are used to this sort of thing Kaylee,' Aylisha said meekly.

'We may be good friends but there are many things you don't know about me. And yes, I am used to this sort of thing.'

Enegene slid her hand up her sleeve and felt the knife mechanism. The loop was still off and she left it that way.

'And Mikim?' Aylisha said, looking at the weapon on his belt.

'Mikim is a trained protector. Today he is going to protect your family. We work well as a team, you are the stray missile.'

Aylisha was about to protest but she didn't get the chance. The house was in sight and Enegene was issuing more orders.

'Go off the path and approach from behind the trees Morvac. Stop where the Drifter will not be seen. Hide it in some shrubbery if possible.'

'There's a group of shrubs around the side,' Aylisha said, 'they look dense, but they have a hollow centre. A drooping Balaca tree grows by the entrance and its branches cover the top.'

'Just right,' Enegene commented.

Luapp found it odd waiting for direction from Enegene; he was normally the one issuing instructions. She turned and looked at him, noticed the wry smile and frowned.

Morvac took the vehicle over a fence and across a field as he came in from the side. Aylisha directed him to a group of shrubs near the centre of the lawn.

He avoided them until he came to a low wide bush near the middle of the group. It had a gap to one side by the tall tree with drooping branches. Although it was a tight fit, he managed to guide the Drifter into the hollow centre.

Luapp moved to the door. He had to use an unusual amount of strength to force it open wide enough to get out. Then he held it while the women left. Morvac seemed relieved to be staying inside.

'Lock everything,' Enegene told him as they left. 'Don't open the door to anything that looks like us unless they give you the name Namrae.'

Outside the Drifter, Luapp pushed his way to the edge of the bush and looked towards the house. There was no cover between the shrubbery and the house, and anyone standing inside by the windows couldn't miss them approaching.

After several minutes' deliberation, he decided that whoever had broken in would probably be too busy to stand looking out the window. They had to chance it. He said as much to Enegene and she passed it on to Aylisha.

He watched for movement for several seconds. Seeing no-one, he strode quickly across to the house with the women close behind.

They stopped beside a large window and he looked inside. With no sign of anyone he tried opening it.

'It's probably locked,' Aylisha said quietly.

'With what?' Enegene said.

'A power bolt.'

'Kindly keep watching behind us Lady Rhalin.' Luapp slid his hand down the window. While Enegene watched Aylisha he used telekinesis to shift the bolt.

When she heard it click, Aylisha looked back frowning. Luapp carefully lifted the window, looked inside and climbed in. With a quick look around he turned to help the women.

Aylisha went first, with aid from both sollenites. Luapp lifted from the front and Enegene from behind. Sitting on the floor of the room she was ignored until Enegene climbed in. Looking around again he closed the window.

Helping Aylisha to her feet he said, 'is everything as it should be, Lady?'

'Yes why?' Letting out a gasp she said, 'you're looking for that thing, aren't you?'

'You're sure?' Enegene prompted. 'Nothing out of place, nothing has a strange glow, anything?'

Aylisha looked around more carefully. 'Sure.'

They moved across to the door. Standing behind it, Luapp listened for movement. As there was no sound coming from the hall he slid it open just enough to see out.

'It's clear,' he said, quietly. 'Where would your mother hide, Lady?'

'In her bedroom; upstairs, fourth on the right.'

Gently pushing the door further open he moved to the side allowing Aylisha and Enegene access to the stairs. Then he followed them closing the door as he left. So far there had been no sound from anywhere.

Outside the door indicated by Aylisha, he stopped and listened again. With no sound from inside he turned the handle. The door was locked. Placing his hand on the door, he searched for the lock.

It turned out to be an old-fashioned bolt. Moving his hand over the bolt, he concentrated and it slid back. Seconds later he pushed the door open and they went inside.

'How did he do that?' Aylisha whispered, amazed.

'Now's not the time for explanations,' Enegene answered.

'The room's empty, but the door was bolted from the inside,' he said, puzzled.

'They might be in the safe space.'

Aylisha pointed to a heavy rug in the centre of the room. Luapp pushed back the rug and knelt down. Now he could see a square shaped crack in the floor boards.

'It's on a spring,' Aylisha said, from behind him. 'Push down and it should release the catch.'

Doing as instructed, he pushed the centre of the square and a hatch lid opened. Aylisha moved forward to stand beside him as he lifted the trapdoor.

It appeared empty, but looking closely he saw a dark material cover. Aylisha knelt beside him and went to pull it away. She frowned at his hand signal to move back and be silent. Pulling the bioscan from the belt pocket he held it over the open door.

'Only salations down there,' he said, glancing at Aylisha. 'Speak to them.'

Pulling up the cover Aylisha leant over the dark opening. 'Mam, its Ayi, are you down there?'

Sounds of movement were heard, and then a second material cover was flung back revealing a tear stained face looking up. 'Ayi, is it really you?' said her mother.

'I'm here with Kaylee and Mikim. We got a message from Ovar.'

Her mother looked down behind her. 'Come on Skye, help has arrived.'

A second face appeared. Luapp reached down and grasped the arms of the child being handed up. Lowering her to the floor he reached down again and pulled up Catailyn Rhalin.

A middle aged woman with silver-streaked dishevelled hair appeared. Aylisha whispered to them to be quiet as they moved onto the bed. The child's eyes were wide with fear and her lip trembled.

'Where is pap?' Aylisha asked her mother.

Tears welled up in her eyes. 'He was being held down in

270

the servant's common room. I told the children to hide in different places, but Skye was too afraid to leave me. I hope your father and Ovar are still alive.'

'Your son was alive a short time ago,' Enegene assured her. 'All we have to do is find him.'

'What about the servants and the slaves?' Aylisha said.

'They were not here for some reason; it's as if they'd been told to go away.'

'They probably had,' Enegene said. 'Or they may be locked up somewhere.'

Leaving the group to talk quietly Luapp indicated to Enegene to move to one side. 'We can't take them around the house searching, we'll be discovered. I'll escort you back to the window. You take them to the Drifter and lock them in with Morvac while I search for Lord Rhalin.'

'There's no way I'm leaving you here on your own,' she retorted. 'What if you run into the Fluctoid? And we have to find Ovar.'

Aylisha caught the end of their quiet conversation. 'I have an idea where he might be.'

'Where?' Luapp said.

'I'll show you,' Aylisha said firmly. 'It's easier…'

'Do you wish your brother to survive Lady Rhalin?' Luapp interrupted curtly. 'The more people moving around this dwelling together, the more risk of being heard. Describe his hiding place and I'll find him. You and Lady Kaylee wait here. It would be safest if you all returned to the compartment until I return.'

Enegene's tight expression suggested a protest, but seeing the petrified faces of Catailyn Rhalin and her daughter she said nothing. Aylisha explained how to reach her brother's hiding place as her mother pulled back the rug.

'Don't be too long,' Enegene said, sternly.

'It'll be a tight squeeze,' Catailyn said, 'but we'll manage it.'

She slid inside followed by Aylisha and Enegene. Skye was lowered in last. Luapp then pushed the trap door shut and covered it with the rug again. Moving to the door, he listened, looked out and left.

A sound of objects being moved made him pause momentarily, then he quickly continued across the landing and into the cupboard. He found the concealed ladder leading to the loft and started up. He'd been surprised when Aylisha told him Ovar's hiding place; obviously the Rhalin family didn't believe in demons.

Once in the loft he considered it slightly safer, but trod carefully just the same. At the far end was the old set of drawers he was looking for. The bottom drawer was the largest and he pulled it out.

He had to feel for the trigger in the gloomy light of the loft, but found it after a short search. The bottom of the draw sprung up and he pulled it out to reveal a startled boy.

'Don't be afraid,' he said, in hushed tones. 'I'm Lady Kaylee's protector. We must move quietly.'

Helping the boy out of the drawer, he replaced the false bottom and closed it. Then they left the loft and returned to the bedroom. Releasing the trap door he helped the women and Skye out.

'I'll escort you to the entry room and Lady Kaylee will take you to the vehicle,' he told the Rhalin family.

'I will take them to the window and return, you can't deal with this on your own,' she replied, giving Luapp a glare.

'I'm the professional, and I have ways of dealing with Fluctoids,' he said calmly in Gaeizaan.

'And I'm your assistant,' she replied, abruptly. 'Once they're outside, Aylisha can get them to the Drifter. I'm staying with you.'

*Arguing with her is not only useless, but probably dangerous,* he decided, and handed the weapon to Enegene.

Pausing to listen he left the room. Moments later he reappeared. Aylisha signalled to the children to be quiet as they formed a chain and followed Luapp down the stairs. Enegene brought up the rear watching for the slightest movement from anything.

As they reached the ground floor they paused. Luapp could hear faint voices, and he was trying to locate the direction they were coming from. Deciding it was safest to continue, he moved them on.

Taking them to the entry room he went over to the window as Enegene guarded the door. Helping Catailyn Rhalin out, he then turned to Aylisha. Next he lifted the children out the window one at a time.

'Take them to the Drifter and give Morvac the name. Lock yourselves in with him.'

'What about you and Kaylee?' she said, looking up at him.

'We'll locate your father and bring him with us. Don't admit him to the Drifter if he arrives on his own.'

After a moment's hesitation, Aylisha took her family to the bushes. Luapp watched them until they disappeared then carefully closed the window and returned to Enegene.

'Switch off your wrist detector; it only works on the ones vaccinated. We'll rely on the general energy detector, and use bio-speak.'

Doing as instructed she followed him out of the room and into the hall. They did a brief search of the ground floor rooms and found nothing.

'*Where now?*' Enegene sent.

'*Staff room and lower quarters.*'

As she had been in the house several times before, Enegene led him to the servants' common room at the rear of the house.

While they moved around, Luapp watched the bio-detector. So far everything was normal. Crossing the space between the stairs and the entrance to the servants staff room, it was unnervingly quiet.

The door was locked. Lifting the ratchet with telekinesis, Luapp opened the door enough to look inside. Drew Rhalin was sat on a chair bound and gagged, and he seemed to be alone.

His head was resting back, with his wavy hair dishevelled. His eyes were closed and his face showed signs of a beating. Several large bruises were clearly visible on his cheek, jaw and forehead.

After a careful study of the sparse furniture Luapp aimed the detector in Rhalin's direction. It registered a human. Satisfied, he went in with Enegene following closely behind.

Their footsteps made Drew bring his head forward and look in their direction. His eyes widened in surprise as Enegene removed the gag and Luapp broke the ropes.

'How…?' he whispered, rubbing his wrists.

'Ovar called us,' Enegene answered, keeping her voice low. 'We must get you out of the house. Don't speak and move quietly.'

'Catailyn? Skye?'

'Safe with my pilot,' Enegene assured him, as Drew Rhalin headed towards Luapp.

Standing by the door, his relaxed stance suddenly became rigid and he looked down at the detector. A Fluctoid was registering. As he locked the door he sent a telepathic message to Enegene to hide.

'Drew, return to the chair; pretend to be bound,' she said, hurrying towards one of the easy chairs.

Luapp loosely tied Drew Rhalin's hands with the rope pieces and put the gag back in his mouth. Then he went swiftly to the tall cupboard against the wall and pulled back into the corner. Seconds later the lock clicked and the door opened.

He recognised the man walking over to Drew Rhalin; he'd seen that rear view many times over the events season. The greenish skin was slightly darker than normal making him look flushed.

As Pellan went to Rhalin, Luapp closed his eyes and shifted the electrical impulses from his cells into his hands. Mentally measuring the distance between him and Pellan, he waited for the right moment. He couldn't afford to get it wrong. With his body working on reduced power, he only had one opportunity to help Drew Rhalin.

'Well?' said the familiar voice. 'Where is she?'

He was now between Rhalin and Luapp with his back to the guardian. Pulling the gag down he grabbed Drew Rhalin's hair forcing his head back.

'Why are you doing this Pellan?' Rhalin said, wearily. 'What have we ever done to you?'

'I wasn't good enough for your precious daughter was I?' Pellan sneered. 'The high and mighty Rhalins whose ancestors were animal herders. My family's as important as yours. An ambassador is a high-ranking occupation easily equal to whatever you do. No more stalling, tell me where she's hiding.'

When Drew said nothing Pellan struck him hard making him gasp. 'You will regret defying me,' he said, viciously. 'I'll make you beg to die.'

With his fingers tingling with bio-electrical energy, Luapp left the corner. As he approached Pellan, Drew's inadvertent sideways glance alerted the man. He spun as Luapp reached him.

His hands landed on Pellan's shoulders and a bright flash of light arced around his head. He screamed, stiffened and collapsed. Rhalin flung off the ropes and jumped up, his face drawn and pale.

'How did you do that?' he said, awe struck.

Hearing the scream Enegene peered over the chair. Pellan was on the ground, Drew Rhalin appeared dazed and Luapp was looking drained. Leaving her hiding place she went over to him.

'Sit down.'

'How...how...? Drew spluttered.

'It would be too difficult to explain,' she said. 'Is he the only one here?'

'As far as I know.' Rhalin looked down at the unconscious man. 'He's the only one I've seen.'

His confused expression turned to horror as Pellan changed shape into an almost transparent being.

'What happened?' he said, hoarsely.

'He's a Fluctoid,' Luapp said. 'He's reverted to natural shape.'

Rhalin looked up at Luapp amazed. 'You are exceedingly knowledgeable for a slave. I can't possibly imagine where you came across something like that wherever you have travelled.'

'I have been on several different planets,' he said, quietly.

Enegene gripped his shoulder firmly. 'Mikim, sit down and remain seated until I tell you otherwise.'

'Things to do,' he answered. 'We've limited time.'

Giving him an annoyed glare she walked over to the Fluctoid and shot it with the weapon.

'Now we have longer. Do as I say.'

Rhalin stared at her open mouthed. 'Why did you do that?' he said, horrified. 'It was helpless; there was no reason to kill it.'

'The Fluctoid isn't dead,' she said, 'just disabled. It freezes its molecules so it can't change shape.'

'If you had a weapon like that you must have been expecting something like this,' Rhalin said. 'I'm going to call the police, and while we wait for them to arrive, you and your slave can explain.'

'I'll get the others while you make the call,' Enegene said. 'Mikim can restrain it.'

~~~

Arriving beside the Drifter, Enegene gave Morvac the code. She pushed her way out of the bush and waited for the vehicle to appear. Then she walked beside it up to the house.

Morvac opened the door for the Rhalin family to leave. 'Shall I wait here Madam?' he said, closing the door.

'Move to the side Morvac, the enforcers will be arriving soon.'

An emotional greeting was going on as Enegene entered the lounge. After giving each member of the family a hug, Drew returned his attention to her.

'While I am exceedingly grateful to you both for rescuing myself and my family, I would appreciate an honest answer. I know Mikim is no ordinary slave, so who is he?'

'Where is he?' Enegene said, looking around.

In answer to her question Drew said, 'Ovar, go to the staff common room and tell Mikim to come here.'

The boy ran off and returned some minutes later with Luapp. Directing him to a seat, she sat down beside him. 'Is there somewhere the children could be?' she said.

'Ovar,' Catailyn Rhalin said. 'Take Skye and Morvac and search the grounds for the servants and slaves. They must be around somewhere.'

Both children hesitated until Drew said, 'it's safe. We have the attacker here, and you will have Lady Branon's chauffer with you. Aylisha, take them to Morvac.'

'Alright,' Aylisha answered. 'But don't start without me.'

Taking Skye's hand, Aylisha led the children from the room.

'What I'm going to tell you is highly sensitive and involves your Coalition Leader,' Enegene said. 'I'm assuming I can trust you to keep what you hear to yourselves.'

She glanced at Luapp but he showed no sign of wanting to take over. 'Mikim is not his real name and he isn't a slave...'

She paused as Aylisha rushed in to the room and sat beside her mother. 'We are both from Gaeiza. I'm a Spyrian, a civilian investigator, and Luapp,' she glanced at him, 'is a guardian commander, a law enforcer from the intelligence division...'

The Rhalin family listened in stunned silence as she explained about the trail of murder victims and their reason for being on Pedanta.

'Now you know why we're here,' Enegene said, as she finished, 'perhaps you can tell me why he attacked you and your family. This is a change of style.'

Drew frowned. 'I have no idea why he - the... shape changer picked on us. It has nothing to gain by it. If you are correct it should have targeted Aylisha, but it was after Catailyn.'

'It's been shadowing me,' Enegene said, frowning. 'Perhaps it decided the guardian was too dangerous to tackle.'

'Do you know why he sent a message to Enegene's dwelling?' Luapp said.

'Enegene?' Drew said, confused.

Luapp glanced at Enegene. 'Kaylee.'

'I didn't know he had,' Drew said.

'He took your shape, and I thought it was you trying to ask for help. But I realised when we saw you it couldn't be you. The contusions on your face would not become visible in the short time it took us to arrive.'

Drew frowned. 'He didn't do it in the staff room; perhaps he was trying to get Aylisha to return.'

'Or it was a ploy to get Kaylee - Enegene here, hoping to attack her with no servants around,' Catailyn said.

'It appeared as if he wanted no one to come back to the dwelling,' Luapp said. 'It was only after receiving your son's message that we came.'

'He arrived only minutes after Aylisha left,' Drew said. 'He told me Antonia Benze had sent him with a message for Catailyn. As I turned to call a servant I was struck. When I woke up I was in the servants' common room, tied to the chair. He wanted my wife, although I have no idea why.'

Looking at Catailyn, Enegene said, 'what made you hide?'

'I was in the kitchen looking over the week's menus. When none of the servants or slaves answered the door, I was curious and went to find out why. I heard Pellan's voice, and decided to leave Drew to it. Then I heard something fall. I looked into the hall and saw Pellan dragging Drew along the corridor.

The children had been playing outside, and I was trying to find a way to get them in when Ovar appeared. He said he'd looked through the window to see who arrived and saw the visitor hit his father. I told him to bring Skye in through the back entrance and I took them upstairs.

When we were in the bedroom I told them to hide in different places. Ovar tried to get her to go with him, but Skye was too frightened to leave me.'

'Asking for you makes no sense,' Enegene said.

'Hopefully he'll enlighten us when he regains consciousness,' Luapp said, wearily. Glancing at Drew he added, 'when the enforcers arrive, I'm still the slave of Lady Branon.'

The doorbell ringing followed by several loud bangs and shouts of "Police!" made the Rhalins flinch. Luapp left to let them in, and returned with a policeman Enegene hadn't seen before.

'Inspector Ghan,' he said, striding over to Drew Rhalin. 'I understand there's been a break-in. While my team collect the assailant and gather evidence I want a statement from you all.'

## Chapter 16

With the Fluctoid safely in jail and the strain of being a target gone, Enegene relaxed and looked forward to the final social event of the year.

Twirling one way and then the other, the elegant cream beaded dress floated around her. Make-up carefully applied, and expensive jewellery hung around her neck, she glanced at her appearance in the mirror. All that remained was her hair.

Sitting on the stool in front of the dressing table she looked around. 'I'm ready now,' she said. 'I'd like a formal style.'

Luapp left the bed and walked over. He collected her hair into his hand and picked up the brush. 'Technically I'm not supposed to do this,' he said, his mind on the task. 'You're not a relative.'

'But you're my slave so technicalities like that don't arise,' Enegene said, watching him work in the mirror.

He divided her hair into two parts. The top layer he twisted and pinned loosely on top of her head. 'You're wrong about that.'

'Which part?'

'I'm not your slave.'

Wrapping a lock of her hair around a heating wand he

made a ringlet.

'I bought you,' she said smugly.

'With gems supplied by the guardians. That makes me their property.'

Carefully working his way from one side to the other, he curled each lock of hair until a line of ringlets was completed.

'Nothing's changed there then,' she muttered acidly. After watching him for some minutes she added, 'it will be interesting to see where your ancestral line originates.'

With the bottom layer finished he brushed out the ringlets making loose waves. Then he started on the top. Wrapping some hair around the wand, he curled her hair again. Finishing the top layer, he brushed her fringe into place, lay down the brush and stepped back.

She studied the finished style in the mirror. 'You're from the city itself,' she said, admiring his work. 'While we wait for the others to arrive you can put this on.'

Taking a jewellery case from a drawer in the dressing table, she opened it. Inside was a golden chain with a bird pendant.

Luapp looked at it but didn't move. 'I don't wear jewellery.'

'I suppose you'll say that to your liana as she's about to clip the ring together,' she said, sourly.

'That would be totally different circumstances.'

'I bought this for you in front of Aylisha; you will wear it.'

'Aylisha and her family are now aware I'm not your slave, and I doubt she'll remember it.'

Enegene remained silent but stubbornly held out the box. They stared at each other for several seconds then he twitched a brow and removed the chain.

Closing the box Enegene watched him place it around his neck and smiled. For several moments, her thoughts were far removed from the mission.

*That white shimmer suit compliments him; he's a real heart speeder. Over the monspa we've been together he's returned to the man I remember; a vision of warm red flesh and well developed muscle.*

*Neat, but not particular about being fashionable. Nails and hair cut to a functional length for the work he does. It's obviously been in the same style for quite a time as he merely runs his hands through it for it to fall into place.*

Her smile widened. *I've been tempted to run my hands through it several times... What is it about Nostowe that stirs me? Not just his looks. I appreciate a good-looking man as much as any female, but I'm not blinded by the physical. There's got to be something more for me; whatever it is, Nostowe has it by the silo...*

He turned and looked at her as the bell rang. 'Shall I let Aylisha in?'

'Cleona will do it,' she said, quietly. Then freeing herself from the perplexing thoughts she added, 'I suppose we should go and meet her.'

As they descended the stairs Cleona stood patiently at the bottom. 'Mr Pellan has arrived Madam,' she announced.

Enegene froze and shot Luapp a glance. He didn't miss a step and she hurried to catch up as he entered the lounge. Pellan was there, nervously twiddling his fingers.

Seeing her he stood and smiled. 'Lady Branon, you are a picture of loveliness.' He reached out towards her. 'If you will allow me,' he said, looking into her eyes.

Enegene looked down at the outstretched hand. After a hesitation, she placed hers into it as she had seen others do. To her surprise, Pellan raised it to his lips and kissed it. As he lowered her hand she snatched it from his grasp.

Glancing at Luapp, he said, 'your slave is coming also?'

'He is my protector,' she said, coolly.

Running his thumbs down the yellow silk lapels of his brown jacket, he smiled. 'You will need no protector while I am with you.'

Enegene gave him an icy glare. She fought the urge to tell him he could no more protect her than the guardian could become ugly.

Instead she said, 'I am sure you will not be offended if I prefer to bring the one professionally taught. I am also sure you're aware slaves are expected. Besides, Lady Rhalin is coming and she wanted someone to go in with.'

'Ah. Lady Rhalin.' The sideway smirk raised Enegene's hackles. 'Yes, I can see the slave would be useful to her, he is about her standard.'

In that utterance, he managed to insult the two people she cared most about on this planet and her temper flared.

'May I remind you that I agreed to go to the gathering with you as a favour? Any more remarks about my friend or my slave and you will be going on your own.'

The smug expression was rapidly replaced by one of fake contrition. 'I did not mean to offend you Lady Branon, but Lady Rhalin is rather young, and tends to do things in a slightly... immature way.'

Her expression suggested she had not been placated. In fact, it probably annoyed her even more. Fortunately, he was saved by the doorbell ringing and Cleona's entrance.

'Lady Rhalin Madam.'

Aylisha entered a little more subdued than usual, but seeing Luapp she smiled broadly. Then she saw Pellan and her mouth dropped open in wordless surprise. Minutes later, she stuttered, 'P-P-Pellan...'

'Didn't Lady Branon tell you I was escorting her?' Pellan said, puzzled.

'It... slipped my mind.' Regaining some composure, she

walked swiftly over to Luapp and slid her arm through his. 'Ready to go Mikim?'

Gently extracting himself from her grip, he said, 'yes Lady.'

Aylisha giggled and blushed. 'Oh! Ah! Uum...'

Her eyes darted from Luapp to Enegene and for a moment Enegene thought she might say the wrong thing.

'Only in the short term,' she said hastily. 'Once we're in we swap partners.'

Aylisha glanced at Pellan in horror. 'Oh no we don't! I'm staying with the handsome slave.'

Enegene laughed at the equally horrified look on Pellan's face. 'Alright, so you and Freeman Pellan go your own ways and I get Mikim.'

'That's not fair.' Aylisha moved closer to Luapp and grabbed his hand. 'I went in with Mikim and I should be able to stay with him.'

Enegene glanced at Pellan. His odd expression managed to make him look smug and silly at the same time. Her smile faded and she added, 'time to go, Morvac will be waiting.'

They left the room in two separate groups. Pellan was in front on his own and the women behind with Luapp.

The journey to the country estate of the councillor was only half an hour, but Pellan's recounting of Lady Benze' reasons for not coming made it seem longer. Enegene let out a sigh of relief as the Drifter joined the queue of aircars delivering their occupants to the front door.

As with all these overnight events, the socialites drifted into the house followed by slaves carrying their cases. Luapp collected Enegene and Aylisha's bags and left Pellan to carry his own.

At the door, a servant asked for their invitations and announced their arrival before letting them pass. Once inside Pellan excused himself immediately.

285

Aylisha stayed with Enegene while Luapp was guided to the luggage lift by a house slave. Placing them inside, he was taken upstairs and she directed him to their rooms.

They were standing at the foot of the stairs conversing with another guest when he returned. As the man left, Aylisha glanced around the hall. 'How is Pellan here?' she said quietly. 'He's supposed to be in jail.'

'It would seem the Fluctoid in detention is not Pellan after all,' Enegene said. 'But I still find him distasteful.'

They wandered into the main room filled with guests and stopped just inside the door. Looking around the crowd Enegene glanced at Aylisha and smiled.

'You'd better go and find yourself a nice young man while I stick with my slave.'

Aylisha looked them both up and down and smiled cynically. 'You can't fool me, I know when I'm not wanted.' Collecting a glass from a nearby table she disappeared into the crowd.

'Better do the rounds,' Enegene said, moving towards a small group near the centre of the room.

Their progress was slow due to the usual time wasting exercise of exchanging useless information. Enegene had got used to it during her time on Pedanta, but she knew Luapp found it irritating.

In the gaps between groups Enegene watched Luapp scanning the crowd. With the Fluctoid safely in a cell, she was confident this event would be trouble free, but he wasn't fully relaxed.

A break in conversation of the current group allowed the participants to disperse to the buffet table and other groups. Enegene then turned her attention to other matters.

She was a little mystified. After attending so many of these events, she had learned to pick out the socialites who were interested in talking to her and the ones who wanted to buy her slave. There was something about the way they approached, and now she had perfected her refusal.

Many a hopeful purchaser had advanced with confidence and left defeated. But this event was different. Not one potential purchaser had been identified.

*Perhaps they've got the message at long last,* she thought.

A voice calling her name brought her attention to a small group a short distance away and she walked over to join them. It was here she got the reason why the socialites had given up hope of buying Luapp.

Her drunken attack on Pellan had convinced her close friends her attraction to her slave was more than a pass time. They then spread the word he was off the acquisition list. Anyone trying to buy him would be an outcast. Not being invited to the circuit events was unthinkable to the socialites of Denjal, so the offers stopped.

'Wonderful,' she said in Gaeizaan, to Luapp. 'Now you can really relax.' Glancing around the crowded room she added, 'Pellan's cousin hasn't come.'

'With the Fluctoid incarcerated, perhaps there was no need to come.'

Giving him a brief look, she headed for the garden. Finding a seat, they sat down and discussed their possible return to Gaeiza. Another couple burst into the garden laughing, and seeing them headed further out into the darkness, Enegene sighed.

'We might as well go in, I doubt if they're the only ones looking for a quiet place.'

Leaving their shelter, they returned through the large glass doors. Halfway across the room they saw Kyrita Chrona walking towards them. Telling Luapp to leave them to talk Enegene went back into the garden with her.

~~~

Tired of her current companion's conversation Aylisha was scanning the room. Seeing Luapp walking towards the stairs, she excused herself from the small group and tried to catch up.

He was already at the top when she got out of the room, so hitching up her skirt, she ran up behind him. Right at the top she dropped her skirt a moment too soon, stood on the hem and fell flat on her face. Cursing under her breath she tried to get up, but found herself tangled in the floating mass of her gold satin dress.

Managing to get onto all fours, she was working on a solution when she noticed someone standing in front of her. Looking up she saw a tall man with a lopsided grin looking down. His russet coloured eyes twinkled with amusement

'Is this a private game or can anyone play?'

'I'm stuck,' she blurted out, in exasperation. 'I can't get up.'

He squatted down so she didn't have to crane her neck to look at him. 'Would you like some assistance?'

'I don't want to stay here all night.'

She attempted to blow away a lock of hair hanging in front of her face. After three tries, she realised it was tangled on the clip in her hair and gave up.

'Then allow me.' With their faces inches apart he said, 'place your hands on my shoulders.'

Aylisha did as instructed as he put his hands around her waist. 'Right, hold on.'

He rose to a stand lifting her with him, and placed her on her feet. Then he steadied her as she pulled the dress hem from under her shoes.

'Thanks. I didn't mean to snap but I felt like an idiot.'

He flashed the lopsided grin again. 'But such a pretty idiot.' He watched her freeing the strand of hair. 'I'm Jym Corder.

And you are?'

Patting her hair into place she smiled. 'Aylisha Rhalin.'

'Are you Lord Drew Rhalin's daughter?' he said, surprised.

Having pulled her dress straight she looked at him. 'Yes, do you know my father?'

'Vaguely, although I doubt if he remembers me, I was six last time I saw him.'

'Really? I don't ever remember seeing you before.'

Aylisha found herself mesmerised by the good looking young man with the black wavy hair.

'Shall we go somewhere to talk, or shall we stay here and block the stairs for everyone else?'

Suddenly aware of where they were standing, Aylisha blushed. 'Back downstairs.'

'Are you safe to go downstairs?' he said, as she turned to face the right way.

Her smile widened into a grin. 'I'm relying on you catching me if I fall.'

'I don't want to make a habit of picking you up off the floor; do you sometimes go in for shorter skirts?'

'Mostly I go in for body suits.'

She lifted the hem of her skirt with one hand and grabbed the stair rail with the other.

'That sounds interesting,' he murmured, following her.

On the way down they talked about his last meeting with her family. From the stairs they went into the ballroom, where she stopped and looked around.

'Lost someone?' he said.

'Not really,' she murmured, continuing to look.

'Didn't come in with someone?'

'I came in with a slave.'

The grin vanished and she heard a note of disapproval as

he said, 'you own slaves?'

'My father owns slaves. He has a philosophy about ownership. But the slave I came in with was not mine.'

'Whose were they?'

He took two glasses from a tray offered by a servant and gave one to Aylisha.

'Lady Branon's.'

She sipped the wine and paid full attention to Jym Corder. He took a drink and smiled once more.

'I've heard of Lady Branon,' he said. 'She's quite a socialite apparently.'

'And she has a good business mind,' Aylisha added.

'And she's a friend of yours?'

They wandered towards the buffet table.

'A very close friend.'

She took the plate he offered and glanced at the food displayed.

'Whose slave you don't mind borrowing,' he said, busily filling his own plate.

She gave him a cool look. 'He's the best escort I've had so far. And, he's the most professional protector I have ever come across.'

Jym Corder held up his free hand. 'Cool down your Ladyship. I just don't agree with slavery in principal.'

Aylisha sighed. 'Nor does Kaylee. It took me ages to persuade her to have the slave. But now she agrees it was the best thing she ever did.'

'So you agree with slavery?' He took a bite from the meat pastry he was holding.

She shrugged. 'I agree with my father. Slavery is evil, but it exists, and while it does, I will do my bit to help a few slaves.'

'Help how?'

He chewed, frowned, stopped chewing and looked at her.

She studied his face for some seconds, struggling not to laugh at his expression. As he put a napkin up to his mouth she decided to trust him.

'He buys a slave, educates them and has them learn a trade. He keeps them in the house until they are proficient.

While by law we cannot pay slaves, we can 'treat' them when they have done something exceptionally well. He treats them with expensive things that are sellable. Strangely, our slaves often manage to buy their freedom.'

'Hm.'

He looked around for a convenient vessel to dump the half chewed pie into. Aylisha glanced past him towards the garden and saw Enegene emerge with Pellan's cousin.

'Here's Kaylee, would you like to meet her?'

Screwing the napkin and pie into a tight ball he watched the tall, elegant, alien woman coming in their direction. 'That would be interesting.'

As she got closer her full lips curled into a smile and her emerald eyes twinkled. 'I see you took my advice literally,' she said, glancing at Jym.

'This is Jym Corder,' Aylisha said. 'He picked me up at the top of the stairs.'

'Odd place to do it, but everyone has their foibles.' Enegene's smile broadened. 'Hello Jym Corder, I'm Kaylee Branon.'

'Your reputation is nothing to the reality Lady.'

Enegene's gaze rested on his face for a few seconds. Her smile remained in place, but Aylisha noticed the warmth in her eyes fade.

'He's a fair talker Aylisha.'

For some reason Aylisha didn't understand, the introduction had not gone well. They were saved more frosty comments when Luapp appeared.

'Relief,' she muttered under her breath.

Jym turned to see what she was looking at. He tried his best to sound surprised when he saw Luapp. 'Is that your slave Lady Branon?'

'He is indeed.'

'Aylisha was right, he is better than most men here. It's understandable you would want to own him, if only to save him from the clutches of more unscrupulous owners.'

'So glad you approve,' Enegene remarked, watching Luapp approach. When he stopped beside her she said, 'I'm tired Mikim and I shall retire. Is my bag in place?'

With a glance at Jym, Luapp replied, 'Yes lady.'

Aylisha watched Enegene and Luapp leave the room then turned her attention to her companion.

'Well, thank you for your assistance. I think I will go to bed also. If you are in the area for a while, call in and see my father, he will be pleased you did.'

Jym smiled. 'I'll do that, and I hope to see you tomorrow before you leave. Do you want help up the stairs?'

Aylisha's cheeks tinged peach with a blush. 'I will go more slowly this time, but thank you for the offer.' With a backward glance, she left him in the room and headed for the stairs.

~~~

Entering her bedroom Enegene went straight through to the bathroom. By the time she finished it was a good half hour later, so she was surprised to see Luapp still there. Like her house, the rooms had side rooms for slaves, and she'd expected him to have gone through.

'What's going on?'

'I'm expecting someone to call on us.'

Enegene smiled. 'Aylisha's found herself a young male and we won't see her tonight.'

Luapp twitched a brow. 'I know Aylisha Rhalin is young, rich, and salation, but I don't think she would trust a stranger so easily after the incident at her dwelling.'

'Who then?' Enegene walked over to the dressing table and sat down. 'Remove the adornments from my hair please.'

He walked up behind her and started taking out the pins holding the curls, and then untangling the small, gem-stone flowers. 'My enforcer contact. Did you obtain the drug?'

He put the flowers on the dressing table. Enegene felt up her sleeve and produced a small vial of purple liquid from her knife belt.

Taking it he held it up. 'It's a different colour.'

'I don't recommend breathing that in,' she said, shaking her hair loose.

'Tomorrow I'll alert the authorities to Freewoman Chrona's alternative activities.'

Putting the vial on the dressing table, he removed the chain around his neck. He held it out to Enegene but she shook her head.

'Keep it; it's yours.'

He placed it on the dressing table next to the hair adornments. 'I don't know you well enough to accept a gift this expensive. I shall be in here but lock the outer door.'

As he walked towards the other room she picked up the necklace and placed it carefully in her bag. Locking the door, she wandered to the bed humming a tune from the evening.

~~~

In her sleep Enegene stirred. Something wasn't right. Her senses slipped slowly into place and she could hear lowered voices. Sitting up she listened intently, trying to identify the direction the voices were coming from. A chill went up her spine when she realised they were in the guardian's room.

Sliding from the bed she strapped the knife to her arm and

293

slipped on a night robe. She approached the door stealthily and listened. One of the voices was his and she let out the breath she'd been holding. The other voice was vaguely familiar. As she tried to remember where she'd heard it, Luapp spoke a little louder.

'Come in Enegene.'

Pushing the door she walked in and was surprised to see the young man Aylisha had introduced. Jym moved position to allow her to sit on a chair while he sat on the bed.

'Jym Corder is the senior law enforcer of Denjal,' Luapp explained. 'He is also my main contact here.'

'The enforcer on the visual sliver?' she said.

'You saw that, did you?' Jym said. 'Pretty nasty.' He drifted into silence and then added, 'I came to warn you the Fluctoid has escaped, and to return those.' He glanced at a small bag on Luapp's bed.

She looked inside and recognised the Fluctoid equipment. 'We thought Pellan or his cousin couldn't be the shape shifter as it was detained.'

Jym frowned. 'You both know how clever the Fluctoid is. My people have never come across one before. Although they were thoroughly briefed and warned, it still managed to escape.'

'How?' Enegene demanded.

'It waited for a change of shift, and then pretended the stop box on its back was painful. The officer switched off the electric field, and then the box to adjust it. Other officers found him unconscious after seeing a pokari running from the cells shortly afterwards.'

'And I suppose no one thought an animal in the detention room was suspicious?' Enegene said, angrily.

Jym shrugged. 'Although they don't inhabit the town, it isn't uncommon to see one in or around the buildings.'

'But they had their orders...' Enegene started.

'There's no logic in condemnations,' Luapp interrupted. 'We're back to the original plan.'

Giving him a glare, she turned her attention back to Jym.

'How do we know you're Jym Corder?'

'Because I've been vaccinated and you can check if you like.'

'Are you really a friend of Drew Rhalin?'

'No. My father is a friend of Drew Rhalin. I used to visit their house when I was a child. Aylisha was just a baby then. Must say she's grown up nicely.' He smiled at the thought. 'Didn't recognise her from the surveillance pictures.'

'Watch out for her then. I assume you know the shifter attacked the family?'

'Yes, although we don't know why. We've questioned it several times but it refused to say anything significant. It just keeps muttering about not changing the target. I must go before we're caught. Good night to you both.'

Enegene watched him go then turned to Luapp. 'Why didn't you wake me?'

'There was no logic in disturbing you for something I could tell you the next morning. Go and get some rest.'

She gave him a glare and returned to her room. Dropping the robe on the floor she climbed into bed again.

The next day she woke in a slightly better mood. Having thought the circumstances through she had to admit the Pedantans had done their best with the alien prisoner.

Pushing her concerns to one side she wandered into the bathroom to have a shower before breakfast. Half way through she heard a knock on the door. With an annoyed frown, she was about to step out when she heard the door open.

She'd momentarily forgotten Luapp was in the other room

and returned to her shower with relief. When she finally arrived in her bedroom she saw him sitting on a chair looking at the vial.

'Who was at the door?' she said, passing him.

'A servant. Firseal is ready.'

She sat at the dressing table and brushed her hair. 'Good. I'm feeling hungry.'

'You can't possibly be hungry after what you ate last night.'

She stopped brushing and watched his reflection. 'I always feel hungry when I'm hunting.'

'What are you hunting?'

He dripped a minute amount of the liquid onto a paper napkin. Immediately there was a strong, bitter smell which quickly dissipated making Luapp pull back sharply.

'The shape shifter,' she said, continuing her observation in the mirror.

Nothing seemed to happen except he looked up and stared across the room.

'Are you ready?' she said, standing up.

'For what?'

Walking up behind him she said, 'firseal.'

'That was for you.'

The words were coherent and sensible, but he sounded distracted.

'Is that what the servant said?' *There's nothing obviously different about him and yet...* 'You are eating with me, so come on.'

He put the vial on a low table, stood up and followed her to the door.

'You'd better put that away before we leave,' Enegene said.

He collected the vial and put it into the top drawer of a chest of drawers by the wall  and stayed there.

'What are you doing?'

He looked at her blankly. 'Nothing.'

Realisation dawned. The best course of action, she decided, was that of owner. 'Come with me,' she ordered, and left.

He followed her to the bottom of the stairs where they were met by the servant. 'The dining room is that way Lady Branon. Your slave will eat with the rest below stairs.'

Enegene gave him a staid look. 'My slave will eat with me. If the Lady of the house has any objection, we shall eat in my room.'

The man backed away. 'I shall inform Lady Vian,' he said, and hastily departed.

'You do that,' Enegene muttered quietly.

A movement caught the corner of her eye and she turned to see Luapp sway dangerously. Hastily grabbing the bannister he straightened up.

Aylisha and Jym were coming down for breakfast and seeing him nearly collapse, Jym hastened his pace. Moving up behind him he said, quietly, 'are you alright?'

He took a few seconds before answering. 'I am now.'

'Not feeling well?' asked Aylisha.

Before he could answer, the hostess appeared from a room to their right. She was a woman in her fifties, slender and looking several years younger.

Her styled hair sparkled with gem strings and her close fitting lilac dress flattered her skin tone. 'Kaylee, 'I hope you we're not offended by the slave rule. In my experience guests prefer to eat away from their slaves the next morning.'

'I am not offended, but my slave is a protector and I prefer he eats with me.'

Lady Vian smiled, her nut brown eyes twinkling as they travelled over the man in front of her. 'I assure you, you are safe here, but a Lady of your wealth and position should never concern herself with others opinions. Besides, you are the first down, so the dining room is yours.' She looked at the two standing close behind and raised her brows expectantly.

'I am perfectly happy for Mikim to eat with his mistress,' Aylisha stated.

'I also have no objection,' added Jym.

Vian looked at Luapp once more. 'If he were my slave, I wouldn't have him eat below either. The view in the dining room is rather dull; anything that brightens it has my approval.'

Enegene raised her eyebrows in mock surprise. 'Cassida Vian! I am shocked! You have a husband.'

'And you, you lucky girl, do not. Follow me. I hope you don't mind if I join you?'

'This is your house Cassida, feel free,' Enegene said following the hostess.

~~~

Enegene's choice of words had unfortunate connotations as far as Luapp was concerned. Cressida sat beside him at the table, and as soon as the meal was served she struck.

Her hand alighted on his thigh and proceeded to caress it continually throughout the meal. He struggled to maintain a neutral expression, and it was a relief when Enegene told him to load their bags into the Drifter.

Collecting both women's bags from their rooms he took them to the luggage lift. Hearing a faint noise as he put them in, he turned and found himself trapped in the cupboard sized space by Cassida Vian. Hastily backing away, he hit the wall and could retreat no further. Cassida was now so close he could smell her breakfast.

Placing her hand on his chest, she said softly, 'you are the most spectacular being I have ever set eyes on. I think I will make an offer for you.'

'Lady Branon is not willing to sell,' he replied, desperately

298

looking for a way out.

'People change their minds for all sorts of reasons, I am sure I could persuade her.'

'She'll be wondering where I am.'

Having scanned the room three times, he concluded there were no secret passageways to escape into. *Teleportation is an option... or perhaps I can get into the lift with the luggage...*

'I'm sure she will be.' Her arm curled around his back and she pulled herself even closer. 'But if we're very, very quiet, she won't find us.'

'Mikim.'

Luapp was startled. He'd been concentrating so hard on a means of escape he hadn't heard Enegene approach the room.

'Help Freeman Corder with his overnight.'

~~~

Vian stepped back with a chuckle as Luapp slid sideways out of her grasp. As he left the room she turned to watch him with a broad smile.

'He is a divine male.'

'He's *my* divine male,' Enegene replied, frostily.

'Surely you do not begrudge me the few crumbs that fall from the table?' Cassida Vian said, moving to the doorway and looking out.

Enegene stepped back and looked Vian over for a moment. 'Crumbs, no. But I do object to you trying to steal a slice. I enjoyed the gathering Cassida, you were a most attentive hostess.'

Cassida smiled, her eyes finally leaving the now empty corridor and resting on Enegene. 'And you are a most attentive mistress.'

'I have to be. It's amazing how many people have more than two hands when Mikim is around.' Enegene smiled briefly. 'Farewell Cassida.'

299

She walked along the corridor accompanied by Cassida Vian. As they started down the stairs she said, 'I hope you won't object if I call on you some time later?'

'He's not for sale,' Enegene replied. Long worded rejections were not useful here, she decided.

'I can be very persuasive. It is surprising what you want or need that you did not realise beforehand,' Cassida persisted.

Glancing briefly at the woman, Enegene replied, 'I had been told the message had got through; he's not for sale.'

Cassida's smile widened. 'They'd never ban me.'

'He's definitely not for sale.'

Aylisha and Jym were waiting by the front door, and seeing Enegene arrive headed out to the Drifter.

'I have vast resources at my command.'

Cassida stopped by the front door and Enegene paused just outside. She glanced at Luapp standing by the Drifter then turned towards the hostess.

'You are welcome to visit my dwelling any time, but he's not for sale. Fairday.'

Settling in the Drifter Enegene let out a sigh of relief as Luapp got in and closed the door. 'That female was the most determined I've met so far.' She glanced at the group and frowned. 'Where's Pellan?'

'He vanished sometime in the night,' Jym answered. 'Along with his cousin. I'll have search out for her as soon as I get back to the station.'

'You can call from home –,' Aylisha stopped at Enegene's smile and then added, 'Jym decided to visit pap today.'

Conversation stopped until they reached the Rhalin estate. Dropping Aylisha and Jym at the front door, the Drifter carried onto Enegene's house. As they returned to the road her eyes were on Luapp. Finally, she said, 'are you alright?'

He brought his attention from the passing countryside to

her. 'Lady?'

'You seem very insular at the moment.'

'I'm considering options,' he replied. 'The unexpected turn of events will have complicated matters.'

A short silence followed. 'Do you realise you were completely blank for some minutes this morning?'

'Only because of the headache and nausea I felt shortly after.'

'What was happening at the table?'

'Which table?'

'The dining table.'

'I was feeling ill.'

'Apart from that.'

He studied her face. 'What makes you think anything was happening?'

'I could tell by the pained expression. Cassida helping herself to more than food, was she?'

'She took your phrase, "feel free", literally.'

Enegene giggled.

'I didn't find the situation amusing,' he said irritated. 'She has an amazing lack of morality.'

Her shoulders shook with the effort of stopping herself laughing out loud. Finally in control, she said, 'your judgement must have been impaired by that drug.'

'What makes you think that?'

'Being caught by Cassida Vian twice in such a short time.'

'She's most tenacious; like someone else I know.'

Sliding him a sideways glance, she grinned. Further conversation was interrupted by the divider being pushed back.

'Lady Vian is calling Madam,' Morvac announced.

'When she said she was going to call, I didn't think she meant this quickly.' Then to the driver Enegene added, 'put her through Morvac.'

Enegene was engaged in talking to Cassida Vian for the rest of the short journey, and every sentence ended with, 'he's not for sale'.

Luapp returned to looking out of the window. When the Drifter finally swept into the drive and came to a halt in front of the house, he left her talking to Cassida Vian. Going to the rear of the vehicle he collected her bag from the boot and disappeared into the house.

Enegene finally got away from Cassida Vian ten minutes later. She went up to her bedroom and looked around. He wasn't there, but hearing the click of the cupboard door she looked out. He appeared a few seconds later.

'Anything?' she said, as he shut the door behind him.

'Nothing registered, but it's back to the extra vigilance and tight security again.'

## Chapter 17


Morvac deposited them beside a grassy hill and left. A short walk later they stopped beside a tree. While Enegene sat on the rug enjoying the view, Luapp contacted Kerran Gyre.

'The data banks of the local law enforcers of Pedanta have been scrutinised. Nothing suggests the slayer has struck elsewhere while you've been there. Nor have there been corpses fitting the method anywhere else in the Black Systems.

With no further slayings using the killer's operational technique reported, the consensus is you are in the right place and have the right shape shifter.'

'Unfortunately, my report isn't so good. The Fluctoid escaped from the salation's detention centre so we're returning to the original plan. The Spyrian obtained a second vial of drug which appears to be much stronger; possibly lethal. I inhaled only a small amount of vapour and lost several minutes real time.'

'We haven't been able to trace the first mix yet,' Kerran said. 'But we're still working on it.'

'I'll send you the analysis of the second drug. You can compare the two and note the differences. Sending now.'

A short pause followed before Kerran said, 'information

received. I have been researching the outworlder Pellan and his cousin. They are Renahs from the Uth'Renahs Systems. Bipedal humanoids descended from reptiles.

There's no immediate explanation for his continuous travelling, but his cousin accompanies him everywhere. She stays in the background, but apparently isn't as timid as she portrays. There are reports of assaults on other females.

There is also a contradiction in her account. Pellan isn't from a lower stratum. His father was an ambassador and always took his family with him when deployed.

The ambassadorial staff that travelled with them described Pellan as a calm but feckless individual. He had no direction in life and tended to drift from one situation to the next. In everyone's view he didn't have the willpower to slay anyone.'

'Strange,' Luapp said. 'That tallies with the Fluctoid's rant at Drew Rhalin. If Pellan isn't the Fluctoid, it must be someone who knows him well. Here on Pedanta I can think of only two people who know him that well. Are there any updates of opinion on the multislayer?'

'Given the Spyrian, the Rhalins and the Garbers were all attacked by someone they thought they knew, the slayer is definitely a Fluctoid,' Kerran said. 'The fact that all female victims were hetro is no longer viable as the slayer is now not necessarily male. Only the strength issue remains.'

'Some females are strong depending on their life style, but whenever we have encountered it, it was either an animal or a male. It's possible the wounds could have been caused as much by speed or anger as strength. It might also explain why all victims were female.'

'I agree female guardians are stronger than salation males, but only because our genus is naturally stronger than theirs. It could be the same with Fluctoids,' Kerran said. 'I'll research their genus in more detail. However, if it's not Pellan, why has he followed the same path as the slayer?'

'His cousin goes with him and she's mixed race. She wants to be his life-spanner but his family oppose it. That would give her a reason.

Benze appears to be defensive with Pellan, but she presents a facade of nonchalance. She has a motive, but apparently has only travelled within the Black Systems.

Judging by embassy staff opinion, Pellan was either a weak individual or he's an excellent dramatist. I'm reluctant to rule him out entirely.'

Luapp paused to think about that. 'The Fluctoid didn't become any recognised gender when it reverted. It was merely a transparent, humanoid shell.'

'Unfortunately, I cannot offer any guidance Commander. The only positive is the lack of corpses elsewhere in the galaxy.'

'Noted. I'll contact you again if I have further information Kerran. Contact ended.'

With the communication finished Luapp looked around for Enegene. He could just see her in the distance and his irritation flared.

*How many times did she have to be warned?*

As she was coming back he decided to let it go without comment this time. Even so, he did a quick check on his mental tag to make sure it was the real Swamplander.

She sat on the mat looking across the meadows to the mountains beyond. Sliding the comunit shut he walked over and stood beside her.

'You seem deep in thought.'

'Just thinking ahead,' she said, quietly.

'To what?'

Keeping her attention on the view, she said, 'to when I get back home.'

305

'You're missing Gaeiza?' he said, surprised.

'I'm missing work and mixing with my own kind.'

'You prefer work to the life of a high born?'

She looked up at him. 'That surprises you?'

'I assumed life in the swamps predisposed you to want wealth and status.'

Silence fell between them and she returned to her contemplation of the countryside. Luapp stepped back and leaned against the trunk of the tree.

After some minutes she said, 'I expect you're looking forward to being a guardian again.'

Ignoring her question he said, 'you can keep in contact with Aylisha when you return home.'

She stood up and straightened her dress. Giving him a dark look, she said, 'you mind tapping Nostowe?'

'Observing.'

'Do you have a female in mind for a life partner?'

'No.'

She leaned on the tree next to him. 'Casual partner?'

'My personal life is not your concern.'

'We've shared a sleeper on and off for some time. I think I should be allowed a little insight into your life.'

His expression hardened. 'The total hours of sharing are eight hundred.'

'Typical of you to be counting... but eight hundred hours is enough to wreck a relationship.'

'Fortunately, there's no relationship to wreck. I remind you yet again we're not here for personal amusement.'

With a sideways glance, Enegene said, 'what have you got against personal amusement?'

'It makes you careless.'

'An ordinary male is supposed to be beneath the uniform. Not with you Nostowe, guardian code is imbedded in your brain.' She walked a short pace ahead and stopped looking across the valley.

Her words irritated him more than he could account for. Pushing off from the tree he looked down to where the Drifter was slowing to a stop.

'Shall we return? Our reason for being here is finished.' He picked up the mat and began folding it.

Enegene turned to face him. 'I want to clarify something.'

He stopped folding the mat and focussed on her.

'Do I get a reward for this operation? Assuming of course I survive it.'

With a trace of exasperation, he said, 'you've already had ten thousand syscred, a dwelling worth several thousand syscred, wealth to cover your stay and servants. What more do you want?'

Picking up the picnic basket he laid the mat on it.

'I'm building a mound here. When we go I'll have to leave it. Am I entitled to keep the value?'

He considered her question for a moment. 'There's no reason why you can't. While the initial bonds were bought with gems supplied by the guardians, if you reimburse the outlay, the rest is yours.'

Her initial flare of intensity faded. 'Guardian Control would agree to that?'

'The income is the result of your own efforts and has nothing to do with the guardians or this mission.'

Glancing down at the Drifter once more he smiled. With a touch of cynicism, he said, 'you could arrange for Aylisha to join with Jym. They could take your dwelling and servants and Aylisha could manage your business while Jym continued his work as an enforcer.'

Enegene stared at him speechless for some seconds. 'I know you're not serious, but that's the perfect solution.'

'Naturally.' He raised a brow and let it drop. 'With the returns and your Spyrian agency back home; you could reach the heights of social achievement once again.'

She slid him a sideways glance and noted his expression. Turning towards him she placed her hand on his chest. 'Why guardian, somewhere in here there's an emotion lurking, just waiting to escape.' Stepping back, she headed for the Drifter.

'Not if I can stop it,' he muttered, following her.

~~~

Back at the house Enegene went straight to her study while Luapp took the picnic items back to the kitchen. When the meal bell broke her concentration, she was feeling much calmer.

Sitting down to eat, she was surprised at how cheerful she felt after her talk with the guardian. Now she could look forward to returning home without regrets. She was even considering inviting Aylisha to Gaeiza after the case was closed.

After the meal, Enegene returned to her study while Luapp went to the loft. It was well past eleven when she decided to stop and go to her bedroom. Entering the room, she looked around for Luapp and was disappointed.

Nearly an hour passed before he finally turned up. Arriving by the bed, he said, 'wake up.'

She opened her eyes. 'I am awake.'

'There's things to be done. When I checked the monitor, it registered a visitor. I've been talking to the staff. They deny hearing or seeing anything. According to Sylata, there have been no callers.'

Enegene sat up. 'The shape shifter was here?'

'Definitely. The screen picked them up outside and monitored their movements as they went through the dwelling.'

'Where did they go?'

308

'Everywhere.'

'Looking for something?'

'Me probably.'

'Why you? Why not me?'

'They wouldn't expect to find you in the servants' quarters.'

'And then?'

'They came into this room, removed the drug and replaced it with something else.'

'But you've hidden the drug up top.'

She opened the drawer of the bedside table, and found a small glass cylinder. 'This is the same as the first one, why did they do that?'

'I took a sample and topped up the vial with water. I doubt they will notice the slight difference in colour. The reason for replacing it is to stop the enforcers from finding the poison.'

She put it back in the drawer and shut it. 'How will they get hold of it?'

'You'll call them tomorrow and inform them of the intrusion. Then you'll tell them about the drug being taken.

They will want to know what the drug was for and where you got it. You'll then inform them about Freewoman Chrona offering it to you. They'll want to examine it and it will be found to be potent but not deadly.'

'Does that mean she's the Fluctoid?'

'Not necessarily. It could be Pellan or an acquaintance of theirs.'

As the words sunk in she said, 'so there'll be just a couple of enforcers here?'

'Possibly a few more. In this society they treat the wealthy with deference. For someone of your status they would send a senior man and a few lesser officers.'

'Why are we doing this?'

'I questioned the staff about an entry and they would

expect you to follow it up by contacting the enforcers. I'm also suspicious the intrusion had another purpose and I'm hoping the enforcers will find out what it was.'

'Why can't you find out what it was?'

'Because I'm a slave. I might be a protector, but in the Black Systems that generally means stopping anyone physically attacking you. The staff and enforcers, with the exclusions of Jym and Ghan, wouldn't expect me to be able to detect the real reason for the entry.'

'You don't have any idea why they entered?' Enegene said sceptically.

'As it was the Fluctoid that entered, and two of its efforts to kill you have failed, I would expect this to be another attempt on your life in some way or another.'

Frowning, she said, 'will I be safe tonight?'

'Anyone trying to enter while I'm here will be stopped.'

'I know I agreed to be the victim, but the persistence of this multislayer is beginning to wear my nerves.'

'That's understandable, but I'm sure Jym's officers will be able to find anything the multislayer did while they were here.'

'And what's my excuse for not calling them today?'

'Tell them you didn't realise anything had happened until you tried to use the drug last night. When I failed to respond in the expected way, you realised the drug had been changed.'

He stood up and turned to go.

'Where are you going now?'

'I'll leave you to sleep and return in the morning.'

'You think I'll sleep after this?' she said, staring up at him.

'The scanners showed the Fluctoid leaving and the detector alarms are set. If it tries to return we'll know about it.'

'If you don't stay here, I'm going to sleep with you in your room,' she said, stubbornly.

After some consideration, he said, 'I understand your anxiety. I'll help you to sleep – '

'You're not going to leave me.'

'I'll remain. I'll get some fresh clothes for tomorrow and return.'

Enegene slid under the covers as Luapp went through the passageway to his bedroom. He returned minus his top clothes and carrying the fresh set. Laying them on the chair, he got in the bed and moved close to her.

'Relax, you won't feel a thing.'

His gentle touch was warm and reassuring as he pressed two fingers against her temples. He closed his eyes as his mind travelled the neural pathways of her brain. Reaching the correct place, he inserted the order to sleep until Cleona arrived in the morning.

As he removed his fingers she said, 'is it done?'

'Yes. I've inserted a few instructions so your unease will appear genuine.'

'That wasn't necessary. My unease is definitely genuine and will still be genuine tomorrow.'

'The Fluctoid will do nothing while I'm here to protect you. I'm going to do a mind and body relaxation procedure, so kindly don't disturb me.'

He lay back, pulled the covers up to his shoulders and closed his eyes. A short while later, his breathing became soft and regulated.

Enegene lay on her side watching him fall asleep. Even with him beside her it was several hours before her eyes became heavy.

With her last thoughts being about the purpose of the Fluctoid's entry into the house, she finally lost the fight to remain conscious.

## Chapter 18

Jym was waiting outside the bathroom for Enegene to emerge. She was kneeling on the floor vomiting violently. Looking around the room, he cast the occasional glance at the pathologist examining Luapp on the bed.

Entering the house after the hysterical call from Sylata, he'd spoken to her briefly and then rushed upstairs. She remained in the doorway, dabbing her eyes as she watched the procession of professional bodies marching up behind him.

The rest of the servants stood in silent disbelief in the hall as Eura Ghan interviewed Cleona in the lounge. Police were everywhere.

Jym's officers had started in the bedroom and spread through the house with their hand-held DNA detectors, print copiers and evidence scanners.

Others were taking fingerprints to eliminate the servants from the ones found around the room. Finally, the pathologist straightened up and packed away his equipment.

'I'm not an expert on Gaeizaans, but by my standards he's dead. No heartbeat, no lung movement and he's cold.'

'Time of death?' asked Jym.

'Judging by the body temperature, I would say about four this morning.'

'Any ideas as to what caused it?'

'There are no signs of physical attack; apart from that it could be anything. Until I perform a PDE I couldn't tell you. Do you know anything about him?'

'He's a sollenite slave who was as healthy as the proverbial stakna the last time I saw him. I wouldn't expect him to die in his sleep.'

Hearing the toilet flush Jym turned back to the door. Enegene emerged, clinging to the door frame for support. While she couldn't possibly look green, she certainly looked ill. The examiner pulled the sheet over Luapp's head and turned to her.

'Come and sit down,' he said, kindly. 'Let me look at you.'

Jym took her arm and helped her over to the chair by the window.

'I've sent for Lady Aylisha to come and be with you. While we wait, I'll begin the interview. Did either of you eat anything unusual last night?'

Enegene closed her eyes. By her tight expression, she appeared to be trying to control the urge to vomit. After a few minutes she glanced up at the medic scanning her, then returned her attention to Jym.

'We had our meal in the house as normal. We are both vegetarians, and the cook and housekeeper have taken courses in vegetarian cookery. Until today the cook has managed to feed both myself and my slave without poisoning us.'

'Did you have any callers?' Jym said, keying in the reply.

'I decided I wanted some fresh air and went out into the country with Mikim. When we returned, he said the alarms had registered someone entering the house.'

313

Jym looked up from watching the words appear on screen.
'Any idea who it was?'

'We don't know. The housekeeper said no one called while we were out, and no one called once we returned.'

'Why didn't the servants hear the alarms?' Jym said.

'They are silent; only flashing lights in a certain part of the house.'

'Did he find anyone around the property?'

'Not inside, and I didn't want him to search outside; I felt unnerved.'

'So your slave stayed inside with you until when?'

'We retired. I must have slept heavily because I knew nothing until I heard Cleona drop the tray and start screaming.'

'You've been ill since you woke up this morning; were you ill last night?'

'No. Cleona woke me with all the noise, and from that moment I have been unwell.'

'Any other symptoms?' the doctor interrupted.

'I have a violent headache.'

They stopped as two men arrived with a stretcher and the doctor directed them to Luapp. They removed him from the bed and placed him in a body bag. Enegene stared at Jym and he raised a brow. Closing the bag, they left the room.

With the body removed the police began investigating the bed. It wasn't long before one of their sensors picked up traces of the drug on the pillow. The examiner hastily took samples and then came back to Enegene.

Holding out a short-padded stick and a small metal spike he asked her for some samples of blood and saliva. As she provided them he suggested she go to the hospital as soon as the police had finished. He was about to leave when Enegene stopped him with a question.

'You will not open the corpse, will you?'

'I have to do a PDE; post death examination,' he clarified at her frown.

'There are ways to do an examination without cutting it open. You must not defile the corpse; it is forbidden.'

Glancing at her Jym said, 'it's their religious beliefs doctor.'

After a short pause, the doctor said, 'in that case, I shall acquire one of those new-fangled deep tissue scanners.'

Collecting his bag the doctor left the room. A short while later Aylisha arrived looking pale and distraught. Jym told her to take Enegene to one of the other bedrooms while the police continued their work in hers.

Helping Enegene to steady herself Aylisha led her slowly into the next room along the landing. As they left she saw Jym look around at the specialists working.

'Make a good job of it people,' he said. 'I want to catch the bastard that did this.'

~~~

Enegene sunk heavily into a chair as Aylisha pulled another over beside her. 'Kaylee... I don't know what to say...' she began, trying to stop the sob in her voice.

With her head resting in her hands, Enegene's reaction was not what Aylisha was expecting. 'Is the door shut?'

Aylisha looked around, 'not quite.'

'Shut it. I'm sollenite; my grief must not be seen.'

Leaving her friend, Aylisha went over to the door and shut it. As she returned Enegene put her hands down but kept her eyes shut.

'I'm so weak; I won't forgive him for leaving me like this,' she muttered darkly.

'I don't suppose he intended to die,' Aylisha replied, unable to think of anything else to say.

Enegene opened her eyes and looked from Aylisha to the door and back. 'I feel like a reactivated corpse.'

She could sense Aylisha's tension as she tried to think of something helpful to say, but Enegene spoke first. Lowering her voice to a whisper, she said, 'come really close and put your arms around me as if you were comforting me.'

Bewildered, Aylisha pulled the chair closer and wrapped her arms around her friend. With her mouth now beside Aylisha's ear Enegene whispered, 'don't react with surprise, just remain as you are. I fear the killer may be here.'

'What? Pretending to be a servant?' Aylisha said horrified.

Enegene took a slow breath in. 'We went out for a while yesterday, and when we came back Mikim said someone had entered the house. The servants knew nothing about it, so I was going to call the enforcers today…'

A sob stopped further explanation. Aylisha waited until Enegene was calm enough to carry on.

'So what happened to Mikim?'

'Someone wanted him out of the way; they put poison on his pillow. When Cleona brought first meal up he was dead.'

She gently rubbed Enegene's shoulder. 'But the shape shifter is in jail.'

'When we were at Cassida Vian's event, Inspector Corder told us it escaped from the detention centre. It could be here in disguise.'

'I'll tell Jym…'

'Inspector Corder wouldn't know what to look for, but I would appreciate you staying for a couple of nights to support me.'

Aylisha sat upright and spoke a little louder. 'Of course; you're in no fit state to remain here on your own. Why are you feeling so ill?'

'I don't know,' Enegene said, weakly. 'The medic advised me to go for an examination when the enforcers finished.'

'The staff are taking it badly,' Aylisha added. 'They are as shocked as I am.'

The door suddenly swished open making them both jump, but it was only Jym that entered. 'I've told the pathologist he will have to be as speedy as possible as Gaeizaan tissue deteriorates rapidly on death.'

Enegene looked momentarily bemused then nodded.

'I'm sorry for the disruption, Lady Branon, but owing to the fact your slave was known to be healthy, we're treating this as murder. Do you know anyone who would want to kill him?'

A movement made her glance at the door, then she returned her attention to Jym.

'Who could he offend? He was my protector, and because of that he stayed with me. The staff got on well with him. Freeborns in my circle never seemed to find fault with him.'

'There was nobody he upset?' Jym said.

'Only one; Freeman Pellan. When I arrived in the city the man seemed to be obsessed with me. He was everywhere I went. It was because of him I bought a slave for protection. He kept Pellan away and he didn't like it.'

'Can you think of anything else that's happened recently that was unusual?'

Enegene told him a revised version of the visit by Pellan's cousin, leaving out the part about them wanting to marry. He asked to see the drug, and Enegene told him where to find it.

A knock on the door interrupted the interview. A policeman came in and told Jym they'd finished with the staff, and the forensics team had gone. He nodded and turned back to the women.

'I want a list of all the people you've encountered since the purchase of your slave. We'll get back to you as soon as possible with the cause of death. His body will be kept at the morgue until the funeral is arranged. What are your customs?'

'We fire the corpse.'

'There's several good crematoriums around the town; Lady Rhalin will be able to make recommendations. We usually dress the deceased for their funeral; if you give Lady Rhalin the clothes, she will make sure the undertaker gets them.'

'There are some clothes on the chair in my room. They will do as he's being fired. As I'm going to the medic centre on the examiner's advice, we can take them with us and give them to the ceremonialist on the way home.'

'No need to take them anywhere but the hospital. Mikim will be taken there to be examined by the pathologist, and we can hand them in at reception,' Aylisha said. 'I'll call pap and let him know what I'm doing, then I'll go and find them, I won't be a moment.'

Enegene's thoughts were going around in circles, and Aylisha's return was a welcome interruption. Watching her put the bag of clothes over her shoulder, Enegene said, 'I must speak to the staff.'

The effects of the nausea were beginning to wear off and she could now move without feeling faint. With Aylisha's assistance she made her way down stairs.

Now the police interviews had finished, most of the staff had returned to their common room. Sending Lydian to fetch the rest, they waited for them to arrive.

She gave them a brief version of what was happening and then asked Morvac to bring the Drifter around to the front.

Half an hour after leaving the house, the vehicle pulled into the private entrance of the hospital. As the Drifter approached a nurse and a porter appeared and helped Enegene into the hover chair.

As Enegene was taken into the office of the consultant for alien medicine, Aylisha said, 'I'll wait out here.'

By the time the doctor had finished all his tests and questions, nearly two hours had passed. It was as Aylisha walked beside the porter to the Drifter, Enegene realised the bag of clothes had gone.

Back at the house they went to the lounge and sat in gloomy silence. It felt cold and unwelcoming with a definite lack of presence. An air of depression settled on them like a heavy mist.

'I'll go and ask for a hot drink,' Aylisha said, at last.

Enegene nodded. Her hands clenched each other tightly as her thoughts ran wild.

*What am I going to do? While Nostowe was here I felt safe, but now I'm responsible for Aylisha's safety as well as my own...*

*Why am I like this? I'm as nervous as a niawl, I never felt like this on Gaeiza, I was confident there. But on Gaeiza I knew what I was facing. This being with its ability to mimic anything and anyone reduces me to a helpless qiver....*

Aylisha's arrival interrupted the dark thoughts.

'The servants are holding a departed service for Mikim. They will be finished in a few minutes. Cleona will bring the drinks then.'

Enegene looked past her to the door. 'I feel guilty making them work when they are as distressed as I am.'

Moving closer Aylisha placed her arm around Enegene. 'They probably welcome the work, it will help to keep their minds off what's happened.'

'You are to sleep in the room opposite mine.' Then with a frown, she added, 'how good are you at firing weapons?'

'I have never fired a weapon in my life.' Aylisha said in disbelief. 'Am I likely to need to?'

'Mikim adjusted the alarms before this happened, so probably not, but I have one for you. Keep it under your pillow. The weapon's for a shifter. You pull the trigger and it stops

319

them from changing. Pull it again and it stuns them. All you have to do is aim it in their direction and fire.'

'What if I miss?'

'You can't miss. As long as you aim in the general direction, it will hit anything in that half of the room.'

Shifting sideways, Aylisha made a small gap between them. 'What about your safety?'

'It's unlikely they'll come back, they tried and failed. But in case I'm wrong, I have my knife.'

With a frown, Aylisha said, 'how can you kill something that can change shape with a knife?'

'It can't do it instantly, and I'll not debate the issue first.'

Aylisha looked around the room and hugged herself. 'It's cold in here.'

'It's psychological; it's no colder today than yesterday.'

'Maybe,' Aylisha murmured.

The door opened and Cleona came in with the tray. Sylata followed her and waited as the maid placed it on the table. As Cleona left, Sylata moved forward.

'May I speak, Lady Kaylee?'

'Of course, Sylata, what is it?'

'The staff has asked me to convey their sympathies on the loss of your slave. We all liked Mikim.'

'Thank you Sylata, and thank the staff for me. I hope your grieving is short. Mikim would dislike you to be miserable on his account.'

'We will do our best. Please excuse me.'

Sylata left and Enegene picked up her tea and sipped it. Neither woman spoke for some time. When both had finished their tea, Enegene stood up.

'Let's go to the games room; I can't stand this gloomy atmosphere.'

'Yes,' Aylisha agreed. 'Let's keep busy.'

When the meal bell stopped play they'd managed to waste most of the afternoon. Aylisha's mood had lightened slightly and she chatted about Jym Corder's visit to her house all through the meal. Enegene could tell by the way she spoke Aylisha was smitten.

After dinner, they went to the study. Enegene wanted to initiate Aylisha into the art of discerning a good buy on the shares market. But before they could get started a tab popped up saying she had several messages.

Opening the message store, she found news of Luapp's death had got around. Most of the messages were of condolence.

'I notice Pellan's is about business,' she said wryly.

There was also one from Pellan's cousin telling her to get rid of the drug as it was incriminating. The final one they read several times. It said: *The obstruction has gone, now for the quarry.*

'I don't like that message,' Aylisha said, with a tremble in her voice. 'I think I will keep that gun under my pillow.'

Even Enegene felt uneasy. There was no identification at the top, and much as she hated to admit it, it unsettled her. Saving the messages, she placed a sliver in the computer and saved them again.

'Come with me,' she said. 'I'll show you how the weapon works. Then we'll take a trip to town to watch a show.'

Putting the sliver in the wall safe she left the study with Aylisha following.

~~~

It was midnight when they returned from their evening. Both were feeling calmer and discussed the show as they had supper.

Instructing Mevil Sylata to lock up and switch on the alarms Enegene walked upstairs with Aylisha. She watched her go into her bedroom, and then went into her own.

As she changed and got in to bed, Enegene's mind was working. Leaning back against the headboard, she made a plan of action in case the Fluctoid had heard about Mikim's demise.

Word had already got around her circle of friends, and if, as she suspected it was one of those, it might decide to return to finish what it started.

As the second hour of the morning approached, she left the bed and went to the bathroom. While in there she heard a noise. Realising she had left her knife under her pillow her stomachs tightened. Still, if she could get in a sudden and unexpected blow, she could overpower them before they recovered and changed into something else.

Her stance became ridged and she tensed her arm ready to strike. After several minutes of waiting and hearing nothing, she eased the door open and peered out. Everything looked normal.

Opening it a little wider, she looked around the room counting the different pieces of furniture and looking for a shimmer. Nothing was visibly wrong.

With the decision to move made, she hurriedly left the bathroom for the bed. Sliding her hand under the pillow, a wave of relief went through her as it closed around the knife case.

Trembling fingers slowed her down as Enegene worked at strapping it to her arm. Occasionally looking up and around as she did so, she was almost finished when a hand landed on her shoulder making her jump. Fumbling the knife release loop, she swore under her breath when he spoke.

'I've just revived from one demise and don't want to end up in the corpse store again; it's cold in those drawers.'

Letting out a sigh of relief she spun to face him. 'What the qess are you doing?' she whispered furiously. 'I nearly ceased!'

322

'You nearly ceased? I could've ceased! Watch what you're doing with that flesh carver.'

'If you must creep up behind me like that...' Replacing the safety loop she relaxed.

'It's unlike you to be this tense Enegene; your nerves are normally tungstrung.'

'Ever since I bought you as a slave things have been going askew and it's wearing me down,' she said, hotly. 'Where have you been? Early evening you said.'

'I was delayed by several minor irritations, but I was here by the first hour.'

She climbed onto the bed and made herself comfortable. 'What irritations?'

'I couldn't get out of the drawer; they're not designed to allow anything out. There's a technician in the cooler whose convinced he's seen a reactivated corpse.'

Despite her annoyance, Enegene smiled. The thought of an assistant seeing a body leave its drawer was amusing.

'Why did you implant the instructions last night? Why not just tell me?'

'I thought the Fluctoid might have positioned more surveillance when it was here. If we discussed plans away from the servants, even in Gaeizaan, it might have become suspicious.'

'But why this... charade of ceasing? The staff and Aylisha are bereft.'

'It placed the poison on the pillow; therefore it expected me to cease. Obviously it wanted me out of the way before attempting to kill you again. By not telling either Aylisha or the servants, we have the correct spontaneous emotional reaction to such an event.'

'That's a rather callous view, Guardian.'

'Better callous than deceased. You can inform Aylisha

tomorrow, but not the servants.'

'Did Jym know?'

'I contacted him yesterday after I spoke to the staff.'

'He puts on a good show; he looked shaken when he came in.'

'Possibly because he doesn't know how a restoration works.'

'It was a risk. Anyone from the enforcers to the corpse store staff could have been the Fluctoid trying to make sure it had succeeded in removing you.'

'A calculated risk. With all the enforcers, the medic and the official vehicles, it would assume it had achieved its aim.'

With a look of panic, Enegene whispered, 'but if it... '

Luapp smiled. 'I went through the dwelling while you and Aylisha were at the medicentre.'

'You were taking a chance with the servants here.'

'They were all gathered in the preparea for some reason, but it worked in my favour.'

'What happens now?'

'While Aylisha is here, you sleep in here and I'll stay in the other room. The slayer can't strike at the moment as the servants will be on their guard.'

'She was supposed to stay for three days, but I can get her to leave before that if necessary.'

'That will be just right. They're releasing me for firing in three days.'

'Won't they discover your corpse is missing when the worker reports what he saw?'

'I doubt if he's inclined to describe what he saw. He'd been consuming alcohol and questions the evidence of his own eyes.'

'Wouldn't he go and look?'

'Usually salations prefer not to know than find out what

they saw was real. I think he'll ignore it and hope I'll be there when they want me.'

'And no-one else will look in on you?'

'Jym told them we had traditions about desecration of the corpse. They included only one source search with a scanner. No one should go near the drawer until Jym comes to oversee my collection on the third day.

I will then be put in something they call a coffin. It's a casket they put their deceased in for burial or firing. So I have to be back in the drawer early that morning.

Once I've been collected by the firing director, Jym's arranging for the coffin to be filled with heavy combustible material ready for the ceremony. He's leaving a message on your intelmac so you know what's happening.'

'I've received several messages but none from Jym. However, I did get a strange message from someone...'

She told him about the message and added, 'it occurred to me later it might have been you trying to let me know things had gone well.'

'Unless they're putting script machines in cool drawers, I wouldn't be able to get to one.'

Raising a brow, he added, 'that puts a different aspect on contacting the deceased.'

Enegene frowned and glanced surreptitiously at her wrist band. In her experience, it wasn't like the guardian to make flippant remarks about serious situations. And at the moment, she didn't trust the mental link.

The non-answer gave her a nervous moment until she remembered he hadn't been vaccinated. When she looked up again he was going towards the bathroom.

'I'll try to track it tomorrow when the place is clear. Let's get some sleep. It's tiring being deceased.'

As he disappeared into the bathroom she closed her eyes

searching the link for an answer. It said he was Luapp Nostowe, even so she decided to be prepared. Moving further up the bed, Enegene leaned against the headboard and released the loop from her knife.

When he reappeared, she watched him walk over to the side bedroom and go in. Sliding between the covers she lay down, wishing she could lock the door.

*It's ironic,* she thought. *I've spent all day wanting Nostowe with me, now he is, I wish he wasn't. It must be the strain of the situation.*

Closing her eyes, she tried to relax and sleep.

~~~

The approach of a maid with her morning drink woke her the next day. Reaching out to the other side of the bed she found it cold and empty.

Moments later, the door opened and Cleona arrived with tea on a tray looking depressed and tired. As she placed the tray over Enegene's legs she didn't even say good morning.

Looking at the tray, it occurred to Enegene that Luapp might find it difficult to eat. Cook was only catering for two while Aylisha was there, and they had such an efficient storage monitor they would notice food going missing.

It was followed by the realisation that with cook, cooking for two usually meant there was enough for four. Pushing thoughts of food aside, her mind then went to recent events.

Their cover story had worked well. Someone was convinced she was a blinkered socialite and were now intent on doing her harm.

She finished her drink and left the bed. Going to the side room she looked in. It looked as if no one had been there. On her way to the bathroom she felt inexplicably depressed.

As she left the bedroom she met Aylisha on the landing. They smiled at one another and walked downstairs talking about the show. Entering the dining room Enegene was pleased the servants had left and they were alone.

Just as they were helping themselves to food, a quiet noise made them turn. Luapp was now standing by the wall.

Aylisha went white and stared open mouthed for several seconds; a potato cake dangling precariously on her fork. Enegene moved closer and placed a reassuring arm around her, afraid she might faint.

'Y- you're dead,' she managed with a hoarse voice.

'Obviously not,' Luapp replied.

'But why pretend you were dead?'

'Because someone wanted me that way. Don't tell anyone I'm still breathing except Jym.'

'Jym knew?' Her tone suggested she had gone from terrified to annoyed.

'He had to know,' Luapp said. 'I didn't want to be killed by the examiner looking for signs of demise.'

'I suppose not,' she murmured more calmly. Looking around the room, she added, 'where did you come from?'

'The passage.'

He joined them at the sideboard and pulled out a plate.

'What passage?'

'The house was built with an alternative set of corridors behind the walls,' Enegene explained. 'The servants are totally unaware of their existence.'

'Why would anyone want concealed passages in a house?' Aylisha dropped the potato cake onto her plate and looked in another tureen.

'For the reason I use them,' Luapp replied. 'To get around without being seen.'

Opening a tureen, he helped himself to the food inside.

'How are we going to explain the extra plate?' Aylisha said, watching him.

'That'll be my fault for not thinking what I'm doing,' Enegene said.

Taking their plates over to the table they sat down one end.

'Now I'm deceased, you might as well call me by my true name,' Luapp said, glancing at Aylisha.

'I've always known you as Mikim.' Aylisha glanced up from cutting a mushroom slice. 'I'll stick with that.'

Enegene placed her fork on the plate and smiled. 'Shall I call you by your real name, Luapp?'

He gave her a long look before answering. 'It would be preferable to the names you usually call me.'

Aylisha looked from one to the other. 'What does she usually call you?'

'Generally, it's unrepeatable.'

Smiling broadly, Aylisha said, 'you two are obviously well acquainted. I think you'd make good partners.'

'No,' he said. 'Our ethical outlook is totally different.'

With a grin Aylisha changed the subject. 'Have you any idea who the shape shifter is?'

'I think we can eliminate Pellan's cousin,' Luapp said. 'She told Jym she was blackmailed into persuading Enegene to use the drug. She doesn't know or is too afraid to say who by. Apparently, she was contacted by intelmac – computer,' he corrected seeing Aylisha's frown, 'and threatened with exposure of her ancestry.'

'And Pellan himself?' Aylisha said.

'He too hides a secret fear of someone, but we don't know who.'

'Where are you going to be today?' Enegene said.

'I'll work on tracing that message in the study. I need you to keep the staff out as there's no escape into the passages. The nearest one is the relaxrom.'

'You go there, and I will tell Sylata we're working in the

study and don't want to be disturbed until mideal. You'd better go; they'll be arriving soon to clear away.'

Luapp left the table taking the plate and utensils with him. 'I can deal with these,' he said, and disappeared through the hidden door.

A few minutes later Lydina and Farin arrived and Enegene and Aylisha left the dining room.

*Strange how things change,* Enegene thought, as they headed for the lounge. *Yesterday the house seemed cold and depressing, today it's comforting again.*

She tapped the call cube on the table and continued discussing plans for the day with Aylisha. When the servant arrived, she said, 'Farin, the Lady Rhalin and myself are going to work in the study for the morning, we don't want to be disturbed unless it is important.'

'Yes Madam.'

Enegene looked him up and down. His clothes were dishevelled and he was slouching. He was not the smart servant he usually was.

'Are you alright?'

He straightened immediately. 'Yes Madam.'

'Nothing wrong?'

He sighed. 'I'm not sleeping too well; none of us are. The thought that someone could break in and kill Mikim has given us nightmares.'

'I doubt the person who did this has any grudge against you or any other member of staff,' Enegene said gently.

'But what could they have against Mikim? He didn't offend anyone.'

'Somebody thought he did.'

'It was Pellan,' Farin said, fiercely. 'He didn't like Mikim.'

Enegene and Aylisha exchanged glances, surprised the servants had picked up on that fact. 'We must not jump to conclusions. We must allow the law enforcers to do their work. You may go Farin.'

As soon as he left, they heard a door sighing open and Luapp stepped from behind the tapestry hanging on the wall. He strode past them, checked the hall and headed for the study. Enegene and Aylisha followed at a more casual pace.

Luapp sat at the desk and the women collected chairs and joined him. 'I think the Fluctoid will attack quite soon now.'

'How soon?'

'Perhaps as soon as Aylisha leaves the dwelling.'

'Then I shall stay on,' she said.

Luapp turned to face her. 'That would be unwise. Their patience will only last so long. If you continue to stay here you could become a target. One more corpse will mean nothing to them. Jym Corder has arranged for your family to go away to recover from your previous experience.'

'Why?' Aylisha said. 'We've got over that already.'

'It was not discovered why the Fluctoid attacked your family in the first place. Therefore, if it decides not to attack Enegene, it may go for you or your family.'

Aylisha visibly paled at the thought. 'I think going away for a while is a good idea,' she said quietly. 'When do we go?'

'Straight after the firing. Jym is taking you to a secure property which has enforcers.'

Enegene placed her hand over his to stop him opening the messages file.

'While Aylisha is here I'm showing her how to manage my business. We can do that while you work on the intelmac. All I need are some print outs before you get started.'

'I suggest you change the name of your business. Anyone trying to forge your identity will then be in for a shock.'

'Forge my identity?'

'We assume the slayer acts for gain. If they killed for

330

another reason, it's been a remarkable coincidence each victim has been wealthier than the last.'

'True, but wouldn't the victim's relatives be suspicious?'

'The Fluctoid can change into the victim. If they can forge the signature well enough, no one will question them.'

'Only Pellan isn't wealthy,' Aylisha pointed out. 'He is desperately trying to scrape some wealth together.'

'As far as we know.' Changing the subject, Luapp added, 'what we need now is some diversion to get the staff out of the house without them asking why.'

'I can help you there,' Aylisha said. 'In just over a week the annual continental party is on. It commemorates the day the different alliances on Gathkara signed an agreement to live in peace. The whole continent stops work and goes out to party for a day.

By now the different states are putting the finishing touches to their themes and pulling it together. I wouldn't be surprised if the servants aren't making their costumes and symbols.'

'Good. Enegene can tell them she's heard about the festivities and wants them to go as intended. That will leave the dwelling to us.'

'They won't want to go.'

'I'm sure you could persuade them. It will give them something else to think about. Come and do your printout.'

'It will take me more than three days to master the business world,' Aylisha said, watching Enegene and Luapp change places.

'You underestimate yourself,' Enegene replied. 'Besides, I'm sure you'll get help.' Moving away from the computer, she added, 'I'll also leave you this dwelling. When you want one, you'll have one complete with servants.'

'I've no idea when I'll need a house,' Aylisha said, amazed.

'Sooner than you think.' Enegene smiled briefly. Glancing at Luapp she said, 'what will you be doing for the next three days before your firing?'

'There are several loose ends I want to tie up with Jym, so I'll be coming and going. But I'll be here by endeal.'

Taking her print outs to a shelf behind her Enegene gave Luapp access to the computer. Scanning through her messages he found the one he wanted and began tracing it.

The women moved their chairs to the shelf and Enegene explained in hushed tones how to read the sheets and find mistakes. Aylisha made a few feeble complaints about not being business minded, but stopped at Enegene's knowing smile.

'You can't fool me Aylisha. You're more enlightened than you make out. This is well within your capabilities, and if you need help, I'm sure your father will help you; or someone else.'

Aylisha blushed at the veiled reference to Jym Corder. 'I don't know what you mean,' she said, quietly.

Ignoring the quiet murmuring of Enegene's explanations Luapp concentrated on the task. Sometime later he linked his hands behind his neck and sat back. Noticing the movement Enegene turned towards him.

'Found it?'

'It came from the Benze dwelling. Unfortunately, we can't tell who in there has access to the intelmac. And we can't go asking questions without alerting the guilty party.'

'Perhaps Jym could get in there on some excuse,' Aylisha suggested.

'Possibly.' Luapp turned to face them. 'But I don't want to discourage their ambitions. The more messages we get the more chance of catching the scripter.

I must contact the Tholman. He should have replies from other enforcers about threatening messages by now.'

'What is the point of the messages?' Aylisha said. 'I thought they disguised themselves to lull their victim's suspicions.' She noticed Enegene's smile and blushed again.

'There could be two reasons,' Luapp said. 'Just to scare the victim more; this slayer delights in their fear. Or it could be to drive them to someone they think will protect them, but is in reality the slayer in disguise.'

Aylisha's face showed her disgust. 'That's horrible... just when they think they are safe, they find themselves in the hands of a murderer.'

'This person is mentally warped. They're not detached about the victim as most multislayers are. There seems to be a personal edge to their activity.'

He pushed back his chair and stood up. Enegene joined him by the door. 'Where are you going?'

Opening the door, he looked around carefully. 'To contact Tholman Gyre. Don't be concerned about the messages; words cannot harm you.'

He quickly crossed from the study to the lounge while Enegene watched. When he was out of sight she returned to instructing Aylisha on the business.

## Chapter 19

Over the next couple of days, Luapp came and went as and when he needed to. In between excursions to the city, Enegene continued to instruct Aylisha about her business and showed her how to watch the market.

Following Luapp's advice, she also contacted the bank. When she went in to change the business into the name of Enegene Namrae, she took Aylisha in to make sure of a smooth transition.

Shortly after returning to the house, she had a call from the police to tell her the cause of death had been established and they were sending an officer around to talk to her.

The women went into the lounge and were drinking tea when the police officer arrived. She was expecting Jym, but when Cleona showed the man in she hadn't seen him before.

Enegene watched him carefully as he crossed to a chair and sat down. The shimmer she was looking for wasn't present and her tension eased.

'The pathologist confirmed your slave died from cardiac arrest, but the PDE showed his heart was healthy,' the detective said. 'The conclusion is that his heart failed due to a drug administered by an unknown. This is now a confirmed murder enquiry.

The drug found on his pillow was an artificial mix designed

to kill sollenites. The quantity put there was enough to kill ten. You were extremely fortunate to escape with mere discomfort Lady Branon. Unfortunately, this means more questions. Within your social circle was there anyone you were aware of that disliked your slave?'

'All my friends seemed to like him. In fact, they liked him so much I was constantly getting offers to buy him. Only a short while before the incident…'

The questioning seemed to go on for ever but finally he left and she sighed her relief.

'I need to talk to the guardian about this,' she said to Aylisha. 'I'll leave a message in the study.'

'And then we can return to the games room; I want a chance to even the score.'

'That will be just what I need to take my mind off the multislayer.'

Leaving the lounge, Aylisha waited outside the study while Enegene went inside, then they continued onto the games room. When Luapp arrived some hours later she told him about the visit.

'I'll contact Jym, this is not a good time to take things at face value.'

They resumed their game as Luapp left the room. Three games later they returned to the lounge. Enegene had just ordered afternoon tea when he appeared again.

'Jym's confirmed he was a genuine detective. He said he wanted to send someone who was "outside the know", as he put it. Apart from the fact he's a good officer and will pursue the case with determination, he felt it prudent to make it look to the uninitiated highers that it's a genuine investigation.'

'Did he warn him about the shape shifter?' Aylisha said.

'Not in those words. He told him he was dealing with a psychotic killer who was an expert in hypnosis. And the way to tell if what he was seeing was genuine or not was to look for the shimmer.'

'That's about as close to the truth as he could get,' Enegene said.

'I'll go to the roof space for now. Tomorrow I'll leave before you rise, I must be back in the cool drawer before the firing official comes to collect me.'

'I don't like this part of the plan,' Enegene said. 'Too many things can go wrong.'

'Nothing will go wrong...' Luapp stopped and looked towards the door. 'I must go, a servant is coming.'

He went swiftly to the tapestry and slid behind it as the lounge door opened. Cleona came in with the tray, put it on the small table and left without a word.

'The servants are so miserable; I wish I could tell them,' Enegene said.

'You're the one I'm worried about.'

Aylisha slid forward on the sofa, collected the teas and handed one to Enegene. Next she brought over the biscuit plate and returned it. 'You will be on your own for a while. That shape shifter could be anywhere or anyone.'

'It won't do anything while there are others around. It'll wait until I'm on my own.'

'You can't be sure of that,' Aylisha said. 'You and Mikim said it has changed its habits, you can't predict what it'll do.'

'Although it's a homicidal psychotic it isn't stupid. In fact, they tend to be more alert than most, so it won't attack at the gathering or while the servants are here.'

Aylisha sipped her tea. 'If you say so,' she muttered and bit her biscuit.

Let's change to a more cheerful subject,' Enegene said. 'How did Jym's meeting with your father go?'

'Pap was pleased to see him...'

With the change of subject Aylisha became more cheerful and chatted about Jym's visit to her home until dinner. Finally interrupted by the meal bell, she fell silent as they walked to the dining room. Luapp joined them as soon as the servants left.

Enegene watched him help himself to food and walk over to the table. 'What are you doing after endeal?'

'I'll go to the roof space and wait until the servants retire. Then I'll come down and sleep in one of the spare rooms.'

Throughout the meal Aylisha aired her concerns about going into protective custody. She paused briefly when Luapp collected his plate and utensils, and continued as he disappeared through the concealed door.

~~~

On the morning of the funeral Enegene woke feeling depressed, and she wasn't the only one. She met Aylisha on the way down to breakfast and for once she wasn't in a talkative mood.

Their brief greeting included the reason for her solemnity. The fact that Enegene was going to be alone in the house for several hours after the funeral was weighing on her mind.

The food was on the sideboard as they entered and Luapp's absence made the place seem all the more miserable. Collecting their breakfasts, they ate in silence and then returned to their rooms to change.

The funeral had been set for eleven to allow the servants time to do their morning chores before coming to the crematorium.

Enegene hadn't issued invitations to any of her social set as she wanted a quiet affair. As the elite did not normally attend the funerals of other's slaves, she felt no one would feel offended.

Apart from the servants, the only other attendees were the

337

Rhalins and Jym. After the funeral, she was holding a life appreciation meeting at the house to which other acquaintances could come.

She took her time dressing and doing her make-up. Despite the ceremony being a sham, she couldn't help being affected by the occasion.

Her imagination constantly ran scenes of Luapp being killed by the murderer disguised as any number of people from the morgue assistant to the funeral director.

By the time she was ready her nerves were near snap point and she was pleased there was only a short time to wait. Aylisha arrived shortly after Enegene entered the lounge.

Joining her on the sofa, Aylisha said, 'that's bright for a funeral dress.'

Enegene looked down at the vibrant orange shaded dress. 'On Gaeiza the clothing can be orange or yellow; it represents the flames. What about yours?' She looked at the white, slim line dress Aylisha was wearing.

'It symbolises the purity of the soul.'

They fell into a sombre silence until the doorbell went. A few minutes later, a solemn looking Cleona came to report the arrival of the hearse. Enegene and Aylisha went in the front vehicle and the servants in the other two.

It was a slow drive to the crematorium and the women silently watched the countryside passing on the journey. The aircars pulled into a gateway half an hour later and made their way up a long straight path to a low-lying building.

Going inside they walked to the front of the room where a large, ornately carved casket was stood on a metal plinth. As Enegene sat in the front row, her eyes fixed on the casket. Aylisha sat beside her and the servants filed into the rows opposite.

'What's that?' Enegene said, her gaze on the casket.

338

'That's the coffin,' Aylisha replied. Noticing the floral display on top, she frowned.

'Will that be fired also?'

Unable to stop the smile, Aylisha said, 'we're not in the habit of reusing them.'

Soft, lilting music started up making Enegene look around. 'You have music at firings? Do you see this as a happy time?'

'No, it's meant to be contemplative,' Aylisha said. 'So you can remember the deceased.'

Jym's appearance at the row end made them move along. 'Don't look so troubled Lady Branon,' he said, as he sat down. 'I assure you everything is as it should be.'

'It had better be,' Enegene muttered.

Aylisha leaned towards Jym. 'Did you request the floral tribute?'

Jym scowled at the flowers on the coffin. 'No, I thought you or Lady Kaylee did.'

'Do you think I would send something like that?' Aylisha said sharply. 'It's disgusting!'

Overhearing the whispered conversation, Enegene said, 'why are you concerned about the floral decoration on the casket?'

'Because that particular design means... It suggests...' Jym started.

Before he could finish Aylisha's parents entered and sat behind them. As soon as they noticed the flowers a quiet discussion took place.

'What message does the decoration convey?' Enegene said, looking first at Aylisha and then at Jym.

'It's a comment, and not a nice one,' Aylisha answered. 'Anyone who knew you well enough to send a floral tribute, also knew Mikim was your protector slave, not that kind of slave. Although the design is not entirely true to the meaning.'

'It's still an insult,' Jym said, taking over. 'It suggests you hired him out for personal pleasure.'

'And the florists would allow a display meaning that to be placed on a funeral casket?' Enegene said, infuriated.

'Orders are taken over the audio, and messages in floral arrangements are an old custom, one that's almost dead,' Aylisha said. 'The florist might not know the meaning, or, when they downloaded the order they did, and tried to hide it. Probably that is why it's been changed.'

'As they'd taken payment for the tribute, they couldn't not send the arrangement as that would be theft,' Jym said. 'The funeral directors would know though, and I'm going to have a word with them after the ceremony.'

All talking stopped as the service official walked down the aisle towards the lectern. As he passed the coffin he noticed the flowers and pulled them from the top.

Reaching the lectern, he dropped them at his feet and was about to start when he stared at the back and stopped. Everyone turned to see what was causing the delay.

A group of Enegene's close friends had arrived and were moving to the seats behind the Rhalin's. To her surprise, Benze and Pellan were amongst them. When everyone was seated, the service began.

It started with a brief résumé of Luapp's life as a slave. He also read out some tributes sent by the neighbours, servants and the group that arrived. The official added it was a comment on how well Kaylee was thought of for the closest members of her group to attend her slave's funeral.

At the end of the service he pushed a button on the wall next to the lectern. Two more plinths rose from the ground with moving belts. They came up under the top and end sections of the coffin and began to roll. The casket moved along them to a curtain. It parted as the coffin approached and closed after it passed.

The official then picked up the floral display and dropped it onto the moving belt. He pressed the button a second time and watched it disappear behind the curtains. Satisfied it would be destroyed he walked to the back of the room and waited.

Aylisha whispered to Enegene it was time to leave. As they approached the back the official stepped towards Enegene. He led her to a small enclave to sign the death forms. Some minutes later she joined Aylisha waiting by the door and continued outside. Here she was met by a funeral bearer who handed her a china container. She looked at it, then at him.

'What is this?' she said, puzzled.

'The ashes Lady Branon.'

'Ashes? What ashes?'

'Your slave's ashes.'

'What do I do with them?'

Aylisha shooed the man away and then explained. 'It's traditional to scatter the ashes of the departed in a place they liked.'

'Indeed?' Enegene whispered. 'How would I know what the object inside the casket liked?'

Aylisha struggled to control the smile. 'Take them somewhere Mikim felt at peace. You open the jar and throw the ashes around the place.'

Jym came over and stood by them as Enegene looked dubiously at the jar in her hands. 'It's time to go Aylisha,' he said, quietly.

She looked at him, then at Enegene. 'Will I see you again?' she said, sadly.

'I guarantee you will see me again before I leave this planet,' Enegene reassured her. 'You'd better go.'

Engrossed in her thoughts as she watched them walk to an

aircar, Enegene didn't hear someone approaching from behind. When he spoke she was startled.

'Lady Branon, may I give my condolences.'

She turned and looked at the man beside her. Had it not been for the look of fear on his face she would have been truly angry with him.

'Freeman Pellan. What is it you want?'

He looked quickly around and lowered his voice. 'Lady Branon, I must speak with you urgently, it is a most serious matter.'

'We are returning to my dwelling - we can talk there.'

She started towards the vehicle with Pellan following. As he walked with her he scanned the surrounding area again.

'No! There will be too many people. I must talk to you and Lady Rhalin alone.'

Looking past his frightened face and seeing no-one watching them, Enegene said, 'Lady Rhalin has gone away for a while.'

'Gone? Where?' Pellan said, surprised.

'I don't know where.'

They stopped beside the vehicle and he looked anxiously around again. 'You then; I must talk to you. It is a matter of life and death.'

'You are being most dramatic, Freeman Pellan.'

'Not dramatic, Lady Branon; truthful. When?'

The driver left his seat and opened the door. Enegene scrutinised him closely and decided he wasn't glowing. Then she mentally went over possible dates.

'I believe there is a festival in a few days' time. The servants will be going to that. If you call the day after the festival, I will receive you.'

His mind flitted over the date. 'Yes, that should be soon enough, but I urge you to be careful. Don't admit any strangers into your house. Nor…' He looked around once again, 'anyone you are suspicious about. Now I must go. Don't mention our discussion to anyone; I will call in four days.'

He paused, and then said louder, 'my condolences are genuine Lady Branon, whether you believe it or not. I must return to my mentor.'

Speeding up he hurried off to a vehicle waiting in the park. Enegene stepped into her own vehicle and laid the urn on the seat beside her. As she travelled home she pensively thought over Pellan's manner. Even she, an untrained talent could pick up the emanations of fear coming from him.

As the funeral vehicle slowed to a stop outside her house, Enegene pushed Pellan to the back of her mind. She took Morvac's offered hand getting out of the vehicle and asked him to collect the urn.

Walking up the steps, she paused outside the door to compose herself. Then she entered the house and took a drink from the tray held by Sylata, and waited for the guests to arrive.

Shortly afterwards, aircars pulled up and emptied. The passengers came up the steps in small groups, talking quietly to each other.

Enegene accepted their murmured condolences as they entered and flowed into the reception rooms. She drifted between the two rooms exchanging pleasantries with everyone, but with none of the people she really wanted there, she felt a little lost.

The afternoon dragged on until the visitors slowly drifted away deciding the decent thing had been done. It was early evening before she was finally on her own. Feeling exhausted she told Cleona she would eat in her room upstairs.

The maid arrived with a tray a while later. Enegene hardly tasted what was on her plate, and finally, she gave up trying to eat. Taking the plate back to the kitchen she locked up and set the security screen.

Returning to her room she waited anxiously for Luapp to turn up. Much to her relief, he did so an hour later and she told him about Pellan's approach.

'From now on,' he said, 'we sleep in the roof.'

~~~

The next morning her eyes were unwillingly forced open. Her head thumped and she had a dead feeling inside. Breakfast was eaten in her room, and then she went down to her study to peruse her business dealings.

The servants interrupted her only to bring tea or to call her for meals. They seemed just as dejected as she was. After dinner, she noticed a distinct bustling going to and fro along the hall and left the sofa to look out.

Cleona and the kitchen girls were carrying armfuls of material and various objects. Noticing Enegene standing in the doorway, Cleona came to a halt. 'I'm sorry for disturbing you, Lady Kaylee,' she said, timidly.

Enegene smiled. 'I'm not disturbed, just curious. Is that for the festival?'

'Just the finishing touches, Madam,' the kitchen girl said.

'Please continue.'

Enegene returned to the room and tried to interest herself in the show on the entertainment screen. By the ninth hour she gave up and went to bed. Luapp arrived when the servants retired and took her to the roof. He returned her to her bedroom at six the next morning.

'Isn't this a little early?' she said, with a yawn. 'The servants aren't up yet.'

'Precisely.'

He watched her climb down the ladder, then opened the cupboard door and looked out. 'They'll be up soon and you will be where you're supposed to be.'

He ushered her across the landing and watched her get into bed. 'I'll see you later.'

Enegene didn't even turn to see the door close. As she drifted back to sleep, the click of the latch registered briefly and was lost.

She woke again when Cleona knocked the door. Rising to a sitting position, she took the tray and waited until the maid had left before lifting the lid on the plate.

When she finished the meal she went into the bathroom. While in the shower, she planned how to fill her days. From now until lunch she would work in the study. After lunch, she would spend a couple of hours in the pool, and then move onto the games room until dinner. From dinner until bedtime she would watch the entertainment screen.

*How hard can it be to fill a day?* she thought.

By the time she retired that evening, she decided she needed something more to keep her busy. It had been a struggle to keep mind and body active.

On the second evening, she was feeling exhausted after a longer session in the pool. While lying on the bed waiting for Luapp she fell asleep. Sometime later, her peaceful slumber was interrupted by a faint noise.

Being a Swamplander used to surviving on her wits, she woke straight away. Alert and listening, she heard it again; a slow release of breath, as if someone was standing behind her.

Sitting upright she turned to look. The only thing behind the bed was the wall. She frowned. *Perhaps I heard the guardian moving through the passage?*

Several moments passed and then it came again, only this time it breathed her name. It also came from a different location; the window. Reaching up her sleeve she released the holding loop and moved off the bed.

She was almost to the window when she heard a breathy

laugh coming from the slave bedroom. Pressing the trigger on her knife she felt it slide into her hand and gripped it tightly.

Engrossed with determination she moved stealthily to the door and turned the handle. With a slight push, she made a gap big enough to peer inside. A quick glance around the room showed it was empty.

Again the laugh came, and then she heard her bedroom door opening. Running into the slave room she hid behind the door and waited in the darkness.

Footsteps came closer and her grip on the knife tightened. Slowly the door moved back and then stopped.

'Enegene? Why are you hiding?'

Releasing the breath she was holding she relaxed and stepped out from behind the door. Luapp was standing in the room looking puzzled.

'Something wrong?' he said, as she appeared in the doorway.

'I heard a voice; it was all around me...'

She left the slave room and walked past him heading for the outer door. Realising he wasn't with her she turned and looked back at him. He walked towards her smiling.

'Your nerves are beginning to fuel your imagination,' he said, as he caught up. 'But this time, your imagination is correct.'

Before she could move he grabbed both her wrists and twisted the one with the knife. Pain shot through her hand and she dropped it. The glow around him was easily visible now as he began to change...

'Enegene...'

Her eyes flew open and she let out a scream. It was quickly smothered by a hand across her mouth. She fought to rise but was held down on the bed.

'Enegene calm down.'

346

He was sitting beside her looking normal. She stopped struggling and he released her.

'I - I was dreaming,' she said, peering at him through the darkness. 'I thought I heard…'

Only now she realised he hadn't actually spoken; he'd used telepathy. The breathy laugh came again and she stared at him. Twitching a brow, he sent, *'be quiet.'*

Leaving the bed, he moved around the room trying to locate the source of the sound. As there was now no noise he sent another message. *'Speak to them.'*

'Who is it?' She didn't have to try to sound terrified.

'Kay-lee,' the sing song voice whispered. 'I'm coming for you Kay-lee.'

Luapp honed in on the bed as the first syllables were uttered and searched around the headboard. Running his hands over it he stopped and glanced back at her.

*'Turn and look.'*

Kneeling up on the bed she peered over the top of the headboard. He pointed to a small ball shaped devise wedged between two pieces of the marquetry pattern on the wall. Enegene's fear evaporated and became fury.

*'Speak again,'* he sent.

'You can't get to me,' she said. 'I know you're outside.'

The breathy chuckle came again and stopped.

*'I think they've gone. But just in case, don't speak to me until we're in the roof.'*

He followed her to the linen cupboard and up into the loft.

'Do you think they know you're alive?' Enegene whispered, wriggling into the sleeping bag.

'I'm convinced it was merely a transmitter. If it was a visual, there would have been a reaction.'

'How could they place that? You removed the last one.'

'It would have been easy for someone to move around the

dwelling and put more in during the life appreciation gathering. We'll see what transpires.'

'I'm surprised they weren't suspicious about the first one failing.' Enegene yawned and lay down.

'They probably thought one of the servants knocked it off when cleaning,' Luapp said, getting into his own sleeping bag. 'At least we know they're still interested in you.'

'That's wonderful news,' Enegene said, sarcastically, 'it's made my day.'

# Chapter 20

Luapp woke in the early hours of the third morning. His mind was working overtime on the ease with which the Fluctoid entered the house and moved around twice. While it now considered him removed, and possibly felt emboldened, he was surprised the servants hadn't noticed anything odd.

*It must have placed surveillance appliances when it entered during our trip to the country. It searched the house suggesting it hadn't known we weren't there. It was just it's good fortune; or was it?*

*After seeing the shadow at the Grand Social gathering I did a complete search through two days later and found nothing. Perhaps I missed it..? Or perhaps it added them during the life appreciation gathering.*

Changing direction he considered Enegene's dream. *It was a symptom of her anxiety, but the voice was real enough. I'd assumed the reason for the entry was to conceal evidence; perhaps it had another purpose.*

*It's intensifying its game and I can no longer leave her unprotected while I have meetings with Jym, they have to stop.*

He looked across at Enegene sleeping in her cocoon. *Being bait worked better than expected. To be a lure for such a twisted slayer would be a mental strain on a guardian, let alone a civilian, even if she is a Swamplander...*

As she stretched and wriggled her way out of the sleeping bag he mentally filed personal concerns away and focussed on the mission.

Going to the hatchway he went swiftly down. He eased the cupboard door open and looked around. It was dark, still and silent in the corridor.

Quickly crossing to her room, he removed the pillows and put them in the side room. Then he returned to the cupboard and waited as Enegene came down.

*'Go back to sleep if you want, I'll be watching you.'*

'I don't want you watching me,' she murmured, tiredly. 'I want you with me.'

She shuffled into her room and he watched her climb into bed. As soon as she was settled he returned to the roof.

~~~

A light knock and the door opening woke her. Lydina brought the breakfast in and placed the tray over her legs. Enegene talked to her about their preparations for the festival but Lydina wasn't very forthcoming. She mumbled they were cancelling the event this year.

After rising Enegene decided to send a telepathic message to Luapp. The last time she did this he was close by and expecting her to try and connect; this time he wasn't. Even so, she would try using the same method.

Firstly, she concentrated on his name, then she sent her message. To her surprise, he acknowledged the contact and replied he would be there.

She arrived in the servants common room some minutes later and told Farin to fetch the missing people. Once they were all inside, Luapp could stand in the corridor and listen to what she said.

It took a short while for everyone to arrive. And then the room was tightly packed.

'I have heard undercurrents from certain quarters that some or all of you are considering not attending the festival this year. I will not permit this to happen. By now you must have made your costumes and anything else you need. Apart from being a waste of time and money, you all need something to lighten your lives.

No one will stay behind. Anyone I find here after the eleventh hour will be dismissed. I order you all to go and have a good time.'

She smiled briefly and was pleased to see some of them smile back. 'I would like cook to prepare some meals which I can help myself to. Apart from that no one is to think of anything but the festival.

'I'm going to my study and don't want to be disturbed. Please return to your duties until it is time to leave.'

As the servants drifted away Enegene left the common room heading for the study. Once Luapp managed to make it inside, they discussed plans to capture the Fluctoid and what Enegene should do if she encountered it on her own.

They were briefly interrupted by the bustling to and fro of the servants with their costumes, and Enegene went out to watch them. She'd left the door slightly ajar so Luapp could hear what was said.

He'd connected the Fluctoid detector to the study computer and watched it as they went in and out. This was an ideal opportunity for a shape shifter to enter unnoticed. Enegene was also watching for unwanted entry by checking her wrist band.

For the first time since the funeral they were smiling and chatting happily. Only when they caught sight of her did they become more sombre and quiet. When most of them had left

351

Sylata passed carrying some equipment to the door. Enegene followed her out and watched her hand the things to Lydina.

'When are you going?' Enegene said, as she came back.

She paused by the doorway. 'I'm not Madam. I'm not in the mood for it this year.'

'I thought I saw you preparing costumes for you and your husband.'

'You did Madam, but we can't leave you on your own.'

'I made my feelings clear on that matter Sylata. I'm ordering you to go. Get your costumes and enjoy yourselves. It's just what you need to cheer yourselves up.'

'But we won't be back until the next day,' Sylata protested.

'That's fine with me. I can look after myself. I'm quite practised at it. Cook probably left enough food for two.'

Sylata's doubtful expression made Enegene smile. 'I have not always been a socialite. On Gaeiza I work for a living. My father believed in learning to appreciate wealth. Go and have a good time.'

Deana Sylata went back to the staff room and shortly after returned with her husband carrying the paraphernalia for the festival.

'We'll be back about ten tomorrow morning,' Mevil Sylata said, as they left the house.

With a sigh of relief Enegene locked the door behind them. For the first time she noticed how the place echoed when the door shut. Returning to the study she expected Luapp to be there and was surprised when he wasn't. The detector was abandoned on the desk as if he'd left in a hurry.

His absence made her feel vulnerable, so she went around the house locking the doors and windows before returning to the study. Sitting at the desk she turned on the computer and a tab popped up telling her she had a message. As she opened it her stomachs tightened.

*Kaylee, beautiful Kaylee, you're wasting your time; I'm already here.*

This time the message didn't scare her; it annoyed her. She was almost certain they weren't there already, but she felt compelled to check. Swivelling the chair slowly she scrutinised each piece of furniture. Seeing nothing, she took the detector with her and went up to the loft.

Retrieving the weapon for Fluctoids she returned to the upper floor. She started in her bedroom and turned in a slow circle. Nothing in here. Next the bathroom, then the slave room. All clean. She made her way along the landing, carefully checking each room and found the upstairs to be clear.

Back downstairs, she systematically worked her way from the front door through all the rooms and down to the servants' quarters. The place was completely empty apart from her.

Her Spyrian instincts kicked in and she began to reason it out. Someone was watching from afar. Obviously one of the guests at the wake was not who they should have been and spy sights had been placed in the house.

*Had they seen the guardian?* she wondered, and straight away discounted that. *I doubt they'd goad me if they knew he was alive.*

Now she was thinking clearly, she decided she needed to get a power detector and find the spies. In a strange way, she was grateful for a useful task to keep her mind occupied.

It took the rest of the morning and most of the afternoon, but by the end of it she had found three spies. Returning to her study she found another message.

*I am waiting to strike. You will not see me until it's too late.*

Having done the sweep through the house, and knowing it to be clean, she wanted to send a message back.

*If they are sending to me, perhaps a message will get to them,* she thought. Sitting at the computer she made her answer short and to the point.

*Show yourself coward. I'm not scared of you.*

353

With a feeling of satisfaction, she left the room to do one more thorough sweep for spies. Returning after finding two more she noticed a third message.

*My eyes are blind, but I hear well. I enjoy a hunt, but I enjoy the kill even more.*

With an odd sense of gratification, Enegene input her reply.

*You think you are the hunter, how sad.*

Within seconds the computer screen filled with profanities making her smile wryly. She'd won that round. Whether this made things better or worse she couldn't tell.

Sitting at her desk contemplating her options she heard the door to her study open. Swivelling to face it she pulled out the weapon and aimed it at the door. At least with only one way in or out, the Fluctoid couldn't creep up behind her. Even so she was relieved when Luapp walked in.

Seeing the weapon, he frowned. *'Trouble?'*

*'Not yet.'*

Bringing up the messages she waited for him to read them.

*'Trying to unnerve you.'*

*'It had the opposite effect. How am I able to answer them in this way? These intelmacs are too ancient for the usual method.'*

*'Either someone has managed to attach a two-way extender to the intelmac, or the slayer is an adept intelmac technician for this society. I'll examine the machine shortly.'*

*'Do you think they saw you?'*

*'I expected some sort of surveillance device so I've been moving through the passageways.'*

*'Where did you go?'*

*'I picked up an urgent message from Jym to meet him. He thought they'd found a corpse fitting the method.'*

*'And?'*

*'It was a vicious attack with a knife, but it wasn't the same kind of mutilation of the multislayer.'*

*'How did you get back in here without me letting you in?'*

354

He smiled briefly. *'Don't think I'd let you lock me out do you?'*

*'What do you think of these?'*

*'I think you've annoyed them enough to step up the programme.'*

*'And what if I taunt them?'* She swung slowly to and fro on the chair as he considered the question.

*'It might work. Tonight would be a good night. They talk of ears. Have you found any listening devices?*

*'Only the spy sights. I thought they must be somewhere close with an antenna.'*

*'Checked for long range high frequency micro receivers?'*

*'Isn't this society too behind to have such equipment?'*

*'The general population is, but their intelligence service has things that come close. As in most societies, if they are wealthy or powerful enough, they can get such things on the sub-market.'*

*'Wouldn't they know you were here if they used those?'*

*'I'm extremely careful when moving around the dwelling, and even more so when I leave it. Besides, they only work through windows not walls.'*

*'I think I'll do a sweep,'* she sent, rising from the seat.

*'I have a wave disrupter in the loft; I'll put it on and see if we get a response. Until then, we communicate in this way. Stay here.'*

A short while after he left, the screen came to life again. *You are more intelligent than the others; this has been an interesting experience. Such a pity to cut it short.*

Swivelling to face the screen she keyed in her reply. *I'm waiting for you; your blood will be spilled before mine.*

Heated words appeared on the screen followed by; *you are an arrogant asinine insignificance. You will scream for mercy before you die.*

*Only through my laughter,* she keyed.

The next message made her eyebrows rise with the foul language. Luapp returned and she pointed it out. His expression remained impassive but he sent; *'I sympathise with the sentiment if not with the vocabulary.'*

355

Enegene smirked. *'You sure you didn't send this, Guardian?'*

*'I would not script such profanities over the mesh.'*

*'I don't know what half of these words mean, although I could guess.'*

*Fortunate. Kindly move so I can use the intelmac.'*

Sitting down he instigated the programme he'd previously put onto the machine. After a few moments, the screen came alive again.

*Who is with you? Who is controlling the computer? You are too witless to do this.*

Ignoring the text, he continued working on the programme.

*Answer me. Answer me. I will make you regret crossing me. You will be sorry you set foot on this planet. I will be exercising my talents on your useless carcass soon. My -*

Enegene stood behind him reading the screen over his shoulder. *'Why have they stopped?'*

*'They knew I could track them if they continued. But the programme tracks the source machine whether they are on it or not.'*

He sat back watching the blank screen. Enegene felt calmer knowing that not only were they not in the house, now they could no longer see and hear what was going on. Added to that, she managed to incense them.

A street map image flicked onto the screen. It showed the search in the manner of a red line travelling up the road. At first it stuck to the main road then it branched off and branched off again. Eventually after several divisions it came to a halt and lit the computer. Then an address appeared on screen.

'As suspected,' Luapp commented.

'We were right,' Enegene said, gleefully. With a sudden sharp breath, she glanced at Luapp and then relaxed. 'I assume it's safe to talk normally as you're doing so.'

'The disrupter is working. All listening devises of whatever kind will be incapacitated, including the enforcers.'

He stared at the screen. 'Again, this does not tell us who in the dwelling the guilty party is.'

'Have profiles been taken of those occupying the premises?'

'Quite a few. Jym managed to obtain them when questioning Benze about my demise. But only those of Benze and Pellan were found here. Naturally they had legitimate reasons for being here.'

He turned towards her and stood up. 'Tonight is probably the night,' he said, and left the room.

Enegene went with him to the kitchen and they helped themselves to food. 'What else were you doing today while I was left alone and vulnerable?'

Carrying their meal into the dining room they sat down to eat. 'Surely viewing a corpse didn't take all day?'

'You were neither alone nor at risk. An intelligence officer came in and watched the monitors while I was out.'

'You mean there was a stranger in the dwelling and I didn't know? Where was he hiding?'

'He thought it prudent to remain unseen as I warned him about your skill with a knife.'

Enegene gave Luapp a glare. 'I used the detector.'

'It's set for Fluctoids, not Pedantans.'

'You didn't answer my question,' she said, stabbing a piece of vegetable roll.

'I was discussing Fluctoids and Pellan with Tholman Gyre,' Luapp replied, cutting the roll.

'Why?'

'If the slayer is not Pellan himself, they have a connection to Pellan. The line of murders has followed his travels closely. It occurred to me Pellan might have met a Fluctoid previously. It seems he had. His father had a placement on a Fluctoid planet for three orbits. Strangely it does not appear on his file.'

357

'So you think the Fluctoid is stalking Pellan?'

'That would suggest it has designs on him. If so, why hasn't it killed him? It's had plenty of opportunity to do so.'

'Maybe not. It could just want to control or frighten him. Or it could point to Pellan helping the slayer for some reason. That would explain its ability to act like him…' She sipped her juice. 'Do you think the files were altered?'

'On the matter of looking like him, it managed to look and act like people the victims knew wherever it went. It suggests someone with a recorder memory or who has the time to study the victim. Personally, I assume it's the second. As for the files, it's a possibility.'

'If Pellan spent time on a Fluctoid planet they had plenty of time to study him. Not too hard for a shape changer I suppose.'

'The other area of discussion was Benze. We knew she was probably not the person named in the demise documents, but I wanted to confirm she was a relative of the former owner.'

'Using biotech?'

'Naturally. The female that arrived here two orbits ago was related to the owner. She was a grandchild.'

'Two orbits? But I thought she arrived not long before me.'

'That was the impression given. She'd been on the planet on several occasions visiting her grandfather before he ceased and was well known to him.

Shortly after he ceased and she inherited, she left Pedanta for another planet on business. It was while she was on this planet she became the benefactor of Pellan.'

'Do you know where she went?'

Luapp smiled. 'To Landrac.'

'Landrac? Isn't that the last planet of the chain?'

'Exactly so.'

Enegene lay down her utensils. 'So Benze travelled outside

the Black Systems and she met Pellan on Landrac.' She noted his brow twitch as she continued eating. 'And up to that point she was who she was supposed to be.'

'Shortly after meeting Pellan she told him she had a business meeting and would be gone for a day. In fact, she was gone for three days. Then she collected Pellan and returned here.'

'Where did she go in those three days?'

'She travelled to a small town in the state of Curt as she had a meeting with the manager of a mining company. She wanted to buy his mines, and he was willing to sell. With business concluded they were due to meet for a meal but she didn't turn up.

He alerted the enforcers, and they found her unconscious in an alley. She was taken to a medic centre but only suffered superficial bruising and concussion. She was discharged the next day.

When she met with the law speakers  to finalise the details there were problems. Her speaker did not want to complete the deal, saying Benze seemed confused and "unlike" herself. In fact, she couldn't even sign her name correctly. He was concerned she didn't understand the implications of the deal.

The next day they met again, this time the papers were signed without concern. The conclusion was she was still suffering from concussion.'

'Possibly the terminator struck and took her place,' Enegene said. 'Has her corpse been found?'

'Until now they didn't know there was a corpse to look for, but the search is on.'

'And Pellan wouldn't suspect a thing because he didn't know her that well.'

'The question is, did she slay to get to Pellan, or is he just a side line and the wealth was what she was after?'

'I would say to get him,' Enegene said. 'She – he - it has followed him across the galaxy.'

'That could be because he can attract wealthy females, and it's just following a fortune finder.'

'The Tholman managed to get all this?' Enegene said, surprised.

'Some of it's on Pellan's travel documents. He had to have a benefactor or he couldn't stay on Pedanta. When they arrived, Benze had to confirm he was her attachment.'

'But what about Pellan coming to see me tomorrow?'

'That's another reason for it to attack tonight,' Luapp said. 'You said he seemed scared and stressed urgency. If Pellan has somehow discovered the truth, they will want to get rid of you before he speaks to you. Or, if Pellan is the terminator, it could be a way to determine whether you can see through his disguise.'

'How could Pellan be the slayer? The law speaker said she was unlike herself; he didn't mention Pellan.'

'The law speaker didn't meet Pellan. Benze could have been still alive and hidden somewhere at that point. If the Fluctoid decided the law speaker was going to be a problem, it might have got rid of Pellan and returned Benze.'

'I looked for the glow, he was normal,' Enegene said thoughtfully. 'But if it's not him, why not kill Pellan?'

'It's a good question. If wealth were the only motivation, they could have found much wealthier prey elsewhere. But if Pellan is the goal, it would explain why the line of cessations follow his travels across the galaxy.'

'And having found out, Pellan realised that by telling Benze I was to be his benefactor…'

'He placed you in danger.'

Luapp frowned and rested his arms on the table. 'I'm concerned; I rely on my instincts, all guardians do. It tells me

Pellan is not a slayer. A syscred seeker perhaps, but not the cold, hate filled being that slaughtered those females. If he was, he would not have been intimidated when I challenged him.'

'Such people can be good dramatists.' Enegene collected her plate and cup. 'That's how they escape detection for so long, they are a completely different personality.'

'Yes, but generally that's because they suffer a medical or mental condition.' Luapp collected his plate and glass. 'Normally, they have something that gives them away. In this being's case I would have expected an underlying resolve. Even if they acted scared of my actions there would be an inner resistance.

I was an inconvenience, nothing to bother about. Merely doing my owner's bidding and as such something to be circumvented. If he/she could have got to you without slaying me they would have. They tried once. Having failed, they realised I would be even harder to get past, so I had to be removed.'

'Surely, when I was attacked Benze didn't know I was going to be the next benefactor, or even if there was going to be a next benefactor.'

'You said he targeted you shortly after arrival here. She may have recognised the signs. Or, if it is Pellan, he was merely testing your willingness to accept him.'

'That's possible, I suppose,' Enegene said, standing up. 'Where does the Garber female fit in?'

She headed for the door and Luapp followed her to the kitchen.

'That's unknown. Jym cannot question them as even he doesn't know where they're hidden.'

'So tonight is the most obvious time for an attack,' Enegene said, opening the dishwasher. 'The servants are out and everybody is in town enjoying themselves. If anyone did come back, the probability is they would be so alcoburned they'd sleep right through any noise.'

She stepped aside. 'if they do attack what happens tomorrow?'

Putting his plates and utensils inside Luapp closed the machine and switched it on.

'If an attack takes place tonight, I hope to apprehend them in the act. The opening above your sleeper is covered in a thin layer of camouflage plastiform. It's easily removed with minimum effort. Once they've been caught we can clear up and you can explain to the servants tomorrow.'

She leaned back against the kitchen table. 'And after that?'

'After that there are some legal necessities to get out of the way and then we can return home.'

Approximately how long?'

'A towk.'

'That should be long enough to finalise my business arrangements,' she murmured.

'I suggest we retire early; it will allow us some rest before the event starts. The slayer is most likely to arrive late night or early morning.'

'I'll sleep with you anytime,' she said, with a wicked smile.

'Fortunately, we have separate cocoons.' After a pause he added, 'one of the things I look forward to when returning home is uninterrupted nights.'

She grinned broadly. 'Until it's time to go to the safe station, I challenge you to a game of blood hunter.'

'You're labouring under the delusion you can defeat me.'

'Not at all, I know I can beat you.'

'Before we do I want to check the detectors. You set the game up and I'll join you shortly.'

While he was gone, she collected the game and set out the

pieces on the board. The box caught her eye and she looked around for a convenient hiding place.

Luapp was bound to want to see the rules; that was the way his meticulous mind worked. Once he had there would be no chance of her beating him. With no obvious hiding place, she put it back in the cupboard and sat down to think of tactics.

Half an hour later, with a huff of irritation she went to the door. *Where's he got to? Typical of Nostowe to go missing.*

Leaving the games room she searched the ground floor and servants quarters. Not finding him there, she went up to the bedrooms and finally to the loft.

The glow of the monitor screen caught her eye and she looked at the picture. The bedroom was empty and it hadn't been prepared.

*Something to do until he turns up again...*

Back at the ladder she started down. Feeling for the light, her hand knocked something on the roof strut. It fell, landing on the edge of the hatch. Brushing it out of the way, she switched off the light and climbed down.

As she left the cupboard she decided to go back to the games room and pack the game away. After that, she went to the front door and made sure it was locked, and set the alarms.

Next, she went up to the bedroom and set the scene. Laying her clothes on the chair as always, she put a glass and the bottle of tranquilisers on the bedside table, and pulled down the covers.

Making herself comfortable on the bed, she looked around the room. *Everything normal...* She yawned and slid down the bed. After another yawn she closed her eyes and waited.

# Chapter 21

A persistent hum grabbed Luapp's attention as he stepped into the loft. Shutting the hatch he was vaguely aware the sound of it closing was muffled. With his mind on the monitors the diminished click of the hatch cover was ignored.

It was the thermo-detector sounding the alarm; it had picked up a rise in temperature outside the house.

A quick glance at Enegene's sleeping bag revealed it was empty and he cursed under his breath. If he left now, he'd miss recording the evidence.

Kneeling by the spy hole he looked down into the bedroom. Everything was set as usual except for one thing; Enegene was asleep in the bed.

After trying three telepathic nudges and getting no response, he then tried calling her. Still receiving no answer he sat back on his heels and considered the situation.

*Drugged? Other victims were awake when attacked. I can't risk her life for the sake of evidence; I must wake her. As I can't rouse her from here I must go down.*

He went to the hatch and pressed the release clip. Nothing happened. He tried again, but it refused to budge. He couldn't see a reason for the hatch not opening so he felt around the edge. As he did, something sharp caught his finger ripping the skin.

Then he tried another tactic. Pressing the clip with one hand he shoved the hatch with the other. It remained shut.

A slightly louder hum from the thermo-detector was quickly followed by the motion monitor flashing a warning.

Luapp returned to the machines and watched a heat shape on the screen change from an upright being to a pool of liquid. It flowed under the front door triggering the bioanalysis monitor.

*I've run out of time; if she doesn't answer this nudge I'll have to shoot it as soon as it appears and lose the evidence.*

He brought the duo-gun close to the spy hole, then concentrated on Enegene below. After several seconds a throbbing pain filled his brain with the effort.

A third beep broke his concentration and drew his eyes to the screen. The fluid had changed into a medium sized four footed creature.

As it wandered through the house, he went back to the hatch and gripped the ladder. Squatting on his haunches, he prepared to push down hard when he stopped and returned to the spy hole. Looking through, he concentrated again, then pulled back.

His mind momentarily blanked. Then, as reason returned he thought through his options.

*If I break my way out I'll probably be heard; my chances of subduing it would be greatly reduced.*

To complicate matters the guardian code came to the fore of his thoughts. **The lives of many supersedes the life of one.**

*If I'm killed, many other females will suffer a degrading and tortuous demise. Enegene knew the risks when she accepted the mission.*

He turned his attention to the monitors. They were

working on day sights so he re-tuned the small vision spies to night sight.

Outside the bedroom door the animal came into sight. It was a creature of the large feline variety. It stopped and listened intently. Obviously hearing nothing, it changed into a viscous fluid and oozed under the door.

Picking up the duo-gun Luapp watched the liquid transform back into a person. It became a green skinned being he instantly recognised.

Pellan crept over to the shutters and opened them to allow moonlight in. Then he returned to the bed and looked down at Enegene; an expression of sadness on his face.

'Why didn't you want me Kaylee?' he whispered. 'Every other woman did; why not you?'

The mournful countenance changed as his lips twisted into an animal like snarl. He knelt beside the bed and felt underneath. A soft pouch was retrieved and he pulled a fine metal collar from it.

After a moment's pause he thrust the collar around her neck. Her eyes flew open as she jumped and took a sharp breath in.

He clenched his jaw, leaned close  and stared into her eyes. 'You made me kill the slave,' he said at last. 'I wanted him alive; but you made me kill him.'

Pellan grabbed her chin and held it tightly. 'Whose the hunter now alien filth?'

Straightening up, he switched on the lights as Enegene struggled to move against the effects of the collar.

'What a shame everyone is out,' he added, sarcastically. 'As the slave is dead there's no one to help you. For that you'll suffer more.'

Watching the scene below on screen, Luapp adjusted the recorder's light meters from night sight to day light again.

Pellan went back to the window and opened it. Then he began to change shape; stretching upward and out. After some minutes he stopped and began to shrink again. In his hand he held a tool roll.

He returned to the bedside and swept everything off the small cabinet. Laying the roll on it, he opened it and studied the contents for a few seconds before removing some instruments.

While he worked, Enegene coughed and her eyes turned towards Pellan trying to see what was happening. Glancing at her, he smiled smugly.

'Don't fight it sollenite, you can't win. I've adjusted it to control your kind. Not so smart now, are we Lady Branon,' he sneered. 'It's your blood that will be spilt first.'

A grunt from Pellan drew Luapp's attention back from calibrating the duo-gun. His expression had changed from gloating to surprise as she forced his hand away from her face.

He slid more muscle into the hand and arm and pushed back towards her neck. But she continued to push his hand away.

Realising he was losing the battle, he frantically searched for a weapon with the other hand. His fingers finally found a thin spike in the roll. Using all his strength he slammed it into her chest.

Enegene's arms flung outwards and her body stiffened. As the rigidity relaxed she shook violently. Then, with a soft gasp she flopped limply onto the bed.

He grabbed her neck and grinned as she struggled to breathe. It seemed like he was going to strangle her, but suddenly released his grip and turned his attention to the tool roll. From it he produced a paper fine blade and turned back to Enegene. Forcing each of her hands open in turn, he sliced the tendons.

A cruel, self-satisfied smile touched his lips. 'Now I can work without interruption.'

He stroked her cheek with the back of his hand. 'Your pretty face is a good place to start. Every beautiful woman fears a scarred face; not that you'll be alive to worry about it.'

The gleeful sneer vanished when her eyes snapped open. She pushed up against his wrist with the heels of both hands. Although her strength was greatly reduced, she was slowly winning.

With a shout of 'No!' he wrenched his arm free. Pellan staggered back, sweat beading his forehead and his hair dishevelled.

Taking a few minutes to recover from the struggle, he leaned shakily against the bed. Then he returned to the tool roll on the bedside cabinet.

'I underestimated you sollenite,' he said, carefully pulling something from the roll. It was a cord of some kind, and he made a loop in one end.

He made several attempts to get it over her hand as she was moving it about. Finally managing to grab her arm he wrenched it down making it crack.

She gasped in pain making him smirk. Tightening the loop, he threw the cord under the bed. He hurried to the other side and rapidly looped the cord around the other wrist. Pulling it down hard, he tied the loose end around the taught cord.

Luapp put the weapon to one side as he again checked the machines. Satisfied everything was working correctly he returned his attention to the Fluctoid.

Pellan removed the sheet covering her and cut off her nightgown. Now his victim was incapacitated he relaxed.

Collecting a small flat box from the roll he placed it just under her collar bone.

'A little present from me to you Kaylee. I don't want you

bleeding to death before I'm done.'

Luapp watched in horrified fascination as Pellan pushed the point of the scalpel into her body and drew it slowly across her abdomen. A perverse look of enjoyment appeared on his face as the skin parted exposing the organs beneath. Next he drew the knife down her leg.

The wounds produced little blood ensuring the victim stayed alive and conscious throughout the torture. After several minutes Pellan put the knife down and pulled a small, sharp ended rod from the tool roll. Chuckling quietly, he stabbed the rod into her arm.

At times Pellan cut deep exposing intestines or bone, other times he sliced the skin just enough to make it open. As he worked he sang a children's rhyming song.

Luapp grimaced. *Thankfully it covers the stomach wrenching sound of nails being pulled from finger tips, and entrails being loosened from their connective tissue.*

Pellan interspersed the song with comments about the social set Enegene mixed with, adding crude statements about them and her. As she could utter no sound, the only outward display of pain was her expression.

The Fluctoid's face contorted with strange waves of skin movement as it worked. It's obvious enjoyment of the torture made even Luapp's crime hardened senses revolt.

A faint intrusion into his thoughts caused him to look away from the screens. After a moment's examination he pushed it aside and continued to watch.

Pellan stood back, smiling. 'You've lasted longer than other victims, sollenite, but I must finish now or I'll be missed.'

Choosing a long-bladed, serrated knife he grinned down at her. 'Let's see if I can get your heart out while it's still beating.'

'*Guardian?*'

The weak and barely noticeable mental call interrupted his

observation again. This time he returned with an abrupt instruction of; *'be silent!'*

The repellent sound of the blade ripping through flesh brought Luapp's mind back to the scene below. Plunging the knife deep into the lower torso, Pellan thrust up under the right side of the ribcage and sliced frantically. Enegene gasped, stiffened and flopped back.

Pellan swore and grabbed the box under the collar bone. Ripping it from the body he pulled several layers of skin with it. Blood flowed freely covering the bed and dripping onto the floor. Hastily jumping back, he swore again.

When the flow finally slowed, Pellan stepped forward and removed the internal organs. As he arranged them around the corpse, Luapp picked up the duo-gun and positioned it into the spy hole. He shoved down hard and fast.

The noise of the material pulling away made Pellan look up, startled. Momentarily losing concentration, his face changed to Benze, went transparent, back to Pellan and finally transparent again in rapid succession.

A yellow beam struck the Fluctoid before it could move. Its efforts to change showed in the rippling on the body surface. In the seconds it took for it to consider escaping, it was hit by a green laser rendering it unconscious.

Pressing his face against the floor, Luapp watched the Fluctoid for any sign of movement. He wanted to be certain it was fully unconscious before leaving the loft.

As the Fluctoid remained transparent he was satisfied it was immobilised. He collected the bag Jym had returned and a remote from the case and went to the hatch. After two more attempts to open it normally, he fell back onto the previous plan.

Gripping the ladder he smashed it down on the hatch. The brain jolting noise made him pause before trying again. It took

370

two more full strength shoves to make a hole big enough and safe enough to lower the ladder and get through.

The bedroom stank with the blood already congealing on the floor. Carefully avoiding the sticky mess, Luapp grabbed the fluctoid by the arm and dragged it to a place where he could work on it.

Securing its wrists and ankles he attached the small control box to the midpoint of its back with adhesive pads. With that done he went downstairs to call Jym. On the way back to the bedroom, he glanced in the study.

*I wonder where…? No time at the moment; I must gather evidence.*

Taking the stairs two at a time he went back to the bedroom. The bed cover was pulled completely off allowing him to record close ups of the wounds on the body with the remote. A light step on the landing was ignored as he added observations to the recording.

'Qess! What a mess, and what's that nauseating smell?'

'Flesh, blood and bodily fluids.'

'I thought it was just a machine…'

Luapp looked up at her. 'I explained it to you earlier. The external layers of the autotron feel like skin, hair and nail. It also has heating elements that bring it to Gaeizaan body temperature.

The internal dried simulations of blood and other bodily secretions became more realistic when water was added, so it smells like a biological being.'

'It did look like me when you activated it, but I didn't think he –; the changer would be so completely fooled.'

She slid her hand up her sleeve as she walked over to the Fluctoid. Stopping beside it she looked down. 'Why is it I can see through it and not see the internal organs?'

Luapp glanced at the being looking like an opaque

humanoid jelly and shrugged. 'I don't know the biological details of Ominarians.'

'Those antiquated wristlinks provided by Jym are useless. It could escape them easily.'

'Which is why I needed it unconscious. The initial shape freezing effect wears off in a quarter, but it gave me time to attach the molecular control box. That will stop it changing until switched off.'

'I could cut its throat and save everyone a lot of time,' Enegene said coldly.

Hearing a faint click Luapp stopped work and looked up to see the knife in her hand. Telepathically searching her intentions, he was concerned. She seemed devoid of emotion.

'It's in my custody and that would be murder.'

Enegene looked back at the mutilated body on the bed. 'Justice,' she corrected, rippling her fingers on the knife handle. 'Many of the planets where it killed have execution. I'd be removing the hassle of trials.'

'It's helpless; could you cut the throat of a being that's unable to defend itself?'

'It did worse than cutting a throat,' she snapped, looking up at him. 'That's quick. What it did to the autotron was sadistic.'

'Put it away.'

She glared at him defiantly.

Luapp turned towards her. 'Sheath it or I'll take it from you.'

Her expression hardened but she released the knife allowing it back into its holder. Walking past him to the bed she looked down at the autotron.

'I assume Guardian Control wasn't expecting this to return, it's not a pretty sight.'

With no comment from Luapp she looked up. He was

examining particular areas of the body and adding quiet commentary on points he'd noticed.

She grimaced as she looked at the pieces of intestines and organs draped across the body and bed.

'It enjoyed inflicting those injuries.' With a frown, she added, 'I thought this thing was only a flexicarbon skeletal interior with an outer cover filled with absorbent material.'

'You saw the digistils on Gaeiza; all the internal organs had been damaged in some way. A filled exterior wouldn't be realistic enough. The Fluctoid would have realised the moment it used the knife.'

'They weren't laid out like a garland around the corpses,' she said disgusted.

'It was your idea to goad it.'

She jerked her head up sharply. 'This is just a mission to you, isn't it? A puzzle to solve.'

He looked up from recording the scene. 'The knife is your weapon of choice and you're exceptionally deft in its use. Only minutes ago you were suggesting cutting its throat.'

'I suppose this has no emotional effect on you at all,' she retorted. 'Ice runs in your veins, Nostowe!'

'On the contrary; I'm pleased we've managed to stop the blood lust of this being saving more females from suffering the same fate.'

'But watching it attack the autotron didn't concern you.'

Luapp twitched a brow. 'It's a machine. It was created for this purpose. For the short time I thought it was you I was concerned.'

Her tone softened. 'You were?'

'Naturally; it would mean a flaw in the plan.'

Her anger flared as he went back to the recording. 'After all this time that's all I mean to you? A flaw in the plan?'

The sound of the doorbell interrupted further outpourings,

and she turned to leave. His hand on her shoulder halted her exit from the room.

'Go into the side room; there's no guarantee this is the only Fluctoid on the planet.'

'No vex guardian; it will only get the flaw in the plan.'

'Get in there now.'

Her back stiffened with determination and she glared at him, but she lost her nerve when he took a step closer. As Enegene went into the secondary bedroom, Luapp picked up the dual gun he'd laid on the table, went to the window and aimed the biodetector through the glass. Pressing a button, he glanced at the readings and flicked it off again.

The weapon was dropped on the chair as he went downstairs. Opening the door, he stood back bemused as a line of experts marched in. Jym had brought not only the local law, but forensics as well.

As he arrived at the bedroom door, froze. 'By the Gods!' he gasped, 'Kaylee!'

Luapp put his hand on Jym's shoulder and forced him inside. 'It's not what you think. This is a machine.'

Jym remained with Luapp as he watched the doctor go over to the body. 'So where...?' he said, the colour beginning to return to his face.

Luapp indicated the secondary bedroom with a glance. Jym watched the doctor walk around the bed describing what he saw into a recorder. Then he went over to the secondary bedroom and knocked on the door.

Enegene came out just as the doctor stood up to talk to Jym. The man went pale and his eyes darted madly from the corpse to Enegene and back.

Aware of the doctor's confusion, Jym went over and put his hand on his shoulder. 'It's alright, Frayn; you're not going mad.'

'But - but the slave died and he's back, now she's ....'

'All I can tell you is this is a highly classified mission. Lady Brannon and her slave are working with intelligence to draw out an extremely dangerous criminal.'

'Looks like they succeeded; twice.' He frowned. 'Wasn't once enough?'

'Unfortunately, due to an officer with too much compassion and not enough regard for orders, the criminal escaped after the first arrest. So they had to do it again.'

This... looks so real. Where did they get something like this?'

'Can't tell you,' Jym said with a tight smile. 'All we want you to do is examine it as normal and write a report in the usual way, leaving out it's a mock up.'

'For...?' the medic's eyebrows rose.

'Yes.'

Turning back to the corpse, the doctor added, 'willdo.'

Joining Luapp and Enegene, Jym grimaced. 'This is a gory scene.'

'Not as gory as watching it happen.'

Jym glanced at Luapp then looked at the Fluctoid. 'It looks male-ish.'

'That's just the shape it was in when I shot it. It could be male or female.'

'Then why the male shape?'

'Psychological ploy. Although a female will fight back against a male attacker, she perceives him as more difficult to defeat. If it was a female attacking, she would fight harder and perhaps even win.'

Jym gave the body another look then hastily averted his eyes. 'And why did it attack Kaylee?'

'Apart from annoying the qess out of it?' Luapp said.

Jym raised his brows in surprise and grinned. 'Yeah... apart from that.'

'It held her responsible for my demise.' Luapp frowned. 'That was a departure from normal practice. Otherwise no explanation was given.

I assume it has something to do with Pellan or Benze. He was coming to see Lady Kaylee tomorrow on a matter of life and death, so he said. We'll see if he turns up. For now, I'd like to clear this away and get some sleep.'

Jym wrinkled his nose. 'Have you something that will get rid of that god-awful smell?'

'Surely you've been near a corpse before?'

'Yeah; but not turned inside out.' Jym moved across to the other side of the room.

'I have equipment to clean the room and furniture and I'd prefer to do it before the servants return.'

'We're just about finished here.'

Scanning the room, Jym watched his team work. 'We'll take the Fluctoid with us and place it in the specialised cell. Then you can clean up. We would like the… body for evidence. If you could leave it on the bed until tomorrow I'd be grateful.'

'Why can't you take it tonight?'

'We haven't got a refrigerated van with us, and the mortuary is closed. Everyone's at the festival.'

'The sleeper's not refrigerated either,' Enegene said.

'Ah but the –,' he glanced around at the doctor by the bed. 'your slave has all sorts of natty little devices supplied by intelligence.' Jym smiled brightly. 'I'm certain he has something that will keep it cold where it is until tomorrow.'

'The servants aren't due back until the tenth hour, and we'll be up before then,' she said. 'Just to make sure we'll lock the room.'

'Thank you, Lady Kaylee, that is most helpful.'

Jym looked around at the various experts packing up their

equipment. To one side, a couple of officers were lifting the Fluctoid to carry it out. The doctor was shutting his case, and the forensic crew were leaving the room.

'We'll be going and I will personally make sure she - he – it's placed securely in the cell before I go to bed. I'll issue written orders that the molecule stasis device not be removed this time whatever it says. No more escapes.'

'That would be appreciated,' Luapp said, watching the team file out. Then he walked down to the door with Jym.

'You realise you can't charge it with the slaying of myself or Lady Branon as we're both alive. The most it can be charged with in connection with us is attempted murder.'

'I know,' Jym replied. 'But with the doc's and your recorded evidence, and the established method of killing of others, we should be able to prove it killed before. Then there's the attack on the Garbers and if we can find Benze' or Pellan's body...' he paused and smiled. 'Get some sleep.'

Looking up at Enegene standing at the top of the stairs, he added, 'both of you look drained.'

When Jym and the experts had left, Luapp locked up and reset the alarms as Enegene returned to her bedroom. After a visit to the loft he entered the room carrying bottles, a cleaning machine, some plastic sheeting and a bag.

'For a brief period I thought it was you in the sleeper; where were you hiding?'

'Why should you care about a flaw in your plan?' Enegene said, petulantly.

Luapp sighed as he dropped the sheeting and bag by the door. 'Stop behaving like an adol in a strop and answer the question.'

Enegene took the fluids from him, and walked around the room spraying the floor and furniture. 'You disappeared first; where did you go?'

'I had an urgent message from an intelligence operative. He insisted I meet him despite me explaining the situation.'

He followed with the radiance machine, drenching everything with a lime green light. Minutes later, the stains vanished leaving unmarked furniture and carpet with a fresher smell.

'Why?'

'One of the breaker politicians has started an investigation into where I came from. He's got as far as questioning the slave master, Goth.'

'And what did he say?'

'The only thing he could; the truth.'

As the bed couldn't be cleaned until the body was moved, Luapp placed the fluid proof sheeting under it. The ends protruded each side to catch any still dripping blood.

Then he took a pale yellow sheet out of the bag, laid it over the body and switched it on. Finally he picked up the cover and pulled it over the cool sheet.

'At least he can't question Langa Cha,' she said.

'He could request a meeting with him, but Langa wouldn't agree to a meet anywhere in the Black Systems. But I doubt he'll bother; we left a trail to be followed by any interested party.'

He stopped and looked down at the autotron. With the collar removed by the police, the grimace on its face made it look as if it was having a nightmare.

The head was turned to one side, the eyes open and one arm dangled over the edge with blood trails down it. Picking up the arm he placed it under the cover, but it fell again. He tried twice more to keep it under but each time it fell out, so he finally gave up and left it where it was, too tired to care.

Enegene walked with him to the cupboard. 'What kind of trail?'

Opening the door he looked up. 'I must do something about that so it won't be noticed.'

'What kind of trail?' Enegene repeated following his gaze. Seeing the hole and splintered hatch cover she frowned. 'What happened to that?'

'I had to break out.'

'Why?'

'Obviously it wouldn't open.'

He started up the ladder with Enegene following him. 'What stopped it?'

'I don't know; something fell and wedged between the hatch and the cover.'

He went to the monitors and shut them off. Then he returned the cleaning fluids to the large case.

'So,' she said for the third time, 'what kind of trail?'

'Before he sold me to Goth, Langa travelled around the Black Systems supposedly testing the interest of various governments to making an alliance with the Zeetan Collaboration. I accompanied him as his guard slave. There is provable evidence of me entering the Black Systems with him.'

Enegene knelt and rolled up the sleeping bags. 'I noticed you didn't come looking for me.' She glanced up as he returned to the hatch with what looked like a second lid.

'Looks like someone overestimated the hatch,' he murmured turning the square cut board over.

'How will we get up now?' Enegene said, as she passed him on the way to a case. 'The strap was attached to the cover. If I attach it to the step base, that will pull it down. We'll have to use one of Mevil Sylata's plant props to push the lid aside. We can get it repaired before we leave.'

'So why did you abandon me? Served my purpose and no longer useful?' Enegene said, joining him at the hatch.

Tying the strap to the ladder end, he said, 'you go down

first, I've got to pull the cover into place.'

As she started down the ladder her hand touched something sharp and she stopped. Looking around the hatch, she found half an object and held it up.

'The remains of a small person made of dried grass,' she said confused. 'And it has a metal spike through it.'

Luapp took the half and examined it. Then he smiled. 'Looks like the demon managed to make its trouble. This is the effigy you were told about. The spike is to secure it to a roof strut. Somehow it fell down and wedged the hatch lid.'

With a huff of disbelief, Enegene continued down the ladder. He waited until she was on the landing before starting down. Collecting the pieces of smashed hatch cover, he left the cupboard.

'I didn't abandon you. Lyndon wanted me to wait until his operatives verified what I told him about Langa's travels. I assumed you went to the safe station and didn't bother to check.'

He collected a chair from the bedroom and took it to the cupboard. Enegene remained on the landing watching him.

'As I got into the loft, the thermo-monitor was showing a shape. I closed the hatch and went to see what it was and only then noticed you weren't in your cocoon.'

He pushed up the ladder leaving the strap hanging down. Standing on the chair he pulled the board across the hole.

'Crude, but it will do for now,' he said stepping down.

'Go on,' Enegene said watching him return the chair and lock the bedroom door.

'I thought I saw you in the sleeper and assumed you'd fallen asleep while waiting. I tried bio-nudges with no response, then I called you. By this time the Fluctoid had come under the door and gone down to the servants quarters.'

Luapp stood in the corridor, seemingly confused. Enegene

gripped his hand and tugged gently. 'We'll sleep in your room tonight,' she said.

Following her to the brown room, he added. 'I tried opening the hatch and found I couldn't; even using all my strength, it must have been the awkward angle...'

She opened the door and watched him go in and sit down to remove his boots. 'Then?' she prompted.

'I tried another bio-nudge and realised I was receiving nothing from the being below. No thought, no emanations; it must have been the autotron. I stopped trying to raise you as it would be fatal if you came from your hiding place and met the Fluctoid.'

Enegene pulled back the cover and slid beneath it. 'I remember you telling me to be silent.'

'I picked you up by bio-speak but I couldn't be sure you weren't talking out loud. As the Fluctoid was busy with its torture I didn't want it disturbed.'

He removed his trousers and joined her in the bed. 'Where were you hiding?'

'I waited for you in the slember, but as time went on, I decided to set the scene and go to the alternative corridor. I hoped the Fluctoid wouldn't know about them.

I took a cover and my knife and made myself comfortable. I fell asleep but a muffled shout woke me. When I went to the observation point I saw what was happening so I returned to my comfort zone and tried to contact you.'

'You chose well. Now the excitement is over let's get some sleep.'

He slid down and made himself comfortable and Enegene did the same. Switching off the light, he relaxed and let out a sigh of relief.

'We'll be up before the servants arrive tomorrow,' Enegene said in the dark, and we can come up with an explanation then.'

As she snuggled close to him he was too exhausted to protest at her proximity and let it pass. Comfortable silence embraced them, and shortly after, rejuvenating sleep.

## Chapter 22

A loud scream pierced the air, swiftly followed by a bang and crash. Luapp sat bolt upright in bed, instantly awake at the first high pitched tones.

'Qessing salations! Why can't they do what they say?'

Scrambling from the bed he grabbed his clothes as the sound of running feet came up the stairs. With his trousers and boots on, he went into the secret corridor and along to Enegene's bedroom. At the spy gaps he pushed back the cover and looked in.

Lydina lay on the floor surrounded by the breakfast tray and its contents. Strangely, for a woman of her age, Deanna Sylata was the first to reach her. Returning to the bedroom he found Enegene almost finished.

'That sounded like Lydina.' She struggled to pull up the boot she'd got her foot into. 'How did she get into the locked room?' She tugged the other one on and stood upright. 'What's the plan now?'

'You go and show them you're still breathing; I'll follow after contacting Jym. I want to make sure the Fluctoid is still in custody.'

Going to the door, they cautiously looked out. With the day

staff having just arrived, it seemed as if every servant in the house was trying to crowd into Enegene's bedroom. With their attention focussed inside the room, no one noticed Enegene walk along the corridor and stand behind them.

Luapp picked up his shirt and went into the passageway. He hurried down to the lounge, came out from behind the tapestry, and quickly crossed to the study.

In there he finished dressing and input the number that was a direct line to Jym. Giving him a brief account of events at the house he returned to the passageways and stopped by Enegene's room. Moving the cover plate he saw her behind the crowd.

Deana Sylata was sitting on the floor cradling an unconscious Lydina in her lap. Mevil Sylata was standing by the bed, bending over the body. He was holding up the cover and sheet and peering beneath it.

Finally lowering the sheet, he looked as if he was going to be sick. The others were half in the room, seemingly unwilling to get too close, but wanting to know what was going on. Sylata stood up, looking first at the floor, then across to his wife.

'We must call the police,' he said, his voice trembling. 'The Lady Branon...'

His sentence went unfinished as he turned towards the door and saw Enegene at the back of the crowd. He stared wide eyed and open mouthed, then started to stagger. Farin rushed forward to catch him before he fell.

Aware her husband had been overcome, Sylata looked in the same direction, saw Enegene and let out a scream. The group in the doorway jostled nervously forwards, wondering what horror behind them was making everyone panic.

Enegene's expression suggested she'd seen enough and was going to do something. 'Move out of the way,' she said, 'let me through.'

The people at the back heard her voice and instantly began to part. As she neared the front, those that could see the body thought it was the police arriving, but went collectively pale when they saw who it was.

Reaching the inner room, she went over to Sylata. The woman stared, speechless with fear and confusion. She trembled uncontrollably as she held the maid.

Farin, still supporting her husband, also looked as if his worst nightmare had come true. His normally healthy bronze skin turned a pale coffee colour, and his eyes bulged slightly.

'There is nothing to concern yourself with,' Enegene said, kneeling in front of her.

The wide-eyed stare was unrecognising. Standing up and turning to face the remaining servants she tried again. 'Go back to the staffroom I will explain the situation in there.'

Luapp watched the people at the back begin to move away. This had the effect of sending a ripple of normality forward, and gradually all but Sylata, her husband, Farin and the faint Lydina were left.

'Sit him on the chair over there,' she said to Farin, as he struggled not to lose his charge to the floor. Turning back to Sylata she added, 'there is really nothing to be concerned about, I have not ceased.'

At last Sylata found her voice. 'But... but the bed...'

'Yes, I know it's a mess. We intended cleaning it up, but you came back too soon.' Enegene stood up and extended her hand.

Gently releasing her charge to the floor, Sylata took the offered hand and stood up. 'We?' she asked, weakly.

'It's a long story and I don't want to explain everything twice, so to you three I give the quick version. Mikim hasn't ceased either.'

'Not dead?' Farin said, 'but we had a funeral.'

'There is a reason for it all. Now kindly join the others downstairs. We will take care of Lydina and then explain everything.'

Mevil Sylata was beginning to recover. He tried his feet tentatively and found them capable of holding his weight. Experimentally putting one foot in front of the other, he walked to the door with Farin accompanying him. The three of them made their way slowly along the corridor to the stairs.

As soon as they left Luapp came out of the hidden door and picked Lydina up. He carried her to the room they had slept in and returned to Enegene.

'That went well,' he remarked, with a fleeting smile.

Enegene smiled back. 'Sylata believes in free walking essences. It's fortunate you didn't come out earlier or we might have had a mass demise.'

'Are they stable now? I don't want them collectively collapsing on the floor when I join you.'

'I think so. Hopefully Sylata and her husband are telling the others all is well.'

Further conversation was curtailed by the doorbell. They went onto the landing and heard Cleona talking to Jym at the foot of the stairs. Enegene started down followed by Luapp.

Jym heard the movement and looked up. Cleona followed his gaze and her expression changed from sad to horrified. Placing her hands each side of her face, she opened her mouth as if to scream, thought better of it, and changed back to a straight-faced stare.

'I thought you were going to tell the servants what happened,' Jym quipped, as he waited for them.

'They turned up sooner than expected,' Luapp said. 'And somehow got into a locked room.' He glanced at Cleona who hurried away.

'Naturally,' Jym replied, 'they're human. We always arrive

late or early but rarely on time. I thought you were familiar with human habits.'

'As you're here, you can explain why we engaged in this subterfuge without confusing them further,' Enegene said, happy to escape that burden.

'By the way,' Jym said, as they walked to the servants' common room. 'I've contacted Lord Rhalin and told him we have the Fluctoid in custody. He said they would be coming home today.'

Arriving at the common room, Jym went in while Enegene and Luapp waited outside. Several of the servants saw him but were too shocked by the day's happening to be surprised any more. Standing by the wall, Jym looked around the room.

'Thank you for remaining reasonably calm in what must have seemed like a repeat of terrible circumstances,' he began. 'There's much I have to tell you, so I hope you're comfortable. The Lady Branon and her slave Mikim have been assisting the police on a murder hunt...'

The explanation and many questions took well over a hour. Finally, the servants filtered out to start their various chores still in a daze. Cleona was sent up to be with Lydina and told to give her a brief explanation when she regained full consciousness.

Sylata brought a tray of coffee to the lounge where Jym and the sollenites had gone to discuss the mission. Taking a sip of coffee, Jym told them the Fluctoid was awake but silent.

'It's female and refuses to offer any explanations for its behaviour, but questioning is ongoing.' He sipped it again. The only reaction we got was when we asked her why she took Pellan's form to attack the Rhalin's and you. She said she wanted him dead.'

'I asked why she didn't just kill him herself. Apparently, she wanted him to have a trial, be found guilty and executed.

She had real anger where he was concerned.'

Jym looked at Luapp with a sideways smile. 'She seemed strangely sorry for killing you, but confirmed Kaylee had been the target from the beginning.'

'Any reason why?' Enegene said.

'No, she refused to co-operate further. Perhaps her own people can convince her to talk.'

When the doorbell rang a second time Farin arrived in the lounge. 'Mister Pellan,' he announced, stepping to one side.

Pellan entered the room, caught sight of Luapp and froze.

'Freeman Pellan,' Enegene said. 'Do you know Enforcer Corder? He's here in connection with an incident last night. Please seat yourself and tell us what was so important.'

He blinked, looked at Enegene, Jym, Luapp and back to Enegene without saying a word.

'I assure you Mikim is no apparition,' she said, tiredly. 'We had an eventful night and would appreciate a swift explanation of what you want.'

Pellan headed for a sofa giving Luapp a wide berth. Every now and then he threw surreptitious glances in the guardian's direction.

Clearing his throat, he said, 'Lady Branon, I have been most concerned for your safety. I was fearful that speaking to you today would be too late.'

'Too late for what?' Jym said.

Pellan looked at him with an expression of mild surprise. 'To save her life. I recently found out we were both in contact with a most dangerous being.'

'How did you find out?' Jym said.

'She told me. She's a changer. She said she was...' he shuddered, 'in love with me. She told me she had followed me across the galaxy. She'd copied the shape of females I became friendly with and... had them slaughtered.'

He paused, disgust and horror on his face. 'Imagine! She thought I could love a changer. My family abhor changers. Because of her ancestry my cousin has suffered terribly.'

'Your cousin is a Fluctoid?' Jym said, surprised.

Pellan frowned. 'She's descended from a Fluctoid. Her family lost the ability to change several generations back.'

'But you don't hold it against her,' Enegene said.

With a shrug, Pellan said, 'she cannot help an inconsiderate act generations ago.'

'Why do you hate Fluctoids?' she pressed.

His face set into an angry grimace. 'They're deceitful. You never know who or what you are dealing with.'

'How did you come to know this Fluctoid?' Jym said.

'My father was, is an ambassador. Because of his work, we travelled to several different planets, including Quarn, where this Fluctoid comes from.

He thought it would help me integrate with the local population if I attended their schools. But I was taunted because I could not change shape. Whenever I spoke to someone to confide my torment, they turned out to be someone else. In time I learned to remain silent.'

'Your father's employment file makes no mention of visiting Quarn,' Jym said, coolly. 'And your cousin told Kaylee Branon you were from a poor family.'

'You checked my background?' Pellan said, agitated.

'You're an outsider and we were trying to catch a serial killer,' Jym said, sharply. 'I was checking everyone's background and I don't appreciate false immigration statements.'

Pellan's skin darkened showing his embarrassment.

'Surely not all Fluctoids are deceitful?' Enegene said. 'Children from all species are crueller than their adult counterparts. They have to learn tolerance.'

389

'Mostly I have found the reverse to be true, children are accepting, they are taught to hate outsiders.' Pellan looked up at Luapp. 'Your slave should understand intolerance.'

'As a child, I was with other slave children and we shared common experiences. As an adult, I have been fortunate in my owners, but I have seen how other slaves were treated. I've also seen there are owners who despite their authority over slaves treat them well and with consideration.'

Pellan stared at Luapp for several moments taking in what he said. 'You're right, not all with power are intimidators, but I could never tell who they were. Some would retain one shape while I was with them.'

He sighed. 'I realise now that changing shape was as much enjoyment as deceit with them. If they got bored with one shape they simply changed to another. My father said it was much the same at work, but he had a way of telling who he was talking to.

Teth was one of the few I became friends with. We got on well until my father was transferred to another planet. It was then she told me she loved me. I told her, as gently as I could we could only be friends. I didn't say it was a great relief to leave her planet and hoped I would never see another Fluctoid again.'

'You may not have actually said it in words, but I suspect you may have passed on the feeling unintentionally,' Enegene said.

'Why was your father's stay on Quarn removed?' Jym said.

'He detested his stay as much as I did. There was some trouble in his office; he never explained what, not to me anyway. He removed it from his records and inserted a note stating he had done a double duty on Rys.'

Jym Corder looked up from inputting information. 'Who was your first female benefactor?'

Staring across the room for a few seconds, Pellan then looked back at Jym. 'She was called Micah Crass. With her I had true feelings. She was not outstandingly wealthy, but we enjoyed each other's company.

We were together for three years. Then she told me she would be taking a husband, and it would be better for me to seek a wealthier benefactor.'

Jym glanced at Luapp and frowned. 'I don't remember this woman on the list,' he said, quietly.

'List?' said Pellan, 'what list?'

'And the next?' Jym said, without explanation.

'There was a gap between her and the next benefactor. I was hurt when she told me of her impending marriage. For a while I decided to give up being mentored and worked in an entertainments hall. Then one of the dancing girls I had been friendly with was found murdered in a most horrific way.'

He shuddered at the thought. 'I'll never forget those pictures...' His voice trailed off as he stared into space. With a blink, he returned to the present. 'We had good times together for a few months before I met my second benefactor.

She was a widow who was slightly older than me. She was only visiting the planet I was on, and I went back to Jel'Lakar with her. After a year her attitude began to change.'

Jym glanced up again. 'How?'

'It was nothing major, just the odd response to a remark, or an unusual way of dealing with something. After three more months, I decided to move on.'

'And her name?'

He looked at Jym. 'Penia Yarth.'

Jym touched his note screen making it scroll information up then he looked at Pellan. 'I'm going to read you a list of names. I want you to tell me how many of these women are connected to you in some way.'

Looking down at the screen again he read the list. With each name Pellan grew more restless. After the last name he said quietly, 'what is that list?'

'They are victims of violent slayings found on a string of planets outside the Black Systems,' Enegene said. 'How many did you know?'

'All of them.'

Looking down at his hands a tear ran down his cheek. 'I didn't realise she killed them all. I thought she only found me two planets back.'

'You were coming to warn me?' Enegene said.

Pellan nodded then looked up. 'After the final social event, I suggested you were considering taking me on as your attachment. When I found out Benze was not herself as it were, I became concerned for you.'

Giving Luapp another curious look he said, 'why did you pretend your slave was dead?'

'Because someone wanted him that way,' Enegene answered. 'Your cousin provided the means; a poison deadly to sollenites.'

'Deadly?' He paled and his lips trembled. 'We were told it was different to the previous potion, but it would only cause temporary inability to function.'

Suddenly realising his cousin could be guilty of attempted murder, he added 'she was forced into it. She was told she would be implicated in a serious crime if she didn't do it.'

'She realised the implications,' Enegene said, unimpressed. 'She sent me a message telling me to destroy the sample when she heard of Mikim's demise. She is much practiced in lying.'

Frowning Pellan said, 'how did a lady and her slave become involved with these murders?'

'The Galactic Council advised the Coalition Master of the killer's progress. They informed him of their possible arrival on this planet,' Jym said.

'Lady Branon was the perfect candidate for a victim, but she needed protection in case we missed their entry into her home. We heard about Mikim before he got to the slave fair at Trhaan and arranged for Lady Branon to buy him.'

Pellan took a while absorbing the explanation, then suddenly looked up alarmed.

'But what about Antonia Benze? She will attempt to attack Lady Branon.'

'She already has,' Jym said, 'twice. And as far as she's aware she's succeeded. The body is upstairs waiting to be picked up.'

'But we don't understand why she attacked me the first time,' Enegene said. 'Surely you had not seen me as benefactor then.'

'When was this?' Pellan said.

'A couple of months ago.'

After a moment's thought, Pellan said, 'that was when I first asked for release from Antonia's patronage. I was surprised by her lack of interest. Normally she would threaten me if she recognised the signs of my restlessness, but she was almost... pleased.

Her only acid comment was that nobody ever left her; she left them if they were lucky. I took that to be another, albeit mild, threat and adjusted my behaviour. I suppose she decided you were the possible benefactor and attacked.'

'That being the case, why did she not attack again straight away?' Enegene persisted.

'I only know from that time on she seemed happier. Instead of asking where I had been when I came in, she gradually ignored me to the point of not bothering to speak at all. That's when I decided it was safe to leave and asked you to take me to that party.

As you know I needed finance to leave. I'd saved a small

393

amount from my previous benefactors, and as you were a successful estimator, I wanted some advice on how to play the markets. Obviously, I couldn't ask Antonia.'

He frowned. 'For some reason, you took against me. What did I do wrong?

'You were the unfortunate victim of a set of circumstances,' Enegene said. 'I was bait for a multislayer, and you kept pestering me.'

Pellan took a deep breath then let it out slowly. 'And you thought...?' He stared at her open mouthed. 'I am most apologetic; if only I'd known, no wonder you felt the need for a protector.'

'If you'd explained what you wanted from the beginning, I would not have marked you down as a potential slayer.'

'When you have lived with a species that can change shape into anything else, you are remarkably careful what you say to anyone,' he replied, sadly.

'Mikim was purchased to protect me from the slayer, not you. You were discounted as the multislayer, but there was interest as to what you did want.'

Pellan looked puzzled. Then a series of expressions flitted across his face as a thought came to him.

'You didn't think...? I never had any real intention of... Lady Branon I give my word...'

Amused at Pellan's fearful expression Luapp said, 'you never had a chance in that direction, sir. The gathering at Lady Kaylee's dwelling put you straight on that.'

'Antonia found that amusing,' he sounded hurt. 'It was then I realised she had no further interest in me. She was obviously working on acquiring someone else. Later that evening I asked her to scrap our contract.'

'Contract?' Enegene's brows rose in surprise. 'You draw up contracts for such things?'

Jym chuckled quietly. 'A contract is a term for a short-term marriage licence in this area,' he explained. 'Both partners agree on a set number of years, after which a divorce automatically takes effect.'

'All the women apart from the first were strictly business based.' Pellan sounded offended. 'They would pay my living costs in exchange for services I performed for them. But Benze refused to pre-set a date.'

'And what did you do for them?' Enegene said, fascinated.

'I... ,'

'How long did you remain with each female on average?' Jym cut in.

'Usually I would sign a contract for about three years. This covered a minimum of ten events, some off planet, which allowed them to make influential business contacts.'

'How did you know about the events?' Jym said.

'Through my father at his embassy. Most of the women, the real women, not the shifter, were pleased with my efforts and were willing to allow me to move on when I wanted to.'

'None of the females allowed you to move on,' Jym said. 'She was adept at discovering who the next benefactor was. Shortly after you were accepted, she lured them to some remote location and murdered them. Then she took their place and released you when the time was up.'

'None were real?' Pellan said, quietly.

Jym shook his head. 'She was obsessed with you. She was happy to let the contract run its course and release you, knowing you would be back with her in a short time.'

Pellan looked from Jym to Luapp fearfully. 'What about the first one? Micah? Did she kill her?'

Jym in turn looked at Luapp. 'You compiled that list, Mikim.'

'She's not on the list,' Luapp told him. 'Possibly you moved on before the Fluctoid located you.'

'You have Antonia in jail?' Pellan said, looking at Jym. Seeing the nod, he sighed and stood up. As he headed for the door he added, 'I'm free of her at last.'

'Where do you think you're going?' Jym said.

Pellan stopped in his tracks. 'To Kyrita, to tell her we're free to do as we want.'

'I have a few more questions first. Do you know a woman by the name of Cyna Garber?'

Pellan's face paled as he walked back to the group. 'Is she dead too?'

'No,' Jym said, 'but it was a close thing. Her husband came home early and interrupted the attack.'

'Yes I know her. She was the first one I approached to help me with investments. I knew her husband worked the stocks and wanted some advice. We met several times and she passed on what he told her.'

'So that's how you knew something about the bonds I recommended to you.'

Pellan nodded slowly.

'You will have to remain on Pedanta for a while yet,' Jym told him. 'I want to question you further, and then Major Lyndon will probably want to speak to you.

After that you will be required to go to the Council planet Padua and make a statement. Benze will be committed for trial under her real name of Teth…?'

'Harat,' Pellan supplied. 'Whose major Lyndon? I've never met him.'

'When you do you won't forget it in a hurry,' Jym said, grinning. 'When the trial has ended, whatever the outcome, I'm informed you'll be offered relocation and physical altering.'

Pellan's mouth opened but no sound came out. On the

second try he managed, 'will I be in danger?'

'You've been in danger all the time,' Jym said. 'Such a being is likely to be violent to the person they claim to love sooner or later.'

'But she's never attempted to harm me.'

'That's not the way I see it,' Jym said. 'I doubt you've gone through life without forming attachments to some of these women. Yet she has slaughtered them in the most painful and degrading way.

She's successfully kept you with her over the years knowing you didn't want to be and then she revealed what she'd done. It was her revenge for your lack of commitment. And from what I have heard, your life with her wasn't easy.'

'No, I admit she was difficult.' He frowned. 'Why didn't I detect a pattern of behaviour?'

'Possibly because you weren't looking for it,' Luapp said.

'And now,' Jym added, 'she'll see you as a betrayer. Yours would be the next name on the list if she ever got free.'

'Hence the relocation,' Pellan said, dully. 'Kyrita and I will carve out a life together somewhere away from the Black Systems. I will no longer search for a benefactor.'

'There is another possibility of funding,' Jym said. 'We're assuming the real Benze is dead. If we can find her body and confirm it, her will may be opened. If she's left anything to you, it's legally yours.'

'Blood money,' Pellan murmured, sadly.

'If it's in her final statement, she obviously wanted you to have it,' Luapp said.

'Did you hint at your feelings for your cousin in Teth's presence?' Jym said.

Pellan considered the question then shook his head. 'I'm sure I've never mentioned her in that context. She knows Kyrita's name, but we were careful not to raise her suspicions.'

'Then she shouldn't require physical altering,' Jym said. 'Perhaps there is something else you could clear up for us.'

Pellan gave him a puzzled look.

'Have you any idea why she went after the Rhalin family?'

'For a while I was hopeful of Aylisha Rhalin taking me on, but I was informed she was not interested. Lady Catailyn met with me and told me she had a certain male in mind for her daughter. Perhaps she thought Lady Rhalin was the one who was to be my benefactor.'

'If she thought Catailyn Rhalin was the benefactor, then she would not have attacked Lady Kaylee looking like you,' Luapp said. 'There is also the fact she was joined to Drew Rhalin. You always targeted unattached females.'

'She took my image?' Pellan said, amazed.

Seeing Jym's stare he shrugged, unable to come up with another suggestion.

'She gave us one explanation for that, I just wondered if you had another,' Jym said.

'What explanation did she give?'

'She wanted you to be convicted for murder knowing you were innocent.'

Before Pellan could respond another ring on the doorbell brought Farin in to announce the collection vehicle had arrived.

Telling him to take them upstairs Enegene rang the servant bell. When Cleona entered, she ordered coffee for her guests. As Cleona left the doorbell rang again.

'It's busier than the swamps during a guardian raid,' Enegene muttered.

Cleona reappeared bringing Aylisha with her. 'Lady Rhalin,' she announced.

'One more, Cleona,' Enegene told her.

As she left Aylisha looked around the group before sitting

398

next to Pellan. 'I assume all is well since we have been told we can return. Someone fill me in please.'

Jym looked at Pellan. 'Keep in mind you can't tell anyone about this except your cousin,' he said, quietly. 'It's classified. One squeak in the wrong ear and you won't see daylight for a hundred years, got it?'

The normal green of Pellan's skin had only just returned but paled again as he nodded.

'Good, sit down and remain quiet.'

Turning towards Luapp Jym indicated he wanted to talk to him alone. Moving to the other side of the room he said quietly, 'thanks for playing along. The C.M. still needs this to be his initiative and not the Galactic Council's.'

'I assumed that would be the case from our previous discussion. It also stops any awkward questions and information leaks.'

While Luapp and Jym discussed the case, Enegene told Aylisha about the events of the last few days. Pellan sat in dazed silence hardly aware of what was going on around him.

Cleona's return with the drinks a short while later brought him back to the present and he listened in to the women's conversation.

Their talk was briefly overshadowed by the noise of feet coming downstairs, and a few quiet comments on how to position the body bag. Shortly after, Farin arrived and announced the bed was now clear and ready for a clean-up.

'I think I'll have that sleeper and everything on it destroyed,' Enegene said, as the servant left. 'It has a darkness to it now.'

Jym placed his empty cup on the table. 'You'll come to the station with me Mister Pellan and give a statement. Lady Branon, we'll be in touch about your assistance in this affair. If you could remain on the planet for another three days I would be grateful.'

'I'll be able to stay for as long as you need me. It will give me time to say my farewells to my friends.' Glancing at Luapp she added, 'I will of course be taking Mikim with me.'

'I would ask pap to throw a party to say goodbye to you properly,' Aylisha said, watching the men walk to the door. 'But nobody else is supposed to know Mikim is alive.'

'Now the case is over, everyone will know how we helped the enforcers. But we'll be too busy for a large gathering. If you would like us to attend a family gathering I'm sure we could manage that.'

'I'll speak to pap.' Aylisha smiled. Glancing at Jym as he left with Pellan she added, 'and Inspector Corder can come as well.'

'We've a lot to get through,' Jym said to Luapp as they left the room. 'But we'll be as quick as we can. I expect you're looking forward to going home.'

Luapp smiled briefly. 'I've enjoyed assisting the enforcers here and it will be interesting to see the home of my ancestors.'

Jim grinned. 'It's been an education working with you Mikim. I'll see you soon.' He followed Pellan out onto the drive and took him to his aircar.

Closing the door, Luapp went to the servant's common room where he found Farin. He took him upstairs to help remove the bed and cleaned furniture to the garden.

They collected axes from the tool store and broke the furniture into pieces. Mevil Sylata had a fire burning in a pit at the bottom of the garden and the pieces were thrown on.

The elderly handyman watched the bed burn for several minutes then walked over to Luapp and placed his hand on his shoulder.

'I knew there was something different about you, lad. Now we all know what it was.'

'Indeed? What was it?'

'You and the Lady Kaylee were working for the police. That made you react differently to other slaves I've met. Didn't the lady trust us?'

'It was a requirement of the police that she told no-one about her or my involvement.'

Their conversation paused as the mattress, linen and pillows were also ferried out by the other servants for destruction. They threw them on and went back to the house.

'It also explains your obsession with house security. Despite my suspicions about your behaviour, I never doubted for a minute you'd protect her.'

A grunt and some heated words made them look back. 'Here's the base,' Mevil Sylata said, watching the two maids and Farin carry it towards them.

The metal sprung base was dropped by the pit and then systematically taken apart and placed in a bin for disposal.

Watching the servant's faces as the furniture burned Luapp was puzzled. For some reason, they seemed to enjoy the destruction. With a mental shrug, he left them to it and returned to the now empty room.

Collecting the fluids from the loft he cleaned it once more. Then he joined the women in the dining room for afternoon tea. Due to the morning's events, breakfast and lunch had been missed, and now they were hungry.

As Aylisha chatted to Enegene, Luapp ate lost in thought about tying up loose ends.

~~~

Aylisha was her normal effervescent self and was busy telling Enegene what she did while they were away. Enegene half listened to her friend's banter, the other half of her attention was on the man opposite. For a year now they had

401

been in close contact, and feelings she'd fought so hard to suppress finally surfaced.

Suddenly aware Aylisha had stopped talking, she returned her attention to her. She was watching her and smiling. 'Husband material?' she said, quietly.

Enegene raised a brow, slid a sideways glance at the guardian and then looked back to Aylisha. 'Not yet, but with work he will be.'

'The g…,' she stopped at Enegene's hand signal. 'Mikim doesn't strike me as a man who is easily moulded.'

'True, especially as slavery is outlawed on Gaeiza, but I could chip a few sharp edges off.' Enegene allowed herself another smile before adding, 'and what about you and Jym?'

'We're doing nicely thank you. Strange it turns out I am attracted to a man whose father is friends with my father.'

'He seems a decent male.'

'My thoughts exactly,' Aylisha said, and sipped her tea.

'Perhaps you will be wanting this house sooner than anticipated.'

Aylisha blushed. 'You're a little ahead of me there.'

~~~

Leaving the women to talk, Luapp went to the loft to pack the equipment. While there he arranged for Kerran to collect it after the servants retired for the night. When he eventually came down, he met Farin in the hall.

'You've come from the roof, haven't you?'

Luapp searched for a way to deny it as they walked to the staff room, but couldn't find anything plausible. 'Yes,' he said at last.

'There's rumours about things in the roof,' Farin said tentatively.

'I know. That's why things the enforcers brought around were stored there.' He stopped by the door. 'I can assure you no demons are hiding there.'

Farin grinned. 'I don't think any of us really believe that stuff about demons, but we don't like to tempt fate.'

Continuing into the staffroom Farin poured two cups of tea from the ever ready teapot. Handing one to Luapp he continued, 'I'll be sorry to see you go.'

Luapp sipped the tea and walked over to an empty chair. 'Why?'

'You were easy to get on with and you made us laugh when you misunderstood things.'

Luapp twitched a brow and smiled. 'I have found you and your companions interesting as well.'

'Sylata will be very sorry to see you go. She was most upset when she thought you were dead.'

He watched Farin sit down and take a sip of his tea. 'I'm surprised you get emotional about an outworlder slave.'

'Most people here don't agree with slavery. There's a political campaign to get it outlawed.'

Farin's gaze rested on Luapp and then he looked down at his tea. He got the impression Farin wanted to ask a question.

'You wish to say something?' he prompted, after several moments of waiting.

Farin looked up from his study of the tea. 'I suppose when you and Lady Branon leave, we'll be out of work.'

'Has Lady Kaylee not spoken to the staff about what happens when we leave?'

'Not a word. But she has been kind of busy, what with your funeral and getting murdered.' A fleeting smile touched his lips and then he frowned.

'There's nothing to be concerned about. If you wish to continue working here it should be possible. I'll ask her to clarify the situation.'

As Luapp finished his tea Sylata came in with a message

about dinner. Putting his cup on the table he left. He went to the lounge and was joined by Enegene and Aylisha returning from the games room.

'Sylata asked me to inform you the meal will be served immediately.'

Walking through to the dining room he added, 'the servants are nervous about their future.'

'I'll do that tomorrow,' Enegene said, sitting at the table. 'What's happened to my slember?'

'It's been emptied with Farin's help. You'll have to purchase new furniture and floor covering.'

'Oh good,' Aylisha said. 'We can go shopping tomorrow.'

'As you are having the dwelling, you should choose the furnishings.'

'I should also buy them. Is Mikim coming with us?'

Both women turned their attention on him.

'I'll be going to enforcer headquarters to finalise details with Jym Corder. Then I must purchase our return tickets.'

Enegene frowned. 'Aren't we getting a pick up?'

'That would be difficult in the political circumstances. We'll have to travel the standard way.'

With a sideways grin, Enegene said, 'remember you're still my slave when you buy the tickets. I have the documentation to prove it.'

'Technically I've ceased, and we have the documentation to prove that.'

'Until you are out of our area there is more evidence that you're alive and her slave, than dead; if you see what I mean,' Aylisha said. 'You still have the brand and Kaylee still has the ownership papers. Someone will have to go with you.'

'As Morvac will be with you, I will take Freeman Sylata.'

The door opened and Cleona and Farin guided the food trolley in. Enegene waited until the first course had been served and the servants had left to  speak again.

'That means you'll be my slave for most of the journey back to the Seven Systems.'

She smiled broadly, apparently pleased with the prospect. Luapp twitched a brow and left the table heading for the door.

'Going somewhere?' she said, surprised.

'I have to make sure there's nothing to link us to the guardians.'

'Cook won't be pleased if you ignore her efforts.'

After a few seconds consideration, he returned to the table. He stayed just long enough to finish the meal then left to get Sylata.

## Chapter 23

Standing by the window Enegene could just make out the figures of Aylisha and Jym on the observation balcony. They'd come down to the space port to see them off. She looked back to Luapp who was reading from a screen. He'd inserted the sliver when they arrived and studied it ever since.

A light vibration went through the ship, and the noise of the engines gathering speed grew louder. Only now did he switch off, come over to the large window and look out.

As the ship rose slowly from the hard standing he raised his hand in a gesture of farewell, then returned to his seat and turned the screen back on. Within seconds they were too high to be seen by the couple so Enegene returned to her place beside the guardian.

'Do you think the Coalition Master will be able to keep the mission quiet? There are several people who knew about it.'

'The elite have been told you were ordered home by your father when he heard about the multislayer. All the enforcers believe the cover story stating we were enlisted to help Jym's team catch a murderer. The servants believe the same story and Pellan and his cousin have left the planet.

Only Jym Corder, Eura Ghan, the Coalition Master and the Rhalins know the truth. All possible trouble areas have been covered, according to the Coalition Master.'

'Yes, he was a most charming man.' Enegene smiled at the memory. 'I enjoyed our meeting with him at his mountain home.'

'That wasn't his home, it's a secure dwelling.'

'What's so absorbing?'

'Detective Corder's report on the Fluctoid and the police work involved. He asked me to review it and inform him of any mistakes or omissions.'

A niggling irritation was manifesting at the back of her mind. It annoyed her he had something that interested him and she had nothing.

'I'm sure he didn't intend you to do it now.'

'Possibly,' he said without looking up. 'But if I do it now I won't have to do it later.'

Her hopes rose. 'Why, what have you got planned for later?'

'Rest.'

Hope died. 'What happened to the Fluctoid?'

'When Jym finished questioning her, guards from Quarn collected her. She's to stand trial on their home planet first.'

'Have they left as well?'

'Two days ago.'

She let out a disgruntled sigh. 'I'm going to look around the retails.'

Standing up she noticed another passenger watching them. In a slightly louder voice she added, 'you remain here and finish that review Mikim. I want an answer when I get back. If you finish before I return you may go to the cabin.'

'Yes Lady,' he murmured.

~~~

It was early evening when she returned to the cabin and her mood was low. While on Padua the continuous round of events and the search for the serial killer had kept mind and body active. Now, she had little to do and she was feeling lost.

Luapp had arrived and changed for the evening meal by the time she  entered the cabin. He was wearing the white suit she'd bought him. It was one of the few things he had clothes wise. His own had been sent back to Gaeiza by Langa Char and the wardrobe she bought him had been packed and sent by freight along with most of their cases. All they carried was a hand held bag each with small amount of clothes for the journey home.

'Purchase anything?' he said, as she went to the wardrobe.

'No, nothing caught my eye.' She walked past him to the bathroom. 'I won't be long.'

A short time later she reappeared wearing a lilac dress with a small flower print in a darker purple. Going to the dressing table she sat down and applied her make-up.

Luapp walked up behind her. 'Do you want me to do your hair?'

'I'm not a female of your family,' she quoted from before.

'And I'm still your slave until we leave Black Systems space.'

With no enthusiasm for arguing, she said, 'I'd like that.'

He picked up the brush and gathered her hair in his hand. When he finished, she added, 'I like your city styles.'

'They're country styles. My mother came from the Azren Plain.'

'Not many people come from the Azure Plains,' Enegene said. 'There's only a small town there.'

'She came from the Azren Plains, on Mintel. What jewellery are you wearing?'

Surprised by his interest, she murmured, 'I'm not sure. I'd not considered it until now.'

Enegene went to the bedside table and took her jewel case

from a drawer. She looked inside, but seemed undecided.

'Perhaps I can help.'

She looked up, surprised again. 'Alright.' She smiled. 'You seem to have a good sense of co-ordination.'

Holding out the case she was puzzled when he went to the wardrobe. Removing a small box from inside he held it out. She looked at it dubiously.

'For me?'

'I would not be giving it to you unless it was.'

Taking the box, she undid the packaging and opened it. Inside was a pendant set with a starglow stone. It was surrounded by small emeralds and was on a delicate silvery chain.

Removing it from the box she held it up. It twisted slightly in her grasp, sending multi-coloured sparkles of light around the room.

Stargems were extremely expensive, she knew. She had seen one in the jewellers on board. It was smaller than this and not such good quality, and yet it had been several hundred syscred. She doubted Luapp Nostowe had used expenses to buy this.

'Could you put it on for me?'

Taking it from her he opened the clasp, lifted it over her head and fastened it at the back of her neck. She studied her reflection in the mirror. The jewel sparkled with every breath she took.

'Why did you buy it?' she said, turning towards him.

'Without your assistance, this mission would have been a failure. You placed your life at risk and you were committed to a successful outcome; most of the time.'

He paused and then added, 'and because I wanted you to have it, as a gift from me.'

Whatever else he might have said; the last sentence was the

only one that held any meaning for her. She smiled, and for a moment was lost for words.

'Shall we eat?' he suggested, breaking the silence.

'Yes, let's.'

As she left the cabin, her depression faded and her mood was so high she felt giddy. She was still floating when they returned to the cabin that evening.

Now off duty, Luapp had relaxed, and she'd found him good company. Despite her efforts to remain awake and hold onto the perfection of the evening, as soon as she got into the bed she was asleep within minutes.

The next day they were woken early by a bell ringing. This was the changeover from medium sized passenger ship to a galactic cruiser on Starport Four. They were leaving right after breakfast. While dressing, Enegene's thoughts went to the previous night.

*Luapp reveals little about his background and is well rehearsed in keeping his private life private. He coaxed many things from me about my qiverhood and maturing in the swamps. But when the conversation swung to him, he changed the subject after the most minimal revelation.*

Glancing at her reflection in the mirror she smiled.

*I hope this doesn't mean he's hiding something major. Ekym Yetok refused to talk about him, and said I would have to ask him. When I ask him, he doesn't tell me anything either.*

*He hasn't worn a ring. He'd take it off for the mission; slaves did not own such things, but there wasn't the faintest mark to show where one might have been.*

*He denies having a serious relationship, but I put that down to his way of ending the questions. Is he the kind of man to give such an expensive gift to a female if he had a liana?*

She doubted it. *So if it's not a liana what is it?*

A knock on the door stopped any further pondering.

'It's time for firseal.' He waited until she appeared and then continued, 'we've been given the cabin numbers for the deep space cruiser; I've placed them in your document pouch.'

'Fine. Let's get firseal.'

It was quiet in the dining room when they arrived. Half the passengers had disembarked already as they had to catch on going ships or the ferry to the planet a short journey on.

Breakfast was buffet style and seating was free choice. After collecting their meals, they talked about their plans for when they arrived back on Gaeiza.

'I'll be going to GSC the next day for debriefing and to hand over the statements of all concerned.' Luapp put his glass back on the table. 'Then I'm going to the medic centre for a few days.'

Enegene stopped eating. 'Are you ill?'

'No. The brand must be removed. Unfortunately, it's not as easy to remove it as to place it there.'

'I don't like the sound of that.'

'Neither do I.'

'They will be able to remove it?'

'I think so. Up to an orbit it's easy to remove, after that it becomes more difficult, but I was told it would be possible.'

'You've had that brand for fifteen monspa.'

'It's not long over; a monspa late shouldn't be too difficult.'

'I'm surprised it bothers you. You've never shown fear of pain.'

'Just because I don't show it, it doesn't mean I participate in anything painful willingly.'

Her lips curved into a wry smile. 'If it doesn't come off, you will be mine forever.'

'I couldn't go back to the Black Systems without you. I'll be pleased to be rid of it, and all it symbolises. What will you be doing?'

Enegene went over her plans for when she arrived on Gaeiza without a comment from Luapp until she said, 'after that I'm going to have a vacation.'

'Vacation? This whole mission has been one long vacation for you. I was the one having to work through it.'

With a smirk, she said, 'I was amazed at your versatility Guardian. The things you can turn your hand to are unbelievable.'

'Now you're being sarcastic.'

'Me? Mock a guardian? But if you ever left the guardians, you could earn a fortune as a muscle manipulator.'

'Guardians are trained in a secondary occupation in preparation for the time they leave the force. We're not guardians for life. The very nature of the occupation means fit, young adults are required.'

The smile widened momentarily. 'Possibly why females from home prefer guardians to other males.'

Ignoring the comment, he continued, 'all but the few who become High Commander or Supreme Commander leave to take up other employment. That said, all guardians are trained in relaxation methodology.'

'Except the ones who don't have to worry about employment.'

Luapp looked up surprised. 'Who are you talking about?'

The fleeting expression on his face made her wonder about the meaning behind it. 'Your friend, Ekym Yetok.'

'Despite his family strata level it didn't stop Kym becoming a guardian. What else did he tell you?'

'A few things as a distraction from not talking about you.'

Looking up at the staff clearing the tables he changed the subject before she could ask any more questions.

'We'd better go.'

They left the dining room and headed for the small side

room that held their bags. After collecting them they left the ship and made their way to the starport's hotel.

It was a short walk from the ship to the hotel, and they appeared to be the only ones staying on. Arriving in the suite, Enegene's attention was caught by the advertising screen on the wall.

Turning to Luapp, she said, 'we have a day before the cruiser arrives. How about a trip to the planet?'

'If you like.'

He touched a button on the desk top and a computer slid out. When the screen lit, he requested tourist information about the planet below. As the information appeared on screen he waited for Enegene's suggestion.

Scrutinising the screen for some minutes, she pointed to one of the activities. 'Have you ever done that?'

Luapp read the information. 'I'm trained in snow gliding, but have never actually tried that. We don't have anything like it on Gaeiza.'

'Neither have I. Let's try it.'

'I'll book one for us to use privately and check the ferry times. We may be able to stay overnight and return in the morning.'

Enegene watched over his shoulder as he ordered a private run and received confirmation. Then he brought up the ferry times and pointed to one.

'Yes,' she said enthusiastically.

As he booked their seats, he told her to collect her bag. 'We have ten minutes to cancel our room and catch the ferry from portal three.'

'And where's that?' she said, fastening her card belt around her waist.

'The other side of the port.'

'Of course,' she said. 'It couldn't possibly be the next one

413

round the corner.'

'This port has no corners, it's circular.' He was contacting reception as he spoke.

'You know what I mean.'

Enegene collected her bag and handed it to Luapp. She grinned at the wry look he gave her as they left the room. Arriving at reception, she signed out, then hurried to catch up. Luapp was already outside and walking towards the dock.

They arrived as the boarding notice was given. Luapp waited as she pressed her thumb onto the portal entry plate, then they headed for the ferry.

'How long does the trip take?' Enegene said, making herself comfortable at a table seat.

'Twenty minutes.'

'In that case, I'll watch a story reel. Dial one up for me Mikim, and get us both a drink.'

Pulling out her card she smiled up at the tight expression as she handed it to him.

Twenty minutes later the ferry touched down at the North Polar Region of the planet. The terminal building was warm enough, but outside a blizzard was blowing.

'Time to get some warmer clothes,' Enegene said, as they passed through port control.

Obviously, this was normal practice. A clothes shop was located a short walk away. It was as large as three shops in one and contained most clothing and equipment wanted for a short stay.

As he had no means to pay for anything, Luapp waited outside. When Enegene emerged, she handed him a bag and said, 'put this on, it's a coat.'

'It's taken you this long to purchase two coats?' he said, pulling it from the bag.

'The rest is being sent on. Lady's in *my* position are *never* hampered by shopping.'

She swept on before him and waited outside while he approached a sledge-taxi. Apparently, they didn't barter on price as Luapp merely spoke to the driver and got on. When it pulled up beside Enegene, he took her bag as she got in.

Entering the hotel almost an hour later, the first thing they noticed was the roaring fire in the lobby. Several large and comfortable looking chairs were arranged around it. At the moment all were occupied.

The woman on reception smiled and her second eyelids blinked as they approached. Enegene gave her name and looked around the lobby as she waited for the receptionist to look up the booking.

'I have it; Madam Namrae and slave.'

She looked Luapp over and smiled again, her pale skin looked almost transparent. 'Yachting today?'

'Yes, I have booked a private yacht for three this afternoon,' Enegene said.

'You need crew?'

'No, merely instruction for my slave. He's quite able, and once shown something he can manage on his own.'

The receptionist nodded. 'Private yachts designed to be manageable by singles. Order you instructor I will.

You return lobby or bar after eat, be paged you will. Instruction is one circumference of timepiece then keep yacht until ninth tonight.

If require basket meal, order one when eat. If not, many small eating houses on route. Be given a map with all marked on you will.'

She paused as she worked at the computer in front of her, then asked, 'have trouble landing, did you?'

'No, why?' Enegene said.

'Ship crashed yesterday, all but one dead. One landing site

been closed since. Directing traffic around must be.' She smiled again. 'Have flavoursome meal, and enjoyable day.' Handing Enegene a slim box she turned to the next customer.

They left reception and entered the lift. One floor up they walked along the corridor to their room. Enegene turned the box over in her hands several times and then looked at Luapp for inspiration.

'Try sliding up or down,' he suggested.

Adding pressure to the front of the box she slid the cover up to reveal four rows of six buttons. 'No combination,' she said, confused.

'Pull the cover completely off.'

When she did she felt something on the inside. She turned it over and saw a panel with six notes and a slim stylus clipped into the frame. Taking the stylus, she played the six notes on the front and the door opened.

In the centre of the room was a small table completely hidden by packages on and around it. Luapp took their overnight bags to their bedrooms, but Enegene remained with the packages.

When he returned, she had opened every parcel and was surrounded by packaging. Handing him his clothes she departed for her bedroom to change.

She returned to the lounge quarter of an hour later to find him sitting on the sofa and the rubbish in the bin. Resisting the urge to comment she walked past him out into the corridor. Locking the door, he followed her to the dining room.

Even with a two-hour gap before the yacht arrived, they only just finished eating in time. A problem with Gaeizaans eating on the planet Freair was highlighted when the waiter arrived to take their order.

Apparently, the population of the planet were mostly carnivores. This meant the menu for vegetarians was so limited the chef came out to discuss what they could eat. After this, they had to wait while the meal was cooked.

The waiter arrived a second time and smiled at Enegene. 'Chef offers goodwill,' he said. 'If slave collect fruit from kitchens; eat it while you wait you can.'

'That is most kind of your Chef,' Enegene said with a smile. 'Mikim will collect the fruit.'

While waiting for Luapp's return, she had the feeling of being watched. A slow look around the room located the source. Two tables back an elderly native woman sitting on her own looked away hastily. Some minutes later, Enegene was surprised by her arrival beside her.

She spoke, but Enegene didn't understand. In a gesture that was recognised the entire width of the galaxy, she shrugged.

The woman smiled and fiddled with her bracelet. 'I said, forgive me for staring. I couldn't help noticing what a handsome man your husband is.'

Enegene felt uneasy under the piercing ice-blue gaze. 'He's not my husband; he's my slave.'

The woman looked shocked. 'You enslaved your own kind?'

Something about this woman made Enegene decide to keep to the cover story suggested by the Coalition Master.

'I bought him in the Black Systems; he was a third generation slave. I'm taking him home with me.'

'Oh I see.' The smile seemed unnatural. 'You rescued him.' She looked up, frowned and then smiled again. 'I must be going; many things to do.'

Enegene watched her leave with relief. Although the woman had said and done nothing suspicious, there was something about her that made her uncomfortable.

~~~

At the kitchen door Luapp was given a bowl of assorted fruit.

He returned to the table and selected a spherical purple one. Breaking open the soft shell he pulled the white, segmented flesh out. Separating the segments on a small plate, he picked up a piece to eat. Noticing Enegene's lack of enthusiasm he said, 'not hungry?'

'What does it taste like?'

'Sweet.'

She took a segment and chewed it slowly. As she ate he studied her expression, it suggested she was mulling something over. He was about to ask when the waiter appeared with their meal. By the time they finished, there was only a short time to wait in the lobby.

As they sat by the fire he said, 'what's troubling you?'

'Did you notice that elderly female in the dining room?'

'There were three. Which one?'

'The one sat on her own; she was watching us.'

'I noted her presence. She was a native of this planet, perhaps she had never seen sollenites before.'

'Possibly...'

A call to reception stopped further speculation. At the desk a young man was waiting. He smiled and held out his hand, palm up with the six fingers spread.

'Felicitations. I instructor. Who I instruct?' He looked from Enegene to Luapp.

'My slave.'

His attention was now on Luapp. 'He strong enough to handle craft. Educated?'

'Mikim is of my species and highly intelligent.'

'Good. Come this way.'

Luapp and the instructor left the hotel with Enegene following. In a small frozen inlet an elegant craft was anchored to the bank. The instructor stopped beside it and smiled.

'This Klaris.' He ran his hand along the polished, wooden

prow. 'Sleek craft, handle well, and fast.'

Built in the traditional style of a water boat, it's low, wide hull was made of a dark reddy-brown wood, with a carved, white painted pattern around the rim.

It was mounted on two long, vicious looking blades that ran the length of it. At the front, the bow was carved in a spiral, and a flattened stern held a rudder.

From the centre of the hull stood a tall mast rigged with three sails. Two went from the top to the bow and stern, the third hung down the centre. The white sails billowed slightly in the weak breeze making the purple emblem fat and full.

'Come see,' urged the instructor.

He brushed back a shock of blue-black hair blowing in the breeze and pulled out a remote. Pushing a button made a gangplank slide out and land on the bank. The last person stepping onto the deck was the signal for it to slide back.

The instructor took them around the boat, pointing out the various parts of the ship, and then he took them into the cabin. Leaving Enegene to look around the compact inside he took Luapp back on deck and started showing him how to sail the yacht.

Standing at the console, he indicated the control panel. 'All controls here except for those in covered area. We start with this.'

He pressed a yellow square on the panel and the two anchors retracted. Pushing a blue square made the engine purr into life.

'Always use engine to enter and leave port you must. Also, when mooring at bank. Wind sometimes too strong for arrival with sails. So take down sails.'

Touching the red square made the sails furl. Now they had a clear view of where they were going. Next he  pushed a small lever underneath the blue square, making the boat slowly back away from the bank. When it was far enough away, he pushed the lever forward and the bow came around.

'If want sails but not enough wind, you engage heater.'

He indicated a white triangular marker to the side of the consol. 'Heats rails, melts ice little, makes sliding easier. If no wind use engine you must.'

He looked up at the shifting sails, then across at Luapp. 'Today the wind god awake; enough breeze for good speed.'

As their pace increased, he continued, 'this turns her right.' He put his hand on a small sphere in the middle of the console, and spun it to the right.

'This left.' He spun it the opposite way. 'When line here, it go straight. If course clear, skate all directions you can. Fins underneath control direction. Rear rudder water sailing only.'

He smiled, making the yacht slide from side to side. Seeing Enegene standing at the bow, he winked at Luapp.

'It go round in circles if spin it.'

Giving the sphere a push it spun the yacht . Enegene turned and looked at them.

'Feeling good you are?' he called, with a huge grin.

She smiled back. 'Wonderful.'

He straightened the course and she returned her attention to the scenery. Two pushes on the red square unfurled the sails.

'Now view obscured, three choices you have. Hope don't hit anything; not good choice. Push this,' he indicated an oval button. 'Screen comes up. This shows where you go.'

He pointed to the screen showing the way ahead. 'Some prefer see naturally. If do, slide this,' he gripped a second leaver beneath the red square, 'and mast moves. Sail gone, see you.' They watched as the mast slid to the left and the mid-sail rose higher. 'Use screen while mast moves.'

As the boat increased speed, the instructor added, 'if want travel slower, press this.' He pointed to a green square. 'One slows little, two more. To reverse, push three times, when almost stopped, put lever in reverse. Questions?'

'You reversed out of the inlet without the green key. Why?'

'Green square to slow speed. Klaris stationary at inlet, she was. Green square not needed. Other questions?'

'What happens if we have an accident?'

'Two ways contacting us there is. Have flares, when cannot be seen; audio unit in cabin. If hit thin ice and yacht goes through, do this.'

On the right-hand side of the console was a set of covered buttons. Flipping the cover up, he pointed to a large, black central button.

'Push first, retracts rails, float you will. Next red. Changes engine from ice to water. Stabilises speed, stop you will. Only use grey if think remain unfound several days. Button instigates ice breaker.'

'When locked, make way to hotel. *Must* be slow. If go fast could damage or sink yacht. Small quantity food in cabin; one day and night. You try.' He snapped the top of the covered buttons down and stepped aside.

Luapp took control and the instructor watched as he guided the boat along the frozen river. Following instructions he took it in a straight line, from side to side, and around in a circle. Speeded it up, slowed it down, and moved the sail and mast. Then he did it again using the screen.

At the end of it all the instructor chuckled. 'Naturally nautical you are. I no fear you in charge. Final instruction. When mooring must slow right down, come along side, slide into reverse. When almost stopped, press one of these.' He indicated two grey triangular markers on the left of the consol. 'Rope go into ring on bank it will. This for right, that for left.

When go ashore lock with voice key. Speak before leave,

saying "lock". Place on consol. Clips here.' He pointed to four small oblong gaps. 'When return say "open". Simple.

Take me hotel then go enjoy yourselves. Leave maps in cabin, I will. If go top of glacier, use engine power, you must, but coming down easy. Good gliding.'

A short while later, they were back at the inlet by the hotel. Just before he left, Enegene walked back from the bow. 'Is there much wildlife around here?'

'Yes, dangerous they not unless scared.'

'Predator canines?'

'Yes, wolves run if approached. Why?'

'I thought I saw one as we were travelling.'

'Was it moving?'

'No.'

'Ice statue, could be. People make them here. Very life like.'

'That must have been it,' she murmured.

They stopped briefly to let the instructor off and consult the map, then Luapp took the boat out of the inlet and headed up the ice lane again.

# Chapter 24

It was peaceful travelling along the various ice lanes. Pristine snow covered everything, and only birdsong and the hiss of the blades interrupted the silence.

Enegene raised her voice to be heard above the billowing sails. 'Where are we going?'

'Half way up the glacier there's an ice sculpture area and an ice bar. I was curious as to what an ice bar is.'

Enegene sat in the prow holding the coat tightly around her. The cold air had paled her skin slightly, and the wind whipped her hair into a mad dance behind her.

She smiled broadly holding her hair back from her face. 'Curiosity guardian? You'll flip your trip if you indulge in too many emotions.'

Luapp stood at the controls making minor adjustments to the direction and speed where required. He glanced at her but said nothing. The year long association with Enegene had taught him ignoring her verbal gibes was the best way of handling them.

*I've managed an orbit without her driving me insane. Surprisingly, the anticipated venomous verbal outpourings didn't materialise.*

*We've become closer than acquaintances, but she's not a friend in the same way as Nommys, Pilih and Ekym. After returning to Gaeiza, I might contact her…*

His thoughts were cut off by having to concentrate on a manoeuvre to turn the yacht onto a different ice lane. This was busier than the previous one and he had to be more in tune with what everyone else was doing. A lot of people in charge of glacier yachts seemed unable to control them. Twice he'd had to swerve to miss someone on his side of the lane.

After a while he moved off onto the stream that would take them to the ice sculptures. With the ice lanes getting progressively narrower he lessened the speed. The sun high in the sky was melting the surface ice and a small spray of water shot up as they sped along.

Occasionally he glanced at the banks. This lane was as quiet as the first and several different animals were walking along undisturbed by their passing.

Briefly checking the map Luapp slowed the yacht. There was only a short way to go now, and as they rounded a corner it was obvious they'd arrived. Huge ice sculptures could be seen in the distance.

A short way ahead were some mooring rings. He tapped the button three times then slid the lever into reverse. The speed dropped quickly and as they drifted up to the ring he pushed the release.

The rope shot to the bank, through the ring and around itself. Repeating the process made the stern rope do the same. With a slight tug, the yacht came to a halt. For good measure, he also ran an anchor into the bank.

Picking up the voice key, he told Enegene to collect anything she needed. When she reappeared, he spoke into it and placed it on the consol.

'How are we going to get there?' she said, looking at the

sculptures. 'It'll be hard work walking.'

'You don't walk; you use those,' he pointed to the bow. Leaving the console, he untied two sets of skis and poles, and brought them back. She looked at them doubtfully.

'Two bits of bent wood?'

Her confusion made him smile. 'You have never snow glided before?'

'Not possible in the swamps,' she said, with a touch of sarcasm. 'And I never felt the need in the city.

'You're about to learn.'

He carried the skis to the edge of the boat and threw them onto the bank. Jumping the short gap between craft and land he turned back to look at Enegene. She stood on the edge debating what to do.

'I can come back and throw you over too, if you want,' he commented.

A deep frown appeared and she pursed her lips as she assessed the distance between boat and bank. 'I'd rather have the ramp.'

'What's the problem? You got out of the boat at the island on Pedanta.'

'But the pier was the same height as the boat then.'

'At least the bank's not going up and down.' He smiled, but her tense expression suggested she was genuinely nervous.

'I must collect the remote.'

He went back on board the ship, released the voice lock and went into the cabin. Seconds later, he returned with the ramp control. Pressing the button, he watched Enegene walk down the gangplank to the bank, and then pressed the remote again. After returning it to the cabin, he voice locked the ship a second time. Then he jumped across to the bank beside her.

He picked up the skis and trudged a short distance to a wooden platform built near the bank. Here he placed the skis apart and stood on them.

Webbing snaked out of the skis, wrapped itself around his boots and up his leg just past his ankle. Squatting on the skis he smoothed the layers with his hands as they solidified into over-boots.

Enegene copied his actions. Standing up, he picked up the poles and waited until she was finished.

'You have to lift your foot on this platform, but when you get on the snow, you just push and you'll glide. I'll demonstrate.'

She watched him walk off the platform onto the snow. It seemed very little effort was needed to move. Shuffling off the platform, she balanced on the little slope and pushed off.

Several things happened at once, none of which happened to Luapp. Her feet got wider apart as she slipped down the slope trying to keep her balance. Unsure what to do with the poles, she stuck them hard into the snow.

The skis went either side and she stopped at a precarious angle. Gripping the poles tightly and unable to move her feet, she was staring face down at the snow.

Of all the training sessions he'd been on, and the many falls he'd encountered, no one had managed to do that.

He glided over and was about to haul her up when her wrists finally gave up their struggle. Hands aching with the compression, Enegene let go and she fell face down, her skis somehow crossing each other.

Luapp was undecided what to do first. Try and turn her over, or unwrap the skis. He chose the skis. Careful not to twist her ankle, he moved them so they lay sideways.

Skiing up to her shoulders he turned her over and told her to sit up with the skis flat on the ground. Finally, he placed one of his skis on top of both of hers and pulled her up.

'How was that?' she said, wiping snow off her face.

'Needs work,' he replied, without a glimmer of a smile.

For the next hour, he patiently coached her in the art of skiing. At first, she spent more time on the ground than on her feet, but gradually she improved.

When she finally managed to walk the skis without falling over, she grinned broadly. 'I did it! I did it! Look!' She shuffled towards what looked like a small slope.

'Good,' he said slightly exasperated. 'Let's try and get to the sculptures before they melt.'

'I'll just try this slope, then I'll come.'

'Enegene, I don't think...'

Before he could say more, she'd launched over the edge. It became obvious it was not as small as it first seemed. She quickly gathered speed down a medium height but steep slope, at the bottom of which was a large tree.

Luapp followed her down. His initial concerns eased as she remained upright and mobile, but the tree was looming and he wasn't sure she could miss it.

With the tree rapidly nearing he saw her aim both skis in the same direction and avoid it. Then he heard a yelp of consternation. She was yanked backwards so rapidly she was hauled off the ground and fell in the snow sitting down. Her skis pointing skyward like flagpoles.

As she sat gathering her senses a creaking noise grabbed their attention. Looking up they saw a large heap of snow slip from the branches above. Unable to move, she was enveloped and looked like a mound with masts.

In all the times he'd taught guardians skiing, none of them had done that either. He couldn't stop the chuckle as he skied over and cleared her face. Now she could breathe, he concentrated on removing the rest of the snow, knocking it from her shoulders and arms.

'We're supposed to be looking at the ice sculptures, not

trying to be one.'

'Very jocular!' she spluttered. 'Typical of you to find my predicament amusing.'

'It was certainly entertaining, and I remember you finding my difficulties on Pedanta amusing.'

He offered his hand and she took it. With a pull, he brought her to her feet and supported her until she freed herself from the snow.

'They weren't life threatening.' She grabbed her hair and shook it vigorously.

'Neither is this if you react correctly. Be more cautious this time.'

He started off in the direction of the ice sculptures. Enegene tentatively slid one ski ahead of the other, and gaining confidence upped her speed to a slow jogging pace.

There were about fifty sculptures altogether. Some towered over them, others were small and delicate, and they covered a range of subjects.

Some were animals or plants, some appeared to be figures from folklore, and some were different machines. All of them had a watery look as they slowly melted in the sun.

As they reached the end of the sculptures, there was a sign carved from ice stating "Ice Bar this way".

'Do you want to go?' Luapp said.

'We're here so we might as well.'

They skied on until a building made from ice became visible. A miniature forest of skis surrounded the building with a couple of jet skis at the side.

Stopping outside, they pushed the small light on the side of their skis. The boots transformed themselves back into straps, unwound and disappeared back into the ski.

Luapp picked them up and stuck them flat end down into the snow. Then he jammed the poles in beside them. Enegene did likewise and followed him through the door into the drinking house.

Everything inside was carved from ice, except the cushions on the seats, and the bottles holding the drinks. Even the glasses were ice.

The barman looked up as they entered. 'What'll have?' he said in Galactic, reaching for some glasses.

'Something warm,' Enegene said, holding her coat tight.

'Warm as chocolate or warm as alcohol?'

'Alcohol.'

'Chocolate,' Luapp said, 'but without lactative liquid.'

'Just water?' the barman said, frowning.

'Unless you have a plant alternative.'

The barman smiled. 'Ooo-kaaay'

Enegene's odd expression was noticed by Luapp. 'You want me to sail back having consumed a drink I don't know the strength of?'

She shrugged. 'Perhaps not. Otherwise I won't be the only thing ending up in the snow.'

As the steaming mug of hot chocolate and glass of spiced alcohol were placed in front of him, it crossed Luapp's mind the mug and bar should start to melt.

Seeing the direction of his gaze, the barman let out a hoarse chuckle. 'Insulated inside and bottom.'

Luapp glanced up at him. 'Indeed?'

'Yeppa. Most folks find strange.'

Handing Enegene her drink, he followed her to an empty table and sat down.

There were several people in the bar, and most of them seemed to be tourists as they didn't have the locals pale skin. A few minutes later, the barman appeared at their table carrying a plate with something on it.

'Compliments of house,' he said beaming.

'What is it?' Luapp said.

'Kwava chips.'

'Define Kwava.'

Placing the plate on the table, he smiled broadly and his second eyelids blinked.

'Kwava; large root Kesttina bush. Cut root, peel and cook. Thinly cut this is, very hot oil cooked in.'

'What's the oil made from?' Enegene said.

The barman looked from one to the other. His round smiling face momentarily serious.

'You cooks? Food inspectors?'

Enegene laughed. 'No, we're vegetarians and we can't eat anything from an animal.'

'Ah!'

His face lit up and he thrust his gloved hand towards her. Enegene tentatively took it and he shook her hand vigorously.

'Vegetarians we too are!'

'We who?' Luapp said.

'We bar. Vegetarian bar this is.' He made a wide sweep with his stocky arm.

'So the oil is made from?' she prompted.

'Seeds; tall grass seeds,' he indicated the height. 'With seasoning; salt from sea, firepowder from seed.'

'In that case we thank you,' Luapp said.

'Eat, you eat.'

The rotund barman waited to make sure they did. Only when they had both eaten a crisp did he happily depart.

'Taste good,' Enegene said quietly.

Chewing his crisp, Luapp frowned. 'Yes, they have unusual flavouring.'

The taste vaguely reminded him of something, but he couldn't remember what. Taking another crisp, he tried to place it. After a third crisp, a niggling inner warning started.

This sense had saved his life on several occasions and he never ignored it, but what could be wrong with eating fried root slivers? Everything was from plants and they wouldn't make them from anything poisonous.

He watched Enegene enjoying the crisps, but felt no urge to warn her. He didn't know what to warn her of. Taking another crisp, he bit on it thoughtfully.

*They're tasty, the more I eat, the more I like them. Slightly addictive?*

That insidious thought halted his reach for more. He sat up straight from the relaxed position he'd slumped into.

'We'd better leave if we want to catch the ferry back to the starport,' he said.

'Already?' Enegene sounded disappointed.

'Yes.' Rising from the table he went over to the bar. 'My thanks to your cook, the Kwava chips were enjoyable.'

The barman beamed again. 'You leaving?'

'We have to catch the ferry.'

'Good, good. Come see us next visit, yes?'

'Yes,' Luapp agreed, and immediately wondered why he said that.

Turning back towards Enegene waiting by the table he continued on to the door. He had his skis on by the time she joined him.

As she laid the skis down and stood on them, she said, 'you were right not to have the brew, it seems to have gone to my head.' Bending down, she made four stabs at the boot button and missed every time.

'Hope you can snow glide; can't carry you all the way to the yacht.' He watched her trying to push the button. 'Suppose I could, but I'd have to drag you by the hair; too heavy over my shoulder; my gliders would sink.'

She stopped trying to hit the button and looked up at him.

'Don't want to be dragged.'

'Your gliders are backwards,' he commented, vaguely interested in her method of skiing. 'Can't see where you're going.'

Squinting up against the sun at him, she then looked down at the skis. Stepping off, she turned around and stepped back on. Then she pushed the button.

'I'm facing wrong way; how do I turn round?'

'Small shuffles, starting with the outside leg.'

'Both my legs are outside legs.'

Luapp thought about that. Then he pointed with a pole. 'This outside leg.'

She shuffled around until the tip of her ski caught the edge of the step into the bar. 'I'm stuck.'

He turned to see. 'Use your sticks and push back, then continue shuffling.'

She did as instructed and finally found herself around the right way.

'Let's get back to the yacht,' he said, watching her set off.

Keeping slightly behind her he noticed she no longer cared when she fell over. She lay in the snow giggling until he helped her up then started off again.

When the boat finally came into view, he passed her and stopped on the bank. By the time she arrived he'd removed his skis and jumped on board. Taking the skis to the bow, he fastened them to the side and returned to the consol.

'Unlock.'

The small devise clicked and loosened itself from its holding place. Pulling it off, he put it inside the cabin, collected the remote and went to the side of the boat.

'I'll get your skis and then lower the ramp for you.'

'Ss alright,' she told him. 'Won't need it this time. Ship's going up and down. I'll jump on the down.'

He jumped from the boat to the bank, then turned and looked at the yacht. As far as he could see, it was as still as the bank. Collecting her skis, he returned to the yacht and headed for the front of the boat leaving her to get on with it.

After fastening her skis, he came back to the consol and checked Enegene was on board. She was sitting on the deck. He didn't know why or care, as long as she was with him.

Luapp touched the key to furl the sails, then started the engine and retracted the anchor. As he released the ropes, they returned to their sockets and the boat moved off.

Sweeping the Klaris around in a tight, neat circle he got her ready to go back the way they'd come. They were in mid glacier when he noticed a wolf racing down to the bank and come to a sudden stop.

'Too late,' he said, as the wind caught the sail. 'You'll have to catch the next one.'

It placed two paws tentatively on the ice, but the yacht was travelling too fast for it to skid across and jump on board. It watched their departure with a snarl.

Enegene uncrumpled herself from the deck and came to stand beside him. 'I feel light,' she said, leaning against the control column.

'Light?'

'Light. Like I could fly.'

'We're moving fairly fast.'

Flinging her arms apart she said, 'feel like I could spread my arms and take off.'

'Doubt it, you're too heavy.'

'I'm not heavy!' She grinned broadly. 'I'm correct weight.'

'For flying?'

She shook her head and wrapped her arms around her body. 'For me.'

'For you to what?'

433

'For me to be me. I'm correct weight.'

It was said with a finality that he saw no reason to argue with; he was feeling slightly light himself.

Coming to the end of their quiet lane he took them onto the busier one. Everything seemed so much more easy-going than before and he was enjoying the ride.

As they rounded the last bend before once again turning off they saw a yacht partially blocking the lane. It was skewed sideways with one blade tip jammed in a bank. There was no time to stop; they would hit it before they could.

His mind went into overdrive. Adding all the sail power he could, he told Enegene to go to the left side and hold on. Then he joined her and their combined weight lifted one runner off the ice as they slid past.

Once clear, they moved to the centre. The airborne runner came back to the ice with a bump, luckily not hard enough to crack it. Then he reduced the sail power and slowed their speed. Enegene turned and looked at the stricken yacht as they left it behind.

'That was tehin clever,' she said, unconcerned about the danger. 'Didn't know you could do that.'

'Neither did I,' he replied, his head beginning to clear.

'Did you see that crate move?'

'No, I was piloting.'

'You nearly took the top off it with the rail. It moved.'

He glanced back briefly. 'Moved?'

The boat was sloping the wrong way for the crate to slide. Although puzzled, he shrugged it off and concentrated on steering.

The close call had done two things for Luapp; it brought his senses back into normal working order at the speed of light. It also allowed him to realise he'd broken the law by being in command of a craft while being under the influence of something powerful.

Flashing Enegene a quick look he could tell she was still affected. But what it was and how it was administered was a mystery.

All he wanted now was to get the yacht safely back. It took another twenty minutes of concentration before they arrived at the inlet outside the hotel.

Making the boat secure, he helped Enegene off and took her inside to reception. He asked the receptionist to call the instructor, and then guided Enegene into the lift. On the third floor, they exited and headed for their room.

By this time Luapp's mind was totally clear except for a slight headache. Ushering Enegene into the room he went through to his bedroom leaving her slumped on the sofa.

He noticed the time as they entered and wondered why it was important. Then he remembered they were in fact boarding at half eight the next morning, not eight this evening.

When he checked on her a short while later, he saw she'd stretched out comfortably on the sofa. As she was apparently asleep, he decided to have a shower. With Enegene sleeping, Luapp didn't bother to lock the bathroom door.

Switching the shower to a pleasant and soothing heat, he undressed and stepped in. For a moment, he just stood under the water allowing its warmth to relax body and mind.

Then he pressed several buttons adjusting the shower head and soap dispensers to his height, and the dryer to hot. Next, he pressed the soap dispenser and began washing his hair, his mind drifting in neutral.

When he finished, he ran his hands through his hair to move it back into place. Then he pushed the soap button a second time, along with another beside it.

A fine spray of soap burst out of the concealed heads covering him from shoulders to knees and he began rubbing it over his body. It was at this moment the bathroom door opened.

Hearing a low curse, he half turned as Enegene catapulted into the shower cubicle slapping him on the rear as she fell. On the way down, she connected with his legs and slithered into the shower tray.

As she hit bottom she tightened her grip around his ankles forcing one leg against the other making him sway unsteadily. Slamming his hands against the sides of the cubicle he managed to prevent himself falling on top of her.

She was now curled in the tray, madly gripping his ankles, giggling and cursing under her breath alternatively. Looking down, he glared at her.

'Let go.'

He moved one leg then the other trying to free himself from her vice like grip.

'Can't let go I'll fall over.'

'You're already over,' he pointed out with rapidly evaporating patience.

Enegene tentatively loosened one hand and tapped the floor. Releasing her grip on his ankles she pushed herself into a kneeling position and squinted up through the water.

'You're a long way up... and you're air-clad.' She exploded into a mass of loud giggles.

'Get out of my shower,' he said, curtly.

Trying to get to her feet, she slid in the soapy water in the shower tray. With no handhold in the shower she gripped his waist and pulled. He winced, grabbed her wrists and pulled her nails away from his body. Then he steadied her as she got to her feet.

'Actually,' she swayed and pushed some damp hair off her face, 'it's my shower. I'm the Lady, you're the slave. I'm going to have a shower and if you don't like it, you can leave.'

Ejecting Enegene from the shower, Luapp held the door shut behind her. He watched her through the opaque glass until she stumbled out of the bathroom.

Luapp's mood of relaxation was shattered. He rinsed himself off and switched on the blower. A blast of hot air enveloped him, quickly drying his skin and hair. When the dryer switched off, he left the cubicle wearing the robe that presented itself from a cupboard at the back of the dry cabinet.

Collecting his clothes, he exited the bathroom cautiously. He looked around for Enegene but there was no sign of her. She wasn't in the lounge, so he went to her bedroom. She was sound asleep on the bed, wrapped in a dry-robe. Giving her a cursory glance, he went on to his own bedroom.

He dressed quickly not wanting to chance being surprised by her again. As he fastened his shirt, the viscom bleeping brought him back to the lounge. The face of the female receptionist smiled out at him.

'Glacial Yacht instructor arrived to collect craft, has.'

'I'll come down.'

The instructor was talking to the receptionist as he arrived, but stopped when he realised Luapp was there. As he handed over the key and licence for the yacht, the instructor took out a small machine and made some notes.

'Safe return of yacht noted, has been,' he said. 'Your lady will receive returned deposit. Notice when she next looks at monetary balance, she will.'

He chatted happily, asking if they'd had a good time. Then he told Luapp they were lucky to have avoided the accident. Although he said nothing Luapp frowned.

*I remember the accident. I should have reported it once we were back, but my mind wasn't functioning properly...*

'Anyone injured?'

'No. Water only half alm deep at this place, but damaged

yacht is. Stupid richie think knows all he did.' The man looked up and smiled. 'Next time visit, look us up.'

He handed over a receipt and left the hotel. Returning to the lifts, Luapp headed back up to their room. He was expecting the door to be unlocked and nearly walked into it. Placing his hand on the door, he pushed gently. It didn't move. He pushed harder but it remained shut.

He searched for the motion sensors and waved his hand in front of them, but it still refused to open. He was considering calling reception to report a faulty door, when a faint sound inside made him suspicious. Leaning against the door, he listened carefully.

'Enegene? Are you there?'

'Yes.' She sounded annoyed.

'Have you locked the door?'

'Yes.'

'Open it, I can't get in.'

'No.'

'Why?'

'You pushed me out the shower,' she replied petulantly.

He stood back, hands on hips staring at the door. 'Enegene,' he said, with an edge to his voice. 'Let me in.'

'Not until you apologise.'

'Alright, I apologise.'

'You don't mean it. Say it like you mean it.'

He took a long, slow breath. 'I apologise for shutting you out of the shower.'

There was a pause. 'You don't really mean it.'

She sounded like a child and it was beginning to annoy. A muscle twitched by his jaw as he placed both hands on the door.

'Namrae, if you don't let me in, you'll regret it.'

'Now you're threatening me. You can stay out there all

night for all I care.'

Standing back from the door he looked up and down the corridor. Seeing no one around, he placed his hand on the door and moved it slowly over the surface.

Finding the locking mechanism, he put his palm over it, checked the corridor again and closed his eyes. It opened with a click followed by a squeak of consternation.

The door opened and he went in. There was no sign of her. Checking her bedroom and not finding her there he tried the bathroom. The door to this was locked.

'You'll have to stay in there all night if you want to remain in one piece,' he snarled through the door.

Chapter 25

The viscom buzzing brought Luapp from his room. The receptionist smiled out of the screen and informed him the evening meal was being served. Glancing at the bathroom door, he picked up the key and left.

In the dining room, he found an empty table and studied the menu until the waiter came over. 'Are you waiting for the lady or starting without her?'

His concern about being refused a meal without Enegene being present faded. 'She's not coming down; she's feeling unwell. Perhaps a light meal could be prepared for me to take back?'

'Of course,' the waiter replied. 'Would you like to order now?'

Luapp was pleased to see the chef had added a few vegetarian dishes to the menu. He ordered the meal and was pleasantly surprised when it arrived only a short time later.

He took his time over the meal enjoying the solitude. When he finished, he called the waiter and asked for the tray to take up.

While he waited, he was surprised to see Enegene walk past the entrance of the dining room. Taking the tray from the man he stopped outside and looked around. There was no sign of her, so he returned to the suite and let himself in.

Placing the tray on the table, he walked over to her bedroom and looked in. A pillow and some covers were missing, and the bathroom door was still shut. Hands on hips he considered the situation.

*Why has she locked herself in the clensrom after going down to the lobby? One minute she's acting scared, then she's walking around unconcerned, now she scared again... is she in there?*

He walked over and tried the handle. It was still locked so he tapped on the door.

'Go away.' She sounded miserable.

'If you wish, but I have something for you.'

'I'm sure you do,' she retorted.

'Come to the door, I'll put it within reach.'

He placed the tray on the ground and removed the covers. There was a soft sound of snuffling, like an animal looking for food, then a low moan.

'You can lose your commission for torture.'

She sounded pathetic and he took pity on her. 'Come and get it.'

'You'll grab me.'

'I brought it up for you; it would be illogical to waste it.'

'I don't trust you, you threatened me.'

'Only once.'

'Once? Try six and each one nastier than the last.'

'I'll stand across the other side of the room.'

He backed up until he was standing by the bedroom wall, questions zipping through his mind. The bathroom door opened just enough for her to peer through and see where he was.

Then she looked down at the tray and glanced up at him again. Edging the door open enough to grasp the tray, she pulled it inside. The door locked and he moved closer. Closing his eyes, he telepathically linked to her thoughts and searched her memory. Although quickly fading as her mind turned to food, he picked up several threats shouted through the door. With a frown, he broke the contact and left the lounge.

Due to the exertions of the day and the strange episode of mind lapse Luapp decided to retire early. As he undressed in the bedroom, he shivered. Despite the hotel's efficient heating system, he felt cold and decided to use the sleep suit provided.

He lay back in the bed with his arms tucked beneath his head and reflected on the oddities of the day.

*Several strange things have happened; too strange to be ignored. The elderly female Enegene mentioned watching us. Inhabitants will sometimes stare at outworlders, but not with such intensity.*

*Then there was the lopar. The animal definitely looked as if it intended jumping on board, even in my mind-fogged state I recognised that.*

*And the crate that slid the wrong way, and finally, she insisted I'd threatened her several times when I wasn't even in the room. Plus, I'd seen her walk past the festrom when she was apparently still locked in the clensrom.*

*It can't all be imagination; hallucination brought on by a drug? I tapped her mind, she was convinced it was me threatening her, and I genuinely thought she walked past the festrom.*

*If it had just been Enegene seeing things I would have suspected the drink she'd consumed, but I'd experienced the same feeling of detachment.*

*Enegene mentioned the woman and the first lopar before she drunk anything alcoholic. Both could be explained logically. I'd already given one for the woman, and as lopars are cautious creatures, they would watch anything passing. But trying to board a moving vessel is another thing entirely.*

442

*Is the atmosphere not suited to us? I hadn't drunk anything alcoholic and my head cleared when we were in danger. It has to be a drug, but how and why was it administered? We were strangers to the owners, and there was nobody in the drinking house that I recognised.*

*I'm now thinking rationally, so why isn't Enegene? Has she had a double dose somehow? Or is she still in contact with whatever is causing the problem?*

The crashed ship came to mind. *The only other explanation is not even worth considering... but perhaps I should investigate that tomorrow; all I want now is to sleep.*

~~~

Light footsteps crossing the floor brought him from deep sleep to awake in moments. The covers moved and a body slid in next to him. A hand touched his shoulder, pulled back the neck of the suit top and soft lips kissed him.

'Mikim,' whispered a familiar voice, 'are you asleep?'

'That's an absurd question,' he said sharply. 'Even if I was, I'm not now.'

'Good,' her voice deepened slightly. 'I have waited too long for this moment.'

*Mikim?*

An icy tingle slithered down his spine and his mind raced. *This can't be Harat; she should have reach Quarn by now, it has to be Enegene...*

Turning quickly to face her he was momentarily frozen with surprise. It wasn't Enegene, it was Benze. Or rather, a gross caricature mix of both. It was Enegene's hair and slim body, but Benze face. She had a strange, sideways grin and a fixed stare.

'I'll take care of your owner when I'm finished in here.'

Her hand went to his face and she leaned forward for a second kiss. Guardian training kicked in and he lashed out with the flat of his hand. It wasn't what she was expecting from a slave, and she had no time to avoid the blow.

His hand landed on her shoulder knocking her out of the bed. Her head hit the bedside cabinet and she lay dazed on the ground.

With Teth Harat temporarily incapacitated, Luapp scrambled out the other side. Hurriedly rummaging in his bag for the Fluctoid weapon, he found it just in time. While on the ground she changed into something resembling a bear.

Rising onto her hind legs, her muzzle wrinkled into a snarl. 'That wasn't the subservience of a slave Mikim, you must learn obedience.'

Raising the weapon, a thought flitted through his brain that freezing her in this shape was not helpful.

*Harat can still shred me and I can't put wristlinks on a manak. I need her to change to something more manageable...*

As she lumbered forward, he dropped the gun into the bag, grabbed the edge of the bed and pushed it towards her catching her knees. She dropped to all fours and jumped back avoiding a second swing. With a ferocious roar she rose onto her hind legs again.

Changing tactics, he raised the bed up on end and shoved it towards her. It fell hitting her muzzle surprising her enough to allow him to snatch the weapon and get through the door. Enraged even further she let out another roar.

He shoved the weapon into his trouser top and pulled the door shut. Bracing his foot against the door frame, he grabbed the handle and held on. The bathroom door opened and Enegene peered out.

'Get out,' he said, get help.'

'What....?'

Splintering wood and a huge paw crashing through the door made her react. Gathering the cover tightly around her she ran for the main door. It slid open at her approach and she almost collided with a surprised manager just outside.

'I to parties no object...' he began in a conciliatory tone.

'We need help,' she blurted. 'There's a wild beast attacking my slave.'

Pulling his communicator from his pocket he called down to reception. He told the receptionist to send up the hunters.

'Often get scavenger we do,' he said. 'No fear, not dangerous they are.'

'It's not...' Enegene's reply was cut off by the sound of hurrying feet and the appearance of a hunter with a weapon.

'What is it?' the manager said, 'torgo?'

'Torgo?'

Another loud crash was followed by Luapp rushing through the door, pulling it closed behind him.

'Torgo?' the manager said, looking at him.

'Manak,' Luapp corrected. Holding the duo weapon close to his side, he kept it out of view.

The manager listened to the translation from his communicator. 'Bear?' he said confused. 'No bear here.'

A huge paw smashed through the door and the guard raised his gun. The bear's head peered through, saw the high powered weapon and jerked back. The hunter let off a shot and moved forward to look through the hole.

Luapp decided he could no longer wait for a convenient shape. Stepping behind the hunter, he looked through the hole and saw her further back.

As the hunter lifted his gun a second time, Luapp glanced back at the manager. He was busy calling another hunter. He raised the weapon above the hunter's head and fired. The laser hit first freezing Teth Harat in shape. With a furious growl, she charged the door.

Luapp and the hunter hastily flattened themselves against

445

the wall as she broke through. Enegene, the manager and the second hunter scattered allowing the bear access to the stairs.

'Shoot!' the manager shouted.

Interested onlookers rapidly returned to their rooms to get out of the way of the furious animal as the hunter beside Luapp fired. Wounded, the fleeing bear staggered against the bannister then continued her rush down the stairs.

'Where did it come from?' Enegene said, throwing the mantle of blame back on the shoulders of the hotel.

'Zaned I know,' the manager replied, bewildered. 'Bear no here.'

The second hunter cautiously climbed into the room through the wrecked door and looked around. Declaring it empty he returned.

'Follow it we must,' he said. 'Dangerous when injured.'

'It seemed pretty dangerous before,' Enegene said, turning her attention on the manager.

He smiled apologetically. 'Move you to another room I will.'

'Good. One without manaks I hope. Mikim, get our things.'

The manager led the way down the corridor to another room and opened it for her. 'Rest of night more peaceful should be.' He wandered off confused.

Enegene waited in her bedroom for Luapp to arrive with the bags and clothes. 'Why have you got the Fluctoid weapon?'

He frowned. 'I don't know; I intended to send it on with the rest.'

'Don't tell me where she came from,' she said wearily, 'I don't want to know, not tonight.'

'I couldn't explain if I wanted to.'

Dropping the cases on the floor and the clothes on the nearby chair he left her room heading for his own.

~~~

446

Enegene woke feeling the effects of the day before. Her head was thumping painfully, and she was feeling slightly nauseous. For a moment, she wondered if Luapp had put something in her food, but had to admit he wasn't vindictive.

She'd felt like this before, on occasions when she'd drunk too much. But she was puzzled; she'd only had one drink and those vegetable crisps. It was a mystery she couldn't be bothered to spend time on.

Having raised herself to a standing position, she carefully made her way to the door. The lounge area was empty so she went to his bedroom. Leaning close to the door, she listened but heard no sounds from inside. Her stomachs tightened as another thought hit her.

*He's gone to the Starport without me…*

Opening the door, she looked in. He wasn't there. *The sleeper's been pulled straight and,* she looked in the wardrobe, *there's no clothes. Clensrom?*

She went to the bathroom door and listened. With no sound of running water, she slid the handle and looked inside. It was empty. Her heart doubled its beat. Back in his room she knelt and peered under the bed.

'Looking for something?'

For a moment her heart stopped. With a gasp, Enegene clutched her head and dragged herself to her feet. Turning to face him she said, 'you.'

'It's not my habit to lurk under sleepers.' For some reason, he seemed irritated.

'After last night, I wouldn't be surprised where you'd be lurking.'

'What do you want?'

'I wondered where you were.'

Twitching a brow, he said, 'thought I'd gone without you?'

'It crossed my mind.'

'It crossed mine too, but I decided not to.'

He returned to the lounge where his overnight bag was standing by the end of the sofa. 'We're leaving in ten minutes. Get dressed.'

She took two strides then leaned against the door. 'Ooh, I can't rush I feel awful.'

'You look awful,' he said, heading for her room.

Summoning her determination she went back to the bathroom. By the time she emerged, he'd packed her bag. She handed him the wash bag and he pushed that in as well.

'Let's go,' he said curtly. 'Hopefully the rest of the trip will be uneventful.'

He marched out leaving her to follow as best as she could. She passed him at reception paying the bill and went outside. When he joined her she was standing by the first taxi in the rank. He put their bags in the rear store and got in the sleigh.

'You direct the driver Mikim,' she said weakly. 'I feel too delicate this morning.'

'Ferry port for star port four,' he told the driver.

The journey to the ferry port was done in silence. Enegene was grateful for that; talking only increased the pain in her head.

The taxi swept into the ferry port, and stopped outside departures. Luapp gave the driver her card as she left the sleigh. Collecting it minutes later he handed it to her as they walked into the terminal.

They passed through passenger control and into the departure room without any hold ups. Everything connected smoothly and the ferry locked into the portal close to the cruiser taking them the rest of the way home.

Three days later they crossed the boundary between the Black Systems and galactic free-space, and Luapp became a free man once more.

## Chapter 26

Disembarking on Gaeiza Luapp and Enegene passed
through passenger control and caught a taxi to the mainland.
In the capital city of Mohaib they went their separate ways.

As the taxi drew up at the Reul apalodge, Luapp paid the
fee and went inside. He stopped briefly to speak to the girl at
reception then took the lift to the 153rd. floor.

Travelling up, his mind drifted to the gap in development
between Pedanta and Gaeiza. The difference between the
rather slow, noisy workings of the lifts on Pedanta and the
smooth, soundless rising of the apalodge riser disc, was a point
in fact.

They had levitating vehicles, but computers for the general
public were only just becoming available. The secret base of
the Coalition Master was almost two decades ahead of normal
housing, even in the more technologically advanced capital
city of Denjal.

The front panel of the lift slid back allowing him out of the
tubular cabin. Walking to his apartment, he said his name and
went inside. The familiar and comfortable surroundings
brought a sense of relief.

The cases were waiting in the iaad room having got through

the underground system straight from the cargo ship. Carrying them through to the bedroom he began unpacking.

A while later, he contacted GSC to tell them he would be in the following morning for debriefing. After that, he made a series of calls to his father and friends. This was followed by a brief message to Langa Cha telling him the mission had been a success and thanking him for his help. This left one last call.

The hospital gave him a list of free appointment times and he booked in. With every personal duty carried out he relaxed and watched the dimensional entertainment screen.

~~~

High Commander Brann appeared to be busy at the computer when Luapp arrived in his office the next day. But he didn't save his work before telling the machine to open a new file, suggesting it was something just keeping him busy until Luapp came in.

The debrief took a couple of hours going over his report and discussing the details of the mission. Finally satisfied, Brann switched off the monitor and sat back.

'The Galactic Council has requested you and Spyrian Namrae go to the hearing on Padua and give evidence. Also, there will be the Pedantan enforcer named Jym Corder, and a law speaker from the council. They will represent all other enforcers involved.

Unfortunately, you and the Spyrian won't be able to travel together. After your leave you will report to HaJaan. He wants you in black and going to Base One East to familiarise yourself with its running.'

Luapp twitched a brow. 'This was supposed to be a temporary secondment.'

'Temporary only in assessment of your adjustment to space duties. You were told this when you contacted us from Freair. HaJaan needs someone of your calibre Luapp, and your sub deserves promotion.'

'Has Padua sent anyone to Freair to collect Teth Harat?'

'Your prompt action in alerting us to her presence enabled the Ominarians to send a collection force. I'm told they'll not leave the planet until they have her.'

'How is Enegene Namrae getting to Padua?'

'We've been given a date and it coincides with Green Commander Yetok's leave. He has agreed to take her.'

'No space guardians available?' Luapp said, surprised.

'Quite a few, but Commander Yetok felt that the Spyrian will be more relaxed in his company. Any other questions?'

'When do I leave?'

'You've been continuously on duty for an orbit; you've got five monspa's vacation. Report to HaJaan during the last week. Have a good rest Luapp.'

As he left guardian command Luapp mulled over the news he was to meet Enegene again. On the journey home, he'd changed his mind about contacting her. She stirred up feelings he'd thought had died.

Transferring to space would mean being away from Gaeiza for many months at a time. That wasn't good for a new relationship and he'd decided a clean break would be best.

Back in his apartment he left a message on her keeper and was surprised when the viscom came to life and her face appeared on screen.

'Just can't get rid of me can you Nostowe?' A broad grin lit her face. 'While we're talking, how about spending an evening with me as a free man?'

Six different refusals came to mind and he was surprised when he found himself saying, 'when?'

'Beon?'

He mentally flicked through dates. 'What time?'

'Eighteenth hour?'

'Agreed. I'll collect you, you decide where we go.'

She smiled again. 'Three days guardian, wear slick.'

Switching off the machine he mulled over the contact.

*Why didn't I refuse? And why am I suddenly edgy? I'd decided continuing contact was unwise. An hour of meditation will calm mind and emotions.*

With a slow, deep breath, he closed his eyes, emptied his mind and relaxed. An hour later, he left the apartment and headed into the country to visit his father.

~~~

The next two days passed quickly. One was spent in the hospital having the brand removed. Although not as complicated as he feared, it had been more difficult than having the top skin peeled and the flesh underneath revitalised. He'd spent the whole day going from one department to the next for a series of treatments.

The second day was less stressful. He remained in his apartment restocking his food stores and catching up with friends while waiting for the ache in his arm to stop.

Arriving outside Enegene's apartment on the evening of the third day he was curious about their destination. He had dressed smartly as she'd asked, and hoped she hadn't been joking.

As soon as he touched the ident plate and the door opened. The room was empty as he walked in, but Enegene arrived in the lounge a few minutes later and smiled her approval.

'Very nice Guardian, that shade of blue suits you.'

Her choice of dark green gown with beaded moonflowers gained his silent approval. 'I feel slightly under dressed compared to you.'

Adding a jewelled clip to her pinned up hair she moved to the sofa, sat down and looked up at him expectantly.

'You can be as under dressed as you like, not dressed at all even.' Her orange frosted lips curved into a wicked smile.

He supressed the instant rebuke that sprung to mind as he joined her on the sofa. 'You're wearing the starglow.'

Gently touching it she smiled. 'It holds special memories.'

'Where are we going?'

'To the Sharron.'

'The new place?'

'New and very exclusive. I've booked for nineteenth. That gives us a bit of time together before we go.'

'We've had enough time together over the past orbit.'

'Tired of me Guardian?' She leaned closer and looked seductively into his eyes.

Moving a short space away, he said, 'I wouldn't have come if I hadn't wished to.'

'That's the kind of thing I like to hear.'

She changed from siren to Spyrian, telling him about what she'd done over the past two days. Luapp listened to every third word. He realised with surprise he was beginning to enjoy the siren as much as he respected the Spyrian.

Now off duty, he allowed himself the luxury of appreciating what a beautiful woman she was. Tuning into the words "we'd better go", he stood and waited while she strapped her card holder to her wrist.

'Taking your ID card?' Luapp said surprised.

'Never been before so they don't have me on record.'

'That's a thought; I'll register as well.'

'You've brought your card?'

Luapp smiled. 'I don't need to, it'll find me.'

'That's the down side of being a guardian, you're on record everywhere.'

'If that was the only downside it would be an easy life.'

With a smile, Enegene left the apartment and walked with Luapp to the exiport. She crossed the silbridge to his cehivo hovering outside, and held on as the seats rearranged for him to get into the pilot position.

It was a short trip across town to the club, and as they neared the building the vehicle flew into the sub-ground park. It stopped by the lifts allowing them out and then parked itself. After a quick ride ten floors up they entered the club.

Arriving home at the fourth hour the next morning, he Thought over their evening together as he undressed. He'd enjoyed it so much he hadn't noticed the time passing. Without work clouding the issue, he'd felt at ease and comfortable with Enegene.

*She's worth meeting again,* he decided as he pulled back the bed cover. As his eyes closed it was followed by the thought; *tomorrow I'm free to do as I like.*

## Chapter 27

Enegene picked up her overnight bag and walked to the door. She greeted Green Commander Yetok with a smile and walked with him to the exiport. He waited as she crossed the silbridge and stepped into his cehivo.

'How long before we get to Padua?' she said, watching him get into the pilot seat.

'Approximately thirteen hours.' He took the cehivo above the city traffic heading towards the country. 'Luapp should arrive shortly after. Base One isn't too far from the council planet.'

'Typical of him transferring to the space division just as we we're getting to know each other,' Enegene said tartly.

Giving her a brief glance the green commander returned his attention to piloting the vehicle.

'Luapp had no choice. High Commander HaJaan requested him, and High Commander Brann thought a change of command would give him scope to advance.'

Outside the city, he increased speed and they arrived at the island spaceport in minutes.

'Advance to what?' she said. 'He's too focussed as it is.'

As the cehivo touched down in the guardian vehicle park

the harnesses and door locks released.

'He's commander of the greys and the only promotion available puts him behind a desk. That's not good for Luapp. Space gives further promotion but still allows him to remain active.'

They crossed the planetary vehicle park to the spaceship area where a sleek arrow-head shaped black craft was standing on a hexagonal marker.

The Dart's door opened as they neared and she followed him to the pilot pod. As they sat down the safety harnesses slid over their shoulders and clicked into the side clasps.

Ekym contacted guardian space control and then its civilian counterpart as he went through take-off procedure.

'Why are you doing that?' Enegene said. 'You don't have to comply with civilian space craft control.'

'It's true we don't have to comply, but we do so out of courtesy. I must also avoid the continuous local traffic between us and the other systems. Only in emergencies do we ignore civilian procedures.'

Given the all clear he took off and headed out of the solar system. Passing the last planet, he put the ship on autofly and glanced at Enegene. Noticing her tight expression, he said, 'what concerns you?'

She scowled at him. 'Giving evidence. The only time I was in a court I was being sentenced.'

'This is a hearing, not a judgement. All they need is your account of what happened on Pedanta. There may be a few questions, but it's just to clarify their understanding.'

'Why is that? Surely they have enough evidence to convict Benze for her crimes.'

Ekym swivelled the chair and got up. Enegene followed him from the pilot pod to the relaxrom. Going to the food machine he pressed the touch screen.

'There's no logic in judging one who is deceased.'

He brought two cups of coffee to where Enegene was sitting at the table. Joining her he watched the steam rise from his drink.

'The report from Freair stated she was killed by the hunters.' He looked up at her. 'They had digistil evidence.

The purpose of the hearing is to close the case to the satisfaction of all the planetary enforcers involved. It also gives some emotional solace to the relatives of the victims.'

Enegene sipped her coffee while gazing at the guardian. 'Luapp and I have been apart for three monspa…' she paused. With Ekym staying silent, she added, 'do you think he would have changed his mind about me?'

He raised a sand coloured brow and let it drop. 'If you didn't irritate him before he left, he'll probably be pleased to see you.'

Enegene frowned. 'What is it about Luapp that you and he don't say?'

Ekym's gaze was steady. 'Anything Luapp wants you to know he'll tell you when he's ready.'

She watched the green commander stand up holding his mug. He sipped his coffee and turned to go. 'Just one question; has he had a liana?'

Ekym appeared to consider his answer before speaking. 'No.' Then he left before she could ask any more.

Enegene cradled her mug in her hands. *He took a long time coming up with a short answer.*

Glancing at the doorway it was obvious Ekym was not going to keep her company so she decided to fill her time another way. She tapped the control on the table and waited as the computer slid up. Giving it her password she linked with her office computer and started work.

Thirteen point three hours later Enegene was back in the

pilot pod next to Ekym. They were watching the galactic council planet Padua turn beneath them.

'I thought this place would be bigger than this,' she said, as they waited for landing permission.

'Size has nothing to do with what happens planetside.'

'But it's smaller than Gaeiza and only has one sun.'

'Orbiting a solo star is extremely common in the galaxy.'

'Don't the inhabitants object to being dominated by the council?'

'Padua was chosen because it had no higher intelligences to negotiate with.'

'But Luapp said it was chosen because it's close to the central position of all membership planets.'

'That too; but for how much longer is debatable.'

'Why?'

'As more systems join it becomes less central, but it will remain the council's planet.'

'So how did they find a planet that had no higher intelligences, was safe and had what they needed?'

'I assume they searched for a long time.'

'But people live here now, don't they?'

'Only short term. Obviously, the various politicians, councillors and ambassadors serve a duty term and return to their own planet, as do their entire staffs.

Equally, all workers no matter what their employment are not permitted to spend more than five orbits continuously on Padua.'

'That seems a bit oppressive.'

Ekym briefly turned his attention from the view to her. 'It's logical. If people were allowed permanent residence, it would inevitably follow they would gain rights of habitation and eventually be able to dictate conditions to the council.

Therefore, there is no infrastructure for families. Most

council members don't bring their families, and if they do they can only stay three orbits. Qivers must be young enough not to need formal education, or adols old enough to be employed.'

'But there's a whole city here; hotels, embassies...'

'There are strict laws about building, employment and ownership of property. Basically, no-one can own a building on Padua except the council. The main council deals with external matters but there's an inner group that determines Paduan regulations. They are supposedly incorruptible, and work for the benefit of all concerned.'

'It must be a logistical night terror to run.'

'They've worked it out as it's gone along and it is continually evolving to encompass new members.'

'Do they control the hotels and amusement areas?'

'They are privately run by reputable firms but are ultimately answerable to the council. They have the power to shut down and evict if they feel the entertainment is mishandled or inappropriate.'

'I'm surprised any firm would agree to that.'

'If they want to operate on Padua they have no choice.'

'So, the council owns the whole city?'

'Most of the city is the galactic council building, its adjoining embassy block, and the archives. As those attending sessions needed somewhere to live, and the normal support industries, they were provided under council supervision.

Hotels are a relatively new addition to the city. With growing membership, the permanent employment of guardians as galactic enforcers, and the training of the MSF located here, it was realised visiting dignitaries and families of enforcers needed somewhere to stay.'

'Why create the multi-species force? Guardians perform all duties within the Seven Systems.'

'While we take on a military role at home, we cannot cover

the entire seventy eight percent of the galaxy council members occupy. We are primarily an enforcer group, so it was agreed to create a multispecies military to act in case of war or invasion. In this way, all members of the council have responsibility for its protection.'

'Why are guardians coming and going?'

'Firstly, we have a Gaeizaan embassy here. Secondly, we do missions for all the sollenite species when required. Thirdly, we do missions for the galactic council when required. Fourthly, this is the centre of the membership's judicial administration. Lastly, we partake in manoeuvres with the multispecies force, and this is the meeting point.'

'Couldn't visiting guardians just stay in the embassy?'

'No. With guardians visiting for routine work and doing manoeuvres with the multispecies, there are around two t'ori on the planet at any one time. The embassy cannot lodge so many.'

'So the only civilians allowed on Padua are the families of the workers?'

A fleeting frown touched his brow. 'Everyone there is a civilian except guardians and the MSF. If I answer what I think you mean, things are changing. Small groups of tourists are beginning to be allowed to visit for short periods to see the council debate on non-sensitive subjects. But this essentially remains a place of work, not a domicile for extraneous visitors.'

'So where will we be going tomorrow?'

'The council building.'

'I thought that was just for council meetings.'

'The council building encompasses the Chairperson and membership representative offices, several small meeting halls and the main debating chamber where business is conducted.

A judicial court and the various workers are contained in a connecting building. While it's separate to the debating chamber, it's part of the council building and can be accessed from it.'

'But…'

She was stopped by a voice coming through the speaker addressing Ekym. With permission granted and instructions received, he broke orbit and started down through the atmosphere.

He landed in the military ship compound and then took Enegene to the hotel. Pressing their thumbs onto the register sensipad, they went up to their rooms. Ekym took his overnight bag to his own room, then arrived in hers a few minutes later.

Noticing he remained by the door, she said, 'what happens next?'

'Luapp will land sometime this afternoon. Until then I can take you into town or you can remain here. Whatever you choose, I have to visit the court and register our arrival.'

'I think I'll come with you.'

Ekym left the room and waited in the corridor for her. She took a few seconds to try and curb her nerves, but her control of her expression was not as good as she hoped.

As she joined him by the lift, he said, 'this is not about you, and there's nothing to be concerned about.'

She gave him a tight smile and was about to answer when the lift doors opened and a happy voice exclaimed, 'Kayleeee.'

Ekym stepped back as Aylisha burst from the lift cabin with her arms flung wide. Jym followed at a more sedate pace.

'Kaylee?' Ekym said, confused.

Enegene allowed the hug and waited for Aylisha to step back. 'Commander,' she said in Gaeizaan, 'this is Aylisha Rhalin, my good friend from Pedanta, and Jym Corder, senior officer in the Pedantan enforcers.'

Switching to Pedantan, she added, 'Aylisha, Jym, this is

461

Green Commander Yetok, Luapp's close friend.'

'We've just arrived,' Aylisha said. 'Would you like to join me in my room?'

Enegene repeated the invitation to Ekym. 'Spend time with your friend,' he said. 'I must go to the court.'

Jym turned as Ekym went to enter the lift. 'Enegene, translate for me. Where is he going?'

Asking Ekym to wait, Enegene passed on the question. 'What language are they speaking?' he said.

'Pedantan.'

Speaking into his helmet, Ekym told the computer to translate Pedantan to Gaeizaan, and the reverse. 'I'm going to the court.'

Suddenly able to understand what was said, Jym paused his next question in surprise. Then he continued, 'do you mind if I join you? I have to go there as well and I know nothing about this place.'

'If you wish, though I doubt you need your luggage.'

Jym looked down at the shoulder case. 'I need a file from inside but I'll leave the bag in my room.'

He hurried off leaving Aylisha chatting happily to Enegene. He passed them coming back and joined Ekym in the lift.

Entering Aylisha's suite Enegene went over to the sofa and sat down. Aylisha took her case into the bedroom. She described her journey from Pedanta to Padua and returned to the lounge without hardly drawing breath.

Sitting beside Enegene, she added, 'it's so good to see you. How are things between you and the guardian?'

'He's been transferred to the space division.'

Aylisha looked momentarily surprised. 'Was that his decision?'

'No, in fact he didn't want it, but his superior thought it was the right move, so he went.'

462

The smile returned to Aylisha's face. 'So he's not avoiding you?'

Enegene grinned. 'No. I was annoyed at first, but I must admit it has its advantages.'

'Advantages? What advantages?'

'When he's away I can concentrate on work, and when he's home, he's home for several months.'

'I hope it goes well for you Kay... Enegene.'

'And what about you and Jym?'

Aylisha's eyes lit up. 'He's so wonderful....'

Enegene allowed Aylisha to gabble on about her romance with Jym. It pleased her to see her friend so happy, and it proved a great distraction from her concerns.

She returned to her room some hours later with just enough time to freshen up before dinner. Luapp should have arrived by now and she couldn't wait to see him. With a final glance in the mirror, she left the room and went to collect Aylisha and Jym.

Passing Ekym's room she wondered whether to call there first, but decided not to. After just one press on Aylisha's door call, the door swished open and Aylisha and Jym appeared.

'The green commander said he and Luapp would meet us in the dining room,' Jym said, as they walked to the lift.

The dining room was almost full when they arrived. After a moment's indecision in the doorway, Jym pointed to a table near the far wall. Wending their way across the room they joined Luapp and Ekym.

'Good,' Luapp said, 'now we can order.'

'Didn't you eat on the way?' Jym said.

'Not worth it. My base is only three hours away and I knew I was going to eat when I got here. A slightly longer journey for you and Aylisha.'

'Yes, never had to travel so far for a case in my life.'

Luapp smiled at Enegene and pulled the menu from its holder. 'And your trip?'

She glanced at Ekym over the menu card. 'It was quiet.'

'I suggest we talk over the proceedings for tomorrow while we eat. Ekym's trip to the court provided useful information.'

'Fine with me,' Jym said. 'How about the ladies?'

'That's what we're here for,' Enegene said.

'Good,' make your choices and we'll start.'

Discussing the next day's appearance at court took little more than a quarter of an hour, the rest of the time was spent reminiscing about their time on Pedanta.

~~~

They arrived at the court offices early the next day and were taken to their appointed places. Ekym being the only one not involved with the case sat where he liked.

As she sat down, Enegene glanced around at the many people there. 'I thought we were the only ones giving evidence.'

'An enforcer from each of the seventeen planets where a slaying took place has come to give their report,' Luapp said. 'This naturally includes us, Aylisha and Jym.'

The arrival of the Judges stopped conversation and the hearing began. It took most of the day to hear the different accounts from the various police representatives involved.

Pellan and his cousin were to give evidence after that, but their account was played on a screen. They recorded their statement the previous day and left before the others arrived.

An Arganite female who had been sitting at a desk in front of the judges podium then stood up. Despite the robes and neatly held back hair, her broad skull and thick frame reminded Enegene of historical mock-ups of the ancient tribes of Gaeiza. With her mind distracted she missed the woman's opening announcement.

'What's she doing?' she whispered to Luapp.

'Reading a report from Freair.'

Pushing the image of the prehistoric tribeswoman away, Enegene tuned into what the woman was saying.

'Teth Harat from Quarn was killed on Freair as a consequence of attacking an officer in their security team. Visual evidence was recorded and sent, but will not be shown. The judges are satisfied the corpse is that of Teth Harat.

The bodies on the Quarn ship that crashed on Freair were the pilots. The log was located and removed. When played, the Freair enforcers discovered evidence of Teth Harat's involvement in the crash recorded on the log. It also included a confession from Teth Harat that she was solely responsible for the many deaths of females across the galaxy.'

The woman turned and bowed to the three judges. They retired to consider the case, then the clerk turned to face the various enforcers and witnesses.

'You are free to leave.'

As Luapp and Enegene left their seat, the clerk pressed a small oblong device into his hand. 'You leave now, you be called when judges ready.'

The deep set amber eyes in the orange tinted skin of her face seemed to bore into their minds.

'Any indication how long?' Luapp said, apparently unaffected by the intensity of the stare.

'Approximately one hour.'

Continuing outside, they joined Jym, Aylisha and Ekym on the steps of the building.

'Where now?' Jym said.

A broad grin lit Aylisha's face. 'I'd like to see the town.'

With no opposition to the suggestion, Luapp called a taxi and gave the driver a location. It stopped in the centre of the town and the group split into two. Aylisha and Enegene walking ahead and the men behind discussing policing methods.

Almost an hour later the device buzzed and lit up. On arrival they were shown to their seats to wait for the outcome.

The judges didn't appear this time. Instead the lawyer that represented the other enforcers came in. He summed up the evidence and gave the conclusion.

'To all concerned. Teth Harat from Quarn, otherwise known as Antonia Benze from Pedanta, was the killer of seventeen women across the galaxy.

The true Antonia Benze' body has been located, and though decomposed, showed evidence of torture.

The one named Harat is also guilty of attempted murder of Lady Cyna Garber, Base Commander Nostowe and Spyrian Namrae. The penalty for such crimes on seven of the planets involved is death. As she is now deceased, sentence is deemed to have been carried out. You are dismissed the court.'

The lawyer smiled. 'Safe journey to you all.'

Leaving the court again Jym said, 'it's over at last. Let's go and celebrate.'

'What have you in mind?' Luapp said.

'Getting mind-blowingly drunk, but –,' looking at the guardians, he added, 'if that's not your style, let's have a real good meal.'

'The meal is good,' Ekym said, as they walked to the taxi.

# Chapter 28

Luapp and Ekym arrived in the dining room before the rest. Apart from sharing a suite, it was installed in them from training to be early risers. It also gave them time to talk without the others being around. Having ordered their meal, they discussed the case.

'Your assessment of the Swamplander being a target was accurate,' Ekym said. 'The fluctoid was most determined and versatile.'

'That's because Harat knew how to read Pellan. She could pick out the next benefactor before it occurred to Pellan.'

The arrival of the waiter with coffee and tea made Ekym look up. When he left, he continued, 'but it's not usual for multislayers to stray from their routine.'

'Enegene wasn't attracted to him.' Luapp stirred his tea absentmindedly. 'Harat's one virtue, if you assess it as that, was she only killed those who took him on.

As Pellan continued to harass Enegene, she became increasingly negative up to the point of buying a protector slave. Apparently this amused Harat so much she decided to let him continue.'

'The Pedantan enforcer, Jym Corder, got this from her

friends and acquaintances?'

'Pellan told us while we were on Pedanta.'

'I don't understand her reason for explaining her actions to the pilots. What logic is there in confessing to people who she intended to slay?'

Luapp sipped his tea, then smiled. 'Other genus' aren't as logical as us. Perhaps she had a need to tell someone how ingenious she'd been. She thought they wouldn't be able to pass on the information and saw no reason to keep quiet.'

'How did Harat manage to be in all those different places without being discovered?' Ekym said. 'The happenings at the dwelling, trying to take the place of the metal worker and the sunseeker that approached the dwelling; why didn't Pellan notice?'

'Their relationship was beginning to break down and he was probably relieved she wasn't around.'

'What alerted you?'

Raising the cup, Luapp smiled.

'I told Enegene I dismissed this incident as there had been other attacks, but not many animals go for a building they can't easily enter.'

'And the incident at the gathering? Pretty basic way of allying your suspicions.' Ekym chuckled. 'Arranged head rests and an artificial scalp!'

Luapp's wry smile broadened to a grin, revealing his drinking fangs.

'It was the early hours of the morning and I was tired. Not even Pellan knew about that. She arranged the sleeper and changed into different creatures.

Apparently, she wanted to hide her weapons of torture and assess whether Kaylee and her slave were together or not. She no longer trusted Pellan to tell her the truth.'

'So why attack on the island?'

'Testing me as a protector. If I was easy to get past there would be no reason to slay me.'

Ekym moved slightly to allow the waiter to place the plate in front of him. 'And Catailyn Rhalin?'

'It was a test and a trap, and also a way getting rid of Pellan. After so long a time having strong feelings for him, she suddenly realised he would never feel the same. Her positive emotions turned negative and she wanted him executed knowing he hadn't committed a crime.

As for us, she wanted to know if we could recognise her over the waves, and she wanted to draw Enegene and I to the Rhalin's dwelling so she could dispose of Enegene. Why she thought I would allow her to do that I have no idea.'

'Totally illogical. Even as a slave you were a protector and would therefore act to save your owner. As for Pellan, she could have got the same result from slaying a servant or even an unknown in the street.'

'The penalty for slaying a servant or a member of the general population is execution but it's painless. The penalty for slaying one of the elite, especially one of the Rhalin's status, was execution by torture.'

'Not quite out of their barbaric law stage then. Why didn't she just kill him herself?'

'Pellan was in a vehicle crash but he survived. It was her first attempt on his life. Then she went for the more indirect approach as she didn't feel emotionally strong enough to try again.'

'She was emotionally strong enough to slay seventeen females,' Ekym commented, dryly.

'I suppose she didn't see males as a threat; only females got in the way of her and Pellan being together. Ironically, a secondary reason for getting rid of Kaylee was Harat's attachment to me.' Luapp grimaced at the thought.

'The Rhalin attack was just a screen. Aylisha was with us, and Harat needed Drew to be alive to bring charges. Catailyn and the qivers were a means to an end. It was a deviation from her normal routine but in her mind, the end justified the means.'

'As she knew you could see her in any disguise you had to be slain. I assume her enjoyment of slaying "Kaylee" was increased because she was partly responsible for your demise.'

Ekym picked up his juice. Taking a drink, he watched Luapp eat. 'And the female called Garber; that was totally different to her usual operational method.'

'I assume that as her interest in Pellan waned, her adherence to the ritual of the slayings lost its appeal. She then went for revenge terminations, slaying anyone Pellan liked or had help from.

Freewoman Garber didn't realise Pellan hadn't told Benze about seeking financial advice. She mentioned it to her and Benze decided to teach Pellan a lesson by slaying Cyna Garber.'

'She was increasingly deviating from her normal methods; it's good you stopped her when you did. There may not have been a pattern to recognise if she escaped from the Black Systems.'

Ekym placed his glass on the table and brought their conversation to a more sensitive subject. 'You and the Spyrian seem to be walking parallel paths.'

Luapp continued eating for a while, then said, 'we are in early stages yet, but the prognosis looks good.'

'There are similarities to Keela.'

A tense silence followed as Luapp stopped eating and looked at Ekym. 'Perhaps I'm attracted to the same kind of female,' he said, eventually.

'The differences are noticeable. Enegene is independent

470

and highly intelligent.'

'Are you saying Keela was unintelligent?'

'Keela had country knowledge. She knew her area and how to read it, but she would have been lost in your life.'

Another lengthy silence followed.

'There are important differences,' Luapp agreed at last.

'One of them is the intensity of feeling. Perhaps it's because I'm more mature....' He drifted off into thought.

'And perhaps enough time has elapsed for you to be able to feel again. It's been a long time Luapp. Possibly Enegene Namrae is the one to replace her.'

Luapp gave his friend another long look. 'And in all that time you haven't sighted one female.'

Ekym smiled. 'I'm too discriminatory.'

Luapp's taught expression relaxed. 'There are of course problems. Most importantly I'm away more than I'm home. That was good timing!'

'Maybe the best timing. Enegene doesn't strike me as the kind who would want you visiting her nightly. I know for sure you're not a regular caller. The distance between you is possibly the substance that binds you.'

'What do you think of her?'

'What does it matter? I'm not involved with her.'

Putting the knife on the plate Luapp picked up the toast. 'You're a good judge of character.'

Ekym poured more juice into his glass and met his friend's gaze. 'Your character judgement is equally as good as mine, if not better.'

'But as you say, you're not involved; sometimes emotions cloud the issue.'

The green commander shrugged.

'She's not a female I would have recommended to you, but that's just the point. You work well together. You've a common

471

interest in the well-being of others, you have similar professions, you enjoy each other's company... need I go on?'

'She's listed.'

Ekym smiled briefly and let it fade. 'You know her listing is harmless. It's the sort of thing any adolescent or secdec can get by being in the wrong place at the wrong time. She served her time and has remained stainless since.'

Luapp stopped eating and frowned. 'How do you know?'

Ekym's smile reappeared. 'I checked. Not hard to do as a commander in GSC. I couldn't have you tied to a cage scat.'

'Did the other two check as well?' Luapp said coolly.

His smile widened .'Didn't need to, I told them. Besides, you don't give a hak about our approval, and that's how it should be. You've been interested in her since you arrested her.'

'I have not,' Luapp said indignantly.

'You have, but you wouldn't admit it. Especially to yourself. That would mean you were getting over Keela.'

Irritated, Luapp said, 'you brought the subject up.'

'Only because you wouldn't. We've previously established keeping things to yourself doesn't work. You need to discuss your problems.'

'I thought I was...'

'You can't mist me; you're deliberately avoiding the real issue. This is more to do with your father than me and the others.'

Luapp twitched a brow. 'You know me too well. My father... it would be awkward in the extreme if he objected.'

'There we agree. He's power absolute, but if he accepted Keela, a floral twiner, why should he object to a female who runs her own successful business?'

'Because she's a Swampy.'

Ekym studied the glass of juice on the table for a few

472

moments. Finally looking up, he said, 'your father would not allow where she was raised to be an issue. Whatever his duties, he's still your father. Have you ever known him to be prejudiced?'

Picking up the second piece of toast, Luapp said, 'no, but I'm not often around when he's deliberating disputes. And we don't get many pleas for assistance from the Swamplands.'

'We have guardians from the swamps.'

'Guardians don't count. Backgrounds are ignored when recruits become guardians.'

A brow twitch from Ekym made Luapp smile.

'It worked for you. But we're drifting from the point. Your other concern is how she would cope with who you are. The only one who can tell you that is Enegene Namrae herself.'

'Am I transmitting or something?' Luapp said, frowning.

'You said I knew you well.' Ekym paused, then added, 'when I escorted her to Pedanta we talked. She's curious and suspicious about your background and she wants to know more.

She unwittingly showed her concern for your welfare, and that was before you worked together. She has true feelings for you.'

'So, you think her a possibility?'

Ekym sighed. 'We've just been through this.'

'I know you as well as you know me. Why are you avoiding an answer?'

'Do I detect a reluctance to continue with the relationship?'

'No, quite the opposite. You're my closest friend and you know how careful I have to be Kym.'

'I think you'd know if I disliked her. We're all ecstatic you've found another female. Now we can stop concerning ourselves with you and think about us.'

Luapp noticed Ekym's gaze shift to someone behind.

473

'Fairday guardians,' came the cheerful greeting as she joined them at the table.

'Sleep well?' Luapp said, watching her pick up the menu.

Now Enegene had joined them, the discussion took a new direction.

~~~

*It was odd meeting Aylisha and Jym again after so long,* Enegene thought, watching their ship take off. *But we slipped back into our friendship as if it had never been interrupted.*

Leaving the observation room, she walked from the public section of the station to the military compound with the guardians. They stopped beside Luapp's Dart.

'Safe journey and interesting experiences,' Ekym said. Looking at Enegene, he added, 'I'll wait for you in the ship.'

'I'll see you in three monspa, be watchful,' Luapp replied.

Ekym walked away leaving Luapp and Enegene alone. She eased herself into his arms and held him tight for a while. As she pulled back, he put his hands on her shoulders.

'Be careful out there; I want you back in the same condition you left.'

'Don't be concerned. I have many orbits experience, and now there's even more reason for returning safely.'

Pulling close a second time she rested her head against his chest. 'You weren't so far away before.'

'There's more chance of being killed on Gaeiza than in space; there's more room to hide out here.'

Enegene stepped back again and looked up at him. 'This is just getting started; I don't want it over before it's begun.'

He released his grip and moved back. 'I'll see you in three monspa.' Walking up the ramp, he stopped inside the door, turned and waved. Stepping back, he waved once more as the door closed.

~~~

Ekym watched Enegene on the view screen. She waited until Luapp's Dart was no longer visible, then turned and walked quickly to his ship. Joining him in the pilot pod she looked out of the window and up at the sky.

'He'll return safely, won't he?'

'Luapp is one of the best guardian's in service,' he said, touching the control console. As she sat in the seat next to him, he added, 'he'd have to be deceased to stop him returning under his own power.'

She turned her head and noted his smile. 'Some comfort you are Yetok.'

Starting the engines he contacted space port control. With permission to leave granted he increased power and the ship lifted off.

Just below penetration point, the ship changed to the upward angle of departure and headed into space. Selecting Gaeiza's location in navigation, he relaxed back as the planet below shrank into the distance.

'Guardians never think about ceasing,' he said, as they left Padua behind. 'We concentrate on living and keeping it that way. It's the positive that brings us home.'

She smiled and rested her head back against the safety restraint. 'Thank you Ekym, let's think positively.'

Having reached the required distance from the system he put the ship into starburst. The sudden rush of power shot them forward so fast the stars blurred into a mass of multi-coloured splurges and fluid shapes.

'It will be good to be home,' she said, with a sigh.

Ekym glanced at Enegene and considered his conversation with Luapp.

*She's not the female I would have recommended to him, but she's the one that will heal his heart and chart his life for the next t'ori, and I wish them well.*

475

## Gaeizaan to English

| | |
|---|---|
| Adol | Adolescent/teenager |
| Alcoburned. | Drunk |
| Apalodge | Hotel on the bottom half of the building, private apartments on the top. |
| Aplirom | Study |
| Befrin | A type of Gaeizaan four horned mountain goat. |
| Biospeak | Telepathic communication |
| Blosips | Biting insects like mosquitoes |
| Carabac | Informer |
| Clensrom | Bath/shower room |
| Drylanders | Anybody not born in the swamps |
| Festrom | Dining room |
| Fehy Music | Folk music |
| Gaeiza | Mother planet of the Seven Systems. |
| Gaeizaan | A native of Gaeiza |
| Galactic Council | United Nations of Space travelling species |
| Gethsana | A Gaeizaan expression of frustration |
| Guardians | Combined services force from the Gaeizaan Seven Systems. Also Galactic Council's police force. |
| Hlystan | Irritating buzzing insect, like a hover fly |
| Iaad room | Internal arrival and departure room (post and travel cases) |
| Intelmac | Computer |

| | |
|---|---|
| Kec | To fool around |
| Keff | Mild curse. Equates to the human expressions damn it, sod it etc. |
| Leg huggers | Tights |
| Liana | Contracted form of the word life-spanner. Means husband or wife. |
| Lopar | Wolf |
| Manak | Bear |
| Mire skiddler | Six legged mollusc found in the Gaeizaan swamps. |
| Monbliss | Lover |
| Monspa | Moon Span; a month |
| MSF | Multi Species Force. Military defence group for the Galactic Council |
| Niawl. | An animal similar to an Aye-aye that lives in trees but feeds on the ground. |
| Orbit | Year |
| Ominarian. | Humanoid beings who are shape-shifters. When in "normal" mode they are semi-transparent. |
| Pedanta | Prime Governmental planet of the Black Systems |
| Pedantan | Native of Pedanta. Fawn skinned humans |
| Poroth | Succulent stemmed fern which is easily blown over. |
| Pretween | Child under ten |
| Preparea | Kitchen |
| Primalin | Baby |
| Pukka | Nocturnal small monkey like a marmoset that lives in underground colonies. |
| Qess/qessing | Expressions of annoyance such as blast, hell or bloody |

| | |
|---|---|
| Qiver/ Qivers | Child/children. |
| Relaxrom | Lounge/ sitting room |
| Restorative. | Self-induced shallow coma to allow the body to heal itself |
| Robstor | Wardrobe |
| Salation | Sollenite word for Human |
| Secdec | Second Decade – someone in their twenties |
| Senicide | The wilful and deliberate killing of a sentient being |
| Sleeper | Bed |
| Slember | Bedroom |
| Spitters | Poisonous toad-like amphibians |
| Spyrian | Gaeizaan Private Detective |
| Sunseeker | Lizard |
| Swamplander/. Swampy | A person from the swamplands on Gaeiza; equates to ghettos. |
| Tehin | Gaeizaan profanity |
| Third Generation | A Gaeizaan slave whose grandparents were born on Pedanta |
| Towk | Two week/fortnight |
| T'Ori | Century |
| Zeetan | A species of blue skinned, willowy humanoids with white hair. |